TALES OF THE
SHADOWMEN

Volume 18: Eminences Grises

also from Black Coat Press

TALES OF THE
SHADOWMEN

Volume 18: Eminences Grises

edited by
Jean-Marc & Randy Lofficier

stories by
**Tim Newton Anderson, Matthew Baugh,
Atom Mudman Bezecny, Matthew Dennion,
Brian Gallagher, Martin Gately, Travis Hiltz,
Matthew Ilseman, Rick Lai, Jean-Marc Lofficier,
Randy Lofficier, Rod McFadyen, Christofer Nigro,
John Peel, Frank Schildiner, Nathalie Vidalinc**
and **David L. Vineyard.**

cover by
Juan Miguel Aguilera

A Black Coat Press Book

ISBN 978-1-64932-103-9 First Printing. December 2021. Published by Black Coat Press, an imprint of Hollywood Comics.com, LLC, P.O. Box 17270, Encino, CA 91416. All rights reserved. Except for review purposes, no part of this book may be reproduced or transmitted in any form or by any means, electronic or mechanical, including photocopying, recording or by any information storage and retrieval system, without permission in writing from the publisher. The stories and characters depicted in this anthology are entirely fictional. Printed in the United States of America.

Table of Contents

Paul Béra

LÉONOX
MONSTRE des TÉNÈBRES

ANGOISSE

FLEUVE NOIR

Introduction
French Pulp and Me

French literature wasn't a subject I knew much about growing up, mostly because, like most Americans, I never learned another language. I was a reader growing up, being infamous in school for always having my nose in a book that had little to nothing to do with schoolwork. My favorites were Jack London, Harlan Ellison, Robert E. Howard, George Orwell, Colin Wilson and many books on odd subjects like history and demonology.

The sole nod to French fiction was in the form of Alexander Dumas's seminal adventure novel, *The Three Musketeers*. I read that book more times than the others put together and watched every musketeer film I could find in the pre-cable television days. My preferences were for the Richard Lester film version, though some of the unofficial sequels from the early days of film were welcome.

Somewhere around high school years, one of my teachers, Mr. McCarthy I believe, gave me a copy of the play *Cyrano* and I was hooked on a second French tale. I looked up Moliere and a few other playwrights, but on the whole, France still seemed a distant concept. I didn't speak the language, though I held a deep reverence for their crime films. French New Wave cinema was a joy in the early days of VHS rental stores. *Le Samourai, Breathless, Bob le flambeur,* were favorites and, thanks to subtitles, easily understood.

This changed when I stumbled into a group of fans of the work of Philip Jose Farmer and his meta-fictional concept, the Wold Newton Universe. One of the members was a name I knew from comics, Jean-Marc Lofficier. Jean-Marc (or JM as we called him) knew about American pulp fiction and comics, having worked with many legends in the field. However, his true expertise was the unknown area of French Fiction, especially pulp and horror. JM spoke on these topics, mentioning names that never crossed my path before.

Suddenly new names and vistas opened before me. I learned of the first true supervillain (Fantômas), Sherlock Holmes's greatest influence (M. Lecoq), and a writer who placed vampires in literature long before

Stoker's *Dracula* (Paul Féval, *père*). Being an obsessional type, I sought out whatever was available in the libraries of New Jersey and the various used bookstores in my vicinity. Sadly, the pickings were often slim, with many of the books being poorly literal translations of the books resulting in stilted tales.

Happily, JM created Black Coat Press, where he and his team of translators—specially the brilliant and prolific Brian Stableford—added new life to the old tales. I bought Fantômas, Harry Dickson, the magnificent works of Paul Féval, and so many more. I read them in paperbacks and later on Kindle, finding new favorites. My tops were the works of Paul Féval, Fantômas after he transformed from a dangerous criminal into the Lord of Terror, Harry Dickson, the evil organization known as The Black Coats, and the first superhero in fiction, The Nyctalope.

As an aspiring writer, JM gave me a shot at joining the ranks of *Tales of the Shadowmen*, joining the ranks of amazing writers like Michael Moorcock, Brian Stableford, John Peel, and dozens of other authors I admire. I followed that with two series, a French version of the Frankenstein Monster as well as a vampire series using the hero of one of Féval's earliest works.

But it wasn't enough! I wanted more! I wanted to read the tales of Bob Morane or Le Commandeur. I wanted to experience the terror the untranslated Fantômas tales suggested, walk the dark streets with Nestor Burma, and see the horrors and monsters that Teddy Verano faced in Paris. Most were out of reach, though I checked with Jean-Marc regularly.

It was during the COVID pandemic that my world changed again. In late September of 2020, during an email chat on forthcoming books and comics from Black Coat Pressd Hexagon Comics, JM suggested I try learning French. His reasoning was that, even if it took me a couple of years to get to a basic reading level, I would one day be able to purchase books and comics that were formerly out-of-reach.

Now I am a negative person by nature, so I immediately dismissed the idea. But having been on the internet in various forms since the 1980s led me to step back and think instead of pooh-poohing the idea outright. I realized that this wasn't the first time I took up a skill set at a less than optimal time age-wise. I ran two marathons in 1999 and 2000 in my 30s. I took up martial arts at age 35, earned my Black Belt at 40, acted as a sparring partner to two pro-MMA fighters at age 39-42, and even earned my certification as a Sensei in that time. I was first published as a writer at age 40, spoke on panels and podcasts in my late 40s and early 50s on subjects involving pulp, horror, and very bizarre films... I guess I'm a late starter by nature. Also, I remembered that, if I made the choice to learn this language, my stubborn Russian/Ukrainian nature demanded I do so successfully no matter how long it took.

A day or so after the discussion, I signed up for an online course and, by the time you read this essay, I will have completed my first year of study without missing a single day. While I am far from being able to read the works featuring Fantômas or Harry Dickson untranslated, I am on my way. I even have a habit of reverting to French unconsciously and answering my wife and friends with *"Oui"* and other phrases when I'm tired. The future looks bright and fun for me.

If this is your first or eighteenth trip with the Shadowmen, I advise you consider diving deeper. French fiction is an untapped universe by much of the English-speaking world, one that I hope will continue to spread far and wide. No matter your interest, there's something wonderful awaiting you as a reader. I can honestly say I'm grateful I took that trip, and I had my friend and mentor Jean-Marc Lofficier as my guide.

Frank Schildiner,
September 8, 2021

Tim Newton Anderson is a new contributor to Tales of the Shadowmen *and he opens this year's collection with a rollicking yarn starring some of our favorite heroes and villains. The star of this story is the fearless young journalist Joseph Joséphin, a.k.a. Rouletabille, at the very beginning of his career, about two years before the famous* Mystery of the Yellow Room *(available in a new translation from Black Coat Press)...*

Tim Newton Anderson: *Thirty Pieces of Gold*

Paris, 1900

Joseph Joséphin almost ran to the Cour du Commerce-Saint-André when he heard about the murder. However, he managed to keep his speed to a fast walk. He was trying to establish himself as a journalist, and there were professional standards to keep up. He had seen too many amateurs race after the Police only to be kept aside as more seasoned reporters were allowed in. This was his first big story and he hoped to sell it to *L'Époque*, as well as his other usual markets.

After pausing for a few seconds at the wrought iron gates to have his shoes cleaned before entering the cobbled arcade, Rouletabille (as he was known in the trade) elbowed his way past the onlookers to where the gendarmes had thrown a cordon around the antiques shop.

He had been in the arcade many times; one of his favorite restaurants, *Le Procope*, was at its entrance on the Boulevard Saint-Germain. Here, the original shop of the Grenouille (now Grenoville) family of fragrance makers stood side by side with a second-hand (or self-proclaimed antiquarian) bookshop, a workman's café where he knew you could get drinks until the early hours of the morning, and a shop selling conjuring tricks. Rouletabille wondered if it was worth visiting the perfumery to see if they could help him identify the scent of the mysterious woman in black whom he recalled had visited him and showed him kindness when he was in the orphanage...

It was ironic that he had dedicated his young life to solving mysteries, but the one riddle he had not managed to penetrate was the one concerning his own parentage and early life. Or perhaps that was why he was determined to unpick puzzles on behalf of others.

Part of the joy of living in Paris was being able to explore the city's hidden corners as he wandered randomly through the streets. The arcades were some of his favorite places, with their iron and glass roofs and small eccentric shops. The Cour du Commerce-Saint-André was one of the oldest, and one of the few on the left bank. It dated back to before the Revolution and the inventor of the infamous guillotine had lived just across the street.

Rouletabille saw a few faces at the front that he recognized: fellow journalist Jerôme Fandor of *La Capitale*, Charles Duroy, the editor of *La Vie Française*, Olivier Molinier and his friend Philippe Roget who had previously mentored him. Obviously, no one was being let in just yet. As the tallest man in the crowd, Philippe spotted Rouletabille easily and pushed some of his fellow scribes to one side to let the sixteen year-old through.

"I was just explaining to Inspector Larsan here that I am an old friend of his boss so I expect to be able to view the scene," Philippe said. "However, perhaps you would like to take my place? I value your young eyes; I have seen too many of these murders to see them afresh. Besides, I witnessed your success in unraveling the mystery of the Magic City Murder and was impressed by the keenness of your brain."

Rouletabille nodded enthusiastically. Although his fellow scribes made fun of him behind his back for his round-shaped head, they had developed a respect for what went on inside. Perhaps it was growing up as an orphan, which had always made him feel like an outsider, but he was able to hold events in a circle of logic inside his brain and weigh facts against a pattern only he seemed capable of seeing. And perhaps it was also to show others that, despite his small stature, his mind was able to match anyone else's in the world.

Larsan was still not sure about allowing the youngster through with Philippe, but then his partner, Inspector Juve, indicated he should let them in.

"I have heard good things about you from your employers," Juve said. "This is definitely a story that will get your by-line on the front page. You were quite helpful with the Mystery of the Missing Marquise. Larsan here thinks your investigative skills may even rival his own someday."

Rouletabille gave a half bow of thanks and followed the Inspector and Philippe into the shop.

The sign on the outside said: *Jurgen Jewelers, est. 1164 Poictesme*, but the imaginary date and location were not the only dissembling element in the shop's description. It was more of a pawnbrokers' than jewelers', as a lance, sword and cudgel hung on the walls and every corner was full of rubbish: African and Far Eastern artifacts including some phallic statues, a pile of *Comedia dell'arte* masks left over from some student ball, a few half-strung guitars and fiddles, a rack of clothes and wigs that had not been in fashion for a hundred years, assorted clocks (none of which told the same time), and a pile of unsorted shoes. What jewelry was on display was of poor quality and obviously paste.

Juve led them through to the back room. As he approached it, Rouletabille could smell roasted flesh and the metallic tang of blood, as well as other less recognizable aromas. He surmised these came from the alembics and other equipment sitting on a bench at the rear.

On the floor was a mutilated body. The man's face and throat were badly burned and there were more burns on his torso. Around the marks were glitters of metal. It was by no means Rouletabille's first view of a corpse. Like many Parisians he made regular trips to the Morgue to view the bodies of those dragged from the river or dumped in alleyways (which he liked to think was due to professional interest rather than simple prurience), but those had at least had some attention from the morticians and were cleaned up and doused in essential oils to mask the smell. This body stank, not least because the dead man had obviously voided his bowels in his final agony.

"As you can see, we are looking at murder," said Juve. "He has had liquid gold poured down his throat and on his chest. A horrible way to die, and not as quick as one might think. The molten metal cauterized the flesh as it flowed, so as well as the shock to his body, our man died from asphyxiation. If I die, let it be from heart failure or a fatal gunshot, not some bizarre murder by a homicidal lunatic."

Rouletabille nodded, although he was concentrating on the crime scene and not the policeman's words. He dropped to a crouch and began minutely examining the floor and then each surface in turn. He could feel the bumps on his forehead warm as his mind's eye conjured the circumstances of the crime.

"If this was a robbery, why did the thief not simply take the gold rather than kill the old man?" he asked. "A knife or a bludgeon would have achieved the same end and there are plenty of weapons available in the shop, even if he had not brought his own."

"I do not believe that simple theft was the motive behind the crime," said Juve. "This was intended to send a message to someone—either the victim or another. It will take us a long while to search the inventory and for what's missing. This Monsieur Jurgen was not the most meticulous of shopkeepers, but I have already spotted several items that would have been worth taking. The safe under the counter has been opened, but there are some nice diamond necklaces and gold rings still in it. The man was murdered because that was the intruder's prime intent. Why, I cannot tell. He lived a quiet life with few enemies, and those who may have wished him harm because of his short-changing on their pawned goods are unlikely to have gone this far for revenge..."

Rouletabille walked around the corpse and made his way to the workbench. Open on it was a thick leather-bound ledger where Jurgen had recorded his sales and purchases and their values. Being careful to put on his white gloves to avoid disturbing any of the fingerprints—the police had now started to use them for detection—he flicked through the most recent pages. The majority of the items listed were straightforward: a few pieces of jewelry and some household goods. However, one stood out for the young reporter and he lifted the book to show it to the detective.

"There is a record here for a valuable Roman coin he bought two days ago," Rouletabille said. "It says '*rare*' and there is a note to talk to an expert at the Louvre. Any sign of it?" He knew that many collectors were obsessive and unscrupulous in their pursuit of their *idée fixe*.

"Not so far," said Juve. "It certainly was not in the safe, where you would expect him to keep it. You may well be on to something there. I will get my men to compile a list of any collectors of Roman coins in the city—although the person for whom the coin was stolen could live anywhere and have simply commissioned a Parisian thief to steal it."

Rouletabille consulted his pocket watch to see how long he had until his deadline. He had another job to do before he returned to file his copy. Something he had seen as he entered the arcade held another element of the mystery and he started to wind back the sequence of events he envisaged in his mind.

"I'm afraid I must go," he said. "Thank you so much for letting me see this and telling me about the crime. I hope you will keep me informed of your progress."

Juve nodded and Rouletabille carefully maneuvered around the dead man again and strode out of the shop, looking all around to record every detail in his head for the article. Philippe could make the first report, but he sensed a far bigger story than the death of a pawnbroker, however sensational that murder may be.

He pushed past the assembled lollygaggers again and walked towards the exit on rue de l'Ancienne Comédie. He looked again at the boot cleaner to confirm his initial impressions. The man was crouched at the entrance, watching and listening intently to all that was going on.

"What did you do with the real boot cleaner?" he asked the man quietly.

The man looked up at Rouletabille and gave a calm smile.

"It was the fingers, wasn't it?" he said. "I would normally have taken time to discolor my hands and nails with mud and makeup to complete the disguise, but I was in a bit of a hurry."

Rouletabille looked at the man again. His back appeared to have the hunched curve of one who spent his life bending over to clean people's boots, but his body was that of an athlete inside the tattered clothing and his face was well fed underneath the disguise. He was being remarkably calm for an imposter who had just been exposed next to a murder scene. Rouletabille wondered if he was an undercover journalist or a secret policeman.

"Can we go somewhere so you can tell me what you know?" he said. "I do not know the reason for your elaborate imposture, but I suspect you do not wish it to be revealed."

The man nodded and stood up. As the young man had suspected, his back was now straight and, although he walked deliberately slowly into the street, the reporter could see this was a conscious charade.

A few minutes later, they were sitting on a bench by the Seine. As this was an area where beggars mixed with the bourgeoisie, they attracted no attention by their odd pairing.

"This is about the Roman coin, isn't it?" Rouletabille asked. His normal desire to show off his intellect was intensified by the need to display his understanding of the crime.

"Coins, not coin," the man replied. "This is a very deep affair and I have no faith in the police to fathom its mysteries."

Now that he had slipped his disguise, if not the bootscraper's clothes, Rouletabille could see the man was a few inches taller than himself, fit and well fed, with an air of opulence about him. Underneath that, however, he sensed something of the street—a disguise under a disguise under a disguise.

"Who are you exactly?" he asked.

"Let me introduce myself," the man said. "I am Doctor Bull and I work for the Diogenes Club of London. I have spent the last six months tracking the roots of this affair through conspiracies of anarchists and occultists, and I believe I'm nearing the end game."

Rouletabille sat silently to draw out more revelations. The man's excellent French definitely had an English undertone.

"I can see you will not leave me alone until I lay out all the facts and I persuade you how dangerous it would be to pursue this," continued Bull. "It is indeed about the coins, but these are not ordinary antiquities."

The tale the man told seemed unbelievable to Rouletabille, but Bull was very persuasive and the young man allowed himself to suspend his disbelief for the moment—he could investigate its veracity later. He sensed the man was telling him only part of the truth, hiding beneath a veneer of veracity. Each word was itself accurate, but what was not said was just as important.

Bull told him that the organization he worked for was an even more secret branch of the British secret service, run by a massively obese man called M who, together with Bull and some other agents, had set up a fake branch of the International Anarchist Council in an attempt to infiltrate the real terrorist organization. Bull had also been charged with joining a group of Satanists led by the sinister Doctor Lipsius, whose group had stolen a gold coin that was the twin of the one missing from Jurgen's shop.

"There were thirty of them, originally," said Bull. "Lipsius told me they had been struck by the Emperor Tiberius to celebrate an orgy, and were thus a key part of his occult ceremonies. However that did not explain the Anarchists' interest in the hoard, or their considerable monetary value. In fact, their history is even stranger. They were made from meteoric gold taken from a fallen star that landed in the Yorkshire village of Wold Newton in the 18th century. The rest of the meteorite was given to the British Museum, but the gold was extracted carefully and made into the coins which were intended for the families who were present at the strike and their relatives. They had only just been created when they were stolen. We thought originally by the Black Coats, but in fact by a third party who concealed them to dig up later.

"I do not know how much you know about astrophysics? There is an interesting monograph on the dynamics of an asteroid which could give you some information… but the key point is that all of the gold and heavier metals on our planet have their origins in space and were brought here by these falling rocks. The particular gold in the Wold Newton meteorite is of a very rare type that has special properties as both an energy source and in its effect on human beings. It is believed to bestow special powers…"

Bull had managed to get his hands on one of the coins held by Lipsius and fled with it to the continent, leaving a forgery behind to try and put the occultists off the scent. Once in France, he had contacted the two groups who had been trying to bring together all of the coins to further their schemes.

"Both organizations appear to have a sense of irony," he said. "I had two meetings in the same street on the same night, with the Anarchist Council of Europe at the Château d'If café, and then the Occultists in the Abbey de Thélème cabaret a few doors away."

Rouletabille was familiar with both premises in Pigalle. The Château d'If was decked out as a prison, based on the more successful Café du Bagne. It was entered via a drawbridge from the street and a large oak door and had imitation cells and dungeons inside. The Abbey de Thélème had a medieval monastery theme whose waiters were monks and nuns and its walls were painted with scenes of debauchery based on Pompeii as well as stained glass windows with the same inspiration. Its name, of course, came from Rabelais. He could see their appeal as meeting places as most patron's eyes would be on the performances as the majority of attendees were too focused on their own enjoyment to see who they were sharing a table with. However, he had never been a fan of the food at either.

"Everyone who is anyone in the world of terror was at the Anarchist Council meeting," said Bull. "I was of course posing as a member of the British Anarchist Council. It is surprising how sinister one can look by simply donning a pair of blue smoked glass spectacles! Their leader, Sir Dunston Gryme, explained they were after the coins for a new mechanical death machine created by Ginochio Gyves. The Brotherhood of the Seven Kings, the Black Coats, the Red Hand, and the Si-Fan were all represented.

"Of course, I didn't let on that I had one of the coins. What I learned was that most of the others would be on display at the Grand Palais as part of a larger collection of special coins during the Great Exposition. That was where they would be stolen. I gathered that a new recruit, a man called Gurn, would do the job. I suspect he is the one behind the murder of poor Jurgen as I spotted him talking to Sir Dunston and I overheard a mention of the Cour du Commerce-Saint André, which is why I was there. As an aside, it was easy and cheap to bribe the real bootscraper."

The second meeting Bull had attended was that of the occultists. Although he only had a few minutes between assignations, he had simply swapped his dark glasses for large plain ones and added some side whiskers to transform into his role as a member of Lipsius' cult.

"The meeting was chaired by Doctor Johannes, a defrocked priest, and his mistress, Madame Chantelouve, who run the satanic society of the Re-Theurgist-Optimates. Others in the room included Quentin Moretus Cassave, who had come from Ghent, and the notorious Mocata. I have some familiarity with the occult scene, and although most practitioners aim to enlighten, these were definitely from the dark side.

"Again, I denied all knowledge of the whereabouts of Lipsius coin. I was unsurprised to learn they, too, planned to steal the collection from the Exposition. Johannes referred to the gold as Paracelsium's metal, which would unlock a range of occult powers…"

"Fascinating," said Rouletabille. "As is your accent. You have done very well to try and sound like an Englishman speaking good French, but I have been working on a monograph on ways in which one can determine the true origin of a person by their voice and I can tell that you are a native French speaker, although there is an underlying burr, perhaps from a parent?"

There was that wry smile again.

"I may have underestimated you," said the man. "A mistake I shall not make again. It is quite refreshing in my line of business to match wits with someone who may be an equal. The story I have told you is accurate except in one single respect. My name is Neil Saprenu. My father was French and my mother Scottish. I was born and brought up here, but spent some time with my mother's family as a teenager which was when I was recruited by M."

"What time are we meeting at the Exposition to stop the theft?" asked Rouletabille.

"We are not meeting there at all," said Saprenu (if that was really his name, Rouletabille thought). "I have told you that this is a dangerous affair and I cannot allow a teenager to compromise my actions, however bright he may be. I would also ask you not to print any of what I have told you in case it tips off the anarchists and occultists. I will tell you afterwards what transpires and which elements you need to suppress. The press has great power, but that comes with great responsibility. I am trusting you to exercise both with wisdom."

"I know you have your plans, but surely there is more than one way to skin a rabbit?" asked Rouletabille.

"You mean, to skin a cat," said the man.

"Why would one want to skin a cat?" Rouletabille replied. "One can eat a rabbit."

"Cat fur is often used in counterfeit coats," said Saprenu. "And if one removes their tail and ears, felines are often sold by the unscrupulous as rabbits."

"Not everything is what it seems then," said the young journalist. "Interesting." He had deliberately misquoted the English saying to see the man's response.

A few seconds after the man had walked off, Joseph attempted to follow him. Unfortunately, he soon lost him in the maze of narrow streets of the Left Bank amongst the throngs of tourists who had come to the city for the Exposition and the Olympic Games. Still, he knew where he would be later, so he headed back to *L'Époque* to file an unsatisfying incomplete story.

His researches in the archives backed up much of Saprenu's story. There had indeed been a meteorite strike at Wold Newton with an unlikely number of remarkable men and women in attendance. He wondered whether the strange power of meteoric gold had been the reason why the eccentric scientist Zephyrin Xyrdal had guided a golden meteorite to Greenland a few years ago.

The names of the anarchist leaders had been linked to a number of outrages across the globe, and Doctor Lipsius was mentioned in connection with the death of a young man in London, also featuring fatal burning on the chest and stomach. Doctor Johannes had been linked to a black mass, not as its leader, but as an anti-Satanist, but as this mention was from the pen of Durtal, who was himself suspected of Satanist leanings, he suspected a whitewash.

All this made for interesting background confirmation, but the only way he was going to get the full story was to go to the Exposition and see the various plots unfold. He had already developed a clear picture within his circle of logic, but needed a few more pieces of information to bring it to its full clarity.

Rouletabille had already visited the Exposition several times. He had covered the Olympic cycle race; he had been there when Thomas Edison had unveiled his robotic Eve in the Hall of Machines.

Although the number of visitors was not as high as had been hoped, it was still considered a success by the French government. Many French inventions had been sold around the world and the visitors left laden with individual purchases.

As one approached the Exposition on the Champ-de-Mars, it was hard to believe that most of the enormous halls and attractions were temporary. Some may stay, of course. After all, the Eiffel Tower had only been meant to stay up for a while, and many still said it should have been demolished rather than spoiling the Paris skyline. His own favorites were the moving sidewalk, the Lumière Brothers cinema, the Globe Céleste and the ethnic villages. He was not as fond of the omnipresent Art Nouveau as many of his fellow journalists were, but then, he was far more interested in science than the arts.

The Grand Palais, built on the site of the 1855 Exposition's Palace of Industry, was one of the constructions Rouletabille thought might outlive its setting. Its iron frame contained even more steel than the Eiffel Tower, although it had the illusion of lightness with its huge windows. It was drenched in Art Nouveau, but even he had to admit its huge skylights and elaborate stairways had an impressive grandeur.

As always, it was thronged with crowds of visitors. Rouletabille was reminded of his visit to the arcade when he saw many were clutching bottles of Grenoville's new fragrance, supposedly based on a formula by one of his forbears.

The first floor gallery was where the coins were exhibited, alongside other precious artifacts. The Exposition curators were taking no chances. Uniformed guards were careful to make themselves visible while undercover policemen mingled with the throng to spot less obvious threats. Rouletabille thought this was as much to give the illusion of security as any reality. It had only been a few months since a concrete gantry on the Globe Celeste had collapsed, killing nine people and injuring many. Since then, attendance had dipped and the sight of uniforms on patrol was supposed to give the public the confidence to return.

His keen eyes spotted a number of questionable individuals, but he thought that may well be due to his suspicious nature. Some of them did turn out to be pickpockets, and he watched with a smile as they relieved some of the richer guests of their valuables. Another day, he might have intervened, but he had bigger fish to fry. He was also amused that, despite the heavy security, only one of the thieves was spotted and apprehended.

While not as used to disguise as Saprenu claimed to be, Rouletabille was more than happy to make his way to the staff room and find a spare security guard uniform which fit. Combing his wavy hair back from his broad forehead and covering it with a cap completed the illusion. He approached a guard just coming on duty with the news that the shift pattern had changed and he would not be on duty until the next day. He had borrowed a snub nosed pistol from his friend Philippe as he expected he may need to take action.

Rouletabille strolled onto the floor of the gallery and made a point of chatting with the other guards so that any suspicions would be allayed. It was amazing what a few words about how sore your feet were and the offer of a cigarette would do to put the professionally vigilant at ease. The last to leave, apart from the guards, was the director of the exhibition who had spent the afternoon wandering through the crowd in his dress suit, top hat and monocle, trying to impress them with stories about the displayed items. The man had apparently spent a year persuading the owners of the artifacts to allow them to be included.

Closing time was now approaching and Rouletabille told his "colleagues" he would be among the reduced overnight security staff. He then helped them close the exhibition and shepherd visitors out.

Two hours later, the guards were happy to let him stay on patrol while they retired to the staff room for supper. He had declined the offer of food and wine, as he suspected the anarchists, the occultists, or both, may have doctored it with a sleeping draught to give themselves free access to the building.

He was right. Half an hour later, he poked his head round the door and saw the other guards slumped and snoring in the staff room.

Rouletabille secreted himself behind a statue just in time to hear a muffled noise above him. A rope dropped from the skylight and four figures, dressed head to toe in black, slid down it in turn. They put down their dark lanterns as the full Moon gave more than enough light to operate by. Two peeled off to check on the guards and the others headed towards the coin cabinet with the glass cutters they had used on the skylight.

Joseph had no idea whether these were the anarchists or the occultists, but was sure the other group would be nearby. His prediction came true a few seconds later as another group of black-clad figures walked in stealthily from the door.

Both sides drew pistols from their belts. The original group had some kind of silencer which rendered their shots as soft pops, while the newcomers were firing darts from their guns. Rouletabille guessed they must work like air rifles as they had round metal canisters for handles.

All of the intruders had taken cover behind display cases and the main sound in the quiet gunfight was the glass in the display cases shattering as they were hit.

While he was no stranger to danger and action, Rouletabille decided it would be wise to stay in hiding until the fight was resolved in favor of one faction or the other—especially when chips flew off the statue he was hiding behind. Besides, he was expecting even more revelations to come.

"Give it up, Joséphine," said a member of the second group. "You are outnumbered and our guns can fire hundreds of rounds to your half dozen. We will take the prize."

"Do not be so sure," said one of the original intruders.

As the woman spoke, the other two members of her gang came back from the staff room and immediately started firing at their rivals from the rear. Two of their opposition were killed or injured, although one of them was hit as the other gang returned fire.

Seeing they were outnumbered, the newcomers put down their weapons on the floor and stood up slowly.

"I warned you, Gurn," said the woman Rouletabille presumed to be Joséphine. "Bring them over here, men."

Her accomplices motioned to their rivals with their dart pistols and escorted them over towards the cabinet with the coins.

Rouletabille was completely expecting what happened next. Joséphine lifted her pistol and shot her two remaining men and the last member of Gurn's gang. He now was the only man standing in front of her.

"Make sure you give an accurate account of this when you take the coins back to Gryme," she said. "I will not stand for you trying to take the whole credit. If it was not still useful for me to preserve my cover as a member of the Re-Theurgist-Optimates, I would bring in the prize myself."

Gurn growled. He was obviously not happy.

"Do not think I will always accede to your orders as easily," he said. "You may fool the others, but I do not trust you."

What happened next was what Rouletabille had been waiting for. The doors at either end of the hall burst open and a platoon of gendarmes burst in, rifles and pistols at the ready.

Gurn and Balsamo turned quickly and both started to shoot at the police. Two men fell instantly and the rest hung back for a moment to catch the villains in their sights. That pause was all they needed and they bolted, still firing at the Police. As all exits were blocked, their only choice was to charge at the big window at the side of the hall.

Rouletabille toppled the statue behind which he had been hiding in an attempt to stop them. He started firing his own pistol, but they leaped over the obstacle, burst through the window, and plummeted to the ground twenty feet below.

Some of the braver police ran to the shattered window and started firing at the fleeing villains, but pulled back as their shots were returned. One officer fell, clutching his shoulder.

"Thank you, Rouletabille," said Inspector Juve. "Your assumptions about the theft were correct."

"Not assumptions, Inspector, Rouletabille replied, "but the result of investigation, observation, and impeccable logic."

"You are a meddling fool," said Inspector Larsan. "I suppose the trick with the statue was your ineffective way to distract them so they could be captured. Shame it was too little, too late."

"If you had arrived five minutes earlier, you might have been more successful," replied the young journalist. "As you can see from the bodies of their accomplices, they were distracted at that point."

The formally dressed exhibition director had also arrived and had gone to the display of the coins.

"At least, they do not seem to have succeeded," he said with a combination of relief, irritation, and even, Rouletabille believed, an element of excitement. "The coins are still here, as is everything else. They have escaped, but they did so empty-handed. Now, if you will excuse me, I will check on my employees."

"By all means," said Juve, "but do not leave the building as we will need to take a statement from you and your guards. You may have seen something during the last few days that will help us track down the culprits."

Rouletabille walked over to the window to see if he could guess where the fleeing thieves had gone, although he had no great expectations of success. If they had any sense, they would be long gone. He was surprised, however, when his sharp eyes spotted a movement over by the Globe Celeste.

The figure was hard to see clearly, however, because clouds were now covering the Moon. The figure was dressed in black. He was not surprised to see the exhibition director exit the building discreetly and run towards the giant globe. The game was still afoot, it seemed, so Rouletabille slipped out of the exhibition hall and trotted down the giant staircase to follow.

He silently cursed the police for not stationing men outside the building. They could have captured the thieves as they were winded from their fall. However, it meant he was unchallenged as he ran after the director.

As Rouletabille arrived at the Globe, he could see the newcomer had reached the top of the structure, with the director following. An unusual feeling of caution made him stay at the bottom and strain his ears to hear the conversation between the two men. Now that he was closer, he was sure that the first man was Gurn. He needed to hear what they said before his mental reconstruction of the entire affair could fall into place.

Gurn sat cross-legged at the top of the Globe as the director climbed the final few steps.

"Good evening," the director said. He tipped his top hat at the villain in an ironic salute. "I presume I am addressing Mister Gurn—or is it Juan North? How are you after this evening's frustrating events?"

Gurn held his dart pistol lightly in his lap. He was surprised the director was so relaxed, given his obvious advantage.

"You may call me Fantômas," he said. "As you can see, I am on top of the world. But I would have thought you would have sent the police to capture me. You are not exactly dressed for combat, although I do like your style. I was thinking of adopting it myself. The evening dress and top hat would quite suit me."

"Oh, but this is personal rather than business," said the director. "I believe you murdered two friends of mine. Monsieur Jurgen was a key part of my enterprise in both providing equipment and selling items which cannot be disposed of through more legitimate channels."

"I'm afraid he took some persuasion to open the safe so I could get the coin," Gurn said. "He was quite loyal—either that or very stubborn.

You will have noticed I did not take any of your other treasures, though. I am a professional assassin, not a common thief. And that is only one person. Who was your other friend?"

The director subtly glanced left and right to see if they were being watched, but did not see Rouletabille standing under the Globe.

"I believe you fought in South Africa," he said, "and while there, you cold-bloodedly murdered Arthur Raffles. He had been a great source of help and advice to me when I was still learning my craft. He did not deserve to be shot in the back by a coward who has not matched one percent of his achievements."

"Not yet, perhaps," said Gurn. "Unfortunately for Raffles, one of his, er, achievements frustrated the plans of the Black Coats, and they don't take kindly to rivals, which is something you should bear in mind."

"Such as interfering in your plan to use the poison you obtained from Sir Dunston Gryme to adulterate Grenville's scent and kill thousands of innocent?" said the director. "You will be disappointed to learn that my associates and I have removed the tainted bottles and replaced them with ordinary scent. The purchasers will be upset that it is not as special as promised, but they will still be alive."

Gurn stood up.

"That is the sort of interference I will not brook," he said. "I had planned to merely wound you as a lesson, but your insolence leaves me no alternative but to kill you. And know that I still have plenty more poison to proceed with my plan."

He sighted the director with the gun.

"I am only at the start of my career, but yours ends here," the director said, grasping the brim of his top hat and spinning it towards Gurn. The assassin tried to brush it out of the way, but was shocked to feel his hand and shoulder sliced open by the steel blade concealed in the brim. He dropped the gun as the director stepped forward and drew a blade from his walking stick. However, Gurn only took a second to recover and pulled a stiletto out of a scabbard at his belt.

"The same poison also coats this blade," he said. "One scratch and you will die in agony. Are you willing to risk your skills against mine?"

The director made no answer but struck a fencing stance. He lifted the blade in an *en garde* gesture and advanced towards Fantômas.

Although Gurn was undoubtedly skilled, the greater reach of the director's sword rendered that moot and he was pressed back. Then his foot slipped and he fell, sliding down the Globe to the ground a hundred feet below. The director again lifted the sword before his face.

"*Touché.*"

Rouletabille did not bother to see where Gurn had fallen as he thought the plunge must have been fatal. That meant he did not see the assassin stab his blade against the side of the Globe to slow his fall and drop the last few feet to the street before slipping away.

The young journalist was waiting at the bottom of the steps as the director descended.

"Congratulations, Monsieur Saprenu," he said. "I presume you have fulfilled your mission?"

"I must pay more attention to my disguises when you are about," the man said, bending to pick up his top hat and place it rakishly on his head. "What gave it away this time?"

"Not your disguise, but your actions," said Joseph. "Who else would be so dogged in pursuit of Gurn? And, of course, no exhibition director would need a fence or associate with so famous a thief as Raffles. You should also consider avoiding aliases that are anagrams of your name— Arsène Lupin. I would also stay clear of clever jokes like the discussion about false rabbits and lapin."

Lupin bowed. "Again, I applaud your perspicacity. If I was less concerned about the police, I would enjoy a longer conversation. Although I had to alter my plans when I learned of others' interest in the coins, I was able to steer them towards tonight's plot which provided a useful smokescreen for my own. The real Doctor Bull had an unfortunate accident while crossing the Channel and he and the other passengers are recovering from their ordeal in Calais. None of them are seriously injured, of course, as the rescue ship I arranged picked them all up a few minutes after their dip in La Manche. It was also no coincidence you were able to see through my disguise as a bootscraper. I knew from your reputation you would be able to see through the disguise at once, and after giving you the story of the two conspiracies, you would make arrangements with the police.

"I had personal matters to resolve with both Gurn and the woman Joséphine, who stole something very dear to me, but I shall leave that matter to another day. I set up the competition between their employers to acquire the coins by passing on information they would be on display here. It was then a simple matter to persuade anarchists and occultists to hire them for their raids."

He slid his sword back into its scabbard and drew a small but deadly pistol from his pocket. He waved it casually in Rouletabille's direction. The young reporter knew his own lack of practice with firearms would make any attempt to draw his own gun moot.

"I'm afraid I must take my leave, but I would enjoy matching wits with you again," Lupin said, smiling. "I believe we have more in common than you might think. The thief and the thief-taker are really two sides of the same coin. You have a bright future ahead of you, young man. A colleague of mine suggested I should keep an eye on you. You may become quite the globetrotter..."

Lupin spun on his heels and ran off into the night. Rouletabille considered giving drawing his pistol and giving chase, but he knew it would be pointless. He also was sure that he would get other chances to battle the gentleman-burglar.

He gazed at the city illuminated by its mixture of gas and electric lights, a field of jewels that was far more precious to him than any diamonds or gold coins. It was a new century and the evidence presented at the Exposition indicated that it would belong to modern scientific people like Lupin and himself, rather than the superstitions of past centuries. A city of light and not of darkness.

As Rouletabille had predicted, the police were able to recover the gold coins and the other precious items that Lupin had substituted a few days before from a hidden safe in the wall of Jurgen's shop. After his report, the French Government decided to take the coins into safe keeping while the other precious items were returned to their owners.

Despite his frustration at not being able to arrange the capture of the criminals, Rouletabille concluded that one positive thing had come out of the affair, apart from his own satisfaction in unraveling the tangled knots of the mystery and the boost it had given to his reputation. It was Lupin's suggestion that he became a globetrotter, which gave his nickname a far more positive meaning and one he would now embrace.

Matthew Baugh returns to the characters of Madame Palmyre the Sorceress and her companion Renée, last seen in his contribution to our Volume 16. The two are borrowed from Renée Dunan's remarkable novel, Baal *(1924) (available from Black Coat Press). Matthew told us that the adventure to which Houdini refers in this story is* Imprisoned with the Pharaohs, *which H.P. Lovecraft ghost-wrote. The chess game featured in here is a real game played in 1991 between Vassily Ivanchuk and Artur Yusupov. Finally, the poem Antinea quotes is* Deathless Aphrodite of the spangled mind *by Sappho.*

Matthew Baugh: *The Long Game*

Cairo, 1925

The woman in white opens with pawn to C4.
The woman in black replies with pawn to E5.

Palmyre and I stepped out of the limousine and gazed up at the elaborate structure. While clearly devoted to the mysteries and the sensuality of the east, the mansion looked somehow out of place in the suburb of Heliopolis.

"It's quite grand, isn't it?" I said.

My friend sniffed. "In a tacky sort of way, perhaps. It would seem an extravagance, even in India, which is where this style comes from. Here it does not fit."

"How so?"

"Just look at the statues." She waved a black-draped arm at a series of carvings depicting voluptuous women, fierce-looking warriors, and a man with the head of an elephant. All of them equipped with an excessive number of arms and rendered in sensual detail.

"I confess, I don't see the problem. We have our gargoyles and grotesques. Certainly, it's not remarkable that these Orientals have theirs."

"Look again, my dear. These are not grotesques; they are gods. The baron's home is not built along the lines of a palace so much as they are a Hindu temple. Egypt is a Muslim land, and these images of foreign gods must seem to them an affront to Allah."

"I suppose, but I can't imagine anyone being too put off by architecture."

"You are a modern woman, Renée. The people of an ancient land may not share your sensibilities. Nevertheless, the baron's eccentricities and his audacity should make this an interesting dinner. Besides, there are several guests whom I simply must meet."

She took my arm and led me to the front doors of the Palace Empain.

The woman in white plays pawn to G3.
The woman in black moves a pawn to D6.

Dinner was not to my taste. Our host served us twelve courses, each from a different country; alas, none of those countries was France. I ate as little as I thought possible without offending our host and noticed that most of the other guests did the same. Palmyre, of course, sampled everything, the more outlandish, the better.

The baron was a smallish man, slim and with military posture even in his 70s. He was Belgian and had come to Egypt as an engineer and businessman hoping to make his fortune. He had succeeded and had even been given the title of baron by the loathsome King Leopold II. The baron's son, Jean, looked a great deal like him, albeit clean-shaven and a half-century younger. I thought Jean a bore, but his wife was a vivacious American named Rozelle, who I took to immediately. She had been a dancer in the burlesque, which is where she had caught her husband's eye.

It had been Rozelle's connections that had brought the famous American magician, Harry Houdini, to their home. He was accompanied by his wife Bess and their factotum, a short, powerfully built man appropriately nicknamed Ape O'Connell.

The other guests included: A dark and diabolically handsome fellow called Gil-Martin, the aged Russian chess master, Stavlokratz, and a pear-shaped man named Major Brabazon-Plank.

The woman in white advances her bishop to G2.
The woman in black plays pawn to G6.

"Why, yes, I am mounting an expedition to the Ahaggar mountains," the major said. "I'm off to Al Qatrun tomorrow to meet my caravan."

"Perfect," Madame Palmyre said. "Renée and I will accompany you, then."

"Surely, you can't be serious, Madame?"

"Perfectly serious. There is something there that I've wanted to see for many years."

"You must be aware it's in the middle of the bally Sahara."

"Indeed. And viewing that splendid desolation, boundless and bare, is one of the bonuses of this trip."

"You make it sound as if you find the desert beautiful."

"Of course I do, major. Don't you?"

"Not at all! It's just a lot of sand and ruddy hot on top of that! You wouldn't like it, I promise you."

"Then why are you going?" Palmyre asked in her most innocent tones.

"Well, it's got to be explored, doesn't it? It won't do to leave places out there that no white man has ever seen. Just not proper at all."

"Of course, major. But if I help to underwrite this expedition…?"

"I suppose it would be wrong with me not to let you come along. Unchivalrous and all that. But I warn you again; it is very dangerous. Likely to get some heathen Tuaregs riding down on us, brandishing their scimitars and howling like banshees."

I saw a touch of mischief in Palmyre's answering smile.

"I thought that the Tuaregs brandished straight, double-edged swords called *takouba*?" she said.

The major's cheeks flushed. He opened his mouth, then closed it again without saying anything. Fortunately, Houdini came to his rescue.

"Just what is it you hope to see in those mountains, Madame Palmyre?"

"Why, Atlantis, of course."

The woman in white advances her pawn to D4.
The woman in black replies by with knight to D7.

"Surely Atlantis, if it exists, is at the bottom of the ocean," Houdini said. "Why search for it in the desert?"

"It is not so strange, monsieur," the baron said. "I have read the theories of Le Plongeon, and he says that Atlantis was an empire of great scope, with outposts from the Yucatan to Egypt. Why should there not be one in the Ahaggars?"

"I suppose there could be, but suppositions are not much to go on."

"I read a great deal, monsieur," Palmyre said. "My studies tell of many such places on the African continent: Kôr, Negari, and Opar to name but a few."

"Yes, but the rumors of many lost cities do not add up to evidence for any of them."

"You surprise me, monsieur," Baron Empain said. "How is it you are so skeptical when you discovered an ancient temple hidden deep beneath the sphinx? That was back around 1910, I think."

"How did you hear about that?" the magician asked.

"It is a popular tale among the locals," the baron said.

"It's a bit of nonsense," Houdini said. "A bad dream I had and nothing more."

"You must tell us so that we can judge for ourselves," Palmyre said.

"Are you certain you want to hear it?" The magician asked. "I guarantee it would be more entertaining to let me escape from a straight jacket or a set of handcuffs."

The woman in white moves a knight to C3.
The woman in black counters with bishop to G7.

"…and there you have it," Houdini concluded. "The whole thing was a particularly vivid dream. My abduction, the temple, the legion of mummies, and the gigantic, unspeakable creature that slumbers beneath the sands, were all the fantasies of an overtired mind."

"So, your escape was just a fantasy as well?" I asked.

"No, mademoiselle. The story is a delusion, but my escape was genuine. All my escapes are genuine." He favored me with a wink.

"It doesn't change your opinion of Atlantis?" Palmyre asked.

"No, Madame, I still think it is nothing but bunk and bewilderment. If you go looking for it, you'll only waste your time."

"Perhaps so, but it is my time to waste. Even if I find nothing, I believe I will take a great deal of satisfaction in the search."

"In that case, safe travels and good luck."

"Yes," the major said. "Just be ready to go first thing in the morning."

"But don't turn in too early," Baron Empain said. "You won't want to miss this evening's entertainment. You've all met Monsieur Gil-Martin..."

We had, but as the dark man bowed his head in acknowledgment, I realized that we knew nothing about him, or at least I knew nothing. Gil-Martin had been a courteous listener to the rest of us all evening, but had said nothing more revealing than, "Please pass the butter." He was as much the man of mystery now as he had been before the meal.

"Monsieur Gil-Martin has been my guest for three weeks," the baron continued. "In that time, we have played a dozen games of chess. While I consider myself quite a good player, he has defeated me every time with embarrassing ease. I have brought around the best players in Cairo, but he has picked them off with the same aplomb. He is a genuinely remarkable student of the game.

"As luck would have it, though, a new player has arrived in town. Anyone who knows anything about chess has already recognized the great Monsieur Stavlokratz. He and Monsieur Gil-Martin have agreed to play this evening. I promise you; this will be a rare and brilliant game.

The dining room doors opened, and we rose and followed our host into a large chamber, where a splendid gold and silver chess set sat atop a small table.

The woman in white moves her knight to F3.
The woman in black plays her knight to F6.

We sent in a row of chairs watching intently. The subtleties of the game were too much for me, but I could read the players. First, I had thought Gil-Martin nervous. He had placed a crystal sphere about the size of a hen's egg on the table and glanced at it occasionally. It was evidently a good-luck piece or some sort of worry stone to help keep his mind calm. He didn't seem to need it, though, for he played with great confidence, seldom hesitating for more than a few seconds before making a move.

At first, the Russian had matched this confidence, but as the game progressed, he seemed shaken. It took him longer to choose his moves, and I could see growing anxiety on his face.

"The Russian is losing!" I whispered into Palmyre's ear. "How can that be?"

"Many things are possible, Renée," she replied, her voice even quieter than mine. "Even a surprising number of impossible things. Keep watching."

The strain was taking its toll on Stavlokratz. After another move, he wiped his face with his handkerchief and requested a glass of water. He reached for a pawn, seemed to reconsider, and having his hand over his queen's bishop for a moment before lowering it to his side. He had still not moved when a servant returned with his water.

Houdini, focused on the board, chose that moment to stand and stretch his legs. He bumped into the servant, knocking the glass from the tray. The water splashed across the board, and ice cubes rattled on the marble surface. Stavlokratz, Gil-Martin, Houdini, and the footman all grabbed for the toppling chess pieces. After a moment of panic, it became clear there was no damage to the pieces or board. Two maids appeared with dishtowels to help the footman clean up the water, and the Russian began to replace the chessmen as they had been. I would have been lost, but he managed it effortlessly.

"My crystal!" Gil-Martin cried.

"Don't worry; I have it." Houdini held out the spherical talisman.

"Give me that!" Gil-Martin snatched the bauble from the magician's hand, and for a moment, I thought he was going to strike him. Houdini stood there calmly, making no attempt to defend himself. Behind him, Ape O'Connell rose from his chair and flexed his long arms.

"Everything OK, boss?"

Gil-Martin took a step back and lowered his hands. "Everything is not OK. Monsieur Houdini. Why did you pick up my crystal?"

The magician spread his hands in a gesture of innocence.

"It rolled off the edge of the table. I was afraid it would crack if it struck the floor."

Gil-Martin glared at him a moment longer, then turned on Baron Empain.

"I must protest this interruption, Monsieur le Baron. And this fool of the footman has disrupted all my careful strategies. You should send him packing immediately!"

"I will attend to my servants in my way," the baron said. "If you would like a break and then resume the game when your nerves are settled, I'm happy to grant that."

Gil-Martin drew in a deep breath. As he let it out, his shoulders relaxed, and when he spoke again, his voice was calm.

"That will not be necessary, baron. Monsieur Stavlokratz, you are a worthy opponent, but I have lost interest in pursuing this game. I resign."

The woman in white castles on her king side.
The woman in black also castles on her king side.

I was brushing my hair at the vanity in the room I shared with Palmyre when I heard a knock at the door. As my friend was in the tub, I threw on a dressing gown and answered the door. I was surprised to find Ape O'Connell standing there, a pleasant grin on his simian face.

"Hi, kid," he said in surprisingly good French.

"Monsieur O'Connell, what are you doing here?"

"I've got a special delivery for Madame Palmyre from Mr. Houdini." He opened a massive hand to reveal the Gil-Martin's crystal sphere.

"I don't understand," I said.

"Ah, she must not have told you. Madame Palmyre wanted my boss to swap out the real sphere for a fake she had. She told him Gil-Martin was using this doodad to cheat. That got his interest all right. If there's anything Mr. Houdini hates, it's swindlers and con-artists."

"But how...?"

"When the water spilled. Honestly, I don't think the boss needed the distraction, but he likes it theatrical, you know?"

"Please tell Mr. Houdini he was brilliant," Palmyre said as she entered the room. Her hair was in a towel, and she wore a silk kimono that clung to her body in a way that made Ape O'Connell's eyes bulge. She crossed to the door and held out a hand.

O'Connell swallowed and dragged his attention back to the task at hand. He dropped the crystal into her palm.

"Mr. Houdini's a hundred percent sure that you were right, and Gil-Martin was cheating. But he can't figure out how he was doing it with that lump of glass."

"I don't think I could tell him in terms he would accept," Palmyre replied. "Just tell him I am deeply grateful for his getting this for me."

"Yes, Ma'am, I'll do that." Ape gave her another lingering glance, then turned and hurried down the hall.

I shut the door and turned to Palmyre.

"I don't understand how you did that."

"Mr. Houdini is a genius at his craft."

"Yes, but how did you know that Gil-Martin was using the crystal?" I said. "And how did you happen to have a duplicate?"

"Some years ago, I heard of a chess player in Cuba who never lost a match. After a time, the locals decided that he must be the devil and refused to play with him anymore. Before he moved on, the man told his secret to a British sailor." She held out the little crystal ball for me to study.

"Stare into the ball, and it will show you your next move. Follow its guidance, and you will always win. If you choose a different move, though, the images in the ball become chaotic. The sailor wanted to buy the ball, and the chess devil agreed to trade it for his soul. The seaman thought that sounded like a good deal, as he was certain his soul was bound for Hell already. He took the ball and held it for a few years until he met his end. I got the story from one of his shipmates."

"But not the crystal ball?"

"That was gone, but when I learned of Monsieur Gil-Martin and his talisman, I knew that the chess-devil was back."

"I see, but why did you want it so much?"

"That, my dear, is part of a much longer game I am playing."

The woman in white moves her queen to C2.
The woman in black moves her rook to E8.

The trip across the Sahara was as unpleasant as the major had told us. We rode camels, which I found smelly, bad-tempered beasts and whose lurching gait left me motion sick. It didn't help that Palmyre rode behind me, her legs comfortably crossed, and wearing a tranquil expression. It helped even less that the major rode in front of me, his massive posterior swaying in time with his animal's strides. This, plus the blast-furnace heat of the desert air, combined to make me as miserable as I have ever been.

After the first week, however, I found that I had developed an affection for my camel. His swaying motion no longer bothered me, and his disposition sweetened. I began to understand the austere beauty my friend found in this barren place, especially at night as I gazed up at the brightest stars I had ever seen. And whenever we reached an oasis, I took delight in the simple comforts of shade and fresh water it offered.

It was three weeks before we saw the mountains, rising in a jagged line from the desert. After so long with nothing but rolling dunes to look at, they seemed magical and impossibly rugged. We found an oasis and made camp, but I was too excited to sleep. That night, while the others were lying in their tents, I climbed to the top of a dune and stood watching the stars rise from behind the mountains' jagged silhouette. Amid that immensity, I felt a sense of wonder.

At least, I did until someone threw a bag over my head.

The woman in white moves her rook to D1.
The woman in black moves her pawn to C6.

In short order, I was bustled away with a strong hand over my mouth, bound with rope, and slung across the back of a camel. The beast lurched to its feet, and I realized very quickly that whatever immunity I had gained to camel-sickness didn't work when I couldn't see anything.

My abductors must be some of the major's Tuaregs. They had seen me alone and unarmed, away from the camp, and decided to take me alive. Even now, I thought they were preparing to ride down on the camp wailing like banshees and waving whatever kind of swords they carried over their heads. I listened intently but could not make out any war cries, gunfire, or other sounds of violence.

Perhaps this was not a full-scale raid after all? They may have seen that our group was too strong to confront it and decided to content themselves with me. I was glad to think that Palmyre was safe from harm, but my relief lasted only a moment. I began to think of everything I'd ever heard about what happens to a white woman when she falls into the clutches of heathen savages. No doubt I would be ravished and possibly whipped. Or perhaps they would strip me naked and parade me in front of the bidders at a slave auction. I could end up being an odalisque in the seraglio of a wealthy sultan where women are forced to wear scanty silken dancers' garments and lavish jewelry. I would be hidden away from the eyes of all men except my master. I would be watched over by merciless eunuchs and subject to the jealousy of the other concubines because of my fair skin.

I thought about this for a while before deciding that I'd probably read too many novels. I began to run through my options. Sadly, there were not many. I didn't have the strength or the skills to overpower my captors. I might be able to slip away, but I doubted I would last even a day in the Sahara after the sun rose. My best chance might be to talk to them and arrange for some sort of ransom. However, since I did not speak their language, and the only Arabic phrases I knew were things like, "I am pleased to meet you," "thank you very much," and "could you tell me where the privy is?" I didn't see this going very well either.

The woman in white plays a pawn to B3.
The woman in black moves her queen to E7.

The eastern sky was growing brighter when they finally took the bag off my head. Two Tuareg men, only their eyes showing through their hoods, lifted me down and undid my bonds. They guided me towards two women standing by a group of boulders, then turned back to their camels and rode away.

I watched them go, wondering what was happening before turning back to the women. They were both taller than I and very beautiful, with Berber features and thick black hair.

"Good morning, Madame Palmyre," one of them said in excellent French. "We are here to escort you to our queen."

Several things struck me at the same time. These women didn't seem to be observant Muslims, or they wouldn't have gone unveiled in the presence of men. Also, they seemed to believe that I was my companion. It must have been Palmyre whom the desert warriors had planned to abduct. Finally, it occurred to me that it might be better not to inform them that they had the wrong woman.

"Good morning," I replied.

"Please forgive the way we brought you here. It is necessary if we are to keep the location of Atlantis a secret." She held out a silken sash. "I'm afraid I must blindfold you for the trip up the mountain. I hope it will not cause you too much discomfort."

I smiled and nodded as if I had a choice in the matter.

"What is up on the mountain?" I asked.

"That is where you shall meet the queen."

The woman in white advances a bishop to A3.
The woman in black moves a pawn to E4, threatening the knight.

The next morning, I woke to the feel of silken sheets against my skin. I was exhausted when they finally had removed the blindfold from my eyes, but I remembered a splendid meal of roast antelope, vegetables, and couscous with a good Sangiovese. I was surprised again by this departure from the Muslim tradition. It seemed that wine and liquor were in good supply in Atlantis. Afterward, I was given a tub of rose-scented water, then ushered into a magnificent bedroom.

I felt better than I had in many weeks and had no desire to get out of bed, or even to open my eyes. I stretched, and my feet bumped into a heavy shape sitting on top of the covers. The body moved and let out a coughing growl. My eyes opened, and every trace of sleepiness disappeared as I saw the huge leopard curled at my feet. Scooting away from the animal until my back was against the headboard, I clutched a large cushion in front of my body as if it could save me from the animal's claws.

I heard the sound of musical laughter from the doorway and turned to see one of the women from the previous day.

"You mustn't let King Hiram frighten you, Madame Palmyre," she said. "He can be fierce when his mistress commands it, but most of the time, he is quite gentle."

"I'm happy to hear it," I said, never taking my eyes from the great spotted cat.

"I've taken the liberty of laying out some clothing for you. Your breakfast will be ready whenever you want it."

She offered me a light smile and a little bow before slipping out of the room. I thought about breakfast. I was not hungry, yet after last night but felt a great desire to explore this place. Could this be the Atlantis Plato had written of? Then I looked again at King Hiram, grooming his paws, and decided to stay exactly where I was for a little longer.

The woman in white moves her knight out of danger to G5.
The woman in black advances her pawn to E3.

I had finally thrown on a dressing gown after King Hiram had curled up for a nap. When I started for the door, the leopard stretched and gave a tremendous yawn, which persuaded me not to try to leave my room again.

I did take the opportunity to explore the room itself, which was a study in contradictions. The circular chamber was made of polished porphyry and paneled with an unfamiliar metal the color of pale gold. The bed, wardrobe, and other furnishings were European, and the bright colors and intricate patterns made me think of the *arts décoratifs* style that was presently the rage in Paris. The bookcase held volumes in English, French, Spanish, German, and Latin, but nothing I could identify as Arabic or Berber, let alone some ancient hieroglyphs as I might have expected. It made a disorienting mix of the exotic and the familiar.

Morning sunlight poured in through a single large window that opened onto a balcony. I stepped out to an amazing sight. My room appeared to be carved into the side of a steep mountain, part of a ring of snowcapped peaks that surrounded lush gardens far below. I could make out a variety of fruit trees and flower bushes not native to this part of the world, but flourishing in the protective circle of stone. I heard the cries of exotic birds and spotted the bright colors of a group of parrots as they rose and circled above the trees. There was nothing I had ever seen in my world to rival this. It had to be Atlantis.

The woman in white advances her pawn to F4.
The woman in black moves her knight to F8.

I spent three days exploring the palace complex without finding my way down to the gardens. Nor did I find a route to the outer world and escape. The maidens who greeted me and the many Africans I saw, I assumed, were slaves. My heart ached for them, trapped by this scourge that should have been eradicated long ago, but I had no common language to share my thoughts with them.

I did not seem to be a prisoner, but I might as well have been. The place was an unending maze of halls and stairs, and while there were no guards, I had the constant feeling of being watched. Several times I turned to spot the watcher and saw King Hiram slink into the shadows.

The following day, a flurry of activity happened. The young women who had greeted me, accompanied by half a dozen younger African girls, bustled me out of bed and into the bath, where they scrubbed me mercilessly. Having dried me off, they dressed me in a regal Moroccan gown. When I saw myself in the polished metal mirror, I was amazed. I had been transformed into some exotic beauty.

"Come, Madame," one of the women urged. "You have been summoned for an audience with Queen Antinea."

The woman in white plays pawn to B4.
The woman in black plays bishop to F5, threatening the queen.

Antinea was as slender as a girl, but her green eyes burned with an ancient fire. With her masses of black hair and hawkish profile, she was a fantasy of Cleopatra come to life. She had dressed to enhance this illusion. Her gold-trimmed white gown could have been taken from a wall painting in Thebes. Likewise, the golden circlet in the shape of a cobra on her head.

"I'm happy to meet you, Madame Palmyre," she said. "Since my friends in Cairo told me of you, I have made it my business to learn more."

"I... I'm very flattered, your majesty," I said.

"You are a woman after my heart. I understand that you speak quite a few languages and know as much about history, architecture, philosophy, the sciences, and the occult as a dozen of the great scholars of Europe."

"Um..."

"I look forward to the conversations we shall have. You can't imagine how I have longed for an equal to converse with. My servants are excellent, but have no breadth of education. And even if they had, they are so submissive that they would never dare to contradict me. The relationship of a slave to their master, by definition, cannot be equal."

"You... that is, I..."

"Precisely!" Antinea said with a smile. "Only a woman like you is a fit companion for the queen of Atlantis."

"Companion?"

"Yes. I have grown tired of male paramours. They are like mayflies, lasting only a little while. Also, like flies, they can be damned annoying."

"Paramours?" This conversation was so bizarre that my mind was whirling. Was this woman mad? Did she want me—that is, Palmyre—as a paramour? I didn't know what that entailed, but the thought of mayflies didn't sound good at all.

"Yes," Antinea said, nodding. "*Para amore* is too romantic a word. They are useful, even desirable, but I would never give my heart to any of them. I choose them for their physical beauty, of course, but also for intellect and strength of will. Those are the qualities that make them the best targets for my revenge."

"Revenge?" My eyes went wide.

"The type of revenge I think you will appreciate, my dear Palmyre. It is the revenge of our sex on those who have abused us, enslaved us, and exploited us since the dawn of time. Let me show you my master-work, then you will understand."

The woman in white moves her queen to the safety of B3.
The woman in black advances her pawn to H6, threatening the knight.

The hall was a massive room of red marble. Alone the sides were a series of niches, numbering probably upwards of a hundred. More than half held standing Egyptian-style sarcophagi, and each of these was open at the front to reveal an unmoving human figure that gleamed pale yellow.

"Statues?" I said, awed by the sight. "I don't understand."

"Look more closely," Antinea said.

I approached one of the niches, which held a small panel that said, *Morhange*. The statue was of a tall man with a broad, pleasant face. It possessed a level of detail I had never seen. It was almost as if…

"No," I whispered.

"Yes," Antinea countered brightly. "Each of these is one of my lovers, preserved in his prime forever. When all the niches are filled, my mission of revenge will be complete."

The woman in white moves her knight to F3.
The woman in black moves her knight to G4.

I walked beside Antinea, feeling numb from the horrible revelation. She chatted gaily as if her collection of dead lovers were a painting or a sculpture she was proud of. She informed me that she had done nothing more than give them what they wanted most. She had, she explained, the ability to inspire love in all men while feeling nothing herself. First, she gave them her company, for she was only interested in men whose wit and intellect were well above the norm. Then she would give them her body, offering them degrees of pleasure they had never experienced. Finally, when the passions she inflamed in them consumed them, she would preserve their bodies in this gruesome way.

She didn't "dip them in gold," she said. For one thing, the metal was *orichalcum*, the metal of Atlantis, which is rarer and stronger than gold. For another, her process was much more sophisticated than dipping. It involved chemicals and electricity, though I was too stunned to understand any of it.

The woman in white advances her pawn to B5.
The woman in black counters with pawn to G5.

Antinea reclined on her lion throne, her green eyes never wavering as she gazed at my face. She had allowed me a pile of cushions which I collapsed onto. She seemed displeased with my weakness, but I was beyond caring. Glancing around the room, I saw that all eyes were on me. King Hiram was there, of course, and the lovely pair of attendants. There were also two Tuareg riders fresh from the desert, with their black robes and blue hoods. In addition, four or five muscular African men had paused from their jobs to watch. They sensed that the queen was judging me and were eager to learn the outcome.

"Do you disapprove of me, Madame Palmyre?" Antinea asked.

"How can you be so cruel?" I replied.

"I am not cruel. Wasn't I merciful by giving those men everything they wanted? More than merciful, I was generous to them."

"You are a murderess."

"I murdered no one. Those men would have used me for my beauty and despoiled my kingdom for its treasures. Every one of them would have done that had they not been consumed by their love for me."

"You are a monster."

"You are a fool! I thought the great Madame Palmyre enough of a sophisticate to see past her culture and narrow prejudices, and understand the splendor of what I do here. I had hopes of a companion who would be my equal, but you have the sentiments of a peasant. Nonetheless, I have set my mind on having you, and have you I will."

"No!"

"You will come to me. You will love me."

"Why should I? So you can have one more body for your chamber of horrors?"

Antinea's face softened. "Of course not. You are not part of my great work of revenge. You're the one I've chosen to share my life with. You will die, of course, but your body will never dwell in the hall of red marble. You, I shall sit on a pedestal here, in my throne room, so that all who come to Atlantis may adore you."

"I will never consent to you."

"…Even if she flees, soon she shall pursue.
And if she refuses gifts, soon she shall give them.
If she doesn't love you, soon she shall love
even if she's unwilling."

I stared at her blankly, my mind too full of horror to form words.

"You recognize the poem, don't you? You must! I chose it especially for you. Can I have been so wrong? Is the great Madame Palmyre a simpleton and a fraud?"

"This woman is not Madame Palmyre!"

The voice had come from one of the two Tuaregs, but it was a woman's voice. I stared at the desert rider's slender form as it raised a large pistol and aimed it at Queen Antinea. The Tuareg's other hand pulled away the dark turban and hood, revealing the face of the true Madame Palmyre.

Everyone in the room froze with shock, except for me. I sprang to my feet and ran to my friend's side, where she wrapped a protective arm around my shoulders.

"How did you find your way in?" the queen demanded. "No one outside Atlantis knows the path."

"Your loyal Tuaregs do," Palmyre said, nodding to her companion. "I'm sure this fellow would never have told me, but I have learned how to dominate another's will with mine. He made a useful guide."

"You sent this girl as a ruse?"

"No, you sent your men to abduct me, and they took Renée by mistake."

"No matter. Now I have both of you."

"You have neither of us. I don't know if you're familiar with modern weapons, but I can kill you before any of your people can reach us."

Antinea laughed. "Yes, I know of such things. That is a C-96 automatic pistol, a very potent weapon. I am certain you will kill me if you fire. Perhaps you will kill King Hiram also before he tears you to pieces. But you can't have enough bullets to shoot everyone in Atlantis. Servants will drag you and your little friend down, and your rescue attempt will have been for nothing."

"A pyrrhic victory is still a victory," Palmyre said. "But I do have an alternative." She nodded toward the west wall where a chessboard with orichalc pieces stood.

"You intrigue me," Antinea said. "What stakes would we play for?"

"If I win, Renée and I are given safe passage back to our caravan. If you win, Renée returns to the caravan, and I remain here with you."

"It seems to me that you win either way," Antinea said. "I will accept, but only if you are both at risk. Your Renée seems to be very valuable to you, perhaps as valuable as the queen in the game. We play, and if I win, you both stay. If you win, you go free, but if I have taken your queen, Renée stays in Atlantis."

I felt myself shiver, and Palmyre's face turned the shade paler. Her expression didn't shift, though. "I will accept that, on one condition; since Renée's freedom is at stake, she should be able to consult with me on my moves. You will play both of us."

"I don't see how that could possibly help you," Antinea said, "but very well, I accept."

The two crossed to the board, Antinea taking white and Palmyre accepting black. It fit with the queen's white finery and my friend's Tuareg black. I leaned close to Palmyre's ear.

"I do appreciate the gesture, but I barely know the rules of chess!" I whispered.

"Don't worry," Palmyre replied. She handed me her pistol, and as I took it, I felt her slip something small and smooth my hand. A glance told me it was Gil-Martin's crystal orb.

Antinea moves a pawn to B5.
Madame Palmyre moves a pawn to G5.

They were eighteen moves in, and neither had taken a piece yet; the tension was agony. Both positions looked strong and carefully crafted to me, though there were too many subtleties in the game to be confident. What worried me most was that twice the crystal had shown Palmyre's best move was to bring the queen out. She had refused, no doubt to protect me, but each time, the images in the crystal had jumped and blurred disturbingly. Looking pleased with herself, Antinea used a pawn to take Palmyre's pawn at C6.

"First blood to me," she said.

Palmyre's only answer was to take the offending pawn with one of hers.

Antinea moved her knight to E5, where it was in danger from a pawn and Palmyre's queen. I looked into the crystal and saw it use the queen to take the knight. The move sacrificed the queen but opened up

44

Palmyre's rooks to wreak havoc. I whispered this into her ear, but she shook her head as one does when a gnat is buzzing in her ear. Instead, she used a pawn to take Antinea's pawn at F4. The crystal began to vibrate in my palm as Antinea moved her knight to C6, taking her pawn and threatening her queen. Without consulting me, Palmyre moved the queen to the safety of G5.

The next few moves were a blur as I looked deep into the crystal, willing the images to come back into focus. Antinea used her bishop to take a pawn at D6, placing Palmyre's knight in peril. My friend retreated again, moving her knight to G6, but Antinea pursued, bringing her knight to D5. My heart sank when Palmyre's reply was to move her queen to H5, as far from the advancing knights as possible.

Antinea moved her pawn to H4, locking Palmyre's queen in place, but then the images in the crystal cleared. I whispered that she should use her knight to take the pawn at H4, and she complied. Unfortunately, this left us open, and Antinea used a pawn to take the knight. We were behind on pieces and trapped in a defensive position.

The crystal showed me our queen taking the pawn at H4, and I whispered the move to Palmyre. She hesitated for a long time, her hand hovering over the queen. The crystal blurred and began to vibrate again. Palmyre moved her hand away from the queen to hover over the rook.

The crystal shattered with a *tink*, and a foul stench emanated from the fragments.

"I thought as much," Antinea said. "You've been using some occult trinket to improve your chances. I should declare the game forfeit for that."

"Perhaps you should," Palmyre said. "You clearly can't win this game any longer."

Antinea stared at her, then burst out in musical laughter.

"You think you can make me do something rash by tweaking my pride? That is delightful, but I applaud your nerve. Since you have no chance of your winning, I shall continue the game. It may be instructive to you.

"We shall see." Palmyre returned her hand to the queen and took the pawn.

Antinea moved her knight to E7.

"Check," she said with a pleasant smile.

Palmyre pulled her king into the corner at H8, and I held my breath.

Antinea played knight to F5, threatening both Palmyre's bishop and her queen. But Palmyre found a way to save both. Bringing her queen down to H2, she placed Antinea in check.

My joy didn't last long as Antinea completely nullified the attack by simply moving her king to F1.

Palmyre advanced her rook to E6 in what seemed to me like a weak move. Antinea moved her queen to B7, significantly increasing the pressure on our king. Palmyre retreated with her rook to G6. Antinea moved her queen to A8, taking our other rook.

"Check," she said again.

Palmyre moved her King to H7, which was the only move she had. Antinea was completely dominating the game now. She moved her queen to H7, and announced "check" for the third time.

For a moment, I thought it was mate, then Palmyre took the queen with her king. Antinea had moved in with no protection. Why had she done that?

My relief didn't last long as Antinea moved her knight to E7, placing us in check again. She was so far ahead; losing a queen didn't seem to have hurt her significantly.

Palmyre brought the king to H7 again, momentarily saving the game. Antinea brought her other knight to G6, and Palmyre took it with a pawn. Antinea brought her knight to G7, and Palmyre moved her knight to F2. Now, the pressure was suddenly on Antinea's king, and I saw her eyes go wide. She moved her bishop to take the pawn on F4, but Palmyre countered by taking the bishop with her queen. We were far behind on pieces, but I was starting to feel more hopeful.

Antinea moved her knight to E6 to threaten our queen. Palmyre brought the queen back to H2. Antinea started to mobilize her rooks, moving one to B1. Palmyre withdrew her knight to B7, placing us in check again. I saw her strategy now. Between the rook and her surviving knight, she could continue to place Palmyre in check until she reached mate in three moves.

As I predicted, Palmyre was forced to move the king back to H8. Also, as I had anticipated, Antinea moved her rook to B8 for another check. What I hadn't foreseen—and neither had Antinea—was that this put her rook on the diagonal from our queen.

Palmyre brought it across the board to take the rook at B8. Antinea replied by taking our knight with her bishop at H3. That left us with only our queen against her rook, knight, and bishop. It seemed almost hopeless until Palmyre brought the queen all the way back to G3.

Antinea saw it right away; it took me a moment longer. Between the queen and the pawn at E3, there was nothing to do to avoid mate in one move.

The woman in white touched a slender forefinger to her king and toppled it.

In the cool of the morning, Palmyre and I left the foothills of the Ahaggar mountains.

"But how did you know you would need Gil-Martin's crystal?" I said.

"I told you, I was playing a long game," Palmyre said. "I knew of Atlantis because of an obscure book I'd found by a man named André de Saint-Avit. I tracked him down and gained all the information I could from him about Atlantis and her queen. His experience there had left him a broken man, but he gave me a good deal of information. This included the fact that Antinea was a fiend for chess and an unbeatable player. I knew that I could coax many of the secrets of that ancient land from her by beating her at the game, but for that, I would need an advantage. From there, you know the story."

"For someone who plans such a painstaking strategy, I thought you would lose it all when you refused to listen to the crystal."

"My dear Renée," Palmyre said, "it is an irrationality that I have developed. I will never sacrifice my queen."

We linked arms and walked out into the desert, where our caravan waited.

In this tale, Atom Bezecny resurrects an obscure French pulp hero who is mostly (and some might say deservedly) forgotten: Fascinax. Introduced in 1921 as the "protector of the weak, the avenger of the oppressed, and the terror of villains everywhere," Fascinax *was published anonymously by the Librairie des Romans Choisis in 22 pulp magazines. He is George Leicester, a British MD residing in the Philippines, who helped Hindu yogi Nadir Kritchna return to life after having been put to death for a crime he did not commit. To thank him, the yogi takes him to a temple in the jungle and, after various mystic rituals, bestows supernatural powers upon him. Fascinax followed in the footsteps of such occult detectives as Sar Dubnotal, John Silence and Carnacki, but never garnered the same success as his more distinguished predecessors.*

Atom Mudman Bezecny: *The Devil Times Phibes*

London, 1928

The only noise in the Stygian darkness was the howling of an infernal wind. This tenebrous abyss held no comforting warmth; the ninth ring of Hell could be no colder. The emptiness seemed to go on forever. Through this dark void sailed a robed figure, whose exposed hands and face resembled those of a shriveled corpse. But even if he could have screamed, the voice of Anton Phibes would not have been heard above the cacophonous hurricane that was now buffeting him.

There were no words for the ecstasy Phibes had felt upon finally reaching the Egyptian River of Life. The subterranean currents he had so recently uncovered were to be his salvation—its enchanted waters would restore his beloved wife to the land of the living, while repairing his disfigured appearance. Ever since his darling spouse had met her death at the hands of his treacherous fellow physicians, Phibes had devoted his life to reviving her. He stood at the cusp of mortality, and beheld the flow of Life itself.

But it was not to be. The holy force turned upon him, deeming him unworthy. He himself had said he was of the dead—not fit to encroach upon this domain. The waters fell away into blackness. His wife's coffin flew away from him, far beyond his sigh; poor Vulnavia was swallowed

48

up by the shadows, and he could have sworn that he'd seen her body torn to pieces.

In an instant, whatever thin thread had held up Phibes' battered sanity snapped. As the winds slashed at him, he begged for his long-ravaged vocal cords to heal, so that he could lament his suffering.

The Devil take you, Phibes... In his quest for resurrection, Phibes had clashed with an immortal whose longevity formula had run out. The man had spat these words at him at his moment of defeat. Phibes had stopped him from claiming the River as his next source of renewal—it could not be shared, after all. But now the man's sinister curse seemed to echo from the void.

The Devil take you, Phibes...

Perhaps that would be relief.

I feel your plight, Anton Phibes.

A voice resonated in Phibes' mind, cutting sharper than any knife, louder than the immortal's curse. Without his sound-device, Phibes could not answer, but his panicked thoughts were answer enough for whatever it was that was speaking to him.

Do not be afraid, the voice said, with a short laugh. *I am here to deliver you from this place.*

Somehow, peace came over the tormented scientist, enough at least for him to consciously articulate a thought:

Who are you? he demanded.

My dear fellow, you know who I am. What matters is what I can do for you.

Phibes once more recalled the immortal's curse, and he indeed knew who the voice belonged to.

Anton Phibes had never been a religious man. He had not cried out to God or any other entity when his wife died. So his reaction to being in the presence of the Devil—Satan himself, perhaps—was one of curiosity rather than fear. He considered the likelihood that this being, whatever it was, chose to play the role of the Devil for its own purposes.

I know that you will charge a grievous price for your help, the scientist said, *and so I wish to know your terms.*

Your salvation will come cheaply, my dear doctor, the Devil replied. *Your brilliance suits you to the task I have in mind, and the challenge will be rewarding.*

Phibes' curiosity increased. The Devil showed him the faces of five men.

These creatures are the heirs of the killers of your wife. When you killed their relatives, they became tremendously wealthy. They have profited from your vengeance.

His point was clear. This was a grave injustice, requiring a brutal rectification.

If you dispatch them, my dear doctor, I will claim their souls for my own. But if you know my rules, you must also know that I am fond of games. And what you do for me shall be a game, to be sure.

In what way will this be a game? Phibes asked.

You will be timed. *I will send a champion of good to stop your meddling. He is very powerful, and you will only be able to elude and subvert him for so long. Carry out your tasks before he catches you, and I will give you freedom to walk the Earth again.*

I see. But what man could be a rival to one such as I?

Again the Devil laughed. The voice growled:

His name is Fascinax.

Phibes thought he heard a finger-snap. Suddenly, the winds were gone from his ears and the void was, once more, empty.

Doctor George Leicester stood over the corpse, seemingly unperturbed by the blood which pooled around his shiny dress shoes. The body was badly mutilated, but it was not the worst he'd seen. He leaned heavily on his walking stick. His face was humorless but calm.

"Excuse me, sir...?" It was the young policeman, the bobby whose name stuck in Leicester's mind as Joe. "Is it true that in France they call you Fascinax?"

"That is true," Leicester replied simply. "I use the name to reflect my own fascination with the universe. But I suppose it was coined by those who were fascinated by *me*."

"It sounds like you're right fascinatin', sir," young Joe said. "In the Yard they say you're bound up in the occult, or so it's rumored."

Leicester smirked. "Rumors are not always truth, PC...?"

"Cuff, sir. Joseph Cuff. I work the family business, sir."

"I see. I'm sorry, PC Cuff, I would like to work alone, if that's alright. Your superiors have authorized it."

The young man seemed hurt that he would not get to see the mysterious investigator in action, but he was compliant.

"I trust you, sir. Good luck in your work, sir."

With a nod he turned to leave. Then, as if on impulse, he turned back around and lamented:

"Poor Mrs. Longstreet, sir!"

And then he was gone.

Leicester silently echoed the sentiment. Mrs. Longstreet, the widow of the deceased, was nearing the end of her pregnancy, and her child would grow up without a father. Fortunately, unlike their mother, the child would live without the memory of their father's butchered corpse.

He hoped he'd not dismissed the young PC too rudely, but he didn't wish to have to explain to him the Satanic meaning of the runes which crisscrossed the dead man's tortured flesh. He had been *sacrificed* by a hand possessing the expertise of a surgeon or a master musician. Many of the cuts were made pre-mortem, but the killer had kept attacking beyond the point of death. Fascinax wondered if maybe his old foe, Numa Pergyll, was behind this, but this was barbarous, even by his standards. No—he sensed a different presence here, one he was somehow both familiar and unfamiliar with…

In the open air, Fascinax drew one of the occult signs taught to him long ago by his teacher, Nadir Kritchna. Though he was loathe to disturb the recently dead, he needed to call on the spirit of Henry Longstreet to ask him what had happened.

The ghost of the dead man appeared in his mind's eye.

"Mr. Longstreet. My condolences for your recent loss." He spoke sincerely, in a solemn voice.

"You can see me?" the ghost asked. "My poor pregnant wife, she can't see me..."

"I'm afraid you won't have to worry about that for long. Soon you will fade into the Light, and you will know peace."

The spirit's face at once twisted up in panic, at the thought of leaving his family behind. Then, as if receiving the knowledge instantly, he understood the inevitable, and relaxed.

Fascinax went on: "I want to know all you can tell me about your killer."

The ghost's voice shook. "H-he was horrible. His face was a naked skull, with only a little bit of burnt flesh covering it. He wore dark robes, and when he spoke, it was through a box attached to his neck by a long cable."

The occult adventurer recalled one of the Scotland Yard files he'd looked over recently—the case of a certain Doctor Anton Phibes, who had slaughtered a group of doctors three years ago, for ostensibly killing his wife back in 1921. Phibes had been eccentric before the car accident which had burnt his whole body—a result of his haste to join his wife in the hospital—but after the crash he had become completely unhinged. While the authorities had hoped the Phibes case had ended with his disappearance at the conclusion of his killing spree, he eventually reemerged, having faked his death. But as quickly as he had reappeared, he had vanished once more, though not without leaving more bodies in his wake.

Now Fascinax knew that Phibes had risen once again.

"That's all I need to know. Thank you, Mr. Longstreet, and again... I am sorry for what happened to you."

"You'd think the worst part would be the pain, or watching him cut up my body. But i-it's not... It's the not knowing, sir. Not knowing how my child will grow up... Or not knowing if they'll know how much I love 'em."

"They'll know, Henry. I will tell your wife of your love for her and your child. Your child won't grow up without knowing you, in some way."

Henry Longstreet breathed a sigh of relief, and his spirit faded from sight. The room had been full of tension before; now, it had only great peace. But the body was still a gristly thing, and Fascinax knew he had a killer to catch.

After extending his condolences to Mrs. Longstreet, and passing on her husband's final sentiments, Fascinax strode out into London streets. There was nothing separating him from the mingling crowds that busied the sidewalks; he looked to be an ordinary man, albeit one dressed in expensive fashions. His black coat and tie were stylish, and though his wide-brimmed hat had many years of wear on it, it was still a fine piece of *haute couture*. He had taken time to clean his shoes, so that he did not leave bloody footprints behind him.

His eyes swept the grayish city. The smoggy air was unpleasant, but in his dreams he had seen futures where the faults of coal had become too obvious and cleaner sources of heat, light, and electricity were found. Consequently, the London of the future would be far cleaner than the one he strode through now. It was one of only a few improvements which he sensed coming. Yet, nothing was guaranteed—only the hard work of those pushing back against the old ways would bring change.

Fascinax walked perpetually between the frontiers of hope and despair, victory and defeat. Endowed with preternaturally long life, the past and future, life and death, good and evil were equally open to him. Witnessing existence the way most people did took some effort on his behalf. As he made his way to his car, he felt as though the world around him was little more than a dream.

Thus, when he turned his head to see a beautiful woman in an elegant white gown with irises that were totally black staring at him from an alleyway, he was hardly surprised. In fact, he had been expecting her. And he knew who she was.

Sensing she desired a degree of privacy, he entered the alley, and tipped his hat to her in a mock friendly greeting.

"I take it you have something to do with the business I've just been attending to?" he asked. He allowed a note of disgust to enter his voice, knowing she'd pick up on it.

"You truly are all-knowing, Fascinax," replied the woman. "You know who I am?"

"In the here and now, you're Lisa, but you've also been known as Iblis, Ahriman, and many other names. Yes, I should say I know you." The occultist tilted his head curiously. "Why Phibes? Why did the Power who controls your eternal adversary, Leonox, choose him as his agent? And why did the Power who controls you choose me to oppose him? Don't they have something better to do?"

She laughed. "You think too small, Fascinax. The Powers who control us are not bound to this time or place. Right now, as we speak, Leonox is tempting Christ in the desert and I am dragging Faust to see my Master..." Her finger looped around a curl of her long hair. "Perhaps the Powers are looking for new champions and whoever triumphs will have the honor of becoming their servants..."

"I sense you're being deceitful, as always. I think this is no more than mere amusement for them."

She smiled eerily at him, with the slightest hint of frustration flashing in her eyes. He knew she hated being caught lying.

"You know where I stand," she said simply. "There is order, and there is chaos."

"And there is power between the two," said Fascinax, feeling his magic swell within him. "I suppose I need to hurry if I'm to stop more atrocities."

"Oh, yes. As a matter of fact, poor Moses Hargreaves is already slipping away from this world."

"What?" Fascinax would act disaffected when he thought it could give him an edge, but Lisa had truly shocked him. He wondered why he had not sensed this, but now, as he reached out with his mind, he saw indeed that a man named Moses Hargreaves was indeed dying—another sacrifice. How had Phibes, who was severely burned, moved that quickly without assistance?

Lisa laughed, enjoying the fact that she had shaken him. "Your time is running out, Fascinax. I suggest you get to work."

And suddenly, she was gone, as if she had never been there. Indeed, for the crowds bustling outside the alley, she hadn't been. And yet, in many ways, she—or Leonox—were with all of them, always.

Fascinax closed his eyes, and visualized the names of the men whom Phibes had blamed for his wife's death. He determined who was more likely to be the next to die—it was David Dunwoody—and rushed towards his car.

When Fascinax arrived at the Dunwoody residence, he was received with great confusion. He couldn't explain how he knew that there was a threat to Mr. Dunwoody, just that there was one, and that he was here to protect him.

David's apple had fallen far from the tree of his physician relative, who had been one of Phibes' victims five years ago. He was a stubbornly close-minded and uncomprehending man, although Fascinax understood his disbelief.

"Why should I believe yeh that the man who killed my uncle is on his way here?" David grumbled. "It seems to me like yer an escaped loonie, trying to intimidate me with somethin' you read about in the papers."

"Mr. Dunwoody," Fascinax said, for what seemed to be the thousandth time, "I tell you that you are in grave danger. I have been working with Scotland Yard in this matter, and I think it would be best if you allowed me inside."

"What, so yeh can steal whatever's not nailed down? That fancy garb doesn't impress me none, mister. Con men can buy them duds too if they save an' scrimp."

Fascinax sighed wearily. He hated to do this, but it was for the man's own good. Taking a step forward, he locked eyes with Dunwoody.

His voice was strong and stern: "You will allow me into your house so that I may defend you from the man who seeks to hurt you."

Dunwoody echoed back, with a hollow voice and wide eyes: "I will allow yeh into my house so that you may defend me from the man who seeks to hurt me."

"Thank you," said Fascinax, allowing himself in.

Dunwoody shook his head, confused as to why he'd agreed to that. But somehow, he was now glad that Fascinax was here. The strange man could instantly change the feeling of any darkened room.

Mrs. Dunwoody took Fascinax to be a friend of her husband's. He did not contradict her. She offered him food and, in return, he offered to cook for her.

The Dunwoodys' unintended guest turned out to be as splendid a chef as he was a dresser. Mr. Dunwoody's confusion faded as he tasted the fine French cuisine which Fascinax arranged, as if by magic, from their humble stores. Fascinax learned that most of the inheritance David had received from his uncle had gone into bills and repairs on the house. It had done very little to change their lives.

As the hour grew late, Fascinax's heart tightened. He knew that Phibes would likely strike at night. On the basis of the quality of his meal and conversational skills, the occult detective was allowed to spend the night. He was offered the room of Mr. Dunwoody's late brother, who had lived there before the Great War. But the small, cozy bed would not see Fascinax rest in it. His focused mind remained awake, psychically scanning the house and the grounds for the faintest trace of incoming evil. To accomplish this, he slipped into a trance. He closed his eyes, his physical body seemed to drop away, and a strange, rhythmic melody entered into his mind.

He was now nothing but his gaze and his private musings—a creature of pure thought. He stood on the edge of the astral void and used its bizarre patterns of swirling mauve to meditate. All the while, he kept eyes on the Dunwoody house, waiting for Phibes' arrival. He stared into the future, reconfirming his certainty of Phibes coming here next. His certainty did not waver for a moment.

He had to wonder what sort of method Phibes would employ. In his previous killings, he had used the services of a servant-assassin named Vulnavia—if the doctor ever struck in person, it was from the shadows, using machinery or poison to kill from a distance. Fascinax understood that Phibes could have already planted something in the house to carry out his crime. But his senses told him there was no such device in the house. Phibes was moving quick, but as far as Fascinax knew, he wasn't superhuman. And yet, he knew he could not underestimate his foe's brilliant mind.

As the night grew darker, the sense of psychic anticipation swelled. Now the music that entered Fascinax's soul at the start of his trance seemed to take on a curious life of its own. He was always captivated when he heard this trance-song, which came both from himself and from the intangible plane around him. It was the song of the universe, the music of the spheres, and it always shifted to reflect how he felt. Now, as he stared into the future, with that music in his brain, he was so sure that this violently-thrumming dread was Dunwoody's impending death. He felt like he was at a séance, or perhaps a demon-summoning—there was the unspeakable sensation of something about to break through. But his resolve held. He did not stop his vigil. His entire focus was on the house, every inch of the garden, every slate the roof, every blade of grass, every note in the wind. Still, he could not see Phibes...

Suddenly, the darkness lashed out into his mind all at once. It struck like thunder. He let out a cry. Something was wrong. Something he had not seen.

He began to wonder if hubris had gotten the best of him. He was not immune to arrogance. Nadir Kritchna had chosen him for his compassion, but the old yogi had also understood that George Leicester would have to find his own way in the use of the mystic arts. But now—

Samuel Whitcombe, whom he'd believed to be Phibes' fourth victim, had instead been the third. His prophecy had been wrong. Fascinax had no one to blame but himself.

The room seemed suddenly calm, as Fascinax reached out to confirm what had happened. When he saw Whitcombe's body, he couldn't help but grieve, just as the dead man's family would later grieve. He tried to steady himself and quiet the guilt of his failure. Despite his powers, he was only human after all. A human bridge to the outer world, but human all the same. And in humanity, there were mistakes. But he could make up for these. He just had to move quickly—he had to predict Phibes' next movements before—

A scream came from down below.

He could hardly believe it. It was Mrs. Dunwoody! He hauled himself up and dashed downstairs.

Once he was back in the dining room, he saw that the worst had come to pass. Mr. Dunwoody was dead, but unlike the others, he was not mutilated with the Satanic runes. His stab wound was instantly fatal, but evidently something had scared Phibes off before he could complete his grisly task.

There was no way that Phibes could move that quickly. Still, Fascinax quickened himself—his steely eyes spotted that one of the kitchen windows was open. Leaving the heartbroken widow, he jumped out the window and into the night. At once, he saw a robed figure running away from the house. He sprinted after it, feeling the wind in his lungs.

Phibes heard him approach, and whirled around. In his hand was his voice-box, attached to his throat with a cable. Fascinax gazed into his foe's dead-seeming eyes, which glared out from a hideously scarred skull.

"Hail, Fascinax!" said Phibes, his voice echoing from the speaker. "Hail, meddler. You are like a snake, who strikes only *after* the boot has come down."

"Phibes," Fascinax said simply, "you can't get away. I don't know how you managed to move so quickly, but I've won our contest. You failed to etch the runes into Dunwoody's flesh. Any sort of ritual you were trying to perform won't work now."

"I am not a sorcerer by nature, Fascinax. The runes mean very little. My, er, *sponsor* will support me no matter what." Phibes began to laugh. "I believe you are about to receive a demonstration of the power granted to me."

Fascinax's nose caught the familiar scent of brimstone, and suddenly smoke poured up from the earth below Phibes' feet. There was a phosphorous flash around the doctor's frame, and, in an instant, he was gone.

Fascinax sensed that he was now on his way to Brian Vesalius—the fifth and final victim. He cursed under his breath, as he ran back to his car. Failures piled onto failures. He should have known the Powers always cheated.

Anton Phibes was at a disadvantage. Only he didn't know it. Thwarting Fascinax had made him more arrogant than ever. He had no defeat to learn from. His guile in subverting Fascinax's prophecy ensured that he'd been able to take his time dealing with the Whitcombe heir. The

Devil had given him no other advantages than the ability to travel quickly and the return of some of his gadgets, so that he could triumph over Fascinax's spells and psychic abilities.

Phibes wondered if perhaps the challenge wasn't fair—perhaps he had too great an advantage over the magician. But that didn't matter to him. If he won, he was free. He would undo his failure at the River of Life. From there, it was just a matter of finding his beloved wife, somehow, somewhere, and restoring her to life.

He stood outside the house of Dr. Brian Vesalius. Like his father, Brian had gone into the medical field. No doubt, he also mimicked his father in cruelly parting men from their wives with his gross incompetence. Vesalius and his ilk were living insults to the medical profession. Fortunately, they would not contaminate such a noble practice for much longer…

When the Devil had taken him to yet another London neighborhood, he had observed a woman walking home. Somehow, as if by instinct, he knew that she was young Vesalius' wife. The hood of Phibes' robe obscured his face. Though he could once again speak, with the aid of his voice-box, he hadn't recovered his wax disguise kit. He kept close to the shadows as he followed her home. He moved silently—so silently that at one point, he was right at her heels, and she didn't notice that her shadow was no longer alone. He couldn't restrain the amusement this gave him.

She led him up to the hedge-enclosed house that her wealthy husband had bought for her. If Phibes had not been a man of privilege himself, at least in the past, he might have been jealous.

From a distance, he gazed into the lighted windows. He could see Vesalius and his wife sharing a meal. Now there was no escaping envy—his ravaged mind flashed back to his own domestic bliss, and once again, he felt the rage which had long ago replaced his grief. It was time to strike. His fingers, surprisingly nimble, opened the window's lock. Like a living shadow, he crawled inside.

Now Mrs. Vesalius saw him. She screamed as she watched Phibes' spidery form cross into their living room. Vesalius turned and shouted a similar cry of alarm. In mockery, Phibes pressed a single finger to his lips. Then his lips split, and from his vocal box came the peeling sound of laughter.

"I did not murder your father, Dr. Vesalius," declared Phibes. "Time did. A heart condition, more specifically. But as I slumbered through the years, I dreamed of killing him. I will satisfy that dream, by completing my revenge against you!"

The elder Dr. Vesalius had evidently told his son of his clash with Phibes. Brian Vesalius had nearly lost his younger half-brother at Phibes' hands, as well as his father.

"I'm not afraid of you, Phibes," Vesalius said. "You couldn't kill my father. You won't kill me."

"The sons and nephews of your father's colleagues have already been destroyed by my hand. None have been able to stop me. Once you are dead, I'll be truly free!"

Vesalius took up a large blade, which he had used to cut the roast he'd prepared for his wife. "I say again: I'm not afraid of you."

Phibes did not fear him, this feeble would-be aristocrat curled up in his cozy mansion. Vesalius flinched when Phibes rushed him. In the resulting struggle, it was easy to wrench the knife from his hand. Phibes raised the blade high, preparing to smite his fifth and final victim.

There was the squeal of tires.

Behind the Vesaliuses, the wall caved in. A speeding projectile darted straight through it. Debris and dust covered the three figures, toppling them over. The shiny steel chassis of Fascinax's sports car glinted in the light, as its driver emerged. A reeling Phibes barked his name:

"Fascinax!"

"Yes, it's me, Phibes," Fascinax confirmed. "And this is your end."

Phibes felt a familiar tingling in his bones—once more he was about to receive the Devil's gift. The light flashed around him, and he was jerked backwards out of Vesalius' house. He didn't travel a great distance—no further than the front lawn. Phibes pondered this, but before he could act, a crash of glass sounded behind him. Fascinax had followed him. When Phibes looked up, he saw the magician walking forward slowly towards him with the determination of an inescapable predator.

The mad doctor was far from helpless. He had snared Fascinax before. From within his robes, Phibes retrieved his greatest tool: his music-box. Fascinax froze in place when it was switched on—the music that issued forth was familiar to him.

Phibes watched the occultist's eyes as Fascinax realized the secret of the music he'd heard in his trance. It had not emerged from the outer Akashic realms, but from one of Phibes' inventions! Too late did he comprehend that this music was responsible for his failure earlier with

David Dunwoody and Samuel Whitcombe. He was trapped inside his trance by his enemy's tune.

Fascinax was now completely paralyzed, as he had been before. While he remained standing, the only part of him that wasn't immobilized was his brain. There was a stormy fury in his unmoving eyes, as he knew that Phibes would complete his murders while he was like this.

But beyond Phibes' perception, Fascinax felt a new strength bloom inside himself. The failure to save Whitcombe and Dunwoody had been the fault of Phibes' trickery, not any arrogance or weakness on his behalf. He celebrated this fact. Yet he couldn't relax for a moment. He knew that the infernal music which held his body stiff—which had blended with the weightlessness of astral projection—would soon infect his mind, holding him in one thought as it had before. He couldn't let his psychic powers be numbed in that way. He reached out with his mind until he touched his car—a wonder-car that he had designed and built himself, that could become an airplane and—soon, he hoped—a submarine as well. Fascinax had a passion was for invention. From within the car's glove compartment, he telekinetically retrieved his electrical gun.

Phibes was now returning to finish off the Vesaliuses. They cringed away as he stepped through the window Fascinax had broken.

Behind them, the electrical gun floated upward, propelled by Fascinax's mind. Phibes saw it too late. A burst of voltage spat out, and the metal of the music box Phibes held attracted this bolt of lightning. In an instant, the box fused and the evil doctor was forced to drop it to the ground. It crackled as it melted to slag.

Phibes heard the sound of Fascinax scrambling to his feet. The magician ran into the room and dove towards the murderer.

Fascinax's tackle was a feint. He knew that the Power who controlled Phibes would try to blink him away again. By diving towards him, he hoped to discourage this—if he touched him at the moment of his disappearance, he would be carried with him, making the teleport useless. His ploy worked.

Fascinax struck the floor of the Vesalius house and where he landed, a fissure split the floor wide open. From the earth itself burst out a writhing tangle of of chains. These chains bound Phibes tightly. The Power who controlled Fascinax—temporarily, he hoped!—had intervened.

Now, it was too late. The other power to take Phibes away, but in vain. The mad doctor felt two forces of equal strength tug hard on him, as if he was on a medieval rack. He could feel his ligaments split.

The charred figure wriggled and writhed for several long moments, before screaming out: "Let me go, or I'll be torn in half!"

It was the Devil who obliged. In an instant, the deal was broken and Phibes could expect no more help. He heard the Devil's breath in his ear. He hadn't realized until now: the Devil's raspy breath had accompanied all of their meetings. He breathed even as he spoke. Phibes stared on ahead blankly as Fascinax put handcuffs on him.

Let me loose! Phibes implored the Devil. *Give me another chance!*

This was our deal, Phibes, and you said at the start of this that you know my rules, the Devil replied. *Fascinax has caught you. You have lost. It's simplicity itself.*

He wasn't wrong, Phibes acknowledged. Any scientist, indeed any musician, knew that glory came from risk. He had risked everything and he had failed.

He kept on staring, heedless of the world around him. The Vesaliuses came up to Fascinax, thanking him for his aid—indeed, their gratitude was boundless. And yet—

"Our house," breathed Brian Vesalius. "I understand your need for *haste*, sir, but our *house*—"

Fascinax was winded, and his clothes were dusty and slashed up by glass, but he pointed out behind the couple.

When they turned, the wall was totally repaired. As if by magic.

The car was gone from their interior. Before they could turn back again, the rescued couple heard its engine turn over. Fascinax had already departed, with his prisoner in tow.

Phibes' stare was still unbroken. He couldn't pull his mind away from what he'd lost. Freedom was only one thing now gone from his life, and yet even for him, the thought—the knowledge—that he would die in prison was more frightful than it initially seemed.

He had failed, and there would be no escape this time—no hidden tomb to preserve himself and hide away in. No somewhere-over-the-rainbow. But he did not care. His wife was forever gone to him, meaning he had nothing left to live for.

Perhaps then, for no other reason than spite, had he sown the seeds of his final revenge…

Months passed quickly.

Fascinax had moved back to Paris, and was looking at some of his old cases, seeking help in his renewed battle against Numa Pergyll. He came across his folder from the Phibes case, which he had not thought of in some time. Slowly, he retraced it all in his head, seeking some spell he had used, some trinket at his disposal, which he could now use to defeat his arch-nemesis. Unfortunately, such meditation only made him aware of something he had overlooked in his mad rush to stop Phibes.

The first victim, Henry Longstreet—his wife had been pregnant. When he revisited Mrs. Dunwoody, he learned she was with child as well. Later, before he'd departed London, he'd received correspondence from the three other widows. He checked his files to see if he still had those letters. He did. As his eyes flew over each of them, he saw they each contained statements proclaiming or implying a pregnancy.

He wondered if each of those women had secretly received a visit from Phibes, before he took their men from them. All a genius like Phibes would need to effect his will on an unborn child was a needle-jab.

Fascinax closed his tired eyes and reached out, trying to sense the minds of the woman he'd previously encountered. His mystical senses at once informed him that they were all happy mothers, and not a one of them had miscarried.

But radiating from the child was a strange energy. It was like something was welling up in them, yearning to be born. He could just barely see it. The vision would need coaxing. Slipping into an occult trance, Fascinax gazed out into the future, to try to glimpse what terror Phibes had brought into the world.

Years passed swiftly.

The grandchildren of Brian Vesalius, David Dunwoody, and the others were born with darkness in their eyes. The doctors and nurses who helped bring them into the world felt inexplicable terror in their presence. It was as if they were immediately aware of the world, and they found an awful, sinister mirth in it.

Their parents were among their first victims. The police found the bodies as desecrated as the children's grandfathers' had been. It took months before the children were caught, and by then, they'd not only killed many more people, but they had all found each other.

The British government didn't know what to do with them. Five children, none older than twelve, had become the most prolific serial killers in the history of the United Kingdom. It was eventually determined by the local magistrates that only an international health facility in the United States would be able to help them. With cooperation from the American authorities, they were sent there at once.

But they would never reach their new home. They escaped the bus transporting them and fled into the wilderness. Knowing that British accents would be conspicuous, they quickly mimicked American voices. And then, they started looking for toys to play with.

In these five devil-spawn lived the legacy of Anton Phibes.

They used to say that one could wait an hour for a London bus, then two would suddenly appear at once. Ditto with Fascinax, who hasn't appeared in Tales of the Shadowmen *for years, but is featured in two stories in this year's edition. In this tale, however, Matthew Dennion did not craft a crime thriller but instead penned a fine and inspiring Christmas parable in the best Dickensian tradition...*

Matthew Dennion: *The Gift That Kept On Taking*

London, 1783

The snow was falling hard as young Ebenezer Scrooge ate dinner by himself, in the dorm room of his boarding school on Christmas Eve. Even the staff had gone home for the holiday and the youngster was left with nothing but a fire, food for a meal to cook himself, and a gift with a note from his neglectful father. The schoolboy grumbled as he took another bite of the side of ham he had burned.

"Confound it! I shouldn't have to cook! It's beneath me! What is my father paying these lazy vagabonds at this school for anyway?" He shook his head. "The very thought of me, a Scrooge, having to cook his own Christmas dinner, while all of the other children are home with their families having fine meals!"

Anger smoldered within Ebenezer as he thought about the other children taunting him as they left the school for Christmas. The other students had all laughed at the boy whose family did not care enough to come and take him home for the holidays. They had called him names such as the boy too naughty for a family, and the kid who would not have a Christmas. Ebenezer spat on the floor as these memories flooded back to him.

"Me, I'm the naughty child? I'm the kid who won't have a Christmas?"

He walked over to a picture of Father Christmas that hung on the wall. The picture was above the dorm's Christmas tree, under which the gift his father had sent him was waiting for Ebenezer to open on the following day. The boy glared at the picture of the Jolly Saint.

"Aren't you supposed to decide who's naughty and who's nice? Aren't you the one who is supposed to leave gifts for the children who behave themselves and leave bad tidings for those who are cruel to others? Yet, after working hard at school all year to please father, while the other kids barely studied, I sit here alone, while they are out enjoying the holiday with their families!"

The youngster walked up to the picture and screamed at it.

"I say you are terrible at your job! I curse you and your holiday for letting the children who work hard be left behind while the lazy and wicked are reworded!"

Ebenezer shifted his eyes to his father's gift. He picked it up and then looked back at the painting of Father Christmas.

"I know you won't be leaving me anything. When I wake up tomorrow, this pathetic gift from my father will be the only present here." He shrugged. "I see no reason why I can't open it tonight. It will be the same gift whether I open it tonight or tomorrow."

The young Scrooge unwrapped the oddly-shaped gift. As he pulled off the last layer of paper, he found an amputated monkey's paw with its four fingers and thumb all extended outward like it was going to shake his hand. The school boy screamed and dropped the paw on the floor. His body shook in revulsion as he looked at his macabre gift.

"Well father, I suppose neglecting and embarrassing me is not enough for you on Christmas. You must scare and insult me as well with this grotesque present."

As he looked at the paw he saw a note beneath it. Ebenezer pulled the note out from under the limb and read it aloud:

Dear Ebenezer,

Our family is very wealthy, and I am certain you have all that you could ever want at your school. Having a child with everything they could desire makes buying a gift for them very difficult. Honestly, I couldn't think of anything you would want so in the end that is exactly what I decided to get you, anything you want!

When I was traveling through India, I came across a yogi who offered to sell me this monkey's paw. He tells me it will grant whoever holds it five wishes. So, my dear boy, hold onto this paw and wish for anything your heart desires! At the end of the semester, please write and inform me if any of your wishes came true.

Sincerely,

Father.

Ebenezer was seething with rage as he looked at the well thought-out prank his father had given him as a gift. He could already hear the other boys mocking him for this terrible gift. They would return with fine clothes, or hats, or family heirlooms, and all he would have was some monkey's cut-off hand. His father had planned out Ebenezer's newest torture well. If he was to keep the paw, the others would mock him for it from now until the day they all graduated. Conversely, if he tossed it away, he would be mocked for receiving no gift at all.

Since his own father was not around, the boy glared at Father Christmas and projected all of his enmity toward the jolly visage.

"This? This sick joke is what I get for Christmas? I suppose you also think this is a great laugh at my expense?"

He looked at the monkey's paw.

"Well, I can laugh too!" He held the paw close to him and said. "I wish that, for every finger on this stupid monkey paw, a rude and cruel child who has used his tongue to make fun of others would have that very same tongue cut out on Christmas night." '

He was seething with anger as he continued to clutch the paw.

"I also wish this pox of tongue cutting to be carried out forever more on the wicked children of England every Christmas Eve!"

Once Ebenezer finished his wish, he walked outside and tossed the monkey's paw in the gutter where it would be washed away by the slowly melting snow. The youngster had decided the scorn for not receiving a gift would fade faster than the mockery he would receive for displaying the paw.

Ebenezer stood there, crying in the storm as he watched as the snow fell down into the gutter onto his gift. Then he wiped the tears out of his eyes, and walked back inside to spend the holidays in solitude.

As the youngster was walking away, two of the fingers on the removed paw folded down into its palm.

After the new year, when his classmates had returned to school, Ebenezer was prepared to see the wonderful gifts they had been given and to be the target of their scorn for being left alone and giftless over the holidays. Much to his surprise, however, no one displayed their prizes or mocked him. All of the boys' attention was focused on their five classmates who had been murdered on Christmas Eve.

Each of the boys in question had had their tongues mysteriously cut out on Christmas Eve, and either bled to death or choked on their own blood. There was talk of a demon who had attacked them in their own bedrooms and, after mutilating them, disappeared into the night.

Ebenezer immediately realized that all five of the boys who had been attacked had mocked him before leaving the boarding school for Christmas. A chill ran through the young miser's body as he thought of the monkey's paw he had thrown away. He briefly looked at his returning classmates and then went back to his room.

As his door closed behind him, Ebenezer considered this another reason why he would always hate Christmas.

London, 1928

It was a dry and cold Christmas Eve night. The chilling wind cut through the coats of the people on the streets and froze them to their bones. A man in a dark cloak and hat sat on the rooftop of a building across an alley from a boarding school. His fierce eyes were fixed on a bedroom window. In addition to the cold wind, the cloaked figure could sense something else near him that was creating a chill. Even as the stoic guardian kept his eyes fixed on the boarding school, he reached out with his supernatural senses to determine the nature of the presence surrounding him.

The cloaked man was Doctor George Leicester, better known throughout Europe as Fascinax! The dreaded crime-fighter had been endowed with enhanced senses, reflexes, and nearly unequalled physical and mystical skills.

Currently, Fascinax's ability to sense imminent danger combined with some detective work he had engaged in over the past several months, had led him to his current position. There was the possibility that a young boy he had been protecting was in danger. For almost a century and a half, every year on Christmas Eve, five young children would have their tongues cut out by a mysterious assailant. Most of the children would die as result of the attack.

Much like Fascinax himself, the perpetrator of these attacks had become something of an urban legend known diversely as Krampus, Hans Trapp, Belsnickle and Père Fouettard. He was something of a darker version of Santa Claus, Père Noël or Saint Nicholas—a sinister counterpart who would whip children that had been naughty throughout the year.

It was after the newspapers had begun to report the yearly tongue cuttings of children that some people began to blame the mutilations on the legendary figure. While most of the media thought they were the actions of a madman and copycats over the years, or the work of some heretofore unknown cult, Fascinax's keen mind and mystical intuitions had led him to suspect that something else for more elemental was behind these crimes.

On the previous Christmas, the avenging hero had learned of a common factor between the five children who had become victims of the tongue cuttings. They each had had a reputation of behaving badly toward their classmates of lesser social standing. With this knowledge, Fascinax had set out on a course of action combining his talents as a medical doctor and a detective along with his mystical abilities, in order to determine the most likely victims of this year's attacks.

In particular, he had chosen to focus his efforts on that specific boarding school which, according to the archives, was the first where the phenomenon had taken root.

As Doctor Leicester, he had spent several months there, studying how some students mistreated their peers, and the factors that allowed them to do so. Once he had reviewed and assimilated all of this information, he had decided to go on a speaking tour throughout the Kingdom. He had hoped to accomplish two objectives: the first was to add to the information he had already gathered; the second was to use his standing as a prominent doctor to educate the students.

Fascinax hoped to stop who or what was behind the "Christmas Cuts" as the papers were starting to call the yearly mutilations. Under this guise, he could deal with threats that were beyond the scope of the ordinary law enforcement. But as Doctor Leicester, he knew that he could also deal with even more wide spread social issues, such as identifying situations where students were the victims of cruel and unusual bullying, and help remedy them.

During his tour, Fascinax spoke about how students should treat their classmates. He addressed instances where they could be verbally attacked and how to defuse such situations. He pointed out that verbal shaming could only exist if the people around the abuser allowed the situation to continue. He offered solutions, like speaking out against the abuser in front of others to dissuade his attacks.

He told students that he had determined that verbal attacks usually occurred when the victim was concerned about either social or physical harm, and faced, what he called, an "unfair match," defined as a situation when one student was unable to engage in or even exchange with the person threatening him, either physically or conversationally.

Most of all, he encouraged the students to report such situations to an adult, like a parent, a teacher, or doctor like himself. He openly made himself available to all of the students to speak to him after his lecture regarding what he had said.

This caused some of the boys to approach him. The earnest ones told him of some truly heinous cases. They also identified some of the most common offenders and their targets. With this data, Fascinax was able to generate a list of ten subjects he felt were the most likely to be targeted by this "Père Fouettard."

With this list, Fascinax could then focus his mystical senses and determine who was the child who was the most likely to be attacked first. His name was Pinkie Brown—at least, that's what his schoolmates called him. Fascinax learned that the boy had been sent to that same boarding school where the "Cuts" had started—a coincidence? Perhaps, perhaps not. It seems that the boy had seen his parents engaged in sexual intercourse. He had been so disgusted by the sight that he had demanded to be sent to a boarding school so that he would never see such abhorrent behavior again.

Pinkie's misplaced anger at his mother and father seemed to extend beyond his parents to his classmates. He was known to constantly insult, degrade, threaten, and even injure them. The boy's actions made him an ideal candidate for the "Cuts."

From his vantage position, Fascinax was observing his target when, suddenly, his uncanny senses detected another, darker presence in young Pinkie Brown's room. Through the dorm room window, he could see a grotesque figure looming over the young boy.

With a speed beyond human comprehension, Fascinax leapt off the roof and crashed through the window. In a fluid motion, the avenging hero rolled with the momentum of his fall, and then sprang at the figure looming over the misguided youngster.

Fascinax had his opponent pinned to the ground when the latter threw him off and sent him flying across the room and into the wall. But the mystical vigilante immediately flipped back to his feet to better see the adversary standing before him.

The demon who had been attacking children for over a century and a half had the overall appearance of man with a dark face and scraggly beard. He was dressed in dark robes with a switch in one hand and a deadly knife in the other. Strapped across his back was a wicker basket in which Fascinax could see the remains of children likely taken on Christmas Eve's past.

Fascinax was still taking his foe's measure when he suddenly another presence slip in through the broken window. Whatever it was, he could tell that it was not a threat to him, or young Pinkie. The boy, who was now wide awake, sat in his bed, transfixed by the supernatural battle.

When he had checked his watch moments ago, Fascinax had noted that it was only five minutes until midnight—until Christmas day. He suspected that he did not need to defeat the evil entity to save the boy; he only needed to keep him busy until the clock struck twelve.

Fascinax looked into the dark eyes of the monster standing between him and the naughty boy he sought to protect.

"Père Fouettard, I presume?" he asked, using the French moniker with which he was the most familiar.

The dark reflection of Saint Nicholas didn't answer, but rather simply hissed.

Fascinax quickly shifted his glance to young Pinkie, his hands now folded in prayer. The young boy was saying *Hail Mary*s over and over in the hope that the Blessed Mother—and surely the angel she had sent in the form of Fascinax—would protect him from the monster. As Pinkie prayed, Fascinax saw the other presence hovering above him. The specter's position suggested that he was trying to protect Pinkie, not harm him.

In the split second during which the hero had taken his eyes off the nightmarish creature, Père Fouettard had spun around and brandished his knife high in the air, as he made his way toward the bed.

As fast as the monster moved, Fascinax moved even faster. The hero sprinted across the room, grabbed Père Fouettard's wrist, and used a judo throw to toss the creature onto the floor.

Like a wraith, Père Fouettard's body seemed to change into smoke the moment it struck the boards. As if it were made of living mist, the cloud then reformed into a solid figure and rose in front of Fascinax, taking the form of Père Fouettard once more.

The creature thrust his knife at the avenging hero, but Fascinax's amazing reflexes allowed him to sidestep the blow and deliver a right cross to the demon's face. The vigilante's punch sent Père Fouettard crashing into the wall.

Fascinax moved quickly toward his foe, only to have the monster once more turn into smoke and float past him, until he was once more looming over the praying form of Pinkie Brown.

The monster reached out and grabbed the boy's face, his knife ready to strike. But Fascinax was there: he kicked the creature's hand and sent the knife flying.

Père Fouettard hissed in frustration again as Fascinax grabbed him and, this time, threw him over his shoulder toward the window. Anticipating what his adversary would do next, Fascinax sprang over Pinkie Brown and the spirit guarding him.

The monster had landed in a vertical position, his feet against the wall on the opposite side. He then pushed off against it with all of his superhuman strength. The monster was leaping toward the child, when Fascinax slammed into him and wrapped his arms around him. The hero's momentum carried both him and the monster out of the open window.

As they fell, Fascinax managed to deliver two more punches to Père Fouettard's face before the monster again turned into smoke and flew back towards the bedroom.

Fascinax heard the clock tower strike twelve just as he hit the ground and fell unconscious. The last thing he saw was Père Fouettard's misty form about to reenter the window…

The mystical hero suddenly found himself in another realm of consciousness. The spirit that had been protecting the boy began to take the shape of an elderly Englishman. He reached out to Fascinax and placed his hand on the hero's chest.

"Be at peace, Doctor Leicester. The boy has been saved." The spirit's face suddenly became filled with sorrow. "Sadly, the curse's four other victims still had to suffer for my ignorance."

"Curse? The creature I fought today was the product of a curse, not a demon or a monster?"

The spirit nodded. "Yes, let me explain. In life, I was known as Ebenezer Scrooge. As a child, one Christmas, my neglectful father sent me a monkey's paw as a gift while leaving me alone at this very boarding school. He attached a note about the paw being able to grant wishes. At the time, I didn't believe in such things, but in my anger, I wished that five children who'd mocked others would have their tongues cut out every Christmas.

"When my classmates returned to school and I learned that several of them had suffered that abominable fate, I was shocked and horrified to see that my wish had come true. That experience, coupled with other difficult days associated with Christmas, caused me to hate not only the holiday but my fellow man…"

The spirit began to weep. "I am sad to say that, as the years went on, I would follow the exploits of my curse every year in the newspapers. Despite the mutilation being carried out, a part of me was happy that children like those who had once tormented me were paying for their cruelty. It wasn't until the very end of my life that an old friend visited me from beyond the grave and, with the help of three spirits, showed me the error of my ways.

"I learned to love what Christmas celebrated. I began to enjoy it and to see how I should use my wealth to assist my fellow man and help those in need. I also tried to use it to undo the evil I had wrought but, despite my best efforts, I was unable to find the monkey's paw, and I passed away before I was able to undo the curse."

Hope returned to Scrooge's face as he looked at Fascinax. "Like my friend before me, my spirit is only permitted to come to Earth on Christmas Eve. For years, I tried to reach out to someone who could help me undo the evil I had wrought, but I found only charlatans and con men, that is, until I found you!

"A man whose magical training would not only allow him to sense me, but a man who could save at least one of the children targeted by the curse. I've followed you for weeks, waiting for the blessed day when I could approach you. I watched as you sought not only to protect those who would incur the wrath of my curse, but their victims as well. You fought the great social evil behind my curse as well pursuing the curse itself. So I knew you would be the one who could help me end it."

Fascinax nodded. "I understand the nature of the threat now. The curse took the concept of Père Fouettard and embodied it into the wraith I fought tonight. Sadly, four other children were attacked at the same time as young Pinkie. Without anyone there to protect them, they have already had their tongues cut out. Since this curse was brought upon us by an enchanted monkey's paw the only way to undo it is with another."

Scrooge took a step closer to Fascinax. "Yes, and I've found one… It is in the hand of a couple… A Mr. White, who inherited it from his uncle… With your training, you should be able to approach them and use the paw safely to end this horror. I also urge you to continue your work to help the youngsters. Had there been someone like you around when I was a child, I wouldn't have been so alone and I never would have made that wish."

Fascinax looked into the eyes of Scrooge's ghost. "You can rest now, Mr. Scrooge. This is the last Christmas during which your curse shall torment the children. I shall do as you suggest, and Père Fouettard shall return to the realm of fantasy where it belongs."

Scrooge's ethereal eyes became filled with joy. "Thank you, Doctor Leicester! This is the greatest Christmas gift I could ever have received! While Père Fouettard may return to the realm of folklore, be careful how you regard his counterpart. He may be jolly, but he is always disappointed when someone stops believing in him."

Fascinax began to regain consciousness. As his senses returned, the hero caught the sound of sleigh bells above him combined with a deep and jolly laugh.

In his bedroom, seven-year old Pinkie Brown looked at the knife left in his wall from the demon that had entered his room. For what seemed like his entire life, the boy had been told that his faith was too strict, misguided, dangerous even. Now, on Christmas Eve, when he was attacked by a demon, his prayers had called forth an angel to protect him. The divine and demonic had fought right before his eyes.

As he stared at the knife, he knew that his views and violent urges had been confirmed by almighty God himself. While the horror of Père Fouettard had now ended, that of what Pinkie Brown would become was only beginning.

Brian Gallagher has now embarked on a new saga featuring Gustave Le Rouge's criminal mastermind, cum mad surgeon, Doctor Cornelius Kramm, once the leader of the criminal cartel of the Red Hand. The adventures of the aptly-named "Sculptor of Human Flesh," originally penned in 1912-13, were translated by Brian Stableford and released as a trilogy by Black Coat Press. They were followed by a sequel written by Brian published in our Volume 10. This is the second installment in Brian's new series...

Brian Gallagher: *The Telepath of Galicia*

Deuxième Bureau,[1] Paris, 21 March 1915

The man in the chair spat out a bloodied tooth. His interrogator had hit him in the front teeth with a truncheon. He had told them everything he knew. Surely his explanation was not that terrible? He looked around him. He was in a small room with just a table against a wall and a couple of other chairs. Two men were standing around. His interrogator was someone he recognized; a policeman seconded to the Deuxième Bureau. His skill in extracting information from criminals was renowned. He looked down at his bloodied military tunic. How could they unleash this man upon him—a French army officer?

The building shook at little. "Release me, let me fight the Hun! They must be shelling us!"

The interrogator was about to hit the man in the chair again, but Simon Hart, the man next to him, dressed in a fashionable suit, raised his hand to stay him and spoke to the man in the chair.

"Maréchal, you are a traitor. Not even worth addressing by your rank. You are a disgrace to our army at the front, including your brother. You are not going anywhere."

"I gave a useless liquid to the Russians—our allies!" replied Maréchal. "I was trying to foster good relations!"

That earned him a truncheon blow in the ribs from the interrogator.

---

[1] France's external military intelligence service, created in 1871.

The interrogator, a large thick-set man named Jacquemain, came right up to Maréchal's face. "You *sold* that liquid to the Russians. We know this because you have told us. It was the property of France, and a state secret."

Maréchal nodded dumbly. He had tried to suggest that what he had done was in the interest of France. However, confronted with his bank statements, the blows of the truncheon had made him reveal the truth. He had not slept for some time, and was not thinking straight, and thus repeated his old story. He knew that this would soon be over. He could not imagine they would execute him. He did no harm, surely?

The man in the smart suit spoke again. "Maréchal, why was Professor Ossipoff so interested in the Lynx? You claim not to know, yet you have corresponded and met with him on cosmology. Indeed, it was this hobby of yours that gained you a place here in this section. I recruited you."

"I don't know," said Maréchal, "They just thought it was something they could analyze, given we could not find out why it is now inert. Ask Ossipoff."

"I would, except he has gone back to Russia. In fact, directly after you gave him the Lynx, he boarded a train and left Paris." Hart turned to the interrogator. "I am not sure there is much more to be gained from him. Still, see what you can do, I must make a report."

The interrogator nodded.

"Monsieur Hart, please! I am a French officer! I have a wife and children," pleaded Maréchal.

Hart ignored him as he left. Jacquemain looked at Maréchal.

"I am puzzled," he said. "You sold out France for just 5000 francs?"

"I wished to make sure that my wife could enjoy the finer things in life," replied Maréchal.

"But what of your mistress? Surely some of that would have gone to her? Who is she, we have not found out."

"I have no mistress; I am loyal to my wife!"

The interrogator looked appalled. "I can see you are no true Frenchman—all becomes clear." He pondered for a moment. "I have good news for you," he finally said.

Maréchal looked hopeful.

"You will soon have a mistress," Jacquemain said, "One who has loved many. Soon, you feel the tender embrace of Madame Guillotine!"

Hart headed down the corridor. The building shook a little. Several staff were coming downstairs from above. He recognized the man he was going up to see, General Charles-Joseph Dupont, the head of the Deuxième Bureau. He saluted him.

"General Dupont, I can give you an update on the Lynx situation."

"Good, come with me, Monsieur Hart."

Along with some of the General's aides they headed towards a quartermaster's office. The General sat down on a chair behind a desk and dismissed his aides. He motioned to Hart to sit down. Hart took his chair. The building shook again.

"Zeppelins," said the General. "The Hun are bombing our city from the air, the savages. It is appalling that we must come down here in the early hours. What is the latest from our prisoner?"

"I can confirm what we have previously found out from him and our own observations. Aside from his military career, he had an amateur interest in cosmology and corresponded with Russian academics, one of whom came to Paris, a Professor Ossipoff. Maréchal told us that he met regularly with Ossipoff and discussed the specialized work in my department. This included the fact that we hold the Lynx. The Professor was very interested and was clearly aware that Maréchal was keen on obtaining money to spend on his wife. This was exploited, with the Professor who offered him money and assurances that was all for scientific use. He claimed that petty rules should not come between allies and that they would publicly publish any findings and claim that they had come up with the Lynx formula themselves. The only positive aspect is that no intelligence outside specialist information was divulged."

The General absorbed Hart's words.

"The Lynx," he said, "was used to read minds. However, it is now dormant? Is it possible that the Russians have found a way to activate this serum?"

Hart nodded. "That is my fear. It was created by the chemist Brion at his institute. When the liquid came into our custody, it stopped working after a few days, mystifying both my section and the Institut Brion. I even tried it upon myself, to no effect. It is puzzling that the Russians are so interested. We know the Okhrana have their Vozduhoplavatel research center, set up covertly in 1909 after the previous year's Tunguska event, to see if there is a threat to Russia from beyond Earth."

"I am aware of that, Hart."

"My apologies, General. It is not improbable that they are looking at matters such as mind-reading. I suspect Professor Ossipoff has some connection with Vozduhoplavatel."

"They may think that the Lynx is of extra-terrestrial origin, although we have no doubt that Brion created it. Is it possible that the Russians think they can re-activate the serum?"

"They would not have gone to this effort if they did not think that they could use it," replied Hart.

"We cannot allow any other power to have this knowledge," said the General. "Russia may be our ally today, but they certainly have not been in the past. If they were able to find a way to use it, they could become the most powerful country on Earth; no nation could keep any secrets from them. Only we French can be trusted with its custodianship—and, in the event of making it work again—its civilized use."

Hart nodded vigorously.

The General continued. "The matter is delicate, given that Russia is an ally during this war. Professor Ossipoff is already back on Russian soil—weeks back. It is unfortunate that our own sources in Saint Petersburg only just relayed the information of Maréchal's treachery. We may never have known some of it was missing, let alone that he was responsible…"

Hart felt a little uneasy. He was all too aware that he had recruited Maréchal to his section. It was why, when the report came though of the officer's possible treachery, he had promptly brought in Jacquemain to swiftly extract information.

There was a knock at the door.

"Enter," the General said.

A private walked in, saluted, and gave the General a sealed file.

"I was told to bring this to you at once, General."

The General took the file and read it.

"Hum. It seems, Monsieur Hart, that the Russians not only know how to use the Lynx, but also plan to do so."

He gave the file to Hart to read. It contained a short summary of the information emanating from their source in Saint Petersburg. Hart turned pale. The Russians, at their cosmological facility at Vozduhoplavatel, had made a breakthrough with activating the Lynx, and now planned to use it.

"Our sources will be telling us more," said the General, "and quite possibly, the Central Powers will find out too. Saint Petersburg is riddled with spies."

Saint Petersburg, Fontanka 16,[2] 9 April

Doctor Cornelius Kramm sat outside the office of the head of the Russian Department of Police, who also controlled the feared secret police, the Okhrana. He looked at the thick wooden door of the office. No doubt its thickness was to ensure that conversations within could not be overhead. He did not like to be kept waiting. These new paymasters had not been keen to meet at their headquarters, but he had insisted, to be certain that it was them who wished to employ him, and not some old enemies luring him into a back street to kill him. Perhaps that is why they were keeping him waiting. This would not have happened in the old days, he thought, when he was one of the leaders of the feared criminal organization, the Red Hand. But those days were gone. Now, he sold his criminal expertise to the highest bidder. As always, he was professionally known as "Doctor Cornelius," rather than by his full name. On the positive side, he thought, this job would provide a great deal of money. Not rubles, but pound sterling, straight into one of his many Swiss accounts. He had insisted on an advance, which he knew had been paid this very day. The money was such that he had agreed to take the job, but he had never entirely trusted…

"…the Russians," said the young man on the other side of the door, looking at it as if he could see through it, "...since some of his Moscow-based Red Hand agents once tried to break away from his organization and set up a rival group. He will take revenge if we cheat him, but if we pay him the rest of the money after the job is done, he will be content."

"He will get paid and will have no idea that we stole all his secrets," said an overweight middle-aged man seated at a nearby desk. He was A.V. Brune de St Hippolite, the head of the Department of Police.

Another man seated behind the desk spoke:

"Yuri Klimkov, is he giving away any secrets at the moment?"

"No, Professor Ossipoff," replied the young man, respectfully. "We need to make him think about them. It needs to come to the forefront of his mind. But I will have plenty of opportunity to have such conversations with him during the mission."

---

[2] Headquarters of the Okhrana, the Tsarist secret police established in 1881.

"We know he speaks English, German and passable Russian. What language does he think in?" asked Ossipoff.

"English," Klimkov replied.

"Your mastery of languages is why we have selected you for this mission," said Brune de St Hippolite.

"Yuri has done well," said the Professor. "Whilst training with us at Vozduhoplavatel, he mastered the use of the Lynx serum, or rather the abilities to read minds it confers."

"Providing he does not read our minds!" said the spymaster half-jokingly.

"By forcefully concentrating on a particular topic, as we have trained ourselves, we can ensure it is not so. Background thoughts are not heard, but this does not last long, although it should be enough for this meeting!"

"He is thinking random, undetailed, thoughts now about his dead brother," Klimkov said, "and something about a favor he is owed by a Russian friend for fixing someone's face… Now he is wondering what has become of a Lord Burydan—an enemy of his…"

"Enough now, Klimkov. As you said you can find out more from him in good time," said the spymaster.

"Yes, sir," said Klimkov.

"We must finish this meeting quickly, so that the mission begins. Time works against us," said the spymaster. "Professor Ossipoff, you have replicated the Lynx?"

"Yes, our chemical team at Vozduhoplavatel has done so. Of course, the Meyral effect will fade soon."

"This Meyral effect, could it return?"

This was Professor Ossipoff's specialty and he enthusiastically went into it.

"The effect has appeared above the Earth for a few months at time. It can be seen with a good pair of binoculars, as sort of a spiral effect, often mistaken for an *aurora borealis*, which is not surprising, given it's in orbit above Finland. It's appeared before and fades away. Our research into psychic abilities at Vozduhoplavatel investigated if such cosmic phenomena had any effect on the human brain. We discovered that Meyral does indeed emit waves effecting it. Its effect is slight, perhaps momentary. Someone with latent abilities can read a mind for a moment or bend a spoon...

"However, Brion's Lynx serum works in combination with the effect, unleashing a much greater power of the mind. Had Brion not developed the Lynx during that period of the Meyral effect, then it would have been near useless, perhaps being able to mind read for a couple of minutes, if even that! Again, it only works in those who have those latent abilities. The French really did not think to consider any other factors, which is typical of them…"

The spymaster interrupted him. "Yes, thank you, Professor. I'd like to know if the effect will return after its current activity?"

The Professor looked a bit put out, then answered: "We have studied the Meyral effect for years now. With each appearance, it moves further from the Earth, longer each time. Currently, our measurements indicate that its effect on the brain gets weaker each time. We believe there are only a few weeks before its appearance ends. The next time it appears, it effects will be negligible. Eventually, it will leave the Solar System altogether. It is not likely we shall ever know what it is, or why it materialized over Earth a few decades ago. Perhaps there is an intelligence directing it, but we think it more likely to be some natural phenomenon."

"We must then move quickly, as we planned," the spymaster said. "Before I can go to the Tsar with this, we must have a successful operation. Then, we can quickly place agents around the world to find the secrets of the other great powers. And of course, the many revolutionaries at home will soon find all their plans exposed."

Klimkov had to restrain himself from reacting. The spymaster's thoughts—his defenses were useless—were clear to him. The reason to delay talking to the Tsar had nothing to do with presenting a successful mission. It was about consolidating control over the entire Lynx project. It seems there were those whom the spymaster feared who would like to gain control of the Lynx, and indeed the whole of the Vozduhoplavatel research.

Klimkov caught a couple of names in the spymaster's mind: Rasputin, and one General Boris Liatoukine… The spymaster intended to use the Lynx to read their minds. Klimkov could see other thoughts; his superior wanted to improve the reputation of the Okhrana, which had been damaged after a series of scandals, and even expand its domain. Klimkov would keep all this to himself, of course. He wanted to remain in the good books of his superiors.

"Let us bring in this Doctor Cornelius," said Brune de St Hippolite. "And no mention of mind-reading!"

They all laughed.

"I had better take my leave," said Professor Ossipoff.

He left via a side-door. The spymaster went to the main door, opening it. He beckoned in Doctor Cornelius and offered him a chair.

"Doctor Cornelius, I take it that what we are offering you is satisfactory? You charge highly."

"I do, but my costs are high, as are my services—including the face changes that we shall need. No one else can do what I do," the Doctor added.

Not for long, thought Klimkov.

"You are of German extraction, are you not?" asked the spymaster.

The Doctor took off his gold-rimmed spectacles and cleaned them.

"I am an American," he replied. "But my only concern is myself. I think my reputation demonstrates that."

Klimkov read the Doctor's mind and saw that the Doctor really did not care about his roots, just money and power.

The spymaster indicated Klimkov.

"Doctor, may I introduce Yuri Klimkov. He is one of our finest agents and a superb linguist."

Both men stood up and shook hands.

"I will swiftly go over the mission," continued Brune de St Hippolite. "You are both to go to Galicia, behind enemy lines. Your task, Doctor, will be to bodyguard Klimkov. Using your skills, both of you will wear different faces. You will use the contacts you claim to have in the area to assist with the following objectives. One: Gathering intelligence on the German and Austro-Hungarian military plans. Two: Gathering information on those Polish politicians who seek to unite Russian Poland with Galicia under Habsburg control. We desire the opposite, of course. Three: If the opportunity presents itself, assassinating the Austro-Hungarian Field Marshal Franz Conrad von Hötzendorf, or another senior German or Habsburg officer.

"Objectives one and two will be primarily achieved by Klimkov using some special listening equipment. Objective three can be done with weapons you, Doctor, claim to have secreted in the vicinity. Klimkov has the authority to change these objectives if the need arises, but within reason."

Klimkov concentrated on Cornelius, starting with more mundane matters, but always with the covert objective of extracting information about his surgical skills and his underworld knowledge from his mind. The so-called "Sculptor of human flesh" was thinking in English of the equipment he would need. He still had a few contacts left from the Red Hand. He thought that some of them might provide him with surgical tools, travel arrangements, accommodation, etc. Klimkov noted that the Doctor realized that, these days, buying loyalty from his former subordinates was more important than instilling fear in them. However, he was not thinking of his surgical skills. Klimkov would have to trigger those thoughts by conversation. There would be plenty of time for that later. Doctor Cornelius's thoughts were beginning to fade. It would soon be time for another dose of the Lynx serum.

"If there is nothing else," concluded Brune de St Hippolite, "I suggest you start on your journey."

Austro-Hungarian Army mobile field hospital, Galicia (Poland),
Austro-Hungarian Empire, 15 April

The Countess Irina Petrovski looked sadly at the lifeless body in front of her. Private Dabrowski was dead. He had lost an arm in a recent battle against the Russians. His life had been saved, but an infection had taken hold and claimed his life.

"He has gone," said the doctor attending him, although this was already clear.

A military priest was also present. He turned to the Countess.

"Thank you for calling me, Countess,"

She nodded her head. "It was important that he receive the last rites. God played a great role in his life."

Later, after the body had been taken away, the doctor said to the Countess:

"You make an excellent nurse, Countess."

She was already making up the bed for the next patient.

"Thank you, doctor," she replied. "It is only my duty."

"You have a visitor, in my office."

"Who is it?"

"I don't know; he had a couple of officers escorting him."

The Countess then knew who it was.

"I shall see what he wants. Thank you for informing me."

With that, she went off to meet her visitor. The doctor looked at her as she walked away. She was a very beautiful, auburn-haired woman. Despite her slightly haughty manner, she was respected by patients and staff alike. She was a widow, although it was rumored that she had been involved with a Croatian U-Boat captain.

Lucky man, the doctor thought, before moving on to his next patient.

The Countess recognized the soldier on guard outside the door, a grizzled-looking man in his late 30s.

"Hello Sergeant Mayr. How is your family?"

"Very well, ma'am," the Sergeant replied in an Austrian accent. "My oldest boy is joining my old regiment, in fact."

The Countess nodded. "He will do the emperor proud, like his father."

She meant what she said, but was uneasy. Would the Sergeant's son end up like the poor boy she had just watched die earlier? The Empire's cause was just, but the cost had been high, and there was no end to it yet.

"Thank you, ma'am. I've heard of your good work here." She smiled appreciatively. "He's waiting. It's an urgent matter, he said."

"It must be for him to leave Vienna," she replied.

The Sergeant grinned and knocked on the door.

"Come," came a voice from the inside.

The Sergeant opened the door.

"The Countess has arrived," he announced to the occupants.

"She may enter," said the same voice. However, the Countess had already done so. She recognized both men who hastily stood up to greet her. Sitting behind the desk was Prince Wilhelm, the head of the section of the *Evidenzbureau*[3] which dealt with threats to the Empire of an unusual nature. On the other side of the desk was Lieutenant Vuljanić, who had joined the section a year previously.

"Please, please, do sit down," said the Prince.

Since the Countess had saved the naval base of Pula from destruction by the lunatic British Lord Burydan, she had become a favorite of the Emperor. She certainly knew it, and the Prince, whilst effectively her superior, knew very well that she would not put up with too many airs from him.

---

[3] The Habsburg Empire's military intelligence service. Formed in 1850, it was the world's first such organization.

The Countess took a seat. They exchanged some pleasantries, regarding her children, who were in Vienna, where she felt they would be safe. The Prince then turned to the reason why he was here.

"We have received information that the Russians have developed a some kind of mind-reading technique. They have sent a man equipped with this ability—apparently a drug addict—to spy on our forces here, and find out about our future plans."

Once, the Countess would have dismissed such a story as outlandish, the fantasy of a degenerate mind. However, experience had taught her otherwise.

"The creature I encountered on the Trans-Siberian express in 1906—the one that murdered my husband and many others—was able to absorb the minds of its victims. So, mind-reading certainly seems possible. However, are your sources impeccable?"

"Yes," the Prince replied. "The information came from more than one source. However, it is not just your experience with such matters that the Empire needs. Another target for this operative is to investigate the Polish Supreme National Committee. I understand you have contacts with them?"

The Countess nodded. "Of course. They're based in Kraków, where I grew up." She noticed an interested look from the Lieutenant. "Lieutenant, are you familiar with the politics of Galicia?" she asked.

"Not in any great depth, I'm afraid, ma'am," he replied

"The Supreme National Committee, of whom I am a supporter, wants to unify Galicia with Russian Poland, under the rule of our Emperor. It is past time my countrymen were liberated from the Tsar. My husband was from Russian Poland, and I moved there to be with him. However, I could not stand seeing my people become part of such a backward empire. I did like the Tsar and the Tsarina on a personal level, but they did not do enough for my people. They have come under the influence of that degenerate Rasputin. Take it from me, monks like him are just trouble." She realized she was digressing. "Yes, I certainly do have contact with the committee, and it's imperative the Russians do not interfere with them."

She knew she was well known as a Polish nationalist, but one working within—and for—the Habsburg Empire. She was also concerned about the part of Poland occupied by Germany. She hoped the Kaiser would be reasonable after they won the war.

"Excellent," said the Prince. "There is a third reason why we need you. The agent the Russians are sending has a bodyguard. It is Doctor Cornelius."

Doctor Cornelius! The Countess had encountered him before. His criminal activities in Sarajevo the previous year had been part of a successful plot to give the French and British a super-weapon that could have won them the war.

"I will appreciate the opportunity to meet him again," she said.

The Lieutenant piped up. "We believe that he has used his surgical skills to change the appearance of both himself and the Russian agent. You won't be able to recognize him."

The Countess nodded. It made sense. The Doctor's description had been circulated to all their agents throughout the Empire. And perhaps this telepath was known as well.

"As you know," aid the Prince, "I would much prefer you to have stayed in Vienna as a journalist rather than coming out here as nurse, but it seems to have turned out well in light of this assignment."

"I had to help my fellow countrymen more directly. This war has not gone so well. I can hardly sit around in Vienna whilst it rages here. Have you any idea of the suffering of our soldiers?"

"I get reports," said the Prince. "My son is on the front."

The Countess softened. "My apologies," she said.

"Accepted," said the Prince. He continued. "Your mission is to stop these two men. The implications of a mind-reader are devastating. Try and capture them alive, if possible. The Lieutenant and the Sergeant will work with you. You are in charge, but they are not to leave your side." He raised his hand. "Please, no protests."

"I had no intention of protesting," she replied. "I am delighted to have their assistance."

"You will have a liaison to the military here as well. General Borojević has been briefed and has agreed to give you whatever you need."

"Borojević has an excellent reputation, due to his actions against the Russians at Przemysl and in the Carpathians. I look forward to meeting him," said the Countess. "One of your countrymen, I believe?" she said to the Lieutenant, whom she knew to be Croatian.

"Yes, ma'am," he said. "It will be an honor to meet him."

"Let us get started without delay, then. The Empire is counting on us."

Kraków, Galicia, 16 April, 8:45 p.m.

Doctor Cornelius and Yuri were in a back street ending with the back wall of the Hotel Central. Yuri had some earphones on, connected to some kind of sucker attached to the wall. Wires connected to the earphones on the sucker were linked to a small box in front him. Both men were dressed poorly. They looked like peasants from the countryside, or vagrants. That had been the Doctor's plan, and thus far, it had worked.

Cornelius looked at Yuri. He was unrecognizable from before. Previously, he had a full head of hair and a young face. Now, he was balding, with a rough, middle-aged face. The Doctor was satisfied with his work. For himself, he had decided to wear the face of an older man with a short beard, wearing cheap, slightly fractured spectacles. He had perfected the technique of face sculpting so much that he was able to change his own features with no assistance. He could also change teeth, but this was difficult and he had not bothered to do so this time. It hardly mattered anyway; he had yet to hear of anyone being recognized solely by their teeth.

Cornelius' thoughts turned back to the street. It was quiet, no one was present. He idly wondered about the machine Klimkov was using; he must take a discreet look at some point. Given that its owner was a drug addict, that might not be too difficult.

Earlier that morning, he had come across Klimkov injecting something into his arm—some kind of pinkish fluid. "It helps keep me alert," The Russian had said. The Red Hand had once been involved in drug trafficking, so Cornelius knew their effect. Whatever Klimkov used, it made him weak and unreliable, but that also meant that he may be able to manipulate him if he had to.

Klimkov had caught the Doctor's thoughts and was pleased the surgeon had no idea of the true purpose of the serum. However, his main concern now was to listen to the thoughts of those inside the hotel. It was fortunate indeed that the Polish Supreme National Committee was meeting on the other side of this wall, meaning that there was a clear line of thought to their minds, with no interference from any others'. However, stray thoughts did occasionally come from hotel staff and clients, the nearby buildings and, of course, Doctor Cornelius.

The meeting inside was ending. At first, it had been difficult to identify who was who. When hearing thoughts, people did not often identify themselves. However, thoughts seemed to have a different "sound" to them when their owner was speaking. So Klimkov would zoom in on those, and at the same time, scan the thoughts of those listening. They would identify the speaker. In a short time, he was able to ascertain the composition of the Committee and felt he knew more about their politics than they did themselves.

A stray thought came into his heard, but not from the meeting. He jumped up. "Someone's coming," he said to Cornelius, but the Doctor saw no one. Then, out of a door halfway down the alley came an old man. They had both prepared for this eventuality and immediately had bottles to their mouths, looking convincingly like a pair of drunks.

The man who had come out of the doorway, turned, and saw them. He came down the street. He was wearing a flat cap and coat, holding a lamp. Cornelius quietly cursed; it looked like a night watchman. They started singing in a drunken manner in German. Since the Doctor knew no Polish, they were to pose as Austrian vagrants, traveling from place to place. The watchman came up to them.

"Go home!" he said in Polish. Then he looked at the box on the floor, with the headphones out. "What's that?" he asked.

"Distract him," Cornelius said in English.

Klimkov complied, picking up the box and talking to the old man in German. "It's where we keep our food," he said.

Meanwhile, Cornelius had taken a small whisky bottle out of his pocket and opened it. The old man looked at him.

"I need a sip of the good stuff; do you want some?" the Doctor said.

Something feels wrong here, the old man thought.

Klimkov knew exactly what the Doctor was going to do. "Look, let me open it for you," he said, drawing the old man's attention back to him.

The Doctor brought out a cloth, poured some of the bottle's contents onto it, then moved swiftly behind the watchman and placed the cloth firmly on the old man's mouth. The watchman dropped his lamp, but struggled ferociously. He was not going to his death meekly. Klimkov grabbed hold of him, but the wily old man deliberately fell over, pulling both men to the ground.

Momentarily freed, the old man stood up. He then gave a horrendous gasp and collapsed.

Cornelius took his pulse. "He's dying. The poison has done its work. We must leave immediately. He will be found, but it will be assumed that he died of natural causes."

Klimkov placed his equipment into the bag and then the two men disappeared into the night.

Later, they arrived at their lodgings. It was little more than a small, run-down room. Klimkov looked at it distastefully.

"Could we not have a better place than this? We could have rented somewhere slightly more congenial and cheaper than your man's rent which you have on expenses."

"Renting elsewhere means we have to register," Cornelius explained patiently, "and that can be made available to the police, who are no doubt checking people's movements, given the war. Certainly, if we eliminate anyone in too obvious a fashion, they will immediately start checking hotels and so on. My contact rents us this room for a high fee, yes, but for this, there is no registration to be shown to the police or anyone else. He uses this building for certain, er, business operations, although it is currently empty, due to the war. Remember also, if we are discovered, he will likely have to abandon the property."

Klimkov seemed satisfied. The Doctor continued:

"If anyone asks, we are here as night watchmen, just like, I suspect, that man was. We need to be more circumspect with your equipment. Once that had made him suspicious, we had to kill him. Incidentally, how did you know the man was going to come out of the door?"

"I head the door unlocking," Klimkov said.

"I heard nothing," replied the Doctor.

"One of my talents is my excellent hearing. That is a requirement when using the listening equipment."

The Doctor looked satisfied. Klimkov decided to move things along.

"I've heard enough information tonight. Your explosive device will be needed."

"The bomb is secreted in this very building," the Doctor said. "My contact has provided us with something that will destroy the entire hotel."

Klimkov was reading Cornelius's mind. He was delighted that thoughts of the bomb-maker came into his mind. Now, he knew who he was and where he was based—Berlin of all places! *The remnants of the Red Hand must work very well indeed to be able to construct and smug-*

gle a bomb all the way to Galicia, he thought. The Okhrana must get hold of the bomb-maker and make use of his talents.

The effect of the serum was starting to wear off. He decided to try for more while he still could.

"It did cross our minds to use your talents to infiltrate someone into the Polish group, someone disguised as one of their members," he said. "However, it was assessed as being too risky. Such an infiltrator may not come across convincingly to those who know him well."

The Doctor simply nodded. His thoughts were in agreement with Klimkov's words, and he wished to get some rest. However, there were some other thoughts in the background, but Klimkov could not hear them. So he pressed on. He had been cautious up to now, but sensed that the surgeon's secrets were within his grasp.

"Your skills must have been hard to come by," he said, raising his hands, "Of course, I don't expect you to tell me how."

And there it was! At the forefront of the Doctor's mind was how he had come by his surgical skills in the first place. There were other thoughts of sinister experiments on humans that came later to help perfect them, but now Klimkov knew the genesis of what had made Doctor Cornelius Kramm the sculptor of human flesh.

"I certainly will not," said Cornelius.

Klimkov laughed. "Let us retire. Tomorrow, we have a long day ahead of us. I need to send a message to my superiors, but first, we must try and find some enemy officers we can eavesdrop on. Our effort came to nothing today. It is important that we find out about their military plans."

Kraków Gendarmerie Headquarters, 17 April

The Countess was seated at a table with a man in an Austro-Hungarian General's uniform. He was balding, fit-looking, and wore a moustache. They had been introduced to each other and had sat down. She was well-dressed, as always, but her garments were all in gray. She felt it would not do to dress too fashionably in a town so close the front.

"It is good of you to come to Kraków and meet with us, General Borojević. Your time as commander of the Third Army must be precious."

"Countess", replied the General, "it is my pleasure. I am aware of your activities last year in Sarajevo and the debt our navy owes you. I must thank you myself for what you have done on behalf of my men, although, sadly, they can never know. I am delighted to be your liaison. Whatever I can do to help, I will. You need only to ask."

The Countess was always impressed by such proper chivalrous attitudes. She would often get negative attitudes due to her being a woman.

"Thank you, General. Of course, we have much to thank you for, given your distinguished efforts to defend us against the Russians. I am also pleased to say that the travel book you wrote, *Durch Bosnian*, when you were stationed in Sarajevo, was of great use in helping familiarize myself with that city."

The General smiled. "I am honored to hear it. Lieutenant Vuljanić? You sound like a fellow Croatian."

"I am sir, from Karlovac, now in the 96th Karlovac Infantry Regiment," the Lieutenant replied, a little nervous for being in the General's presence.

"A fine town. I'm from Banovina, myself. Now, I believe you both have a remarkable story for me?"

The Countess related what the Prince had told her.

"It is almost unbelievable—a mind-reader? And this Doctor Cornelius, he is able to shape faces at will? But I must believe this not only because of the high regard the Emperor has for you, Countess, but also because I am aware of some of the materials the Empire keeps in Sarajevo—the advanced technologies, artifacts from other worlds and so on. Mind-reading would be a powerful weapon, one that could change the fate of this war."

The Countess responded. "It is difficult to know how to counter it effectively. We chose to meet you here as it's less likely that these men would be watching this station. We assume that places where soldiers gather would be their first target. Nonetheless, all the rooms around this one are empty—although we do not know the range of the thought-reader, or telepath as such people are called."

"I will issue orders for my senior officers to limit their interactions with anyone they do not know—something which they should be doing anyway—and to immediately report anyone who may acting strangely. That might help us in avoiding this thought-reader and also any infiltration by a lookalike. I could bury this town under troops, checking everyone to help you find these men, if you will?"

"No, General. The telepath is likely to able to sense troops around every corner. Furthermore, we need to catch him and Cornelius. They could elude your troops and head elsewhere. This threat must be dealt with here and now."

"At least, let me provide you with some troops. Some of my men are from this city; their local knowledge could prove useful to you."

The Countess pondered this. "We already have the local gendarmes' cooperation, but I suppose that a reserve of a few soldiers could be useful—but they would have to await our call."

There was a knock on the door. The Countess and the General simultaneously said "Enter," then both laughed.

A Sergeant entered, swiftly saluting the General. "Mr. Jaworski has called," he said to the Countess. "He is waiting for you at the Hotel Central."

"General, I am sorry but I must leave," said the Countess. "I think time is of the essence. Lieutenant, please liaise with the General's staff in order to arrange for his reserve."

They made their farewells, with the General bowing to the Countess. Then she and the Sergeant left the station.

Outside, there was an armored car. On closer inspection, it appeared to be an open-topped civilian roadster, but it had armor plating all around it. The Sergeant opened the back door, letting the Countess in, then went to sit at the driver's seat.

"How are you finding driving *Elizabeth*?" she asked.

"Not a problem, Countess," he answered. "It seems able to ride smoothly on any terrain, and at high speeds too."

"Excellent." She only let trusted people drive her *Elizabeth*.

It had been a gift to her from her British friends, Professor Saxton and Doctor Wells, before the war. It was given to her on the condition that she would never share its technology. The *Evidenzbureau* were keen to learn its secrets, but she had kept her word. The car remained a mystery; it was not clear who had built it, or indeed if there were others like it. Her friends had told her that they thought it would be best used in her hands. Certainly, a fleet of such vehicles had not been deployed by the British, deepening the mystery. It had served her well, and she had allowed its use as an ambulance, saving many lives in the recent battles against the Russians.

"Proceed, Sergeant," she said.

The car drove off.

Klimkov and Doctor Cornelius had changed into more respectable garb, and the surgeon had changed their faces slightly. That, coupled with a wash and shave, made them look like the salesmen from Salzburg they claimed to be.

They were seated at the Wierzynek restaurant on the main square, eating lunch, not far from several officers enjoying their lunch. The Doctor was puzzled by Klimkov's tactics. How would they be able to use the listening equipment? And what did they expect to hear if they did? It was not a given that these officers would be discussing military plans. They had already visited three cafés that morning, and Klimkov had been displeased by all of them. What was he up to?

Klimkov looked at him and smiled. "I think we are done now here, but we can take our time. Our next engagement is not until the evening."

The Doctor wondered as to this change of mood.

Klimkov was indeed very pleased. He had been scanning the minds of the officers and the soldiers they had passed or sat nearby all day. The cafés had provided scraps of information. However, the German colonel sitting at the next table had been thinking about an offensive by the Central Powers that was to take place on 5 May. This was vital information, which he had to get to Saint Petersburg at once.

Tonight, they would kill some Polish politicians and tomorrow, they would assassinate a top Habsburg officer. On top of that, he now had the secrets of Doctor Cornelius. He started thinking of his future. He would be well rewarded for this. His work may well ensure Russian victory here in Galicia. Perhaps he would become a favorite of the Tsar and Tsarina? He would certainly give better them advice than that damned monk of theirs. He started laughing.

Dr Cornelius looked at him. "What amuses you?" he asked. And Klimkov simply laughed more. *An effect of his being a drug addict*, the sculptor of human flesh thought.

At the hotel, the Countess was meeting with Władysław Leopold Jaworski of the Polish Supreme National Committee. They were in the manager's office, with the door slightly ajar, and the Sergeant standing outside. They had made small talk at first, reminiscing about the past. They had known each other for several years.

"You say, Irina, that there is an espionage effort against us?" said Jaworski, a man who looked around fifty, balding with a beard. "I must say that we had assumed that already."

"I am glad to hear it," replied the Countess, "but there does seem to be a particular effort, of which I cannot say too much. It is very real."

"And you cannot tell me what this effort is?"

"I fear I cannot."

Jaworski looked affronted. "Am I not to be trusted?"

The Countess soothed him. "Of course, you are. You know that I hold you in the highest regard, but you must know that there can be no exceptions in security matters. However, as you can see, I have chosen to share these concerns with you. I have little doubt that you can help us deal with it."

He looked placated. "Of course, I will do whatever I can to help," he said.

"Thank you. Tell me, have you noticed any strange behavior amongst your Committee? Anyone acting out of character?" The Countess was trying to determine if the Doctor had already infiltrated the Committee with a lookalike, having satisfied herself that Jaworski was not thanks to their initial small talk.

"No, not all. Are you suggesting that we have a traitor amongst us?" he asked, horrified.

"Not necessarily. Has there been any strange incidents? Anything out of the ordinary? Any incidents of any kind?"

Jaworski pondered for a moment. "Well, there was the death of a night watchman at the back of this hotel. He was starting his work early, and it seems he collapsed from a heart attack."

"That is unfortunate, but is there a connection with the Committee?"

Jaworski looked awkward. "Yes, we were having a meeting there at the time the gendarmes think he died. That's why I'm here today, preparing for another meeting tonight."

"What meeting? I was not aware of it."

"It was a meeting of some delicacy."

Now it was the Countess's turn to feel affronted. "I may not be a member of the Committee, but my work for the Polish people, I think, does entitle to me to the courtesy of being informed about such meetings. Kindly tell me what transpired."

"We are trying to set down the groundwork for the union of the Austrian Poland with Russian Poland, after our armies defeat the Russians, of course. As you know, Piłsudski's incursion was not the success we had all hoped for."

"I strongly supported that incursion myself. However, I have lived in the Russian Poland. I can assure you that the fear of the Tsar is strong. Hopefully, with imminent military success, that will change."

The previous year, the Polish activist Józef Piłsudski had led the First Company of Poles from Kraków into Russian Poland in the hope of starting an uprising there, but it had failed. The Countess had been disappointed, but not entirely surprised.

"Tell me more," she continued.

"We have managed to bring here, to Kraków, a couple of important Polish figures from Russian Poland. We hope they can help mobilize the population in our favor when our armies start to liberate them. Secrecy is paramount. We are also hoping they can cause dissent in the ranks of the Poles in the Russian army."

The Countess understood then why the Russians had selected this as a prime target for their telepath. "Whilst I am disappointed that I was not privy to all this, I am pleased at your initiative. The current situation, where our people are fighting each other on different sides, is truly horrendous. A united Poland under our Emperor would prevent this from happening again. You say there is another meeting tonight?"

"Indeed! We hope to finalize various matters before our compatriots return to Warsaw—they face a difficult journey. Then, we intend to inform the authorities of what our plans are, which will no doubt be of great help to Field Marshal von Hötzendorf."

"That previous meeting—where did it take place in the hotel?"

Jaworski stood up and pointed at a layout of the hotel on the wall. "Here," he said, pointing to a room at the back.

"Did the night watchman die on the alley behind the hotel?" she asked,

"Yes."

The Countess realized that this could be significant. This would be the perfect place for a mind-reader to operate, assuming the wall was no impediment. It was probable that the night watchman had disturbed the spies. Doctor Cornelius no doubt had found a way of murdering the poor man, making it look like natural causes. Poison most likely.

"Władysław, this is what you must do. Proceed with the meeting as planned. However, you must arrive thirty minutes late. Please do not ask me why. You are to tell no one that you have met me, or share anything of what I have told you."

Bemused, Jaworski nodded. The Countess knew that if he was there at the beginning of the meeting, the telepath may be tipped off immediately, and he and Cornelius would escape before being captured. And that would not do.

Having bade farewell to Jaworski, the Countess and the Sergeant returned to *Elizabeth*. She briefed the Sergeant on what had been said.

"We will have to observe that alley from a distance, and hope that our thoughts won't tip them off. We cannot have gendarmes or troops nearby; that, too, may tip them off. When they arrive, we must be sure it is them, and not anyone else who may have business in the adjoining properties."

"I have some ideas on that, Countess,"

"Excellent. Let's discuss them when we meet with the Lieutenant. Take me to the Royal Cathedral on the Wawel Hill. I wish to pray for our success tonight."

The Sergeant nodded and drove her to the Cathedral. It was well known that the Countess was a devout Catholic. He often wondered about God's ways himself. He came from a poor background in the village of Kandersfeld in Austria. Yet, here he was, an army Sergeant having a conversation with a Countess and dealing with strange phenomena. God—and the *Evidenzbureau*—did indeed move in mysterious ways.

Doctor Cornelius was escorting Klimkov to a bench by the river Vistula. They were back in their peasants' garb. After lunch, they had returned to their safe house, where Klimkov had assembled a lengthy coded message for Saint Petersburg. Now, they were headed for a drop off point, a bench with a view of the river.

Klimkov beckoned the Doctor who sat next to him. Klimkov discreetly stuck a cigarette packet containing the message under the bench.

"That will be picked up later today," Klimkov said. "As we are by ourselves, I think I can mention that, in addition to the chaos we shall cause tonight, I think we can do one final thing before we leave. Tomorrow, we shall assassinate General Borojević."

"Not Field Marshal von Hötzendorf?" asked the Doctor.

"Too difficult to get to him. I have the authority to choose another target. Borojević is a competent officer. Once he is dead, we can leave."

"It sounds a bit risky to me. What is your plan?"

Klimkov could see that the Doctor was not keen on doing this at all. He could not be told that, in the process of reading the thoughts of the officers earlier, he had learned the details of Borojević's whereabouts. He had also discerned the high regard that his men had for him. Killing him would help when the Russians would launch their own offensive to counter the one the Central Powers were about to start.

"I need your expert opinion," Klimkov replied. "After the General is dead, you will have earned your fee."

Klimkov could see that this had worked. The Doctor was very keen to get the money that had been promised.

With binoculars, the Countess and Lieutenant Vuljanić were watching the alley behind the Hotel Central from the Sandomierska tower on Wawel Hill. Although it was dark, the street lighting would enable them to see if anyone showed up. The Sergeant was ready at the wheel of *Elizabeth* outside.

"Are you sure we can get there in time if we see them?" asked the Lieutenant.

"You know *Elizabeth*'s capabilities. We can be there in a couple of minutes after the Sergeant starts her up. Running down the stairs may take us longer than the actual journey by car. Meanwhile, we must stay at a distance so that the telepath cannot detect us. He may well sense us when we drive down the alley, but there will be nothing they can do at that point." She looked at her pocket watch. "It's now 8:55 p.m. The Committee will soon be starting their meeting. Cornelius and the telepath should turn up soon."

A couple of minutes later, they spotted two shabbily dressed men with a large bag turn the corner of the main road into the alley.

"This can't be them, surely? They're just vagrants," said the Lieutenant.

"That is precisely why it could be them, Lieutenant. Spies do not dress as gentlemen—at least most of the time."

They could see them standing by the wall, talking.

"Look! The way they move has changed. They're no longer acting like vagrants," said the Countess. "They think they can't be seen. Now, they are indeed talking like the gentlemen they no doubt think they are. We must move swiftly."

They ran down the stairs.

Klimkov was perturbed. He could sense the minds on the other side of the wall. However, he heard the thoughts that Jaworski had not yet appeared. And he was keen to kill the chairman.

Cornelius was taking a box out of his sack. It was a simple-looking wooden box.

"And that will be enough to destroy the building?" asked Klimkov.

"Not as such," answered the Doctor. "It's been designed so that the explosion will blow against the wall, affecting this building only. It will blast inwardly with great force, smashing most of the ground floor. It will likely bring the rest of the building down. These Poles you dislike so much will not stand much of a chance."

Was this Russian not listening when I told him this earlier? He was probably a peasant elevated to his position by his betters because of his linguistic gifts, Cornelius thought.

Klimkov heard the thought. He would enjoy the moment when Russia had mastered the secret of changing people's faces and relish the fury he knew the Doctor would feel when he would discover that fact.

"Excellent," he said. "However, let us wait a few minutes, just in case there are latecomers."

Then, another thought hit his head. And another. It was a woman's thoughts, in Polish. It said:

They may detect us now! We are close. They may be reading my mind!

He turned to the Doctor. "Set it for two minutes! We've been discovered!"

Cornelius had no intention for setting the bomb for two minutes, discovered or not. There must always be time for any delays in escaping a bomb set to go off.

Suddenly, they were bathed in headlights. A car was roaring down the alley. Cornelius set the bomb for five minutes and affixed it to the wall, where it held. That was enough time to get away—or to bargain with if caught.

"Through that door," the Doctor shouted. Klimkov was already heading towards it; it was the same door that the night watchman had come through the previous night. It opened. Klimkov ducked as a bullet whizzed over his head. The two men went in, slammed the door shut behind them and bolted it. They were in what looked like a kitchen. No doubt the night watchman had come here to find something to eat before doing his rounds. Had he not instructed the staff here to bolt the door at night?

"Exit?" shouted Klimkov in Polish at a startled cook.

Before the man had time to point, the Russian was already running off. Mystified, Cornelius followed, carrying Klimkov's bag which the Russian had left behind in his hurry to escape.

Their pursuers clambered out of the vehicle. They tried to go in, but the door refused to budge.

"We must go round," the Countess said.

The Sergeant noticed the box on the wall.

"I am sure that is a focused bomb. It could destroy the hotel," he said. "Drive back down. I'll head into the hotel and get everyone out."

The Countess nodded. She had heard of such devices, used by elite criminals.

They drove back, with Sergeant hanging on the outside. She was going to admonish the lieutenant for shooting at the men, but there was no time, and anyway, it may be better to shoot them dead than let them get away.

The Sergeant got off at the end of the alleyway, whilst the Countess turned *Elizabeth* around the corner, driving down a small road that backed onto the alley.

Suddenly, she and the Lieutenant saw Cornelius and Klimkov, who had managed to leave the Hotel, running down that same road.

"Split up!" shouted Klimkov as he took one side of the road. The Doctor simply doubled back the way he came. He heard a woman's voice shout: "Stop or I'll shoot!", but he kept moving. Then he heard several shots—presumably at Klimkov.

He found himself back in the alley where the bomb was. He knew it was going to explode away from him, but he had never run faster in his life. He crossed the alley and went down another street. He finally stopped when he was certain he was no longer being followed. He caught his breath and started walking again at a normal pace. He had to keep moving; he had run past some people who would report him to the gendarmes, perhaps thinking he was a thief. He knew who the woman in the car was—Countess Irina Petrovski. How was she involved? For now, he had to make his way back to their safe house, which was the plan if and Klimkov were forced to split up. But first, he would a make a quick detour…

The Countess and Lieutenant Vuljanić had taken shots at the fleeing Klimkov from the *Elizabeth*. However, the Russian ducked and weaved, eluding all the bullets.

The Countess stopped firing. She was concerned that she may inadvertently injure a passerby. She also realized the man they were chasing this had to be the telepath.

"Stop firing, Lieutenant," she said. "We will run him down."

Klimkov listened around him. There were a number of voices he could hear, all talking about the shots they had heard. *Are the Russians here?* he heard. Some windows were opening. He took full advantage of the incipient panic and shouted out:

"The Russians are here! They are bombing the city; they are in the next street! Run, now!"

A few people began to leave their homes in a panic. Kraków had been briefly under siege by the Russians the previous year. Klimkov saw someone exit a house and onto the street. He quickly ran into the now abandoned house just as *Elizabeth* was turning the corner.

"Where did he go?" a frustrated Countess said.

Then there was an explosion.

Doctor Cornelius had returned to the drop off point. He heard the explosion and was satisfied that the bomb had done its work.

He went to the bench and retrieved the cigarette packet. He took out the piece of paper and unfolded it. It was written in code on both sides. Clearly, Klimkov had a lot to say. He took out a pencil, and some scraps of paper he had on his person. It was a simple code, and he could hardly believe the Russians were still using it. A nearby lamp provided some light, and he had to strain to see, but he started decoding the message.

Halfway through, his blood started running colder with every word. First, there were details about a Central Powers military offensive along the Gorlice-Tarnów line to be launched on 2 May. How on Earth did Klimkov know this?

Briefly, it also mentioned their plan to assassinate Borojević beforehand. Then there was a mention of the Supreme National Committee of the Poles, and the bombing action to be taken. Both these actions would certainly help a Russian strike before 2 May, which was likely to happen when they read the message.

Finally, there were details about him. Cornelius became more disturbed with every word. It was revealed how he had become the sculptor of human flesh. As a young medical student, he had hired sailors to engage in some drug running, to help live more luxuriously. One of these men had had facial deformities which, as an aspiring surgeon, he had noted. This sailor had later journeyed to China, and returned with seemingly a new face, all his deformities removed. The young Cornelius Kramm could not believe it, but ascertained it was indeed the same man, not least due to the same tattoos.

The sailor told him that he had saved a Chinese from drowning. In return, the sailor had taken him to his home village where some kind of surgery was performed on him to change his face.

When he qualified as a doctor, Cornelius and his brother Fritz had journeyed to China, looking for opportunities for their fledgling Red Hand organization to smuggle opium. He had left his brother for a while to travel to the hidden Ling Valley, where the sailor said he had his face changed.

There, he found a village that was known for healing those with deformed or damaged faces. The villagers told him that, many years ago, two brothers had come from the West and had stayed in the village. Their names, translated from the local dialect, was Ténèbre, or Shade. They knew the secret of making flesh soft, pliant and malleable, and had used it on some locals, either to repair their damaged faces or to punish them by turning them into monsters. They had eventually left, forced to flee to escape the wrath of a man named Kronos, but some of their secrets had been left behind. It involved a mysterious serum used to loosen the flesh, which could then be molded in any shape one desired.

Cornelius had told the villagers that the process was evil; that those who it was used on should be watched carefully, and that it should never be used again. He generously offered to take all the serum left behind by the two brothers to be destroyed safely elsewhere. He never got to the bottom of who the brothers were, but he now had the means become a sculptor of human flesh.

Klimkov had spelled out a concise version of all this in his message, along with a suggestion that someone should be sent to the Ling Valley at once to obtain information, and if possible samples of the serum, from the villagers. Cornelius had always suspected that the villagers, should they overcome their fear, might be able to provide more samples of the serum—not all of them had cowed in terror when he had told them the process was evil. He had once considered sending a Red Hand force to wipe out the entire village, but it would have attracted attention, and the Tongs might have had something to say about it.

The Doctor looked at the message again. There were other details about him, such as the identity of the Red Hand contact who had provided the bomb.

How could Klimkov know all this? He certainly had not told him. However, Klimkov had asked him questions on these matters. He had thought about them... Could he then be a thought-reader? A telepath? He had read of research into these matters, usually concluding that the alleged mind-readers were frauds. However, could it be done? Perhaps the drug Klimkov had injected into himself gave him these abilities? It would explain everything, including how the Russian seemed to know things in advance, such as the appearance of the night watchman, and even ducking in time to avoid a bullet.

Cornelius looked into his bag, to examine the so-called listening device. Opening it up, all he could see where a few wires and a stone taped inside to provide weight. It was nothing more than a prop—ideal to provide cover for a telepath!

He formulated a plan of action immediately. He would destroy the message, then kill Klimkov, but not just yet. First, they would assassinate the Croat General; then he would eliminate him. He would return to Saint Petersburg with some plausible story about the man's death and point out that they had wiped out the Polish committee and killed an enemy general, which should be enough to claim his payment. It was a risky, but he needed the money.

As for now, he would try and think in Mandarin. Klimkov's language skills were clearly European; he was not likely to know that Chinese language. And if he was proved wrong, or Klimkov got too suspicious, then he would kill him at once and deal with Borojević himself, but it would be useful to have a telepath on hand for that job.

"I believe that's for me," a voice said.

It took Cornelius by surprise. He had been careless, getting wrapped up in his thoughts. The man had spoken in Polish, but the Doctor knew immediately that he was here for the message. He was a small man in an old suit.

The Doctor pulled out a knife and stabbed the man in the stomach. He staggered back in shock and Cornelius stabbed him again, right through the neck. The man toppled over and fell.

The Doctor realized that he had been angry. He was furious that his secret, which even his late brother had had limited knowledge of, was known.

He took the body and tipped it in the Vistula. He ripped up the message into bits and cast them into the river. No one saw him do any of this. He had blood all over his clothes. He headed back to the safe house, hoping that that the dark would help disguise the stains.

The Countess surveyed the wreckage of the hotel with the Sergeant. She was still holding her firearm, a Doppelpistole M1912, effectively a double-barreled hand-held machine gun—a favorite of hers. She had used single shots, to prevent stray bullets from hitting civilians.

"You did well, Sergeant Mayr," she said. "It seems there were no casualties."

"There were few people in the hotel, essentially just the Poles and the hotel staff. Had the place been full, it might have been different story," he replied.

"I miscalculated; I thought they would be spying tonight. Furthermore, we have lost them," said the Countess.

"We did save the Polish committee and the hotel staff. Had we not been here at all, then they would have succeeded in their aim," said the Sergeant.

"We must at least be thankful for that."

The Lieutenant came up to them. "The gendarmerie has already searched the buildings where we lost the telepath. The found no one, although they reported a man shouting. 'The Russians are coming.' That was probably our man, trying to cause a panic to cover his escape. I've told the gendarmes to make inquiries in the city, I have given them the descriptions of the two of them. The troops General Borojević promised are already helping. Some of them will patrol the city during the rest of the night, although I suspect the spies have gone to ground."

"Very well," said the Countess. "There is not much more we can do now. We should get some sleep and reconvene first thing in the morning."

When Cornelius arrived back at the safe house, Klimkov was already there. The Doctor was already thinking in Mandarin.

"What happened to you?" Klimkov asked, pointing at the blood stains.

"I had to deal with a gendarme," Cornelius replied. "There is an organized search. I must destroy these clothes at once. We must abandon the peasant disguise. How did you escape?"

"Someone left his house open. I took cover there and came out after out pursuers had moved off."

"They were led by Countess Irina Petrovski. She may be a woman but, believe me, she is a formidable foe. Someone in Russia must have leaked that we were here."

"Nonsense!" replied Klimkov, outraged. "The Okhrana is the most secure organization in the world!"

Cornelius rolled his eyes. "Nevertheless, she did not appear out of nowhere. That will not disturb or plans, as she knows nothing about that. It is correct that you changed your plan from assassinating the Field Marshal to the General only yesterday?"

Klimkov nodded.

"Excellent!" the Doctor said, clapping his hands. "You know, I am quite enjoying this. It reminds me of my younger days, back when I was in the opium trade in China. Those times certainly set the blood pumping!"

In fact, the sculptor of flesh could not stand being so close to the action; in the old days, his Red Hand operatives would have dealt with the more physical elements of the business. However, he thought that this story might help explain why he was suddenly thinking in Mandarin.

Klimkov had certainly noticed it. In fact, he had done so before Cornelius had even opened the door. He could not understand what the Doctor was thinking. He was known as being mysterious; the Okhrana were unaware of his previous activities. There were thought flashes of English, but nothing substantive, just disjointed words. Had he somehow found out about his thought-reading? Or perhaps he was merely reliving his glory days in China?

Klimkov was uneasy. He wondered if it might not be safer to eliminate Cornelius at some point soon. He had only enough of the Lynx serum for one more day.

18 April

The morning came. Doctor Cornelius had not slept well. He had kept an eye on the door to his room all night, catching moments of sleep now and then, but always with his gun in hand.

He grabbed two large bags from underneath his bed and went into the front room. Klimkov was already awake and refreshed, reading a newspaper.

No doubt he has taken the drug, thought the Doctor in Mandarin. He tossed a bag to the Russian.

"Put this on," he said.

Klimkov took out the pike grey uniform of a Lieutenant in the Austro-Hungarian army.

"I thought we may need these, and had them prepared before our arrival here," the Doctor said, bringing out his own—a Captain's uniform. "It was made to your size," he added.

The Countess was also awake and breakfasting in the gendarmerie that served as her base of operations. Lieutenant Vuljanić came in.

"One of the gendarmes had a woman approach him. She said she saw a blood-stained vagrant heading into a neighboring house. They're looking into who the owner is. They also fished a dead man out of the river. It looks like he was stabbed to death. They are awaiting our orders."

The Countess got up. "Send the Sergeant to look at the body and see if he can find out more. That house may well be their hideout. We need to get there at once, in force."

Minutes later, she stood outside by the *Elizabeth* with the unit of soldiers that the General had detached to her.

"Lieutenant, take these men; we're going to search that house. The telepath may 'hear' us coming, but with so many men, their room for escape is limited."

The Lieutenant and the soldiers ran down the street, efficiently smashed the door and stormed in. The Countess drove down slowly after them. The Lieutenant came back out.

"There is no one here."

The Countess went in. The Lieutenant beckoned her up some stairs to the first floor.

"This looks like where they were staying," he said.

The Countess entered. The room was sparse, with two doors which led to the bedrooms, which were also empty. There was a table on which lay some discarded newspapers. She went over to them and looked. There were different papers dated from the last few days. One was folded to a page with an article on General Svetozar Borojević. Could they be planning to assassinate him? Would they be so stupid to leave such an obvious clue behind? Or was it a diversion? She had no choice but to follow this up.

Klimkov and Cornelius approached a small barn on the outskirts of town. Their walk had been uneventful, gathering a few salutes on the way. They still had their vagrant faces, but cleanly shaved, with their uniforms and caps, they now looked very different.

The Doctor entered the barn. In front of them was an armored car, with machine guns sticking out of the front over the engine and on the sides.

"My contact obtained this for me," the Doctor said. "It is a prototype called the Junovicz P.A.1 used by the Austro-Hungarian army. Money can obtain anything, especially these days."

Klimkov looked astounded. "What are we to do with it?" he asked.

"It's very simple. We drive up to General Borojević's HQ and kill him," the Doctor said, pointing to the machine guns. "Then we drive away at great speed."

"You're insane! I thought perhaps we should use a sniper's rifle."

"Are you a sniper?" Cornelius asked, coldly.

Klimkov shook his head.

"Neither am I. You're also assuming we could get a decent line of sight. This way, we're sure to get him, and the shock of his death will help us get away. I already have a route planned for escape. The criminal world can do things faster than the authorities. This is why I charge so much. Now, you say you know the General's movements. A morning walkabout at around 7 a.m.?"

"I also know the passwords the sentries use," Klimkov said.

"I somehow knew you would. Your espionage skills have impressed me greatly. Be ready to use them. As it's a Sunday, let's hope some of the soldiers are sleeping in."

The Doctor did not ask for the passwords; he knew that Klimkov would only know them when he read them in the sentries' minds.

"Let's waste no more time, then," he concluded.

They got into the armored car and started the engine.

It was at that moment that the Countess and the Lieutenant sped by in *Elizabeth*, too fast for Klimkov to pick up their thoughts or even hear them due to the armored car's noise.

Klimkov went to open the barn door to let the armored car out. By the time their vehicle had come out of the barn, *Elizabeth* was already out of sight.

"Are you sure, Countess?" asked General Borojević.

The Countess had just arrived and asked to see him. His standing orders were always to let her through.

"Not really, but that article indicted that you were at least of interest to them. According to the investigation, that house was being used by two men who recently showed up, saying they were employed locally as night watchmen. Now, they're gone, leaving behind nothing but burnt clothes and the newspapers I mentioned. They may have simply escaped, or they may plan something more sinister yet. Doctor Cornelius has used infiltration doubles of officers before."

"After our meeting, I instituted extra security measures. Passwords may be useless against a thought-reader, but anyone who wants to come near me must also be recognized by my staff."

"I think, General, that you should stay inside for a least a few hours more while we investigate further."

The General looked a little exasperated. He needed to focus on the coming offensive. "I cannot do that, Countess. However, I will ensure that there is always a guard with me today. The Captain here," he pointed to an officer next to him, "has been with me continually for the last few hours and, if he were a double, he could have easily killed me by now and made his escape. Now, I must do my rounds."

Outside, Doctor Cornelius's Junovicz P.A.1. had passed through a number of checkpoints. They knew the passwords and their reason for being here—they wished to show this new armored car prototype to the General--as plausible. They even let some soldiers look inside. They were coming to the last checkpoint.

"Damn!" exclaimed the Doctor.

"What's wrong?" asked Klimkov.

"The Countess's vehicle is parked right there." The Doctor was beginning to think that the Countess had telepathic powers, too. It could not be coincidence that she was there.

"What should we do?" asked Klimkov

"We proceed. Don't you want this assassination done? And while we're at it, we can dispose of that meddling Countess as the same time."

He drove the vehicle towards the next checkpoint. Klimkov opened the door and gave the guard the password and told him they were there to see the General and demonstrate the Junovicz for him.

"Sorry, sir, but you have to wait," said the guard. "Before you can proceed, we need to ensure that you are both known by someone here. Do you know of an officer who could vouch for you?"

The guard peered inside at Cornelius, noting his rank. *These men are not expected* he thought, which Klimkov heard.

"We have no time for this," Klimkov insisted. "Please direct us to the General. This vehicle is top-secret, and we've not been able to send specifications to senior officers. They need to see it for themselves to see its capabilities."

At that moment, the Countess exited, followed by the Lieutenant, the General and his aide. She went over to her car, clearly about to leave. Cornelius saw a chance and started to mount the machine gun. The quick-witted guard saw what was happening and shouted "Stop!" at the Doctor.

He raised his rifle, only to be rewarded by a bullet in the head by Klimkov. But his cry had had the effect it needed. Cornelius was still grappling to move the weapon into a better firing position, but was now too late. The Countess and the General had dived into *Elizabeth*, while the two officers with them had taken cover elsewhere.

Cornelius fired. His bullets hit *Elizabeth*, but only made small dents. Other troops started firing back. The Doctor was forced to return fire lest a stray bullet enter his vehicle.

He slid back into the driving seat and turned the vehicle away.

"Get behind the gun and fire at anything that moves," he told Klimkov.

There was a sudden jolt and then they were spinning. Cornelius cursed. The Countess had rammed them with her own vehicle. It gave Borojević's men a chance to attack the Junovicz.

The Doctor completed the turn of his armored car. *It was time to retreat*, he thought. A sword stuck through the front observation port, missing his neck by inches. Outside, soldiers cheered. It was Borojević himself on the vehicle who had attacked with his ceremonial sword.

The Doctor swerved the vehicle and threw the General off. Then he drove off, heading away from the camp.

"Go back! We must kill Borojević!" shouted Klimkov.

"You go back!" shouted the Doctor. "They will attack ups with grenades and all kinds of weapons now. Why, that sword almost killed me! We do not have to go far to escape, and I don't intend to let them catch us!"

Klimkov pointed his pistol at him. "Go back now," he ordered.

"Shoot me and we crash. At least, with my plan, we escape and can try again."

Klimkov looked uncertain, but kept the gun aimed.

I will kill him the first chance I get, thought the Doctor. But he had slipped. He had thought in English, and Klimkov had heard him.

"What is your escape plan?" the Russian demanded.

"We will stop at the next village. There, I have a house and a cart ready to take us to the next step in the escape route," Cornelius replied.

His thoughts, however, told a different story. He would shoot Klimkov dead immediately. He would then see if the Countess was in pursuit and try to lure her out of her vehicle, or somehow disable it, before heading off toward the city where the real escape route started. Klimkov also heard thoughts indicating that the Doctor had read, and destroyed, his coded message. He decided he would kill Cornelius as soon as they stopped. Then, he would deal with the Countess himself, and would somehow get back to Kraków and get word to Saint Petersburg about the new offensive before it was too late.

"Very well, proceed," said the Russian.

Back at the camp, pursuit was being organized. General Borojević had been thrown off the vehicle, but his landing had not been too hard; he was already back giving orders. The Countess went up to him.

"I can catch up with them. My vehicle has certain, er, properties, including that of speed."

"Properties that also include somehow your not being injured when you rammed his car?"

"A certain shock absorption design, General. Now, I must go."

She climbed into *Elizabeth*, the Lieutenant jumping in on the other side. She closed the door and sped off. General Borojević wondered where that technology came from.

The Junovicz had come to a stop.

"After you," Klimkov said to Doctor Cornelius, indicating he should get out. Then he would shoot him. Suddenly, new thoughts popped into his head.

"The Countess!" he said.

The speed of her arrival meant that her thoughts were suddenly becoming clear, so he was distracted momentarily. Cornelius leaped out of the car, ran around it to confuse Klimkov, and headed into the village.

Klimkov try to run after him, but the Doctor had already disappeared. And the Countess's car was rapidly approaching. The Russian decided he would eliminate her and the Lieutenant—a dangerous Polish aristocrat—first. Then Cornelius.

He moved towards them, preparing to shoot. He knew he would know ahead of time when they were about to fire. Indeed, the Lieutenant fired first, but Klimkov had ducked and fired back at him, hitting him. He then read the Countess' mind a moment before she brought out her own firearm. Unfortunately, it was the Doppelpistole!

In panic, Klimkov ran towards the village, hoping that the Countess would not fire that way. But he was too late. She fired, moving the gun left and right, bullets spraying forward. Klimkov avoided the first few, but other bullets hit him, right in the chest.

He died instantly, his body crashing to the ground.

The Countess looked around for the Doctor, but could not see where he had gone. Behind her, Lieutenant Vuljanić was bleeding to death. She could not abandon him for the likes of Doctor Cornelius.

She went over to him and administered aid.

"Thank you," said Cornelius to a bemused villager as he took his horse.

The villager could not speak German, and simply assumed that this officer needed the horse for war purposes.

The Doctor rode off. Things had not gone well. However, he still needed his money. Perhaps his friend in Saint Petersburg might help.

Saint Petersburg, 10 May

Spymaster A.V. Brune de St Hippolite was in attendance at a social function at the Alexander Palace. He hoped to meet with the Tsar soon, in order to ask for an increase in his budget. The mission with Klimkov had been a disaster. No word had been heard from either Klimkov or

Doctor Cornelius. The hotel had been destroyed, but with no loss of life. That must have been a bungled attempt to kill those damn Poles. Nothing had been achieved, and the Central Powers were enjoying a successful offensive. Had the two men been captured? Had the Lynx serum fallen into Austrian hands?

He saw the Tsarina with that monk, Rasputin. And next to him was a balding man with gold rimmed spectacles—Doctor Cornelius.

Rasputin beckoned him over. Cautiously, the spymaster went over. He decided to try and get his side in first.

"Your majesty, this man is…"

"A valued agent of yours," interrupted Rasputin, "who has not been treated well by you, it seems."

The Tsarina spoke. "The Doctor has told us of his attempts to find out about our enemies in Galicia. It seems that the man whom you sent with him was... I cannot speak the words…" She looked distressed.

Rasputin patted her arm. "Fear not, your majesty. I shall speak on your behalf. This man, Klimkov, we are told by Doctor Malbrough here…"

"A top agent," the spymaster interrupted, trying to control the conversation.

"A top agent?" exclaimed Rasputin, his voice rising. "He claimed to have unearthly powers, to read minds—powers that can only be obtained by consorting with satanic forces!"

The monk gesticulated wildly, with his eyes rolling upwards. Brune de St Hippolite saw that a few of the other guests looked their way, including General Boris Liatoukine, another dangerous character.

"And now," the monk said, "you refuse to pay this brave man what you promised. A payment that will barely feed him for a month!"

"I would like an explanation for all this," the Tsarina said.

The spymaster knew he was in trouble. Lying to the Tsarina could have serious consequences. What story had been concocted by the Doctor? And how did he know Rasputin?

The monk came to his rescue. "I suspect that our friend here was unaware of Klimkov's true nature, and that he sent these men on their brave mission in good faith. He was not to know that Klimkov would desert the Doctor, getting shot whilst fleeing the Austrian gendarmerie. However, we can fault him for not paying the Doctor. Russian honor can be restored by payment. Full payment," he added meaningfully. "Then, we will refer no more to this sordid affair."

Brune de St Hippolite saw his way out and took it.

"Of course, I shall see to it immediately."

"See that you do," said the Tsarina. "I wish to hear no more of this."

The spymaster sensed he was dismissed, thanked the Tsarina, and walked away. He hoped that their Vozduhoplavatel base would provide better projects soon.

Later, Rasputin and Doctor Cornelius spoke together.

"Is my debt settled, my friend?" asked Rasputin.

"It most certainly is," replied the Doctor.

He recalled how previously he had healed the face of a man Rasputin had disfigured in a brawl, an act the monk had later regretted for whatever reason. Doctor Cornelius had been contacted and repaired the injured man's face. He had asked Rasputin—who was already influential—for no payment, merely a favor to be repaid at some point. It had been a wise decision. The sculptor of human flesh now had something to celebrate.

"Let us drink more," he said to a delighted Rasputin.

Deuxième Bureau, Paris, 12 May

Simon Hart read the report from their agent, Leo Saint-Clair, a.k.a. the Nyctalope. Saint-Clair had gone to Vozduhoplavatel and located the lab where the Lynx serum was. He had scared Professor Ossipoff into revealing the secrets of how they had unlocked its power—the simple knowledge of this Meyral effect upon certain individuals with latent psychic powers.

Had their own department not halted their research into the Lynx, they may have noticed the correlation with the Meyral themselves, Hart thought.

The Nyctalope had then destroyed the Russian's serum supplies and the entire lab, although he had not killed the professor which would have been against his code of honor. He had even brought back some of the Russian produced Lynx serum. Only a man with such powers could have ventured out into Russia and back.

As for the other part of the plan, that had gone very well too. Their spies in the Okhrana had told them of the plans for the Lynx. They had no assets in Galicia, and so information was fed to the *Evidenzbureau* via certain channels. It included the idea the telepath was a drug addict, to mislead anyone who might have seen him injecting the serum. The *Evidenzbureau* was led to believe that it had found out these secrets from Russia, rather than being fed them by the French.

It had been decided that this was a separate matter to the war. Russia had committed an act of aggression against France with its theft of the Lynx. No other power could have the serum, although it did appear that the fading of the Meyral effect made it useless in any event.

Best of all, was the act that he had planned these operations. His hiring of the traitor Maréchal had been forgotten. It was now time to leave the office and relax.

Jacquemain saw Hart leave the building and cross the road to meet an attractive woman—one who was certainly not his wife, but the sister of one of the other officers.

Hart is a good Frenchman, he thought approvingly.

Austro-Hungarian army mobile field hospital, Galicia (Poland), Austro-Hungarian Empire, 14 May

The Countess was back in her nursing uniform, albeit off-duty, sitting next to the hospital bed of the sleeping Lieutenant Vuljanić. He had been shot in the stomach and, despite an infection, would recover.

Sergeant Mayr had already been there to report on their hunt for Doctor Cornelius. It seems that the former lord of the Red Hand had commandeered a horse and disappeared. She doubted that this would be the last she would hear of him.

The Gorlice-Tarnów offensive of 2 May had been immensely successful, liberating much of occupied Galicia and Russian Poland. It was good news for the Polish people, who, like so many others, had suffered during the war, either as refugees fleeing from the Russians, or under Russian occupation. It looked like Poland may become unified as she had dreamed, but a cost no one had anticipated.

Her thoughts turned to the telepath. It was doubtful there were others like him. The Russians would have had advance warning of the offensive if there were.

But for now, her patients needed her.

Martin Gately, like Brian Gallagher, has also embarked on a new saga, this one featuring Jules Verne's Robur—more precisely, Young Robur, since this is about the early days of the future would-be Conqueror and Master of the World. As a side note, the Amazons of Dahomey featured in this tale really did exist and were the inspiration for the Dora Milaje of Marvel's Black Panther...

Martin Gately: *Young Robur Over Africa*

Western Africa, 1916

Everything hurt. His mouth was full of blood and dirt. The interminable, out of control spinning had stopped. And, somehow, a pitiless noon-day sun was beating down. He was sure he hadn't been knocked unconscious, yet he had lost all sense of time. The red dirt-dust beneath his fingers wasn't the right shade for Arizona or Nevada. He was somewhere else. He rolled over to get his bearings and spat to clear his mouth. The function of memory reasserted itself as he saw the wreck of Robur's aero-vehicle—*The Storm Petrel*—not ten yards away. The fuselage was split open like a rusted tin can on a garbage pile. One wing had been ripped off completely and was not in evidence; only a jagged stump remained. The other vibrated half-heartedly, no longer capable of the hummingbird-like action which had kept the ship aloft. Somewhere in there was Robur, either alive or a corpse. Frycollin stood up painfully and limped towards the crashed machine.

Thankfully, the boy was still breathing. Robur's hands still gripped the controls tightly, his knuckles bone-white. His eyes were open, yet unseeing and glassy. And a goose egg-sized lump was busily forming high on the left-hand side of his forehead. It was most likely just a mild concussion.

Frycollin unlatched the boy from the buckles and straps of the pilot's harness and carried him bodily out onto the long, desiccated grass of the endless plain upon which the aero-vehicle now rested.

He smelled the beasts before he saw them. The pungent aroma was evocative of a visit to the Philadelphia Zoo. Lions. An entire pride of lions was starting to circle the *Storm Petrel* wreck, some creeping low in the grass, while others, more daring, did not bother to conceal themselves from their prey.

Frycollin reached reflexively for his Colt Navy pistol. It was not there in his holster, and he couldn't remember if he'd abandoned it while climbing into the aero-vehicle or if it was still somewhere within the hull. How the devil had they flown so far? That was a question for later. If they survived.

Frycollin carried Robur back into the shelter of the fuselage, laid him down on the deck and commenced to search for the pistol or anything which might be used as a weapon. The hunt for the revolver proved futile. It had either fallen from the *Storm Petrel* while it was in flight, or it lay on the rock floor of the Anu Sinom hive, back in Arizona.

Looking in the small lockers next to the pilot's seat was more productive. Here Frycollin found the electric crossbow of Robur's own invention. He connected the battery cylinder's charging wire to one of the arrow-like bolts and loaded the weapon, then put the battery cylinder over his shoulder by means of its leather strap, like a hiker's backpack. He flipped the activation toggle on the crossbow's pistol grip and the weapon came to life with a low hum.

A large male lion nosed its way curiously into the interior of the ruined metal shell, sniffing as it came. The beast saw Frycollin and prepared to charge at him, a roar already building in its throat. Frycollin aimed and then shot the bolt in the same split second. The bolt struck the lion's upper lip and the roar turned into a piteous whimper. The enormous feline jerked spasmodically and then lay still.

Frycollin turned off the current and then tugged the bolt out of the creature's flesh, slightly nervously since he had no real idea how long it would take to recover. Yes, it was still breathing, and its rasping purrs had taken on the quality of snores. God bless Robur's ingenuity! The thing was out cold. And seeing this, its family members had slunk away to a safe distance. Not wishing to be caught inside the wreck with the lion when it came around, Frycollin evacuated himself and Robur back onto the grassland.

Robur was now starting to regain consciousness. He cradled his sore head and moaned as his senses returned. Frycollin became aware of an unaccountable droning sound from somewhere above in the heavens. It was partially mechanical sounding, almost like a distant locomotive, and partially musical. But he did not dare take his eyes off the pride of lions in order to ascertain what it was. But Robur was under no such restriction. The young man shielded his eyes from the glare of the noonday sun with the flat of his hand and looked straight up. The sight was so wondrous that the throbbing of his head immediately abated.

"It is undoubtedly the most beautiful thing I have ever seen," said the boy.

A long shadow was cast over them. The lions turned tail and fled—for now, at least. Frycollin put his head all the way back to better drink in this astonishing sight. It was an airship of colossal proportions, perhaps over one hundred and fifty feet-long. Shaped like a cigar with two rounded ends, it was a dull pale gold in hue, except on its fins which were painted in the style of the red, white and blue Union Jack of Great Britain. Integral to the design was an armored gondola, and protruding from its decks were the long barrels of heavy armaments.

"That vessel is a ship o'war for the air," said Frycollin.

"It's also quite impossible. The craft is immensely superior to the airships of the Aerial Navigation Company in New York. It is astonishingly futuristic. What genius could have designed it?" queried Robur.

Now that the lions had learned the British airship meant them no particular harm, it was merely a slightly noisy and narrow cloud which partially blocked the sun. So again, they crept nearer, hunger being a powerful negator of fear.

Robur noticed that the airship was dropping slightly lower. He wondered at the nature of the mechanism which produce this altered buoyancy effect. He swore he would gain knowledge of it, and he grieved somewhat that his mentor, Professor Oxalis, had not lived to see this astonishing iteration of aerodynamic principles. It was similar in some ways to aero-vehicles they had planned to build together, though they had always favored the aeronef model over the airship.

The lions were getting too close. Frycollin activated the current in the electric crossbow, standing ready to defend them. Then, without warning, heavy lines dropped from beneath the gondola and crew members began to descend down them in harnesses. The crewmen were armed with pistols or carbines, and they took pot shots at the advancing lions. Two were hit and killed; the others fled at their maximum velocity, disappearing into the taller swaths of verdure.

One of the British airmen touched the ground not more than five or six yards from where Robur and Frycollin stood. The man untethered himself and, as he approached, Robur saw he was wearing the greyish blue uniform of something called *The Royal Naval Air Service*. The airman was about twenty-five, broad in the shoulders and short in the legs, a man of iron, with one of those enormous heads characteristic of a Hogarth illustration.

"Good day, sir," said the airman, addressing himself exclusively to Robur. "I am Chief Petty Officer Tom Turner of *HMS Venger*. We saw your aeroplane go down and headed over to rescue you. We have accommodation for both you and your servant aboard, and your aircraft can be winched up into our bomb bay for storage until repairs can be made."

Frycollin was only mildly vexed by being mistaken for Robur's servant. It was perhaps understandable in the circumstances. But he also had to stifle a guffaw at the prospect of the *Storm Petrel* being repaired. Though if anyone could do it, it was these men.

"Thank you, Mr. Turner," replied Robur. "I seem to have suffered a slight head injury, and I'm feeling rather faint."

"Don't worry, sir," replied Turner. "We have a medical officer aboard and you'll be able to recuperate in our sick bay. It is as well appointed as the best military field hospital."

"That is good to hear," said Robur.

"Ah, I can tell by your accent that you are American. Was your craft a reconnaissance vehicle? Do you think the United States will soon enter the war?" asked Turner.

Before Robur could begin to mentally assemble an answer, Frycollin cried out in loud surprise. With a throaty growl the previously stunned lion had stalked out from inside the fuselage. Frycollin fumbled with the electric crossbow while Robur remained rooted to the spot, too weakened to even attempt to make a run for it.

Coolly, Turner drew his heavy Webley service revolver and emptied it into the advancing predator. It faltered, then keeled over, blood pouring from the half dozen yawning mortal wounds in its chest.

Not long after, Robur and Frycollin were in harnesses and being winched aboard the British airship called *HMS Venger*. Robur wondered at how this extraordinary piece of technology had been kept secret. For years, Oxalis and him had smuggled news cuttings about the development of balloons and dirigibles into the Woodlanders' Haven, but British airships such as this had never rated a mention in the American press.

Their point of arrival aboard *HMS Venger* was a metal gantry within the spacious bomb bay compartment. A party of men unhitched them from their harnesses and ushered them along a walkway to the exit at the far end of the bomb bay. There were many wooden racks of aerial bombs, the largest of these perhaps 200 lbs.

Robur was familiar with the concept of aerial bombs being dropped from balloons. It had been something pioneered by the Italians some years ago, but he had never heard of them being constructed in such size or volume. Suspended by chains directly above the twin bay doors was a devilishly large aerial bomb. He hesitated to guess its weight, and because it was of such different construction and configuration to the others, he wondered if it was an incendiary. If so, the resulting fire could probably burn down most of a city.

Frycollin was allocated a hammock at the far end of the enlisted men's sleeping quarters, and told to rest while his "master" received medical attention. Assisted into one of the double bunk beds in the sick bay, Robur was astonished to see the adjoining room was an operating theater. And rather more astonished to be examined by a woman physician, who identified herself as Dr. Louisa Garrett Anderson. She was a formidable woman in her middle years who deftly, albeit slightly roughly, bandaged the boy's head. She then prescribed complete rest along with 24 hours of observation.

Robur was sitting in his bunk propped up on pillows and drinking hot, sweet tea when the prescription for rest was interrupted by the arrival of the commanding officer of *HMS Venger,* Captain Albert Ball. It was truly a day for surprise and astonishment. Captain Ball was scarcely any older than Robur. Smooth-featured, almost angelic of face, with glossy, jet-black hair, there was a quiet charisma which wrapped around him like a cloak. Within his pale grey eyes could be seen both pain and determination. This was a man exuding both moral and physical courage—in spades.

After formally introducing himself, Captain Ball said, "Actually, I am relieved you aren't German. I much prefer the prospect of a dinner guest to one of the Hun cluttering up my brig. I've just been examining that extraordinary aircraft of yours... Oh, don't worry, it is securely stowed in our bomb bay now. A high altitude, rocket-powered ornithopter! I had no idea the Americans were working on such a thing. I wonder what else you have up your sleeves?"

Robur decided to be extremely circumspect, if not evasive, from this point on. It was one thing for the development of a new British airship to have escaped the attention of the American Fourth Estate, but he most certainly would have heard about a war between Great Britain and Germany. It occurred to him that the head injury gave him the opportunity to feign amnesia.

"Captain Ball, I am in something of a predicament since the head injury I've suffered seems to have robbed me of my knowledge of recent events. I recall that I am an American inventor with no connection to the government of my country, but other than that, my recollections are hazy in the extreme. Perhaps you could bring me up to date?" asked Robur.

"Of course," began Captain Ball, "do interrupt if any of this sounds familiar. Great Britain and Germany have been at war since 1914, following the assassination of Archduke Ferdinand in Sarajevo. It has become a global air war with virtually every country with an aerial navy taking sides, all except the United States and China, who have both insisted on remaining neutral. Many strategic battles are fought here in the skies over Africa, particularly here in Benin territory where rich seams of the miracle metal duralinium can be found. It is duralinium which allows the construction of massive airships. Now, I would not normally reveal our objective to a civilian, but since you are aboard, you will find out soon enough. Our mission is to drop one of the new radium bombs on the duralinium processing plant in the German held city of Ketou."

Robur's brain reeled at all this shocking new information. First of all, it was obvious the strange green energy doorway above the Arizona Territory had displaced them in time as well as space when the *Storm Petrel* had passed through it. Furthermore, he was pushed into deep despair and depression at the dismal realization that the advent of powered flight had not ushered in a utopian age, as he had hoped, but rather an era of war across the entire world.

"What is the current year?" asked Robur.

"Why, it is the summer of 1916," answered the captain. "We are most earnestly hoping that America will shed its neutrality and enter the war to aid Britain. What do you think are the chances?" asked Ball, somewhat ignoring the stumbling block of Robur's purported amnesia.

"Tell me more about this radium bomb," said Robur, with a slight edge of insistence to his voice.

After he had been resting for a little while, Frycollin was visited by the airship quartermaster, who issued him with a change of clothes which comprised a *Royal Naval Air Service* uniform bereft of all rank insignia and emblems. Serviceable, neat and comfortable, he felt immediately at home in it. The quartermaster had given him directions to the mess, as well as the sick bay, so he could visit his master later, and Frycollin was surprised to learn that only the command bridge was off limits to him. So, after partaking of the rather bland mutton stew that was on offer in the mess that day, he headed to the gunnery deck.

The long-barreled repeating cannons had an almost graceful look to them. There were three cannons on each side of the gunnery deck; each one had its muzzle poking through an open port. The warm African wind howled through the deck. It looked as if it was permanently open to the elements. In the central aisle between the weapons were cradles filled with dozens upon dozens of slim brass artillery shells. At present, a maintenance crew were lubricating one gun, and the only other people around were a sergeant and a single gunner.

Frycollin's overriding thought was to wonder what a ship like this could have done against the Confederate forces during the War Between the States—if only it had been around! Might have the war been one in just a week, or perhaps a single day?

He passed along and was given a friendly nod by the gunnery sergeant as he started his quest for the sickbay. Following the directions to the best of his recollection, he headed up metal ladders and along gangways, and was then able to home in on the antiseptic iodine aroma military hospitals the world over seemed to have in common.

Frycollin didn't want to interrupt Robur's recuperative rest, so he sat down on the metal and canvas chair by his bedside and waited for him to wake up. This merely resulted in a word of admonition from the boy when, some half an hour later, he finally started to stir.

"You should've woken me earlier. We have much to discuss."

"Didn't like to. Besides, you need your beauty sleep."

"This is no time for joking. What year is this?"

"1866," said Frycollin, automatically.

"And there you'd be wrong. Somehow, our journey through the green curtain of energy has propelled us fifty years into the future. It is 1916."

"Robur, whoever told you that must surely be pranking you. It's against all common-sense and reason."

"There you are wrong again. This futuristic airship is incontrovertible evidence that we have left our own time behind. Its crew have no reason to lie to us."

"So, what else have they told you?"

"We are caught up in a global aerial war. The skies over Africa are a chessboard upon which battles are played out. Only the United States and China remain neutral. All other countries have thrown in their lot with one side or the other. But there is the possibility that America will enter the war soon on the side of the British and French."

Frycollin's mind reeled at all this information. A global war meant that there was no country in which they might find refuge away from the conflict. Also, such a war might continue for years, as long as there was the will and materiel with which to fight it.

"How…how do we get home?" asked Frycollin, falteringly.

"We have a more pressing problem than our own self-interest," said Robur in hushed tones. "I have always despised war. I have always feared the advent of war. I have always thought—naively, it would seem—that with greater technology would come wisdom. And that Mankind would outgrow war, just as a malicious child might one day outgrow pulling the wings from flies. But I was wrong—the mission of this airship is to rain down doom by means of a poisonous bomb onto an entire city of men, women and children. The whole population will suffer a lingering death."

"Good God! Why?" asked Frycollin.

"Merely because the city is the location of a processing factory for the metal duralinium, which is essential for the manufacture of these colossal airships. The city is occupied by the Germans, so everyone there must die. Our moral duty is clear. We must prevent such an enormous loss of life at any cost."

"And that cost will be our lives! Are you crazy, Robur? If we take any action against this crew, they'll think we're German agents, not neutral Americans, and toss us out of the bomb bay. If we're lucky, they'll shoot us first."

"Nevertheless, we must find a way to commandeer this vessel. Once we've done that, we'll need to get the crew off. Only then can we pilot this ship through the green curtain back to our own time."

"The brains must have spilled out of that great noggin of yours during the crash. Has it occurred to you that we are just two people? One deputy sheriff and an injured boy? We can't overpower an entire airship crew. And even if we could, do you really think you could control this thing on your own? It's not *The Storm Petrel*—it's huge. And here's the clincher. I've been looking out of the gunnery ports and portholes and I can't even see your green aurora curtain. Back in Arizona, you could see it even during the day time. If it's not there, we don't have a way home. We'll just have to make the best of being here."

"We need to get to the command bridge," judged Robur. "There is nothing to gain from idling here."

"It's off limits to me, but I'm sure they'll admit a fellow aero-vehicle pilot. Get your boots on, if you are feeling up to it."

Dr. Garett Anderson was busying herself in the dispensary storage cupboard and did not see them go.

If the after-effects of the concussion were still bothering Robur, he did not show it. He led the way as if he knew the layout of the *HMS Venger* well and ascended the ladders until they were confronted by the guarded entryway into the bridge.

"Please tell Captain Ball that Captain Robur wishes to see him," opened the boy, conversationally, with the British airman barring his path. Frycollin shot Robur a quizzical look in reference to his dubious claim to be any kind of captain. If the two Americans had expected resistance to the request, they were mistaken. Captain Ball came out as if eager to speak to them, he was polite, but extremely somber.

"Mr. Robur, I am glad you are here. I had meant to come down to the sickbay immediately to relate some news we received just moments ago via the wireless telegraph. I am sorry to have to tell you that President Walter Trump died last night."

Captain Ball paused to allow the import of this sad news to sink in. Of course, the name meant nothing to Robur and Frycollin, but they did not feign sadness, so much as show the necessary respect due upon the passing of any stranger.

"Was he assassinated?" asked Frycollin with a slightly bowed head. There was still a raw and bleeding wound in his soul caused by the assassination of Abraham Lincoln. Ball showed just a little surprise to be questioned by a servant, but responded nevertheless.

"No, not assassinated. His constitution was never strong due to the near fatal injury he received in Texas decades ago," said Ball. "The ramifications are already enormous. Vice-President Phil Evans has immediately taken his oath of office, and lost no time expressing his hawkish sentiments. It seems a foregone conclusion the United States will soon enter the war on the side of Great Britain and France."

"Sad news indeed, and yet for Great Britain and her allies, a time of hope," said Robur as noncommittally as he could. He wondered what sort of man President Evans could be, as well as how he had risen so high in public life without the repulsion at foreign military adventures shared by most Americans. "Since we are here, perhaps you could show us the command bridge. I have long been fascinated by the control systems of airships."

"By all means," agreed Ball. "Such a distraction can only serve to lighten your mood in the face of the tragic death of President Trump."

Captain Ball ushered them inside and Robur had to restrain his reaction—the proverbial starving waif in a candy store could not have faced greater temptation. The great brass-trimmed control wheel, the copper and ivory-tipped engine throttle levers, the speaker tubes through which orders could be barked to the engine deck, the cherrywood navigation chart table—it was all so perfect. How often had he imagined himself helmsman of such a vessel? And in those imaginings, he had always had to design and build the whole thing from scratch. He had no choice but to admit that this reality had exceeded his imagination. Though never once had he suspected such heavily armed dirigibles would be created. For he had always imagined hydrogen rather than helium would be used in their gas envelopes, thus rendering them useless for purposes of war, though with caution and care, they still might have had enormous potential for trade and exploration.

"You can see here on the chart our current location," advised Ball.

Robur edged closer. It looked as if they were now on the final run to drop the radium bomb on Ketou. They had passed beyond the boundaries of the Oyo Territory and, beyond was the impenetrable wilderness of Benin, and a place Robur had never previously seen marked on a map—Dahomey.

"Increase altitude to ten thousand feet," ordered Ball.

"Is the target in sight?" asked Robur.

In answer, Ball moved past the steersman to a pair of great lenses which could be pulled down from the ceiling on adjustable brackets; they acted like a powerful telescope through which several people could peer at the same time. Robur was astonished to see he could make out the detail of the city in the distance. There were people, carts pulled by horses, and some kind of self-propelled carriages. On the far side of the city, were clustered the slim chimneys of the duralinium ore processing factory, wispy bluish smoke emanated from these and undulated towards the horizon. At ground level, the factory was befogged by clouds of brown dust. It looked like it must be a hellish place to work. But, not as hellish as it would be once the radium bomb was dropped.

A desperate idea formed in Robur's mind—a poor and fanciful idea, which in other circumstances he would have rejected out of hand without a scintilla of consideration. Such a ship as this ran on discipline, and the obeying of orders without question. Could Robur grab a speaking tube and order the premature use of the radium bomb? What would be the correct words? Could he convincingly imitate Captain Ball's English accent? He'd been told once at the Woodlanders Haven he was an excellent mimic. And also, that he had picked up a smattering of Oxalis' British intonation, having spent so much time with him. But Robur's dislike of violence extended to a dislike of tawdry physical confrontation. How could he strike insensible a man who had treated him with such decency? No, the whole thing was fated to fail. He'd need Frycollin's skill in unarmed combat to stand a chance. He tried to guess what Frycollin's reaction would be if he suddenly punched Ball in the jaw. More likely, he'd think he'd gone crazy than wade in to back him up.

"What the hell is that?" demanded Frycollin, pointing up to the limits of what could be seen at the top of the bridge's windows.

The eyes of Ball, Robur and the steersman all followed. It was another airship, swooping down on them from out of the clouds which hung above Ketou. It was difficult to judge the scale of it at this distance, but it looked a little smaller than the *Venger*. It was black with red trim and fins; a dozen or so engines were attached to its hull, and an army of propellers whirred as the beast of a machine powered down towards them. The airship's nose was emblazoned with a gold and black design. It was still too far away, but Robur guessed it could only be the double-headed eagle—the national insignia of Germany.

"It's the *Devil Bat*," said Captain Ball, with an almost detached resignation. "Lothar Von Richthofen's ship. He's pursued me here from the skies above France—anxious to obtain vengeance for the humiliations I have dealt him."

Robur suddenly had a sense of merely being a supporting player in the mythic duel between Captain Ball and his nemesis. He had wrongly thought the bombing run against Ketou would be unhindered by defensive action from the Germans. Now the true nature of this global war was being demonstrated to him. The two sides were evenly matched. There were courageous men of tenacity and skill on both sides—perhaps even good men on both sides. But did that even matter? The enemy of both sides was the war itself. Of course, the participants would be blind to this—blinded by duty and the prospect of glory.

"Civilians leave the bridge, we're going into combat!" shouted Ball.

Robur and Frycollin immediately moved to comply. They strode swiftly out and slid the steel door shut behind them. As it shut, they heard Ball cry out: "Evasive turn to starboard!" and they then felt the deck reel beneath them. Momentarily, they staggered like drunken men before regaining their footing and clawing for the ladder which led to the decks below.

"You're the inventive genius. What are we supposed to do now?" asked Frycollin. "I dearly wish we could find a way off this thing"

"Dropping the radium bomb prematurely might still end this conflict," said Robur. "We should get to the bomb bay."

From far below on the gun deck there was a muffled fusillade of shots from the repeating cannons. Then answering blasts from the *Devil Bat,* followed by an appalling cacophony of explosions, screeching metal and screaming men. They were high pitched and piteous death-screams which might almost have been the crying out of tortured children.

"That came from above us on the command bridge level," said Frycollin. "We may be able to help get the injured to sickbay."

Robur had anticipated they would have to pry open a damaged door to the bridge, but the door was gone. It would have been an exaggeration to say that the corpse of the airman was still guarding the door. It was really just shreds of flesh and uniform accompanied by splintered segments of gleaming bone.

Robur bottled up his terror and cast it into the most remote section of his soul. Crippling fear was no use to him here. He pressed on and felt the pressure of the screeching banshee wind which clawed through the wrecked carcass of the command bridge. It was as if two huge invisible hands were pushing him back. He fought against the wind, as did Frycollin by his side. All of the windows had exploded out, and the forward section of the bulkhead appeared to have taken a direct hit. There must have been a fire, initially, but the strength of the air gusts had extinguished it. The rudder wheel was missing. Only the plinth upon which it should've been fixed remained. There was no sign of the steersman. He was, by now, in the hands of his creator.

Frycollin tapped Robur hard on the shoulder to get his attention and pointed to the rear starboard section of the deck. It was Captain Ball. Curled in a semi-fetal position, his lacerated face was a mask of blood. Both his hands had been blown off. And yet, he was still alive. Robur knelt down next to him and saw the brave young man was mortally wounded. Frycollin was about to remove his belt to use as a tourniquet when he arrived at the same conclusion. Even had the injured man been on the operating table of a fully equipped hospital at this very second, he doubted anything could have been done to save him. Then Ball started to speak and Robur put his ear to the man's lips in order to stand some chance of catching the words.

"Tell my parents I love them," said Ball.

And then he did die.

It was at this moment Robur swore a solemn oath to God to prevent wars any way he could. Perhaps even prevent this war, if it was humanly possible to do so.

Robur made his way to the controls to assess the damage. There was no way to steer left or right, but the aileron pedals were still in place. He pushed the dual throttles to maximum revolutions, and slammed down his foot on the ascent pedal, setting them into a steep climb.

Meanwhile, the *Devil Bat* was executing a graceful turn, coming around for another pass, but somewhere far below on the *Venger's* gun deck, someone was still alive—a single repeating cannon was taking pot shots at the adversary.

"Do you know what you are doing?" bellowed Frycollin, directly into Robur's ear.

"I'm using basic aeronautical principles to get us out of the cannon sights of the German airship. If I can keep us above them, we can avoid further damage," shouted Robur.

Chief Petty Officer Tom Turner passed through the shattered portal into the command bridge. He had prepared himself for the strong likelihood his captain and the bridge crew were dead, but he was astonished to find their recently rescued guest now in control of the vessel and taking evasive action to keep her out of harm's way.

As *The Venger* entered a cloud layer, Robur eased off on the throttles and removed his foot from the ascent pedal. The craft leveled off, and Robur assumed, quite correctly, that *The Devil Bat* crew would lose sight of them.

"The steering cables have been sheared away," declared Turner. "With no way to control her, this ship is doomed; it's just a flying wreck."

"But the throttles are still working," said Robur, close to the man's ear. "We can use engine power to steer. I was just about to experiment with it."

Robur then demonstrated his idea. Pulling back on the starboard throttle while maintaining power to the port engines, he took the airship into a right-handed turn. It was all very sluggish compared to normal rudder steering, but Turner was impressed with the young American improvising it so quickly. They weren't just a rudderless hulk after all. There was fight in the old girl yet.

"As the most senior surviving crewman, I must take control of the airship," insisted Turner. "Go down to the bomb bay and see if you can drop some ordnance on the *Devil Bat,* if it comes into view."

Robur nodded his assent, but had no intention of complying. He would not take life unless it was completely unavoidable. There had to be another way to drive off the German airship. He gestured to Frycollin to follow him and they descended down the ship's ladders to the lowest level of *The Venger.*

While some crewmen were still going about their duties, there were a few that were either catatonic with shock or immobilized by their injuries. Robur had to curb his natural instinct to bring assistance to anyone in trouble or pain and press on until they got to the bomb bay.

When the pair arrived, Robur saw a bombardier in overalls, goggles and leather flying helmet hunched over his optical aiming sight, his ear not far from the speaking tube through which his orders would be given. He could not know this linkage between himself and his commanding officers had been severed. His orders would never come, at least, not by that means. Of course, the huge bay doors were wide open and a slim 100 lb bomb was poised on its drop cradle. But also suspended over the open doors, hanging by thick chains from a gantry, was the wrecked *Storm Petrel.*

Robur experienced a pang of loss and regret at the sight of it, yet also some inspiration. The destroyed aero-vehicle might be the answer to all their problems. Robur swiftly trotted to the ladder that would give him access to the gantry and, thereby, the *Storm Petrel,* which swayed vertiginously above the abyss. Frycollin caught up with him and restrained him with a firm grip.

"Where the hell do you think you are going?" he demanded. "You've just had a concussion. You could blackout while climbing up there and fall to your death. If you need something out of our ship, I can get it for you."

"At the right moment, I want to turn on the wing motors. I'm sure they are still working," said Robur.

Robur snuck a look downwards at the thinning cloud below them. He could see *The Devil Bat* just a few hundred feet below them, still executing turns, still looking to find and finish off its adversary.

"You set those wings to flapping and the *Storm Petrel* will tear itself loose from those chains and drop down onto whatever is below us."

"Precisely," agreed Robur, already imagining the damaged wing blade striking the duralinium skin of *The Devil Bat* like a giant stiletto; rupturing and gashing as it went, causing the airship to swiftly lose buoyancy and crash-land.

Seeing the point, Frycollin ascended the ladder and inched his way along the gantry. He was no balloonist, and wrestled with a crushing feeling of vertigo which manifested itself as the impression a nest of rats was trying to gnaw their way out of his stomach. He would rather have taken on any number of men in a fistfight or gunplay, and it was disconcerting to discover he had such a weakness. But how could he know? He was generally not much further off the ground than the height of a horse.

Gritting his teeth, he swung into the open cockpit door. He recalled the two coral-colored throttle toggles which controlled the beating of the wings, but he could also hear Robur calling out a description of their location. He pushed them forward to the maximum, and then got out of there as if the devil was on his tail.

The Devil Bat was still below them, but it was in the lap of the gods as to whether this improvised secret weapon would plummet harmlessly past her, or deal her a fatal blow.

The bombardier looked on incredulously as the *Storm Petrel* started to shudder and jerk, before slipping its bonds like some automated aerial escapologist, fragments and lengths of shattered chain falling with it.

Robur stood as near as he dared to the abyss, the bomb bay having no guardrail, and watched the tumbling progression of his crippled aerovehicle with one damaged wing and one wing stump.

The Devil Bat's steersman was like some unknown ally or accomplice, perfectly lining up the enemy airship beneath them. The impact was even more perfect than Robur could have hoped for, albeit his heart jumped in anticipation of a near miss. The port wing with its beveled end stuck into the top edge of the airship's gasbag like a knife thrown in a bar fight. The *Storm Petrel's* fuselage then acted as a counterweight and dragged the vibrating wing blade down the side of the envelope all the way to the craft's belly, slicing open multiple helium gas cells en route.

Almost immediately, the airship lost trim and altitude. Its engines took to maximum revs in a futile effort to compensate. It resembled nothing so much as some great shark which had lost its hunger and decided to slink back into the deep.

"They'll be wondering what hit them," said Robur with some satisfaction.

"I hope you don't end up regretting showing mercy to our enemies. That bomb could have achieved the same ends," said Frycollin.

"The Germans are not my enemy. My only enemy is the war itself. Now let's get back up to Turner."

By the time they got back to the bridge, word of their temporary victory against *The Devil Bat* had reached Tom Turner. Incredibly, a damage control party were already re-glazing the shattered windows, and the corpses, such as they were, had been removed to the tiny morgue located next to the sickbay. Two mechanics were also seeking to reconnect the rudder cables to a jury-rigged steering lever.

"That was a clever stratagem to drop wreckage on the German ship," observed Turner. "It saved us a bomb for another occasion."

"What's our heading now?" asked Robur, conscious the charts and navigational equipment all appeared to have been destroyed in the initial attack.

Turner consulted a pocket compass.

"South by Southwest, I'm relying on my best recollection and some guesswork, but I should be able to get us to Ouidah," said Turner.

"What's in Ouidah?" asked Frycollin.

"An airfield where we can refuel and make proper repairs. The Dahomeans are nominally allied to the French, though they distrust them, and not without good reason," replied Turner.

"Once you are fully repaired will you seek to bomb Ketou again?" queried Robur.

"More likely, I will signal for replacement crew. All of our senior officers are dead or seriously wounded, save our medical officers. I think we will be holed up in Dahomey for some time."

Robur suppressed a smile. Frustrating the progress of a war was a rewarding activity. The crew of the German airship and the citizens of Ketou would never know to whom they owed their lives. But what did that matter? With the crisis over for now, Robur realized how brutally fatigued he was, and his severe headache had suddenly returned. Frycollin noticed at once how deathly pale the boy looked.

"You're still unwell. Let's get you back to sickbay for some rest."

Robur simply nodded.

Seraphina got up, walked across her bedchamber and flung open the door which led onto the balcony. The morning light was almost blinding. The golden sunbeams bathed her black skin, and for a moment it seemed to Frycollin she was transfigured by the light. No longer merely human. Impossibly beautiful. A goddess.

The girl looked back at the bed, and Frycollin, just as he stubbed out his cigarette.

"You are always looking at me... watching me... like some kinda spy," said Seraphina, laughing.

"And why shouldn't I drink you in? You are the most beautiful girl...the most beautiful woman I have ever laid eyes on."

She laughed again, but there was nothing mocking in it. She was just as in love with him as he was with her. It seemed they had been in love since their first encounter at the King of Dahomey's court some three weeks ago. There'd been about two minutes of flirting, then they both realized just how deep the attraction was, how enduring it was likely to be, and how there was nothing either of them could do about it. Forty minutes later they were in bed.

While Frycollin had the girl again and again, Robur and Turner worried about whether their associate had been abducted by enemies so sudden was his departure. And King Andandozan II wondered why the captain of his Amazon bodyguards had deserted her post. Seraphina's young maids wondered at the reason for the loud gasps and cries which arose uncharacteristically from her bedchamber. Turns were taken to press eyes and ears to the keyhole, and only then did it become apparent their mistress was not crying out for help. They continued to peep for some time, wanting to be assured of their employer's safety, or such was the excuse they would have given had they been caught. They suppressed giggles, and they wondered even more at the sudden change in character of their mistress who was normally so serious, severe and prim.

There was a knock at Seraphina's door, the strident, rhythmic knock which was only used by the King's corps of Royal Messengers, all of whom were female. Without bothering to grab her robe, Seraphina answered the door, only to find Robur push brusquely past her.

"How dare you invade my bedchamber?"

"Be quiet, Seraphina. I have no time for your Amazon nonsense to-day. There are important matters at hand," replied Robur.

Seraphina's first instinct was to throw the youth from her balcony, but seeing the intense expression of worry and concern upon his face she decided to ignore his rudeness. For his part, Robur momentarily observed that he had to be becoming accustomed to the unclothed female form. Having been brought up in a strict religious community, he had not seen a naked woman until three weeks ago when they had arrived in Daho-mey, and had been invited to the Amazon equivalent of the ancient Olympic games. Naturally the athletes all competed nude, as had the male athletes of long-ago Greece. His instinct to blush and be tongue-tied had obviously abated.

"Get up and put your pants on, Frycollin," ordered Robur. "There have been two crucial developments since late yesterday."

"Well then, why don't you tell me what they are?"

Frycollin knew this had to be something big, but for all the theatri-cal seriousness Robur looked like he was taking partial pleasure in im-parting awful news.

"The king received a communiqué last night from the American government via wireless telegraph. By executive order, President Evans has re-instituted the practice of slavery. All black people are now the property of the state, but will be auctioned into private ownership in the coming months and years," said Robur, gravely.

"That's just insane. It has to be some kind of hoax," said Frycollin.

"Not at all. The message came through official diplomatic channels. King Andandozan seemed jubilant when he spoke to me," said Robur.

"Jubilant? Why the hell should he be jubilant? This is dreadful news," said Frycollin.

"Tell him, Seraphina," instructed Robur.

"It will mean a time of great prosperity for Dahomey—a return to our old ways."

Frycollin looked shocked as realization broke over him like a wave of ice water.

"Hadn't you guessed?" asked Robur. "This country was founded on the slave trade. Founded on capturing and selling their black neighbors into slavery. While you have been engaging in more fleshly pleasures, I have been busy researching our hosts. Did you know that they still prac-tice mass human sacrifice for religious reasons? This place is rotten to the core, and the sooner we are out of it, the better. Which brings me to my second point…"

Robur gestured to the now fully-dressed Frycollin to follow him onto the balcony. The youth pointed high up into the bright morning sky. It was faint, but unmistakable.

"The green curtain," said Frycollin. His voice full of relief and hope.

"Yes, the doorway which may lead us home. It reappeared last night. But it is drifting away at speed. We must act quickly or risk being stranded here."

Frycollin looked back at Seraphina, glancing instinctively at the woman's belly, suddenly certain that new life, his child, their child, now grew within.

"I want her to come with us," said Frycollin.

"Then I suppose she must," said Robur, resignedly.

Frycollin drove the commandeered horse and buggy like a madman onto the airfield in the direction of the skeletal metal docking tower to which the *HMS Venger* was moored by its nose anchor.

More than once Robur feared the buggy would overturn and ended up clinging to Seraphina, who was now dressed in her military uniform of blue shirt, red scarf and white-and-blue striped trousers. She was also armed with a loaded blunderbuss—her weapon of choice—which only added to Robur's discomfiture, since he feared it might go off with each judder the vehicle experienced, each rut they crossed.

Less than five minutes later, the trio stood at the foot of the tower ready to commence the ascent of the steel spiral staircase. The airman guard recognized them and did not seek to bar their way, and Robur bade him follow them with haste since the airship would soon be engaged in an emergency departure.

Robur decided it would be best if he spoke to Tom Turner alone, and, in the absence of a convincing reason for leaving Dahomey, settled on the expedient of simply lying and being prepared to justify it to his creator at a later date.

"Mr. Turner, it has come to my attention that there are strong rumors in the capital that an attempt will be made by enemy agents to sabotage the *Venger* this morning," opened Robur.

"German agents are here in Dahomey?" said Turner.

His tone was both incredulous and fearful. Turner had every reason to trust Robur, and think that he had the ship and crew's best interests at heart rather than his own.

"Yes, my suggestion would be to unmoor immediately and gain as much height as possible."

"Not quite everyone is aboard. Dr. Garett Anderson has already left on a shopping expedition to the bazaar for certain medicinal herbs. But the safety of the ship must come first," said Turner.

Without further consideration, Turner ordered the docking anchor to be disengaged from the tower and for the engines to make maximum revolutions.

The helmsman then put the airship into a steep climb. There was then a sharp whistle from one of the speaking tubes, the one assigned to the gunnery deck lookout. Turner immediately responded and put the flexible end of the tube to his ear.

"Two enemy airships approaching from the east. Range approximately two and a half miles, altitude is low. Estimate eight hundred feet."

Turner was flabbergasted.

"A sneak attack! Captain Robur, your warning was not without merit," said Turner. "We were very nearly caught napping."

Turner moved the viewing lenses and focused them on the incoming ships. Two similar, though not identical, red-and-black German dirigibles were approaching. One was *The Devil Bat,* now repaired; the other could only be *The Angel of Death,* the personal ship of Baron Manfred von Richthofen, also known as the Red Baron, commander of the elite squadron of brightly colored airships known as *The Flying Circus.*

"We beat Lothar von Richthofen before through the miracle of your stratagem, Captain. Do you have any more ideas for evading two enemy airships?" asked Turner.

"Only one. This newly-discovered phenomenon of the equatorial aurora. It is above us—above Dahomey—right now. If we can somehow hide within it, we might be difficult to target," said Robur.

Robur pointed out the phenomenon of the green energy curtain, and Turner put them into an even steeper climb in order to intercept it.

At this point, Frycollin and Seraphina arrived on the command bridge. The latter was somewhat dumbstruck since she had never had cause to travel on an airship before, and now she found herself caught up in terrifying aerial combat.

The *Venger* impacted with the energy curtain as if it were a physical barrier in the sky. Pale green lightning played across the ship's exterior and probed inside like a living thing, where it could.

"We're stuck to it, like iron filings on a magnet. I've lost the ability to maneuver," said Turner.

"Why haven't we passed through it like before?" asked Frycollin desperately.

"I don't know... I don't know," admitted Robur, but then he tried to reason it out. "It's a curtain of energy... sometimes weaker... sometimes stronger. What is the source of its energy? Perhaps the magnetic field of the earth? Perhaps rays from the sun? Perhaps both... It seems weaker, less bright. It is lacking in energy and this airship is much larger than the *Storm Petrel*. It doesn't have enough power to pull us through to the other side."

"What's on the other side?" asked a baffled Turner.

"If we live long enough, you'll find out," said Frycollin with a weak smile.

"We need to make a contribution of energy and we have only one source of unusual energy aboard, your radium bomb," said Robur. "If you detonate it with a short fuse, you may be able to free us... and we'll pass through."

"Bombardier swap out the standard airburst timer on the radium bomb for a two and a half second delay and drop it immediately," ordered Turner via the speaking tube.

Turner looked despondent.

"I've probably just signed our death warrants. At this range, we'll be badly irradiated—a slow, unpleasant death."

The two German airships closed cautiously on the *Venger*. They could see how it was stuck to the sickly green barrier in the sky as if it were flypaper, and they did not wish to share its fate.

They moved to a station keeping position about five hundred yards away and readied their cannons. Then there was a rainbow burst of color just below the British ship, an explosive blast which was sucked upwards and into the barrier, which then brightened intensely until it resembled a blinding pyrotechnic.

The *Venger* became a translucent ghost—a dirigible *Flying Dutchman*—then it was enveloped, swallowed, by the reinvigorated green lightning. Swallowed, and then after a nausea inducing rollercoaster ride, spat out, like Jonah from the belly of the whale.

"These new British airship commanders are of a different breed," observed Lothar von Richthofen. "They would rather destroy themselves, their ship and their crew, than be defeated in fair combat. It is both suicidal, and simply not sporting."

Frycollin looked down at the terrain below them. One thing was for sure, they were no longer over Africa. Then he thought his bleary eyes were playing tricks on him—but they weren't.

"I know this area. That rounded mountain is the Great Eyrie, just outside Morganton, North Carolina," said Frycollin.

"Then we are home, after a fashion," said Robur.

"One hell of a fashion," sneered Frycollin. "I was almost lynched in Morganton!"

From tale to tale, Travis Hiltz is building a tapestry of time-strewn events across different eras. This new story features the return of his most unusual detective agency introduced in Volume 12, comprised of detective Camparol, the giant ant Spiridon (from André Laurie's eponymous novel, available from Black Coat Press) and the Selenite Astarte (from Alfred Drious's The Adventures of a Parisian Aeronaut, *also available from Black Coat Press), but it also connects with Doctor Omega, the Timeslip Troopers, the Morlocks, and a host of other characters who have previously appeared in Travis' past stories…*

Travis Hiltz: *The Case of Where Does The Time Go?*

Paris, 1910

The sitting room was small. It had a cluttered, comfortable air. Most of the furniture was mismatched and showing its years. It was not made for sophisticated entertaining, but it was rather a relaxing oasis from the bustle of the city outside.

On a well-worn, high-backed wing chair, a young man with dark hair and a suit that, like the furniture, had seen some use, was comfortably slouched. The other occupant sat nervously perched on the edge of a settee with a faded flower pattern.

"What can I do for you, Oscar?" the dark-haired man asked, guardedly.

"Ah, well, yes," replied the other man, who was smaller, with a round head fringed with a bit of black hair. He nervously stroked his well-groomed mustache. "Well, my dear Camparol, a case has been brought to my attention, but, as I am currently, er, engaged in some other investigation, I had hoped you might be available to pursue the matter?"

"I am currently between cases, at the moment," Etienne Camparol said, noncommittally. He clasped his hands across his stomach and raised a questioning eyebrow.

"A young gentleman—a vague acquaintance—has been accused of theft," explained Mazamette. "The details are… where did I put those notes…?" He patted his coat until he came across a much-used notebook. Licking his thumb, he flipped through the tattered pages. "Let's see…

Need to pick up shoes from the cobblers... Bring home a head of cauliflower and bottle of Riesling... Ah, here it is! Young Privat is a clerk for a prominent firm of solicitors... Seems a diligent and earnest young man. He was tasked with delivering some documents... bonds, financial listings, that sort of thing, to a small brokerage firm..."

"Seems fairly straightforward," Camparol nodded.

"Yes, well, that changes once he reaches the office... A little unassuming, four-story building... He entered—that was witnessed by a passing gendarme and two residents. He then exited the building within minutes, disheveled and claiming he'd been attacked and robbed of his charge."

Someone waiting in the lobby who knew of his errand?" Camparol suggested.

"Except, Privat claims he was attacked outside the office that was his destination, which is located on the third floor."

"Curious. Did he receive a blow to the head during the attack?"

"Possibly," Mazamette shrugged. "His story is a muddle."

"What do you want from me, Oscar?"

"Other affairs are keeping me from taking the case myself, but I feel for the lad. It's a modest fee and most likely an afternoon's work. I do not have high hopes that young Privat will be cleared, but feel an effort should be made."

Camparol studied his fellow detective for several moments. If it had been anyone else, he would suspect he was being duped, but Oscar Mazamette, for all his faults, was not a conniving soul. It didn't hurt that his own caseload had been practically barren and he had been looking for any excuse to leave the house.

"Give me your notes and I'll see what I can do," he said.

Mazamette did and, after a great deal of heartfelt thanks and vigorous handshakes, the little detective was on his way, leaving Camparol to study the case.

The more he read, the more pronounced the furrows upon his forehead became.

"What was that all that about?"

Camparol glanced up.

Sitting in a straight-backed, wooden chair by the door, was a young woman. She was tall, her posture ramrod straight; her hair was long and midnight black; her skin was pale, while still retaining a healthy luster;

and her dress was white, pleasant, without being overly frilly or fashionable.

"How long have you been there, Astarte?" Camparol asked, not looking up.

"Long enough to doubt your associate will remember to purchase any cauliflower," she replied.

Camparol usually told people that his young partner was a foreign student and new to Paris. What he left out was that Astarte's home was a city on the Moon. She'd left her immortal family to come to Earth and learn about humanity. She'd come to Paris specifically, hoping to stay with a balloonist that had encountered the Lunar Angels during one of his flights. Being immortal, her estimate of time had been off; the balloonist had passed away a decade before, and Camparol was the current owner of the house where he had lived.

While she looked human, Astarte needed to breathe less and, when at rest, adopted a stillness that could lead one to mistake her for a statue. Most people found her off-putting, but the detective had grown used to her.

Camparol nodded and continued reading.

"That frown leads me to believe your friend has misled you concerning this case."

"No, not really. He didn't paint a rosy picture, but Oscar is not devious. The fact is that being so honest and trusting is one of the reasons why he isn't more successful as a private investigator."

"What concerns you then?"

"On the surface, it seems a fairly basic case: is young Privat the victim of a robbery, or an inept thief?" He shrugged and flipped through the pages. "Then, troubling details merge: the Inspector in charge of the case is one Justin Ganimard..."

"Ah! The one who doesn't like you," Astarte nodded.

"The same. And then, there's the identity of the man who owns the firm Privat was delivering his papers to: Maurice-Ernest Favraux. I can see why Oscar was reluctant to become involved..."

"Who is this Favraux?" his associate asked.

"A banker, a man with vast financial interests and a nasty reputation." Camparol explained. "There's a great many shady enterprises in Paris that he's rumored to have his fingers in. There are rumors, of course, but no proof tying him to anything illegal."

"It would seem this 'basic case' is sandwiched between two worrisome complications," Astarte said. "What do you plan on doing?"

"See what we can discover for ourselves and if we can earn our fee without attracting the attention of either Ganimard or Favraux," Camparol replied, getting to his feet and tucking the notebook into an inside coat pocket. "While I'm fetching my hat, could you leave Madame Jouvence a note? We should be back in time for supper?"

"What about the Doctor? Should we bring him along?"

"No, leave the little menace here," Camparol said. "We may have enough difficulties without bringing one more along with us. I'll bring the car around front."

Once she'd informed their housekeeper of their plans, Astarte found her hat and a spring-weight wrap and was on the front steps just as Camparol pulled up. His car, like his home and wardrobe, was several years out of fashion, and a bit threadbare. The black roadster had the top down.

Astarte held onto her hat with one gloved hand, as Camparol always tended to drive with a bit more urgency than she felt was necessary.

Parking a few buildings down from their destination, the detective glanced about the neighborhood, as he and his associate strolled.

"What are we learning?" Astarte asked, anticipating a lesson on not only detection, but earthly customs and behaviors.

"That we can trust the witness accounts," Camparol said. "This is a grey neighborhood."

"What does that mean?"

"Rich neighborhoods are a nightmare for witness accounts. Everyone stays in their fancy homes, behind fences. In poor areas, it's generally healthy to mind your own business; you must pry information loose. This street is in the middle. Not too much money, not too little. People are friendly with their neighbors and the local businesses. They know each other and they trust the police, rather than being disdainful or afraid of them."

He nodded greetings to a shopkeeper and several passing pedestrians, as they strolled along.

Camparol's observation had been correct. Most of the buildings they passed sported a business on the ground floor, with frugal apartments on the floors above. The buildings were clean, if plain and light on ornamentation.

Their destination was a weathered, four-story building, grey and functional. Camparol put a hand on his hat, as he tilted his head to peer up at it.

"Couldn't be more unassuming and mundane if it tried," was his conclusion.

Astarte reached into her sleeve, bringing out a small hand mirror on a long, thin ivory stem. She paced in front of the building, peering up at the brick building and then at the small mirror.

Despite looking like the bauble of a vain aristocrat, the mirror was, in fact, a piece of advanced selenite technology. Camparol hadn't the least idea how it worked, but he had seen his companion use it for a variety of tasks.

A corner of her lip went down briefly.

"What?" he asked.

"The energy readings are…odd," she replied, absently.

"What now?" Camparol asked, this time sounding more annoyed than concerned.

Since taking on Astarte and the aforementioned Doctor as housemates and assistants, the cases Camparol seemed to acquire tended toward the odd, if not the outright fantastic, and he, for one, had grown a bit peevish about it.

"There's an energy trace. It's minute, but…?" She shrugged and tucked the mirror back in her sleeve. "Most likely background radiation… Sunspot activity ,or possibly…"

Camparol rubbed at his cheek, while he contemplated informing his associate that he barely understood a word she had said. He was distracted by the realization that he needed a shave and then continued walking.

Astarte frowned at his behavior, then followed.

The gendarme assigned the area nodded in response, when Camparol showed his credentials and explained the purpose of their visit. Obviously bored with his current posting, the man then continued his patrol.

"What do you suggest?" Astarte asked.

"Stay here, keep your eyes open. I'm going to take a look, see how far I can get in the five minutes our client is said to have been inside."

She nodded and Camparol climbed the three steps into the lobby. It was, much like the exterior, showing its years, but clean and functional.

The concierge gave the detective a disinterested glance and then returned his attention to his newspaper.

Camparol glanced at the directory plaque but, not spotting any familiar names, he began his trek up. He was approaching the second floor, when he consulted his pocket watch.

"If he was younger and eager," Camparol said to himself, "he'd likely have gotten here or maybe even to the second-floor landing…"

He tucked his watch back in his vest pocket, and then glanced around, taking in his surroundings.

"If we believe Privat's story," he muttered, stroking his chin, "then he was pounced on roughly here… On one of the landings, but which presents the best opportunity for our mysterious thieves?"

The first floor had several office suites, with too much potential foot traffic during the early afternoon. The second floor seemed quieter, its landing more dimly lit, giving it an air of seclusion.

Consulting Oscar's notes, Camparol read that the second floor contained only three offices, two of which being unoccupied at this time.

"Almost too good to be true for an enterprising cutpurse," Camparol concluded, recommencing his journey.

Several steps from the second floor, the detective paused. He rested a hand on the worn banister, and with his other hand, pushed back his hat to rub at his forehead. He felt slightly lightheaded and reached out, leaning against the aged wallpaper.

He blinked and shook his head, but neither action did much to dispel his dizziness. The rest of the building sounded far away and muffled.

Camparol sank down, onto the third stair from the top. He rested his head in his hands and, slowly, the world returned to normal. He exhaled, and raised his head, intently, anxiously studying his surroundings.

It was too coincidental that his dizzy spell had occurred so near the possible scene of the crime. The investigator frowned at the wallpaper, accusingly, as though its faded patterns were somehow hiding vital clues.

Camparol sighed and, hat in hand, stood up and slowly started walking. He plodded back down to the lobby, juggling ideas and theories, while struggling out of his mental fog. He noticed the concierge eying him more intently than when he had arrived, but was too preoccupied to analyze it further.

Back on the front step, blinking in the sunlight, Camparol frowned. Standing in front of the office building were three gendarmes, Astarte and a diminutive man nearly swallowed up by his oversized black overcoat and Homberg hat.

His face appeared oriental, but his features were puffy, almost exaggerated to the point of deformity. The sleeves of his coat were too long for his stubby arms, so his hands were hidden.

"What's going on?" Camparol asked. "Why is he here?"

He gestured at the odd individual they referred to simply as "the Doctor."

Camparol raised an eyebrow, as his usually stoic female assistant, had actually changed expression. Astarte looked vaguely concerned.

"Where have you been?" she asked.

"What? I barely made it to the second floor," he explained. "Had a bit of a dizzy spell... Why call in the cavalry? I was only gone only... ten minutes?"

"You have been gone three hours," Astarte told him, quietly concerned.

"What?"

Camparol rubbed his forehead and sat down on the front steps. Both the Doctor and the constables moved in. As he reached forward to take the detectives' pulse, a large claw poked out of the Doctor's floppy sleeve.

Camparol waved him away and then reassured the constables he was fine and there had just been a misunderstanding.

Once they'd gone back to their patrol, Camparol stood up and starting to walk away from the building. The other two hurried after him.

"Where are you going?" Astarte asked.

"I need a drink and I need to do some thinking," he explained, gesturing towards a nearby café.

They were soon settled at a small outside table. Astarte sipped delicately at her glass of water, knowing there was nothing to be done until Camparol had sorted his thoughts and had had his drink.

Halfway through his second glass of wine, the detective sighed, put his glass down, and rubbed his eyes.

"So, what did happen to me?" he asked. "I was only in that building for ten minutes."

"There are numerous scenarios that would explain your time loss," Astarte explained, reaching into her sleeve and retrieving her mirror.

"It could have been some form of gas?" Camparol muttered, thoughtfully. "It would explain the dizziness and time loss..."

"Except, it does not explain why we could not find you when the Doctor and I searched the stairs," the woman from the Moon countered.

The small, malformed Doctor nodded his agreement, before reaching out a claw to snatch a piece of bread off Camparol's plate.

They sunk into thoughtful, yet frustrated silence. Camparol toyed with his wine glass.

"We can piece together a scenario that fits," he muttered. "Except for the matter of lost time…"

"Lost time," Astarte quietly repeated, toying with her mirror wand. She glanced at its polished surface. She then held it up, as she peered at the building down the street.

"What?"

"That energy trace," she explained, not looking away from the small mirror. "It is quite possibly temporal energy…"

"So, Privat and my time loss incidents really happened? There's something wrong in that stairwell?" Camparol asked, struggling to keep up with his associates' train of thought.

"It is sporadic… more a flicker than an active energy signal, but it is there nevertheless." She moved the mirror slowly from side to side. "It is most definitely a temporal distortion of some kind," she concluded.

"What does that mean?" Camparol asked.

"Time generally moves in a straight, linear flow," she explained. "On rare occasions…"

"Wait," Camparol said, holding up a hand. He paused in mid-thought, then drained his glass. "Let me see if I, a mere mortal from Earth, can make sense of this…"

Astarte nodded, a stern teacher indulging a student with some hope of potential, and took a sip of water.

"Time moves in a straight line, from past to future, but occasionally there's a… ripple or something… which muddles how time works in a small area," Camparol mused, earning a nod from the tall woman.

"And when you're inside the time ripple," Camparol continued, his brow furrowed in thought, as he absently moved his glass about. "Privat and I were briefly… stuck in that moment and didn't… 'catch up' until the ripple faded or whatever it is they do… Have I got any of it right?"

"Enough of it," she replied.

"OK," Camparol nodded, knowing from the stoic nature of his partner that he'd just been highly praised. "So, I now understand the basics. How does it happen? Are these ripples a natural phenomenon or are they, er, orchestrated… caused by someone?"

Astarte raised an eyebrow and sat up a bit straighter.

"Interesting," she said, thoughtfully. "Both are possible. Natural temporal eddies are very rare, but known to occur…"

She paused, gently tapping at the corner of her mouth with a finger.

"Well?" Camparol asked, frowning, as he peered into his empty glass.

"It is also possible to cause a temporal disruption, but the necessary knowledge, technology, or even required energy is hardly to be found here, in Paris," she explained, with a shrug.

Camparol, having encountered the Lunar Angel's bias before when it came to judging mankind's intelligence, merely sighed.

"I can think of at least two people who have the knowledge or equipment to interfere with space and time without leaving Paris," he said, "so there must be others."

"Yes, Doctor Omega is capable, but who else?"

"She's sitting at this table," Camparol replied, looking up from his glass.

"What? No!"

"Your people, the Lunar immortals," Camparol continued, "are, by your own accounts, knowledgeable, capable of building whatever machinery was required, and have shown no reluctance to interfere with… whatever celestial powers suited their purpose. Why shouldn't they be on the suspect list?"

"I object to your phraseology in describing my people, but I cannot dismiss your logic. There are scientists amongst my people who would be quite capable of temporal manipulation, but we have a very strict moral code concerning its use as well as… you are smirking."

"Yes, well, we can discuss your people's 'strict moral code' some other time," Camparol said, "but I'll go along with you for the moment. So, this… time ripple… bubble, what's your best guess? Naturally occurring or created by someone?"

"I have not gathered enough information to form a solid theory," she replied, frowning.

"Give me your best guess," Camparol prompted, "your hunch."

At the word 'hunch,' the lunar immortal made a face similar to the one society matrons made when one uttered a rude word in their presence.

"I know," Camparol said, "it's unfair of me, but, we're lost in the weeds."

"Lost? No. We know what occurred. Do we have to do all of the police's work for them?" she asked, indignantly. "We should tell them about the temporal rift..."

"...And they would lock us in a padded cell next to young Privat," Camparol interrupted. "We understand what happened, but what we need to do is to find some kind of proof that exonerates our client: proof that the bonds were stolen from him. Somewhere in all this are the actual thieves. We need to investigate the time disturbance in the hope that it will lead us to the thieves or the stolen bonds."

"You think they are still in the building?"

Camparol shrugged. "Who knows? But even if they are not behind the time disruption, the odds are quite good that they frequent one of the offices." He held up two fingers. "Opportunity and location," he continued. "The bonds wouldn't attract the attention of just some grubby snatch thief. This was done by someone who knew the comings and goings."

"The concierge?" Astarte suggested.

"Not bad," Camparol said. "Possible, but there's only one way to learn more. We need to search the building further."

He gestured to the waiter for their bill.

"How so? What are we looking for?" she asked.

"We need to locate the source of the time disruptions and hopefully, we'll find evidence of whoever robbed Privat," Camparol explained, standing up and rummaging through his pockets for money to pay for their snack. "Let's split our forces: you're the expert on exotic devices and strange phenomenon, so you'll know what to look for where the time disruption is concerned. And I know a thing or two about crime and how to spot a thief."

Astarte nodded as she stood up. The two detectives stood, waiting expectantly for several moments for the Doctor. The odd, little figure was still sitting, continuing to slip pieces of bread under his mask, oblivious of his associates.

He finally glanced up at them, made a exasperated clicking noise and stood up, while scooping up the remaining bread and tucking it into his over-sized pockets, before shuffling along behind the duo.

"Do you have a plan?" Astarte asked, as they walked.

"No, but I'm full of ideas," he replied. "If there's a machine causing the time bubble, what size would it be?"

"We are probably dealing with fairly primitive technology, judging by the erratic nature of the disruption," she mused. "So, something roughly the size of that old wardrobe you have in the spare room."

They reached the building and stopped at the front steps.

"You take the ground floor, then move down," instructed Camparol. "Search any storerooms and the cellar. I'll head upstairs. I'm convinced that the thieves are connected to one of the offices. To have been a planned job, someone had to know the schedule of the other businesses."

Astarte nodded.

"What about the Doctor?" she asked.

Camparol turned and focused his gaze on the bizarre, little creature in the over-sized coat.

"He will wait in the car," he said, raising his voice and enunciating distinctly, as though speaking to a difficult child. "The Doctor will stay in the car until either we return, or one of us comes to fetch him."

The Doctor looked up at the detective, his grotesque mask giving no hint of what lurked beneath it. A terse clicking sound came from one floppy sleeve and then the bundled-up creature turned and sulked off to the roadster.

After a quick word to the patrolling gendarme and a couple francs slipped to the concierge, the duo split up and began their search.

Astarte, her little mirror in hand, roamed the ground floor, moving with a quiet, fluid grace that, combined with her all-white wardrobe, might have lead some occupants of the building to mistake her for a ghost.

She first checked the ground floor studio, which was currently empty, paying close attention to a little kitchenette but found no appliance that seemed capable of causing damage to the fabric of time.

She was also skeptical of the junk piled in the storeroom under the stairs, so she moved towards the cellar.

Down a narrow, rickety flight of stairs, Astarte found herself in a low-ceilinged room that ran the length of the building above. It was dimly lit, and haphazardly packed with old furniture, cleaning supplies, and a variety of boxes and sacks whose contents the Lunar immortal could only guess at.

She had to stoop slightly in order to avoid having the top of her head brush against the ceiling. She looked around, peered at her mirror, and occasionally nudged a dusty box with the toe of her white shoe.

While her path seemed random, she was guided by her mirror, which was detecting traces of temporal energy. Squeezing past a behemoth of a furnace, and ducking under one of its pipes, she suddenly discovered a door set into the stone wall.

It was small, pristinely dust-free, and sported a sign that read *Beware the Leopard.*

Astarte tried the doorknob, which stubbornly refused to turn. She studied it and the lock.

Reaching under her hat, she extracted a hair pin that looked as though it had been made of crystal. Tapping it against the knob, it rang like a tuning fork. The knob turned, the lock clicked, and she eased the small door open.

She then stepped into a large room that resembled the collision of a bookstore and mission control for a space launch. Shelves were choked with books, which were also piled on top of banks of computing equipment far beyond the technology of Earth in the first decades of the Twentieth century.

"Oh dear!" she breathed, frowning.

Delicately, Astarte made her way through the maze of bookshelves, worn Victorian furniture and sophisticated computer equipment.

At the center of the room was a large, mushroom-shaped control console made of white plastic. It was littered with discarded teacups, scribbled notes and of course, more books.

Shuffling around the console, pausing occasionally to adjust a control, reread a scrap of paper, or take a sip from one of the neglected cups was a figure, every bit as eccentric as his surroundings. Short and burly with a bushy, brown beard streaked with silver, he was dressed in academic tweeds, a pair of worn carpet slippers on his feet.

Astarte stepped up behind the bearded man and glanced over his shoulder.

"Don't you want to set the frequency modulator lower in order to counter the Blinovitch Limitation Effect?" she asked.

Irritated the bearded man turned around, peering gruffly over the top of his glasses at her.

"I'll have you know... Wait... Who are you?"

"Stella Astarte," she replied, straightening up, haughtily. "Daughter of the first house, vestal of the scared..."

"Oh, good lord, a Lunar Angel!" the bearded man exclaimed, turning fully to confront Astarte.

"No, stop!" she said, holding a hand up in a placating gesture. "I have not come here for any sort of confrontation, or to rehash conflicts between my people and yours. Whatever you are up to is causing temporal disruptions in the building above and is starting to interfere with the inhabitants of this... the citizens of Paris."

He peered up at her intently for several moments.

"Oh, bother!" was his pronouncement, before returning to his work.

Astarte followed him, on his journey around the console.

"If you would just tell me what you are doing, Mister...?"

"It is Professor. Professor Helvetius."

"Of course! Doctor Omega's colleague."

"Omega! Don't mention that scofflaw to me. Insufferable know-it-all!"

"Professor, could you please explain, what you are doing?"

The bearded savant frowned up at her, then nodded to himself and began self-consciously polishing his glasses as he spoke.

"A bit of research, I was conducting went, er, awry and I inadvertently sent a small, insignificant number of Morlocks through a temporal rift," he said, avoiding his guest's incredulous and disapproving gaze. "The problem itself was simplicity to repair. Unfortunately, while attempting to return the Morlocks to their proper time, they encountered a group of French soldiers that had gotten their hands upon some make-shift time machine, and the resulting chronal feedback sent both groups hurtling through space-time... Most bothersome! I do detest when rank amateurs start dabbling in temporal science!"

Astarte had some opinions herself on that topic, but thought it best to bite her lip and let the Professor continue his rambling explanation.

"After that, it became such a chaotic mess, I realized I couldn't fix it, entirely, on my own.... I'm not one for gallivanting across the timeline! But, finally, I came upon the idea of, rather than scurrying all through history, settling here, where I've been constructing a transtemporal... Well, it's complicated and you would most likely disapprove... So instead, I have been attracting the time-lost Morlocks to me."

"You did what?" Astarte asked. "You planted a trans-temporal activator in the middle of a pre-galactic industrial culture in order to attract a life form from a millennium in their own future! I cannot possibly convey how irresponsible, if not senselessly dangerous, that is."

"You can't stop me now!" Helvetius protested, jamming his pince-nez back upon his nose. "I'm nearly finished!"

"I have no intention of stopping you," Astarte said, rolling up her sleeves. "That would be nearly as dangerous as connecting a flux capacitor to your console with... Is that duct tape? Never mind, I am going to help you complete this before any more damage is done. Hand me that sonic probe."

Two floors above, Camparol had conducted a fairly thorough investigation of the hallways and the offices.

While he was sure that the dentist on the first floor was also illicitly dealing narcotics, and was quite intrigued to have spotted the actress Musidora entering a lawyers' office, neither seemed to connect to his current case.

He finally reached his original destination, the modest accounting firm on the third floor. It was as tedious and nondescript looking as you'd want your illicit business to appear for it to be effective.

He made an excuse to enter and chat for a moment with the clerk, before returning to the hallway and his contemplation.

"Awfully calm, for a den of thieves," the detective mused, before shaking his head. "No, it doesn't fit."

He turned and began to retrace his steps.

"Second floor," he muttered as he walked. "Both Privat and I had our dizzy spells there; so it has to be one of the unoccupied offices..."

Rubbing his chin, walking almost without any motivating thought, he let his mind and his gaze wander and allowed his body to follow.

Camparol wasn't entirely sure what he was seeing or what, if anything, it contributed to his theories about this case, but he found traces in the dust, scratches on the lock of one of the office doors, a discarded cigarette butt, and a button.

Back in the basement, tempers were wearing thin.

"Don't touch that dial!" Helvetius snapped.

"It is set too high," Astarte replied, in a quiet, terse tone. "Perhaps you should focus on the chronal oscillator. If the stasis bubble becomes unstable, anything could jeopardize its integrity!"

Camparol was now leaning on the railing, of the first-floor landing. He nodded to the occasional passing clerk or janitor, as his brain sorted the various crumbs of information he had gathered.

He glanced, over his shoulder at one of the doors. He nodded to himself and walked over to it. A quick twist and a few seconds with a bit of wire and the door eased open.

Allowing the enraged Morlock to pounce!

"See, the stasis bubble integrity is weakening," Professor Helvetius barked, frantically flicking switches and jabbing at buttons.

"If you are not careful, you are going to fracture one of the mercury fluid links," Astarte responded from the other side of the console.

"I have the situation completely under control," Helvetius said, as he twisted the end of a loose wire and stuck it into a nearby cup of tea.

Camparol punched the squat, bestial creature.

"Humph!" he exclaimed through gritted teeth.

Shaking his aching hand, the detective dove at the Morlock, driving his shoulder into the creature's midriff, driving him back into the empty office. The Morlock leapt about, swinging his arms like an enraged gorilla.

Camparol took up a fighter's stance, unsure if he could beat the bestial creature in a straightforward fight. He was going to have to outthink him. Scanning his surroundings out of the corner of his eye, he stepped back as he and the Morlock circled each other.

The room was dusty and contained only a few pieces of discarded furniture and what at first appeared to be a pile of rags.

Until it moved.

Startled to realize it was a person, Camparol ended up back-handed by the Morlock, stumbled backwards, and collided with the wall. He slid down and immediately flung himself to the side, as the Morlock lunged at him.

The man-beast struck the wall, cracking the plaster, and slumped in a heap. Camparol got to his feet, and with the toe of his shoe nudged his unconscious opponent over onto his back.

"Aren't you an ugly one," he muttered.

Rubbing his shoulder, he walked over to the other prone form. It was a young man in the modest attire of a clerk. His suit was torn and his face bruised. He also seemed to be clutching a parcel of papers.

"Well, well, what have we here?" Camparol muttered, squatting down next to the other man.

The disheveled clerk groaned and blinked his eyes at the detective.

"Who...?" he mumbled. "How are... Is it still here!"

He clutched fearfully at the lapel of Camparol's coat, nearly pulling the detective off balance.

"Calm down," Camparol muttered, with minimal effort to be comforting, as he reached across for the bound parcel.

"No," the young man said in an anxious hush, while he grasped Camparol's wrist.

"It's... It's still here!"

Realizing what the other man was trying to say, Camparol glanced over his shoulder in time to see the Morlock get to its feet and propel itself across the dingy office at the two men.

"Don't touch that!" Helvetius snapped. "This is a delicately balanced collection of machinery and science!"

"These two wires are held together with a paperclip," Astarte replied, exasperated.

Helvetius' grumbles were unable to escape his beard, as he reached over and vigorously twisted a large dial.

Camparol braced himself, frantically contemplating an escape route or something he could use as a weapon against the Morlock.

The creature's breath hit him, rancid and hot; stubby, clawed fingers dug into the fabric of his coat.

Then the enraged creature grew translucent and passed through him. The clerk shrieked in fright as the Morlock passed through Camparol and reached for him, before fading like morning mist under a sunbeam.

"So," Camparol said, once the thief had been turned over to the police, along with the stolen notes and bonds, and the trio had returned to the neighborhood café. "Your Professor Helvetius created the, er, time bubble to trap wayward Morlocks and inadvertently caught the thief."

A large brandy was soothing Camparol's various aches and pains acquired during his tussle with the time-lost creature, as he slumped in his chair.

"Yes," Astarte nodded, sighing at the memory of the curmudgeonly scientist. "But he claims his work is now done and has scampered off to... Cambridge, I think. Hopefully, he meant it when he said he is done experimenting and wants to return to his quiet, scholarly ways. So, what now?"

"We rest and see how generous a fee we get for having helped Oscar."

"Shouldn't we be doing more?"

"What?" Camparol replied, with a shrug. "We caught the thief, returned the bonds, and young Privat has been exonerated. With the thief freely confessing to anyone who will listen his obviously fabricated tale of how he was attacked by an albino gorilla, no one will look too closely at the case. But it will also get enough notice to keep us, Privat and Oscar safe from any retribution from whoever was behind the robbery."

"Do you mean, the thief?" Astarte asked, raising a puzzled eyebrow.

"No. He was just an errand boy," Camparol explained. "There was planning behind this. I don't know who, but they now know about us."

"So, this harmless favor for your friend Oscar may have gained us a mysterious enemy?"

"All in a day's work."

Matthew Ilseman is an infrequent collaborator, but his contributions to Tales of the Shadowmen *are always clever. This new story borrows elements from the tales of the famed Belgian horrormeister Jean Ray (the man who penned many of Harry Dickson's best adventures), and throws him a notorious black bird...*

Matthew Ilseman: *Unknowable Powers*

Hamburg, the 1930s

"We are being followed," said Joel Cairo.

Casper Gutman pulled him into the doorway. He looked up and down the Hamburg alley. It was empty. Rain fell heavily. Puddles collected on the street. The old houses loomed on either side.

"I see no one," said Gutman.

"Nevertheless, I felt someone following us," said Cairo.

Gutman took him by the arm and led him through the street. They entered a decrepit tavern. The lights were low. They took a table in the back. Gutman sat facing the entry way to watch anyone who came in.

"You've been like this since we were on the *Endymion*," he said.

"There was something wrong with that ship," said Cairo. "I felt it."

Gutman sighed. Cairo had always been too sensitive.

"Of course, there was something wrong with that ship," he said. "That is precisely why I chose her. We minded our business and they minded theirs."

Gutman did not doubt that the crew of the *Endymion* had been smuggling something. They had been closed-lipped. There had been a cabin in which they were not to go into. Possibly, there was some fugitive hiding out on the ship.

"I don't mean something criminal," said Cairo. "There was something inherently wrong with it."

In all the years that Gutman had known Cairo, the years he spent chasing the Falcon across the world, he had never seen Cairo like this. The Lebanese man had always been of a nervous disposition, but now he was seeing things that were not there.

"What do you mean?" said Gutman.

"There was someone else on the ship. Someone we did not see."

They had boarded the *Endymion* after they had lost track of the Falcon. For years, they had chased it. They thought they had found it in San Francisco, but it turned out to be a fake. Gutman had been shot there, and almost died. They had then gone back to Constantinople, but had not found it.

Not that they searched for that alone. They had made a play for the treasure of the Black Coats, too. Now, they were in Hamburg planning to burgle another treasure. Gutman planned to search for the Falcon as long as it took, but they needed money. So he had found another prize.

"Your nerves are getting the better of you," said the fat man. "At least, I hope it is your nerves and not your conscience?"

"No," said Cairo. "We are being followed."

Just then, the door to the tavern opened, but no one came in. It was the wind, Gutman told himself.

"I don't mind robbing this… what's his name?"

"Gockel," said Gutman. "They are a wealthy family of antiquarians. They can afford the loss."

"Oh, I am sure they can," said Cairo. "But something has not felt right since we began this. Ever since you found that infernal book."

The book had been *The Wickstead Grimoire*, a treatise by an occultist named Samuel Podgers on otherworldly entities. Gutman had found it on the *Endymion*. According to that book, the family Gockel had come into wealth from dealing with an ethereal creature called the Horla. He had read it with interest, but not believed it. Casper Gutman was a man of the world and he did not believe in invisible beings. What he did believe in was money.

"Come now," said the fat man. "You cannot believe in invisible creatures living among us."

"But you believe in their wealth."

"I believe in the Gockel's wealth, which they undoubtedly got through some illicit means. They did not get it from any supernatural creatures that live on an imaginary street. I checked a map. There is no street in Hamburg called Sankt Berengonnegasse. It is just a local legend, like Marlyweck Cemetery in London."

"But I know that we are being followed," said Cairo. "I heard footsteps."

"I heard nothing," said Gutman. "Still, someone from the ship could have found out about our plans…"

Gutman looked out the window of the tavern. The rain had stopped.

"All right," he said. "We will keep our eyes opened. The rain has stopped. Let's leave."

They got up and went out the door. The air was cool. The sky was still grey. It seemed that the clouds were merely waiting to pour out a torrent of water. Gutman scanned the street looking for anyone suspicious. It was empty.

They stepped out on the sidewalk and headed down the road. Behind them the door swung open, yet no one was seen to come out. There was a splash in a puddle as if someone had stepped in it, but no one could be seen.

Before the burglary, Gutman decided they should reconnoiter Gockel's place of business. He posed as an American businessman who was searching for a certain antique. This was essentially true. He had found that an element of truth made a lie more believable. Besides, if they happened to have knowledge of the Falcon, he wanted to know it.

After perusing Gockel's shop, he had struck up a conversation with Gockel himself. He mentioned the Falcon while giving no indication of its worth, but Gockel had not heard of it. Gutman liked to talk and the conversation turned to various figures of the past. Ever ready to show off his erudition, Gutman discussed the lives Mattias Tannhauser and Gotfried Von Kalmbach.

"They sound like rogues," said Gockel. "But truth be told, I have a certain fondness for rogues."

"As do I," said Gutman. "I would like to give you my contact number if you hear anything about the object I want."

"I will let you know. A black statue of a Falcon, you aid?"

"Yes," said Gutman. "It is not worth much, but I would greatly desire to have it. I must say, you seem to be quite prosperous. Forgive me, if I seem to be like the crude Americans who are always talking about money."

"Not at all," said Gockel. "We were once a poor family, but we have become quite wealthy. It was around the time of the great fire here in Hamburg that my family came into its fortune."

"The great fire?"

"Yes, during my grandfather's time; some lunatic set fire to the city. No one knows who. While many people lost their homes and fortunes, we were spared. In fact, my grandfather became quite well off"

"What an enterprising fellow he must have been!"

"I suppose he was; but we were lucky in that we found, er, trading partners of considerable wealth."

"That was lucky indeed."

"Yes, it was."

It was just as Gutman suspected. The Gockels had come into their wealth through illicit means. He spied a large strong box in the backroom behind the antiquarian. Earlier, he had checked to make sure that Gockel had no account at any banks in Hamburg, which meant that he had to keep his wealth elsewhere.

"Well, I've enjoyed conversing with you, sir, but I need to be going." Gutman turned around and headed to the doorway. He stopped. A thought had struck him. He turned and asked, "Have you heard of something called the Horla?"

Gockel's face went white.

"Yes," he said. "An invisible creature from a tale by Guy de Maupassant, but sailors down at the docks talk about it as if it were real."

"I must have read the story a long time ago," said Gutman, before leaving.

Outside, he met Cairo. He asked, "Have you seen any invisible men?"

"Don't joke," said Cairo. "That is mean of you."

"Sorry, my dear fellow," said Gutman. "It'll be tonight. I know where the strong box is. Do you think you can crack it?"

"Please," said Cairo. "I've cracked safes all over Europe and America. Only, Lupin ever had more experience."

"Good. We will wait until dark, then burgle the place."

Night had fallen. The streets were empty. From an alley, Cairo and Gutman watched Gockel lock up his shop and leave. When they were certain he was gone, they crossed the street to the door of the shop.

Cairo pulled out his lock pick and began to work on the door. Gutman watched the street. He saw no one. He acted nonchalant. He had learned a long time ago that if you were going to do something that you were not supposed to do, you should act as casual as possible. Nervous people attracted attention.

Cairo, on the other hand, was furtive.

"Calm yourself, man," whispered Gutman. "No one is looking at us."

The truth was that Gutman was more worried than he looked. He had a bad feeling about this venture. He wondered if Cairo's nervousness was getting to him.

After what seemed like a long time, there was a click. Cairo slowly opened the door. The two stepped inside. Leisurely and quietly, they closed the door behind them.

Gutman took out the flashlight in his pocket. Aiming it at the floor, he turned it on. Keeping the beam low so it would not light up the windows, he scanned the room. The various bric-a-brac cast long shadows as the beam went back and forth.

"The safe should be in the back," Gutman said and headed to the backroom. Just as he expected, he found it there. "All right get to work," he said.

From a satchel that swung at his side, Cairo removed a stethoscope which he placed against the safe. Listening, he slowly spun the dial one way and then another. Gutman stood quietly, knowing it was best not to break his partner's concentration.

As he did so, he passed the beam over the room. It was old and dusty. Cobwebs hung from the ceiling. For furniture, there was only a desk and a chair.

Gutman turned back to Cairo. There was sweat on his brow. He wished he had found another partner for this venture. Cairo was competent, but his lack of nerve could be trouble. He wished someone else could be with him, but he did not have anyone else. The boy Wilmer had disappeared after their encounter with Spade. His daughter Rhea was not even talking to him.

He could not trust Cairo not to betray him. He had done so in the past. So he planned on betraying Cairo first.

Suddenly, Gutman felt a draft. As if someone had opened a window or a door. There was a creak of the floorboards from the other room. He pulled a revolver from his waistband.

He hoped he was wrong. He preferred to let someone else do his killing. Poking his head through the doorway, he looked in the front room. He could see nothing in the dark.

There was another creak. He scanned the room with his light. There was nothing there. Yet, the boards creaked again,

He could sense someone—or something—coming toward him, yet there was nothing. He stepped back and closed the door. He turned off his flashlight.

There was more creaking of the floor boards.

"Cairo," he said.

"What?" the little man said, annoyed.

"We are not alone."

Cairo stopped spinning the dial. He removed the plugs from his ears. He pulled a tiny automatic from his waist band.

Slowly, the door opened. Gutman raised his revolver. There was only enough light to see the door move. He expected to see a dim silhouette behind the door, but there was nothing. The door seemed to be moving on its own. Then, he heard a footfall. He fired reflexively.

There was a scream. Something fell against the floor. Gutman turned on the flashlight. He pointed the beam at the door. There was still no one there. And yet, he heard moaning. He had hit someone—something.

He went forward with light and the revolver before him. Cairo followed. They could find no one in the next room. Still, he heard moaning from a dark corner. He pointed the light toward it. He saw nothing but he heard a single word:

"Horla."

Gutman was not a man that frightened easily, but when he heard that word, fear swept through him. He pointed the revolver at the corner and fired repeatedly until the hammer fell on an empty cylinder.

"What are you doing?" said Cairo. "We need to get out of here. Someone might have heard you and call the police."

"There is something invisible here."

"Yes," said Cairo. "And there may be more of them. We have to leave."

The little man tugged at his arm. They went out the front door and ran down the street. They saw no one outside, but they could not be certain no one was there.

There was the knock on the door. A shiver went down Gutman's spine. He reached for his gun that lay on a table beside him. Then he went to the door.

Gutman and Cairo were in a hotel room. It was run down and seedy. Both would have preferred more luxurious surroundings, but because they were low on funds, and to keep a low profile, they had chosen a dilapidated hotel in a less savory neighborhood of Hamburg. They had stayed in the room since the incident at Gockel's. It had been three days.

When Gutman peered through the eyehole, he saw Gockel waiting outside. He thought he looked like the antiquarian was alone, but he could not be sure. Now, he could never be sure.

Slowly, he opened the door without unlatching the chain.

"What do you want?" he asked.

"We need to talk," said Gockel.

"I don't have time to talk. Go away."

"If you value your lives, you will let me in. Otherwise, they will come for you."

Gutman slid the chain and let Gockel in. He then closed the door swiftly before anything else could get in.

"I'm alone," Gockel said.

"How can I be sure of that?" said Cairo.

"You are right. You can't," replied the antiquarian.

"What are they?" asked Cairo.

"Maupassant called them Horla. Sometimes they are referred to as Striges. What they call themselves, God alone knows. Either way, for your sakes, I have convinced them to offer you a deal instead of killing you—or worse."

"Even after I killed one of them?"

"You did not kill one of them. If you had, there would be no hope for you, but fortunately, they are hard to kill."

"What is the deal?" asked Gutman.

"It's a simple one. They want you to work for them. They have need of agents in the outside world. Particularly, agents who, like you, live on the wrong side of the law. There are others: my family; the captain of the *Endymion*…"

"So he was in league with them…" said Gutman.

"You figured that out?"

"I have had a lot of time to think. There was one of them on the voyage over. That's how they knew we were planning to, er…"

"Burgle my place?"

"Do business with you."

"Anyway, the captain has made a fair profit for himself by transporting them all over the world. So has my family. It's the only good thing about them. They pay well."

"And I am to become their agent?"

"Yes. Sometime, they, or one of their other agents, will make contact with you. Whatever they ask of you, I suggest you do it, no matter how horrible."

"So we are to be their slaves," said Gutman.

"Not quite. It's possible that that time will never come. In the mean time, you are free to continue your search for this Falcon. In fact, they might even help you if you behave yourself. If not, you may be killed, o, as I said, worse."

"What is worse than being killed?"

"Believe me, you don't want to know," said Gockel.

"We don't have any choice, do we?"asked Cairo.

"No."

"Very well. We accept," said Gutman.

"I will tell them." Gockel walked to the door. He stopped and turned to the two and added, "Do not think of betraying your agreement. They would not take that kindly."

He opened the door and went out.

"What are we to do now?" asked Cairo.

"Whatever they ask," replied Gutman. "We have no choice. I believe I can handle just about anything human, but this is another matter. Still, there is one thing they will not stop me from doing, and that is to find the Falcon."

"We don't have any idea where it is," said Cairo.

"No, but as I said, I have been thinking. We lost sight of it in Constantinople. It is time we return there and see if we can pick up the trail."

"What happens when they come for us?" said Cairo.

Gutman was silent. Then he said, "Then, God help us all."

Rick Lai's stories are part of a vast jigsaw puzzle, all the pieces of which fit with remarkable precision. This new story will remind our long-time readers of incidents mentioned in his earlier tales, going back all the way to our Volume 2! Irene Chupin and Josephine Balsamo continue their deadly dance, with a dollop of martial arts thrown into the mix. We should also recommend Rick's two similarly-themed collections, Shadows of the Opera: Retribution in Blood *(2013), and* Sisters of the Shadows: The Cagliostro Curse *(2013), both available from Black Coat Press, which expand on his clever tapestry...*

Rick Lai: *The Prisoner of Countess Cagliostro*

Provence, 1885

The young girl unlatched the window in the large attic above the second floor of the residence. Taking a deep breath, she contemplated the irrevocable action that she had chosen. Having lived on this earth for fifteen years, Irene was about to terminate her own existence. In Paris, she had been taught by the nuns that all suicides were sent by God directly to Hell, but her continued confinement in the den of depravity posing as a school already placed her on a road to damnation.

Clad only in a long white nightgown, Irene positioned her feet on the sill and her hands the sides of window. While the wind blew her hair sideways, she looked towards at the moon and the stars. Her gaze then shifted downward towards the large gate separating the boarding school from the Provence countryside.

"Holy Mary, Mother of God, have mercy me!" she yelled.

Before Irene could fall forward, her shoulder was grabbed by a blonde girl behind her.

"Rochelle! Orianne! Help drag her inside!"

Two other girls seized Irene's arms.

"I have her" asserted the blonde. "Let her go." The other two girls released Irene's arms. Resting on her back, Irene struggled to break free. Straddling her younger opponent, the blonde's hands pressed down on her captive's shoulders.

A girl with curly red hair closed the window. "Shall I inform Madame Fourneau?"

"No, Orianne," replied the blonde. "Madame must remain totally ignorant about this."

"I don't understand, Josephine," stated the blonde's other companion. Unlike the others present, the brown-haired girl's nightgown was black rather than white. "Surely Madame would want to punish our fellow prefect. Such behavior merits a flogging."

"Don't be a fool, Rochelle!" snapped Josephine. "Your own conduct merits a flogging."

"For what offense?" challenged Rochelle.

"Negligence," declared Josephine.

"I performed my duties" argued Rochelle. "I escorted Irene from our sleeping quarters to Madame's office at the midnight hour. I waited patiently outside while Madame performed the initiation ceremony. A half hour later, I escorted the new prefect back to our bedroom."

"And foolishly forgot to ensure that the door was locked before falling asleep," added Josephine. "You are responsible for the new recruit fleeing to the attic."

"Only you have a set of keys," pleaded Rochelle. "You were sleeping."

Josephine smiled as she touched a ring of keys hanging from a chain around her neck. "You should have awakened me."

"Perhaps Josephine is correct," volunteered Orianne. "We should handle this matter ourselves."

"No need for further debate," decreed Josephine. "Leave me alone with Irene."

After Rochelle and Orianne had departed, Josephine's eyes stared directly into Irene's.

"You have a choice to make, my sweet *protégée*," she said. "I am going to release my hold if you agree to listen to my offer. Once I have finished, you will be free to reject my proposal and seek the oblivion of suicide. I promise not to intervene. Do you agree to my terms?"

"Yes."

Releasing her grip on Irene, Josephine stood erect. Irene lifted herself up. Tears filled her eyes. "Madame Fourneau... She..."

"I know," asserted Josephine. "But if you perform a certain act at my request, I will ensure that Madame will never place her filthy hands on you ever again."

"Why should I trust the word of her chief prefect?" replied Irene "You've tormented me since my arrival. You've forced me to become a prefect. Your hand held the lash when my coerced punishment was ordered. Whatever immoral act you want to perform, I won't do it!"

"The act isn't immoral. I want you to forgive me."

"What?"

Tears began to fall from Josephine's eyes. "I have sinned against you. Irene. I beg your forgiveness," she said.

Irene hesitated for a moment before giving her reply. She was clearly struggling to decide on answer.

"I forgive you," she finally whispered.

As Josephine hugged her, Irene murmured:

"Something beautiful may have been born here tonight."

Paris, 1898

Regaining consciousness, the female operative of the Chupin Detective Agency was greeted by the mocking voice of her captor.

"Your ring is very appropriate, my old classmate. Once more, we cross swords."

These words were uttered in the spring of 1898 by Josephine Balsamo, the notorious criminal feared as Countess Cagliostro. She made this observation in the cellar of a house in Paris. Clad in a green dress, she stood next to a table. Resting on its surface was an umbrella in which was sheathed a sword, a Cordobes hat, a pair of silver bracelets with very sharp edges, a large brooch in the shape of a silver pentagram, a telephone, an old magazine, a bottle, a hypodermic needle, and a notebook with the words *Rahilly Project* written on its cover. On a smaller table was a lantern, the only source of illumination for the room. The bulk of the cellar was shrouded in darkness.

Josephine's blue eyes stared triumphantly at the slender woman whose black hair was bound in a French braid. Wearing an orange dress, her hands were encased in elegant black gloves. Over the fourth finger of her gloved right hand was a ring bearing the image of two swords intertwined.

"In lieu of wedding ring, you bear a representation of the lengthy duel that binds our destinies together," continued Josephine. "I appreciate the symbolism. I shall adopt your standard as my own when I resume my vendetta against my half-brother. Would you like to hear my plans concerning him?"

"Not particularly. The only person whom I despise more than Arsène is standing before me," replied Irene.

"In the thirteen years since we first met, you have been known as Irene Chupin, Irene Tupin and Irene Lupin. The surname would vary, but you were always Irene. Now your nom de guerre is Irina Putine. For old times' sake, may I address you as Irene?"

"I prefer Irina."

"As you wish. Relish your false identity of a Russian émigré while you can. Your true identity is known to the highest echelons of the Black Coats. A mere whisper into a journalist's ear would expose you as the sexual predator who tormented girls at a notorious boarding school. The public that worship you as a fearless investigator would recoil in disgust."

"Enough empty threats! The Black Coats want the public to forget about the Fourneau College for Young Women. We are not the only prominent ladies who attended that institution. Two High Council members, Professor Chauvain and Madame Koluchy, as well as several of their top lieutenants, learned their diabolical talents at our former *alma mater*. Any further inquiries in the school would disrupt their criminal operations."

"Very perceptive. Any objections to reminiscing about the good old days then?"

"None. A question has long perplexed me. Why did you prevent my suicide?"

"Such a death would be too quick for the daughter of the man who lured my mother to her death."

"For the record, a witness claims that your mother was trying to lure my father into a trap. One of my father's innumerable lovers fatally stabbed her."

"Don't be ridiculous! Théophraste Lupin betrayed everyone foolish enough to trust him. He even allowed you to be punished for one of your brother's thefts. I heard the details of my mother's stabbing from her own mouth as her life slowly ebbed away. She wasn't slain by an inconsequential rival for your father's affection. My mother's life was the price paid by your father to share the Revenant's bed!"

"The Revenant! She was the woman who stabbed your mother!"

"My mother made me swear an oath of vengeance against the family of her betrayer. You were the first victim of my vendetta. I saved your life in order to corrupt it. I groomed you to succeed me as Fourneau's chief prefect. In the false security of your position as the *de facto* ruler of the school, you were an easy target for the assassin that I had cultivated. I remember my College Girl Murderer fondly. Do you?"

"Your killer failed! I still live! He later died by my hands!"

"But they aren't really yours, my sweet. Doctor Cerral grafted to your wrists the flesh of another victim dissected by my underling's knife."

"Part of that girl's soul still resides in these hands. Her fingers crave to snuff out your life."

"I forget the names of inconsequential casualties. Who was the other girl?"

"Teresa Grévin. She was far from inconsequential."

"Oh yes, I remember her from the newspapers accounts. She was the daughter of Violette Mathilde Grévin, an overrated singer at the *Tivoli* cabaret in Avignon. Having been nearly bored to death by attending one of Violette's performances, I feel no guilt about causing her offspring's death."

"Teresa didn't deserve to die!"

"Mademoiselle Putine, you are being foolishly sentimental," suddenly interjected another feminine voice. "Teresa was merely a pawn in the deadly chess game which you and Countess Cagliostro play. My own role closely resembles a queen's."

The new speaker emerged from a dark corner of the basement. Clothed in a white dress worthy of a pagan goddess, the woman's neck and back were exposed. With the exceptions of two thin straps that prevented her dress from falling to the ground, her shoulders were bare. Two long thin creases ran along the front of her dress along her long, smooth legs. Her naturally pale skin had been rendered bronze by long exposure to the sun. As dark as her probing eyes, her hair was pinned to flow upward. Each of her earrings was in the shape of a silver lotus.

Irina's eyes flashed with recognition "I see! You pretended to trip on the sidewalk while exiting a carriage. Bumping into me, your hand rubbed against my neck, and that's why I lost consciousness."

"Yes. I caused you to sleep by pinching a nerve," explained the gloved damsel. "It was child's play to place you in the carriage and bring you here."

"Your jewelry links you to the Wu Fang Clan, the pirate confederation of Formosa," noted Irina.

"An astute observation," replied the woman in white. "My name is Fabiana Mata. I was born into a family of Portuguese merchants in Macao. Denied a role in the family business due in my gender, I led the pirates of the South China Sea. The flag of the Wu Fang Clan is a silvery white lotus. It indicates that the criminal dynasty founded by Wu Fang is subservient to a far more formidable organization, the White Lotus Tong. Every year, the Wu Fang Clan delivers a percentage of its plunder to Temple of the Five Hundred Steps, the headquarters of the White Lotus Tong. While delivering our annual tribute, I enchanted the reigning High Priest and became his pupil in the martial arts. I eventually became his Divine Consort. I am the first High Priestess in the Tong's history."

A grim realization was suddenly reflected in Irina's eyes. "I foolishly assumed myself to be Josephine's principal target. I was wrong. The real target is my associate, Blythe Furnace."

"You're finally beginning to see the big picture," concluded Josephine.

"Mademoiselle Putine, please explain the connections between your colleague and the White Lotus Tong," requested Fabiana. "I enjoy the sound of your voice."

"Blythe was trained by the Iga ninjas. Blood Flesh, a female member of the Koga ninjas, the historical rivals of the Iga clan, forged an alliance with the White Lotus Tong by seducing its ruler. After Blythe slew Blood Flesh in combat, the High Priest sought vengeance. He severely wounded Blythe. I won't go into details!"

"But I want to go into the goriest details!" proclaimed Fabiana. "The high priest plucked out Furnace's right eye and then raped her. This was my husband's ultimate revenge; Furnace was forced to bear his child. She gave birth to a daughter and christened her Legacy. Hearing of his daughter's birth, my beloved searched for her. However, Furnace had hidden her child in one of the secret Iga villages in Japan."

"So that's your game!" exclaimed Irina. "Three weeks ago, Madame Koluchy, Josephine's rival in the Black Coats, abducted Legacy and brought her to France as part of a scheme to destroy Blythe. My colleague rescued her and humiliated Koluchy before scores of her followers. Word of Legacy's kidnapping by Koluchy must have reached the White Lotus Tong. Their leader dispatched you to gain possession of Legacy."

"My original intention was to purchase Legacy from Koluchy," said Fabiana, "but Furnace had rescued her progeny. Koluchy had retreated from Paris in disgrace. I hired Countess Cagliostro to find Legacy."

"The Black Coats have always had informants inside the Paris police," asserted Josephine. "We know that Blythe and her daughter are secretly staying at house of Chief Inspector Jacques Lefebvre. Rather than launch an immediate assault on their household, we intend to eliminate Blythe first, and then seize Legacy."

"Which means that I am the bait in your trap," concluded Irina. "You're being a fool, Josephine. As Koluchy and her underlings found their detriment, Blythe is ruthless when protecting her daughter. She will not hesitate to take your life."

Josephine laughed before replying, "I have no intention of engaging Blythe in physical combat. Fabiana is quite capable of single-handedly eliminating Blythe. Her Tong has created several invincible warriors by bathing them in a fluid that enables the skin to harden if properly controlled by the mind."

"Your friend's ninja skills are no match for my steel-skin Kung Fu," boasted the High Priestess. "I can make my body impervious to harm from knife, swords, and even bullets."

"I am familiar with your so-called steel-skin methods," claimed Irina. "You have at least two weaknesses."

"You must have read Kegan Van Roon's recently published *Secrets of the Thirty-Sixth Chamber*," deduced Fabiana. "He argued that steel-skin fighters are vulnerable to blows to their eyes and to the organs between their legs. I have developed tools to protect my eyes. As for Van Roon's other assertion, it applies only to a male combatant."

"There are other weaknesses that you aren't even considering!"

"I have heard enough!" decided Fabiana. "Countess Cagliostro, silence this chattering upstart!"

Reaching into left her left sleeve, Josephine pulled out a handkerchief and stuffed it into Irina's mouth.

"Black Eyebrow, step forth," commanded Fabiana.

Another woman emerged from the darkened areas of the basement. She was wearing a corset made from the skin of the snow leopard of Tibet. Black pants covered her legs and her feet were encased in sandals of the same hue. Her long black hair covered her shoulders. Her most remarkable features were the thick black eyebrows that situated over her sparkling green eyes.

166

"Did Putine speak long enough?" asked Fabiana.

"Yes, Divine Consort," the newcomer replied.

"Repeat her last sentence."

"There are other weaknesses that you aren't even considering."

"A perfect imitation of Irina's voice," declared Fabiana. "Proceed with the plan."

Black Eyebrow picked up the telephone. After contacting the operator, she connected to the Lefebvre residence.

"Hello, Madame Lefebvre, it's Irina. Could you please put Blythe on the line?... Blythe, I'm calling from a restaurant near the abandoned Black Coat base from the Bluebeard III case. Yes, the old mansion in the Rue St. Claude... I searched that house and found a secret room which the police overlooked. Inside were more than twenty filing cabinets full of documents written in Japanese. I need your expertise to determine their significance. Could you join me there? Wonderful! *Au revoir.*"

Black Eyebrow hung up the telephone.

"Countess, remove our guest's gag. Well, Mademoiselle Putine, were you impressed by Black Eyebrow's vocal skills?"

"Not at all! Her American accent was quite evident in her pronunciation of the French street. Blythe will deduce that she spoke to an impostor."

A flabbergasted Fabiana slapped Black Eyebrow's face.

"Fool! You assured me your French was impeccable!"

Black Eyebrow seemed totally unfazed by Fabiana's scornful slap.

"Nothing is wrong with my French," she said. "Putine wants to trick us into quarreling among ourselves."

"How could she have deduced your American nationality?"

"She has a memory for faces. Countess, please show my mistress what you showed me yesterday?"

Grabbing the magazine on the table, Josephine brought it to the High Priestess. It was the spring 1894 issue of *La Vie Française*. Opening it to the middle, Fabiana beheld an illustrated article bearing a lurid title: *The She-Devil of San Francisco: American Heiress Flees Country After Beating Child to Death*. The subject was Wilfreda Tillman, a young socialite who'd succumbed to a murderous rage when a ten year-old boy had bumped into her on the street. Next to the article was a full-length photo of the murderess in an evening gown.

Fabiana glared angrily at Irina. "You read that article years ago. Memories of that photograph prompted your identification of Black Eyebrow as Wilfreda Tillman. There were no flaws in her pronunciation."

"I was hoping that your anger would result in her being *hors de combat*. Van Roon wrote that a single face slap from a steel-skin expert could break an opponent's neck, but your sycophant suffered no injury. Perhaps you exaggerate your skills?"

"You misread the evidence," argued Fabiana. "Black Eyebrow is no one's sycophant. Today was not the first time that I unjustly struck her. In order to protect her from my temper tantrums, I trained her in steel-skin combat. No one's hands can harm her, including my own. The former Wilfreda has evolved into a cunning advisor. Unlike me, she has mastered her anger."

"A notable achievement for a murderous slut."

"Putine, you have a sharp tongue!" shouted Black Eyebrow.

"I have an even sharper sword."

"Your blade is a trivial inconvenience against a woman of my talents. The Divine Consort's agreement with the Countess prohibits me from tearing out your tongue. I must only relish this gesture of contempt."

Black Eyebrow spat in Irina's right eye.

"Bravo!" shouted Fabiana. "My husband imported a Tibetan snow leopard to fight me in the arena at our Temple. After breaking the beast's neck with my bare hands, I gave the carcass to Black Eyebrow as a gift. Her lovely corset was the result. After I snap Blythe's neck, her corpse shall become my *protégée's* property. Undoubtedly, she will find a creative use for the remains."

"Not if Blythe creatively causes your last breath," warned Irina.

"As you may have guessed already, the house where we are is also Rue St. Claude. Black Eyebrow, get our coats. Even though we will merely be crossing the street to where we've set our ambush, we don't want to shock Parisians with our exotic dress on this rainy afternoon."

Black Eyebrow briefly entered the darkened area of the cellar. She returned with two hooded coats. Quickly donning them, the pair departed the cellar via the stairs. As the two women crossed the street, Black Eyebrow complained about Irina.

"That skinny detective went out of her way to insult me!"

"Perhaps she harbors a secret grudge against you."

"She looks a lot like that kid Fritz the Dealer had me discipline. Maybe she's his mother?"

"Furnace might be compelled to answer that question. According to the Kunoichi Rules of Engagement, a defeated female ninja must answer one question truthfully."

"Now that my allies have left, we can resume our chat," said Josephine. "Our long duel has scarred our bodies. Your wrists bear the stitches from Cerral's radical surgery. Your first victory over me resulted in my shoulders being branded. Do our souls bear scars as well? My life is not the destiny I yearned for in Provence."

"Remember how you convinced Madame Fourneau to allow our *Mardi-Gras* celebration?" asked the detective. "You dressed up as the legendary White Stalker, the woman who fought vampires and werewolves. You claimed that she was your great-grandmother, the original Josephine Balsamo."

"She was—truly. I am proud to bear her name."

"You regaled me with accounts of her exploits. One of those stories involved your ancestor traveling to the Far East to combat the White Lotus Tong. I doubt that your great-grandmother would approve of your current allies."

"Alliances shift with time. Take the two of us, for example. Didn't you love me once?"

"Yes, but now I feel only hate."

"No, there is a force more powerful than love and hate, and it consumes us both."

"What are you talking about?"

"Haven't you noticed something strange about our vendetta? We are constantly squandering opportunities to kill each another, Whenever I have been your prisoner, you invent a lame reason to spare my life. You want to see me publicly beheaded, or face a Black Coat tribunal, and so forth. As for me, all my schemes involving your demise always take place at the end of our battles. You're always the final victim in a series of planned murders, instead of the first... My worst mistake was preventing your suicide. Since those steel-skin assassins were listening, I gave a false rationale for my unusual act of charity..."

"What is the true reason?"

"Lust. Ever since we first met, I have craved your body. Lust is one of the most potent forces in the universe. Since our school days, my dependency on it has grown even greater. Through studying my ancestor's occult writings, I am able to use the psychic energy generated by lust to accelerate healing. But my lust for you continues to cloud my judgment. I suspect that your own decisions about me have also been hampered by lust. Your hidden desires are a reflection of my own."

"Hidden desires? In the past, I merely underestimated your ability to survive. If these hands ever touch you again, they will quickly dispatch you to Hell."

"I was hoping to negotiate a temporary solution in which you would satisfy my needs, but you force me to pursue another," Josephine said, picking up the hypodermic from the table.

She filled it with the liquid in the bottle. Holding up the needle, she smiled at her bound captive.

"Fourteen years ago, a Cornish doctor invented a super-aphrodisiac that unleashed hedonistic tendencies. Driven insane by the drug, he committed suicide. The formula was believed lost, but some samples had been taken by Mary Rahilly, an accomplice who carried payments from brothel keepers. Recently recruited by the Black Coats, she gave the drug to her new employers. Fearful that the passage of time has weakened its potency, the High Council entrusted its testing to me. Poor Mary tragically perished in a police raid before I could do so. I honored her sacrifice by naming the project after her. So far, a third of my test subjects responded as expected. The other two-thirds went into convulsions and died. Let's see to which of those two groups you belong..."

Raising the hypodermic, Josephine prepared to drive it into the artery on the right side of her captive's neck. But suddenly, Irina's hands were no longer behind her back. They tightly gripped Josephine's wrists.

As the Countess struggled futilely, Irina's left hand turned her foe's right hand and drove the needle into her carotid artery.

Losing consciousness, Josephine fell to the floor. Her body began to shake uncontrollably.

A triumphant Irina gazed down at her squirming adversary. The sleuth then looked at her ring bearing the symbol of the crossed swords. She pushed in the secret blades on both sides of the ring. They had cut through the ropes binding her. After putting on her pentagram brooch, hat, and bracelets, she pulled a sword out of her umbrella.

Josephine ceased writhing on the ground. Her eyes were closed, and no breath appeared to escape from her open mouth.

"Our deadly game of chess is almost over, my sweet Josephine," concluded Irina. "Even though you have conceded the match, your queen and her knight are still making moves."

Across the Rue St. Claude, another woman approached an abandoned house. She was dressed in black pants and boots, as well as a black shirt and cravat. White gloves covered her hands. A black Inverness Cape completed her ensemble. Her right eye was covered by a patch. Hanging from her neck was an amulet in the shape of a cat. Combed backward, her short brown hair gave the impression of a bird's crest. She was Blythe Furnace, ex-ninja, ex-assassin for the Black Coats, and current operative for the Chupin Detective Agency.

Finding the door to the house opened, Blythe entered and was surprised to see two exotically dressed women standing twenty feet away. The room was lit by two lanterns hanging on opposite walls. The women introduced themselves.

"I am Black Eyebrow, the Steel-Skin Siren. My voice lures fools to their doom. Your name shall be inscribed on my scroll of victims. My voice imitated Irina's on the phone. The real Irina is being entertained by Countess Cagliostro."

"I am Fabiana, High Priestess of the White Lotus Tong. The Siren is my obedient servant. Our goggles are constructed from the Unbreakable Glass of Yian. Our eyes are protected from your ninja trickery. In the Temple of the Five Hundred Steps, my husband has a jar containing one of your eyes. He wants a matching pair."

Blythe pulled out a small tour-barreled gun from a coat pocket. She fired all four bullets at the steel-skin assassins, but the White Lotus executioners swatted them aside with a swift movement of their arms. The room then erupted into a medley of punches and kicks.

Blythe's blows proved ineffective against her two assailants, and the fists of the White Lotus assassins took a devastating toll on the former ninja. After Fabiana delivered a series of kicks to Blythe's stomach, the latter dropped to her knees. Extending her arms in order to push her palms against the floor, Blythe prevented herself from falling further. Her right palm rested against a bullet deflected by Fabiana.

"Our foe is exhausted," concluded Black Eyebrow. "Divine Consort, may I ask the question?"

"You may."

"I invoke the Kunoichi Rules of Engagement. Does Irina Putine have a son living on the Island of Lynched Women?"

"Irina has no. children," murmured Blythe.

"Not the answer I expected," noted Black Eyebrow. "Divine Consort, who shall have the honor of the final blow?"

"We shall share that honor. You shall remove her eye. I shall break her neck."

"Get away from her!" shouted Irina suddenly bursting into the house.

She swung her sword at Black Eyebrow. The blade broke in half upon striking the steel-skin fighter's forearm.

Black Eyebrow laughed.

"Your puny sword is useless against..."

The assassin never finished her sentence. Irina had driven her truncated blade through her open mouth and down into her throat. The self-styled Siren had never considered an open mouth to be a potential weakness.

Fabiana only briefly opened her mouth wide in shock, but that interval was long enough for the kneeling Blythe to throw the bullet into it.

Instinctively Fabiana tried to swallow it, but it became stuck in her windpipe. The inability to breathe overwhelmed her.

"Countess Cagliostro is dead, Fabiana," declared Irina. "So is your precious Black Eyebrow. This game of death now reaches its climax. The queen falls."

Gasping for air, the haughty Fabiana expired.

Irina spat on Black Eyebrow's corpse.

"Filthy child murderer. I detest swine like you!"

Blythe spoke with a quivering voice. "Irina, the back of my amulet has a small compartment containing pills. Shove one into my mouth."

After swallowing the pill, Blythe displayed renewed vigor and strength. She was able to stand.

"The Purple Sacrament," she explained. "A rare drug that accelerates healing. A gift from my ex-lover, Antonio Nikola."

"The game of death is not over yet!" suddenly uttered a male voice, "The King still lives!"

A panel opened in the wall facing the two detectives. It revealed a muscular Chinese man wearing a white business suit. His shoulder-length hair was vividly white as was the beard extending to his belt.

Even though he wore goggles, his most prominent feature was his long white eyebrows.

"*Mon Dieu!*" exclaimed Blythe. "The White Priest! Pai Mei! Irina, put on the goggles! Quick!"

Removing the goggles from Fabiana's corpse, Blythe swiftly donned them. Irina did likewise with the goggles of the deceased Black Eyebrow.

"A wise precaution, Nevermore of the Iga clan," said Pai Mei.

"I no longer use that alias. Address me as Blythe Furnace."

"Your change of name shall be noted on the official inventory of my eyeball collection."

"Nice suit."

"The House of Crafts in London made it for me."

"You can wear it to your wife's funeral."

"Twice you have slain a woman dear to me. Now you shall suffer a similar loss—the death of your best friend. Irina Putine shall be the first to die, then you!"

Blythe delivered a series of blows into Pai Mei's body, but they were ineffective. By contrast, a mere slap of Pai Mei's hand against her face rendered her almost unconscious.

As the High Priest slowly approached, Irina knew that she had only one chance to kill him. With all her might, she kicked Pai Mei below the belt. Pain overwhelmed her. Her right foot felt as if it had kicked a fire hydrant.

Losing her balance, she fell backwards. Lying on the floor, she saw Pai Mei grinning at her as he stroked his beard.

"I know the Japanese trick of pulling my lower body organs into my abdomen. You are probably wondering why an unbeatable fighter like myself would entrust Furnace's removal to two accomplices and watch from a secret room? Frankly, I enjoy watching women fight. Additionally, I judged my wife and her assistant more than capable of killing Furnace. Your unexpected intervention shifted the tide of battle. An excruciating death will be the penalty for your intervention. I shall tear out your eyes, tongue, arms and legs in quick succession."

Bending down on one knee, Pai Mei pulled the prostrate Irina's goggles down around her neck.

"Such lovely blue eyes. A superb addition to my collection. Which would you prefer to lose first? The right or the left? You have sixty seconds to decide. Failure to answer will cause me to decide for you."

Irina's only available weapon was the pentagram brooch on the right side of her dress. Its five points were as sharp as knives, but she had no clear plan of attack. Pai Mei's only apparent vulnerability was his mouth when he opened it to speak. Stabbing him there would only minimally damage his tongue. And unlike the bullet which had doomed Fabiana, the brooch was too large to trick the White Priest into swallowing it.

"Your time has expired," said Pai Mei pulling back his right arm to strike.

Unexpectedly, a whip with a silver tip shot through the air and coiled around his right arm. Pulling on the whip, its owner prevented the Priest from injuring Irina.

The whip belonged to a woman dressed in a white tunic with long wide sleeves. Her pants, boots and gloves were also white. A white belt circled her waist. She looked just like Josephine, except she had black hair.

"I am Rylee Balsamo, granddaughter of Cagliostro. I am the woman who unveils the secrets of the human soul. I am the White Stalker."

Grabbing the end of the whip that had wrapped around his arm, Pai Mei yanked the lash out of the newcomer's hands. He then quickly looped the whip around her neck.

"Stalker, die by your own whip!"

But before the High Priest could tighten the whip, Irina attacked from behind. Standing on her injured foot, she ripped off his goggles and rammed one of the sharpened points on her pentagram into his right eye and into his brain.

Falling away from Rylee, the Tong leader uttered his last words:
"Pah Mei shall avenge me."

The White Stalker untangled the whip around her neck.

"*Gracias*, Señorita Putine, your timely intervention saved my life."

"As yours did mine."

"I recognize you and Señorita Furnace from your photographs in the newspapers."

"Call me Irina. Please help me awaken Blythe"

After Blythe had been revived, Rylee explained her antecedents.

"Surety the Chupin Detective Agency has genealogical charts for the Balsamo family?"

"Yes," affirmed Irina, "but your name doesn't appear on any of them."

"Does the name Isabella Riley appear on them?"

"She was the second wife of Joseph Alexander Balsamo, a controversial French scientist who settled in Mexico after being publicly ridiculed for his claims that vampires actually existed. His mother was the first Josephine Balsamo, the original White Stalker."

"Joseph and Isabella are my parents," professed Rylee. "They kept my birth a secret because the Black Coats have been targeting members of my family for years."

"For the updating of our Agency's files, I'd like to get the correct spellings," insisted Irina. "Our files spell your mother's last name as "R-E-I-L-L-Y.""

"That's incorrect. My mother's family uses the spelling of R-I-L-E-Y." Furthermore, my first name, a variant of my mother's maiden name, is R-Y-L-E-E. I can list all the other variant spellings of my mother's maiden name if you wish."

"That won't be necessary. Please clarify your family relationship to the second Josephine and her daughter."

"Born in 1845, the second Josephine was my half-sister, the oldest of my father's children. When she reached the age of 22, a serious schism developed between her and my father. He refused her request to succeed her grandmother as the next White Stalker. Because my grandmother died heroically fighting an unspeakable foe, my father feared that my headstrong sister would similarly perish if she became the White Stalker. Thus, he refused her request. This refusal combined with my father's decision to move the family to Mexico angered my sister.

"Rebelling against our father, she joined the Black Coats. In 1868, my father, by then a 52-year-old widower, married my mother. I was born two years later. Recognizing that his efforts to preserve his firstborn's life had resulted in her corruption by the Black Coats, my father wisely granted my request to become the new White Stalker. I never met my late sister or her daughter, the third Josephine. Although we are roughly the same age, I am technically her aunt. My niece is a vicious criminal who must face justice. I came here to end her reign of terror."

"What caused you to come to this address?" asked Irina.

"In a London bar, I encountered a drunken old man with a harmonica tied around his neck. Calling me 'Countess,' he asked why was I was wearing a black wig. Realizing he had mistaken me for my criminal niece, I loosened his tongue with more liquor. His name was Larry Parker. He works at the House of Crafts, the London clothing firm which is controlled by the Black Coats. On a recent business trip to Paris, Josephine had him deliver a white suit to a mysterious Chinese gentleman at this address."

"I know Parker," admitted Blythe. "He's an old crony of the late Professor Moriarty. The High Council uses him for minor errands. I knew he played a Galician harp, but I was unaware of his expertise with a harmonica."

"Are we sure that there are no other Tong members lurking about?" wondered Irina. "Pai Mei said that Pah Mei will avenge him."

"Don't worry about Pah Mei," insisted Blythe. "He's in China. Contrary to popular belief, Pai Mei isn't a single man, but a succession of High Priests hiding their real identities beneath a shared alias and an unruly mass of facial hair. Upon his coronation, a new High Priest adopts the name of Pai Mei and alters his physical appearance to conform to that of his predecessors. He also names another steel-skin fighter to be his successor. This Heir Apparent is called Pah Mei. The designated successor lives in seclusion at the Temple of the Five Hundred Steps until his elevation to High Priest following the death of the reigning Pai Mei."

"Then Josephine is our only surviving adversary. Where is she?"

"She's in the basement of a house across the street," volunteered Irina. "She tried to inject me with a deadly drug, but fell victim to it. She's dead."

Rylee briefly sighed. "I should feel sorry that my niece is dead, but I don't. May I see her body?"

The two investigators concurred. Before departing, Blythe reloaded her four-barreled silver-plated gun with bullets from one of her coat pockets. Irina reattached her brooch's pin to her dress, even though it was covered with Pai Mei's blood.

Since it was getting dark, Irina took one of the wall-lanterns with her. Having taken one of Blythe's pills, she no longer limped. It was now raining hard. Despite running fast, the three women were drenched when they reached the first house.

"The one time I need my umbrella to act like an ordinary umbrella rather than a sword, it's broken," joked Irina.

"At least, your hat protected your hair from the rain," observed Rylee.

"It also protects my hair during fights. The chin strap prevents it from falling off my head."

"My tunic is soaking wet," admitted Rylee. "I'm going to take it off.

Removing her tunic, Rylee revealed a white corset underneath. Her shoulders and back looked extremely attractive.

Holding the lantern in front of her, Irina led her two companions through the cellar doorway and down the stairs.

"Josephine's body! It's gone!"

Irina bent down near the spot where her nemesis had fallen. She picked up an object from the floor. It was a harmonica tied to a cord.

"Larry Parker's harmonica!" professed Rylee. "He must have moved her corpse."

"But that makes no sense," objected Blythe. "You last saw him in London. Why would he suddenly come to Paris?"

"Parker is the High Council's errand boy. Irina mentioned that Josephine was experimenting with dangerous drugs. Maybe the Council dispatched Parker with new orders regarding those experiments?"

"Look over there!" indicated Irina. "There's a door."

Opening the door, Irina revealed an entrance to a closet. Inside were whips, chains and various costumes of a scandalous nature, ranging from a parody of a nun's attire s to a female version of an American cowboy.

"It seems Josephine had some unusual hobbies." commented Blythe. "Someone's also been extremely careless. There's broken glass of the floor."

"I never imagined that a member of my family would behave so disgustingly."

"Irina, could you tell us more about the drug that killed Josephine?" asked Blythe.

"According to her, it was created by an unnamed Cornish doctor. She identified one of his underlings as a woman with her surname written on the cover of her notebook."

Irina held Josephine's notebook with the words *Rahilly Project*.

"Rylee, does this name means anything to you?"

"*Ra-hil-ly*. Other than rhyming with *Swahili*, it has no significance to me."

Blythe shook her head. "I don't recognize the name, nor do I remember any scandal in Cornwall involving a doctor."

Irina moved directly in front of Rylee, "Will the new White Stalker do me the honor of holding hands with me?"

The two women intertwined their fingers.

"Rylee, look into my eyes. I know the truth. You and Josephine mispronounced the name on the notebook. It has only two syllables. The name R-A-H-I-L-L-Y is a variant of Riley, and pronounced exactly the same. If you really were the daughter of Isabella Riley Balsamo, you would have known that the project's name was actually a variant of her maiden name. Your mother was actually the second Josephine Balsamo."

For a moment, Rylee shivered, but Irene's soothing voice calmed her.

"You were worried that Blythe and I might reject you because you lied about your past, but we are guilty of the same offense. Just as Irene Chupin became Irina Putine, and Berenice Fourneau became Blythe Furnace, the third Josephine Balsamo has been transformed into Rylee Balsamo. Josephine called the drug's inventor 'a Cornish doctor' not because the doctor lived in Cornwall, but because his name originated in Cornwall. That doctor actually lived in London. In 1885, he became the center of a scandal so bizarre that the French press covered it extensively. His real name was Henry Jekyll.

"It is falsely believed by many that his serum releases the evil side of the human soul. I read his confession in a French newspaper. His belief was that the human soul has multiple personalities hidden inside it. But in reality, his potion just releases one of those personalities. In Jekyll's case, it was an evil persona. It could be a good persona. I have spoken enough. It is time for Rylee to tell us tell us the truth in her words."

"I was a prisoner inside Josephine's body for decades. I functioned as a static observer. I could only watch. I could never interfere. Josephine and I greatly admired our great-grandmother, but she only managed to live up to our ancestor's high standards on a few notable occasions. I watched Josephine descend to the farthest depths of self-degradation as she feasted on the fruits of vengeance.

"My other self has had innumerable romances with both men and women. Of all her lovers, only two instilled romances inside my heart. The first was a young circus acrobat in Normandy. I am not at liberty to discuss him. The second is standing before me. Irina, I can't dissect Josephine's true feelings towards you. Her mind is a complex maze of love and hate. Nevertheless, I do know that Josephine's decision to stop your suicide was not motivated by lust as she earlier asserted. That night in 1885, she was consumed by the same love that fills my soul anytime you are near.

"You thought the comatose Josephine had died, but she was slowly transforming into me. Once the transformation was complete, I heard you leave through the door at the top of the stairs. Rising from the floors, I looked into a mirror. My eyes and hair were now a different hue than Josephine's. Feeling my shoulders and back, I knew that the scars of Fourneau's whip and Koluchy's branding irons were gone.

"Deciding to assist you and Blythe in fighting the White Lotus assassins, I opened Josephine's shameful closet to get a whip that could be used in combat. Josephine had created a replica of our great-grandmother's clothes and whip. Whereas she had denigrated them in sinful practices, I used them to become a new White Stalker. As I was removing the costume from the closet, a harmonica fell on the fell on the floor. It came from an American cowboy custom. Josephine based the costume on reports of a harmonica-playing outlaw.

"Fearful that you and Blythe would reject me if you knew my true origins, I concocted the elaborate fiction of being Isabella Riley Balsamo's daughter. Since Larry Parker had actually delivered the suit to Pai Mei, I used him to justify my knowledge of the street address. I even falsely portrayed Parker as a harmonica player to explain Josephine's disappearance.

"Josephine's closet also housed also the remaining bottles of Jekyll's drug. I used the silver tip of my whip to destroy them all. Not only have I deprived the Black Coats of a powerful weapon, but I have made my flesh the perfect prison to hold Josephine. Only another dose of Jekyll's drug could reverse my transformation.

"I know that the battle seems won, my friends, but it isn't. Irina, your brother is in great danger."

"Normally I would say something nasty about Arsène, but he is my only brother."

"No, you have another brother, only six years-old. He's the son of the Revenant, Kenton Lupin."

"Where is he?"

"The Black Coats are holding him prisoner in a remote location. I have to show you on a map. There are atlases upstairs."

"While the two of you are looking at maps, I'll call the police," said Blythe. "We can't just leave three corpses in a deserted house without promptly notifying the authorities.

"Yes. We waited far too long."

Embracing each other, the two women passionately kissed. Irina's eyes followed Rylee up the stairs.

"Rescuing your brother should be easy. I'll just impersonate Josephine, and Kenton's jailers will surrender him to my custody."

They reached the living room of the house. Rylee's gray eyes sparkled as she smiled at her companion.

"Irina, there is something we both want."

Embracing each other, the two women kissed passionately. Irina briefly closed her eyes. But when she opened them, she was staring into the eyes of Josephine Balsamo.

Blythe ran up the stairs. Reaching the living room, she beheld Josephine holding Irina in front of her, her left arm wrapped around the other woman's neck. The Countess' right hand gripped the pentagram brooch. One of its sharp points was already close to Irina's throat.

Blythe pointed her gun at Josephine's face.

"Blythe, you know that before your bullet reaches me, I'll have slit Irina's throat," said Josephine. "So let's skip the banter and strike a deal now. I'll release Irina and surrender the brooch. You let me put Rylee's tunic to cover my scarred shoulders and allow me to escape before the police arrive. Agreed?"

"Agreed."

Releasing Irina, Josephine dropped the brooch. Picking up Rylee's tunic, she quickly put it on.

"How did you return?" asked Irina.

"As I told you earlier, I can use Cagliostro's magic to manipulate energy generated by lust. There was enough lust in that kiss to fuel my resurrection. Poor Rylee! By destroying Jekyll's drug, she's doomed herself to be my prisoner forever. It's tragic that she never told you where I've imprisoned Kenton. Such a darling boy! He looks just like you. His guardians are finding the best teachers for him. They even allowed the late Black Eyebrow to tutor him. Irina, our game has ended in stalemate. You forgot to protect your queen."

And Josephine fled into the night.

An emotionally devastated Irina fell to her knees. Tears flowed down her cheeks.

"I've lost everything tonight."

Blythe gently lifted her back up.

"You're wrong, Irina. You can still rescue your loved ones."

"But there's no way to bring Rylee back."

"If magic can bring Josephine back, it can also bring Rylee back. We need an occult scholar who's opposed to the Black Coats. Rylee mentioned such a person..."

"Josephine's grandfather."

"Yes. We'll go to Mexico after we rescue Kenton from the Island of Lynched Women—a secret criminal colony in the South Pacific"

"How do you know that's where Kenton is?"

"Black Eyebrow asked me whether you have a son living there, and Josephine's parting remarks put that question in context."

As the women in the Cordobes hat and in the Inverness cape continued to formulate a plan to rescue Kenton, their shadows seemed to merge into a single entity—a frightening figure in a hat and cloak.

This TV extravaganza which begins with characters from House *and mixes characters from* Nikita *(2010),* Buckaroo Banzai *and* The Thing *(1982) also features the duo of Leonox and Lisa, the envoys of extra-dimensional powers beyond human ken, who appeared earlier in Atom Bezecny's story, but play a much greater role here. They are the creation of French writer Paul Bérato (1915-1989) who penned numerous popular adventure, genre and juvenile novels from the early 1940s to the mid-1980s, using a myriad of pseudonyms such as Jean Vier, Michel Avril, Jean Mars, Paul Mystère, Yves Dermèze, John Luck, and Paul Béra. Leonox and Lisa were featured in six novels published by Fleuve Noir in the early 1970s...*

Jean-Marc Lofficier: *The Taste of Death*

New Jersey, The Early 2000s

I watched from a distance in the hallway, waiting for my check up.

"She's crashing," shouted Dr. Cameron.

"Get the pads, stat!" shouted Dr. Chase.

The grim sound of a patient flatlining came from the devices attached to her body, immediately followed by Chase's voice screaming "Clear!" and the characteristic zap of the resuscitation device.

"She's back," said Dr. Foreman as the "beeps" restarted.

But as it turned out, the patient—Victoria Madsen—my sole reason for being there—wasn't back at all. Unbeknownst to the three doctors at this stage, she had rabies. And, despite all of their efforts, she passed away a few days later.

What Dr. House's remarkable team never learned was that her body vanished from the Morgue at Princeton-Plainsboro Teaching Hospital a few days later. An administrative error was blamed, the paperwork quickly buried, and things soon returned to normal. But the real culprit was I, Percival "Percy" Rose, the head of Division.

Division is a secret U.S. government-funded organization responsible for what we called "black ops" in the trade, but which other, less genteel folk, would dub sabotage and assassination, with a dash of under-the-table, private murder-for-hire on the side. Pension plans aren't what they used to be, and one has to take care of one's own golden years.

But in the case of Ms. Madsen, I wasn't working on Division's clock. In fact, my colleagues would have been greatly surprised to learn the reason I was there wasn't for a checkup. (I'm in very good health, thank you!)

Because while Virginia Madsen was the one transported to Princeton-Plainsboro, it was someone else entirely who walked out—yes, I did say "walked"—a few days later after her death, wearing her body.

It was Lisa.

I can see that an explanation is in order.

First, there are other, let's call them "dimensions," above (or is it below or sideways?) our own. And in these dimensions live nameless "Powers" who occasionally interfere with us. From what I can gather, there are also other superior dimensions with other Powers who also interfere with the former, and so forth and s on. On Earth, the Powers operate through agents and pawns. For the time being, I'm a pawn; I hope someday to become a full-fledged agent, hence my concern about squirreling away enough cash for my golden years which, I hope, will last a very long time indeed.

I was told all this by my predecessor, a French journalist named Francis Dalvant; he was a pawn who never became an agent, but he had a good run before, er, "retiring." He had been a serial killer named Lacana who was resurrected into Dalvant's body. I don't know what happened to him, but he had lived two lives—perhaps more. I hope I can do this too; it sure would beat a condo in Cancun.

The agent is the person who "runs" me—her name is Lisa. She is constantly at war with another agent called Leonox. Like Dalvant, they switch bodies; they are resurrected time and time again in the body of a freshly-deceased person. Mind you, they don't look like the deceased—it would create to many problems, and the Powers have seen to that—but for the process to work, there must be a fresh corpse.

Lisa generally works alone, but I usually receive a message from the Power who controls her about when and where she's going to reappear next, so I can be there to, shall we say, facilitate the paperwork. Leonox works in fancier ways: he has an entire sect of pawns who worship him; when he comes back, they steal a body, lock it up for a night inside a stone coffin, and presto, at dawn, Leonox steps out.

Pawns like me can always recognize Leonox and Lisa, no matter what their incarnations look like. Lisa has ink-black irises and Leonox a crooked smile—only the right half of his mouth smiles, never the left. I have no idea why that is, but it does make our lives simpler.

When the Power who controls Lisa told me she was about to return, I knew Leonox would soon be back too, so I started a discreet watch on neighboring funeral parlors, cemeteries, etc. More corpses disappear than you might suspect, and Granny's ashes are not always hers, if you see what I mean. It's a cutthroat business, not as cutthroat as mine, but close enough.

It didn't take me long to zero in on a suspect; it helped that the Sect was anything but subtle. A second-tier mobster had just died in a car accident, one Christopher Moltisanti, and my educated guess was that his body had been snatched between the undertaker and the burial plot. I said "car accident," but Leonox, unlike Lisa, only used bodies that had died a violent death, so I suspected there may have been more to it than what the official report claimed, but none of that was my business.

There may be other agents operating on Earth than Leonox and Lisa, but I have never met any. Dalvant told me of other entities he'd met, projections of those higher beings, but so far, I've been spared that.

One last word: don't assume that Lisa is good, and Leonox evil, or that one stands for order and the other for chaos. That is the stuff of cheap melodrama. The truth is, I don't know why we do what we do. Is it all a game? A form of nourishment? Is there any purpose at all to this? I honestly don't know. I don't think anyone, including Leonox and Lisa, knows.

Now that I've explained all this, we can go on.

So I picked up Lisa outside Princeton-Plainsboro's Morgue in a black Optima. She didn't look too different from the Madsen woman, but I recognized her right away thanks to her ink-black irises.

I gather that she and Dalvant had a closer relationship that involved more banter, but chit-chat has never been my bailiwick. So it was down to business from the get go.

"Where are we going?" I asked.

"Have you heard of Outpost 31?" she replied.

"No. What is it?"

"I don't know. The Power who controls me is keen on stopping something that's connected with a place called Outpost 31. I thought you might know."

I smiled. Lisa is… ageless. She's probably been around for a thousand years, maybe more… She does her best to keep up with the times, but sometimes her understanding of our environment is partial, at best. She knew who I was and what I did—that is, after all, why they had recruited me. You don't get to become a pawn of the Powers if you're an accountant or a scout leader. But she didn't grasp that I didn't have all of Uncle Sam's top secret information at my fingertip.

But I could get it.

"Let's go to my office," I said.

Division employs a terrific hacker named Seymour Birkhoff (real name Lionel Peller) once known in the trade as "Shadowwalker," whom I had recruited while he was in prison for having gained access to the Pentagon's files from his college dorm room.

It didn't take long for Birkhoff to find what Outpost 31 was, and I impressed upon him the need for the utmost discretion, probably giving him a few more nightmares in the process. That search would never appear in Division's records,.

Back in the Optima in Division's underground lot, I told Lisa what I'd found.

"Outpost 31 is—was—a U.S. research station in Antarctica twenty years ago. It had a crew of twelve men. They all died and the station was totally destroyed under mysterious circumstances. My guy had to dig very deep to get at the truth—SHADO, UNIT, the BPRD, none of them had anything on it. We finally found what we were looking for not even online, but in a pamphlet published by a bunch of kooks known as the 'Lone Gunmen.'

"What destroyed Outpost 31 and its crew was a hostile alien they— or a Norwegian crew—the details remain hazy—buried under the ice. Some kind of metamorph who could perfectly mimic the life forms it encountered and take them over…"

"Like those pods in San Francisco?"

"They may have been related. In any event, a helicopter pilot R.J. MacReady succeeded in killing that Thing although it cost him his life. The Government, who'd gotten a report of the attack, at first decided to drop a tactical nuke on the place, but someone though it smart to use Ice-9 instead…"

"Ice-9?" asked Lisa.

"A secret compound developed by Dr. Felix Hoenekker in the 1960s," I explained. "It acts as a seed crystal upon contact with liquid water, causing that water to instantly transform into ice. In effect, they turned the entire outpost and all it contained into a giant, forever ice cube."

"Smart," remarked Lisa. But she, like me, knew that was not the end of the story.

"But since 9/11, the Pentagon has more money than they know what to do with. Some smart alec in a basement office thought there might be something they could use down there. And being in the blessed enlightened times we live in, they decided to entrust it to the private sector. So someone to Antarctica, picked up the ice cube and brought it back here, where I gather they're preparing to thaw out that Thing. Needless to say, this can't end well."

"Someone—who?" asked Lisa, sensing the end game.

"Yoyodyne," I answered.

The Yoyodyne Corporation founded in the 1930s by one Clayton "Bloody" Chiclitz has been a blight on the already well-blighted American Industrial-Defense complex. You know the motto, "Success has many fathers, failure is an orphan?" The opposite is true of Yoyodyne who has fathered failure upon failure. At some point in their chaotic existence, they were even infiltrated by reptilian humanoids. I think they were defeated, but I couldn't swear to it.

It turned out that the "ice cube" had been taken to their top secret facility located not too far from here in Grovers Mill, which explained why both Leonox and Lisa had decided to spend some time in our beautiful Garden State.

Lisa knew at once that Leonox intended to resurrect that Thing und unleash it on the East Coast, while her job was to stop it. Even if the Powers hadn't been involved, I would have been happy to assist. Fortunately, I wasn't without resources myself.

I immediately called in for a strike team from Division, led by that insufferably priggish Michael, and ordered him to "clean" the Yoyodyne Grovers Mill facility. Presumably, Leonox's Sect had already rid us of the few scientists and employees Yoyodyne kept there to study the

Thing. But I had dealt with the Sect before—compared to Division, they were amateurs. There was no way they could withstand a full frontal assault by Michael's team.

The only "x" left in the equation was the Thing itself.

My predictions came true. Michael's team dispatched the Sect quickly and efficiently. The Yoyodyne facility was already ablaze when Lisa and I arrived. We were met by Michael and his young protégée, Nikita.

"I lost eighteen men to that… Thing…in there," he complained. "We barely escaped, and that was only because Nikita blew up the entire facility with a Q-bomb."

"I thought the Q-bombs were off limits without my specific authorization," I said, peeved and yet relieved at the same time.

"Tell that to Nikita," grumbled Michael.

The chief interested party in this discussion only smiled, showing no remorse at all.

At that moment, Lisa came out of the shadows and grabbed my sleeve.

"Let me," she whispered.

"Let me—what?" I replied, taking her away from Michael and Nikita.

"Your men can't kill the Thing," she said matter-of-factly. "But I can."

"You can? But how?"

I knew that, apart from her ability to be resurrected time and again, and some extra-sensory perception, Lisa didn't have super-powers. She wasn't a Jaime Sommers or a Goldine Serafin. She was just plain Lisa.

But I couldn't stop her. She walked towards the fire, towards the blazing building, just as the Thing, aflame but seemingly unharmed, shambled out of it.

I saw it grab Lisa—envelop her with its very substance, *taste* her… absorb her until there was nothing left, but the Thing.

Then it took two, three steps forward… and stopped.

It remained still for what felt like a long time, but which I found out later from Michael had only lasted two minutes and twenty-five seconds.

After that, it began to rot. I don't know how else to describe it. It rotted on the spot, quickly and completely, until there was nothing left but a pile of putrescent ashes which, as we found out when we went to examine it, smelled like rotten eggs.

Michael and Nikita went back to Division; unlike Berkhoff, I knew they weren't easily impressed with melodramatic threats, so I didn't bother. Besides, to whom could they report what had happened that night?

I drove away in the Optima. While on the turnpike, I let my mind wander and, as is often the case in such situations, I finally understood. At least, I think I did.

When Lisa had been resurrected in Virginia Madsen's body, she was till infected with rabies—for which there is no cure. The Power who controlled her knew that it would be fatal to the Thing, and when the alien creature had ingested Lisa, it had also sealed its fate. Rabies was what had killed the Thing.

I started whistling Bobby McFerrin's *Don't Worry, Be Happy*. I knew Lisa would be back and I was looking forward to our next encounter.

I only wished I could say the same of Michael and Nikita,

Randy Lofficier carries on with the new adventures of the Phantom Angel, a.k.a. the Sleeping Beauty of legend, who was awakened in modern times by Doc Ardan, and has since set up her own detective agency in Paris. In this latest tale, a prologue for more stories to come, our fearless heroine acquires a new partner, one which fans of 1960s & 70s British TV will remember fondly...

Randy Lofficier: *Angel and Hopkirk (Deceased)*

Paris, Today

I was in a terrible mood. You would think that being a semi-immortal being from a world of fairy tales, yet living in what most people would call the "real" world, everything would seem wonderful all the time. Sadly, though, like everyone else, I have my bad days. Today was one of those. And, worse, I had absolutely no idea why I felt the way I did.

Once upon a time I was a princess. I had supposedly been "cursed" by an evil fairy. However, the truth was somewhat different, as it often is. My fairy godmother, a wise woman whom some would have called a "witch," knowing how unhappy I was with the life that women were required to lead in my era, offered me the chance to go into a magical sleep and wait for more enlightened times.

Hundreds of years passed by and a roving adventurer named Francis Ardan stumbled upon my chamber and awakened me from my slumber. Angry at first, I quickly forgave him when he explained to me that times had, at last, changed, and I took the opportunity to explore the strange new era in which I found myself.

I undertook many wild adventures and was soon dubbed the The Phantom Angel by the journalist Joseph Rouletabille. I loved that name, but it was not one I could use in my daily life, so I instead chose to call myself Rose L'Ange.

Thanks to the help of Francis and his wealthy family, I was able to access the money of my ancestors and used it to settle into a *hotel particulier* in the Marais district of Paris. I soon discovered that there were many others from my realm who also lived in this brave, new world, living side by side with the mortal citizens who had no idea who, or what, they truly were.

Many of my fellow fairy tale friends had real world problems, however, and needed someone to help them navigate them, while at the same time, not wanting to give away their true natures to just anyone. I quickly discovered that I had the skills and desire to help them, so set up my own, very specialized, detective agency: *L'Agence d'Investigations & Recherches L'Ange*, orAngel Investigations.

My reputation has become known to a select few outside of the Fairy Tale community, and I have even helped members of the Police Judiciaire solve a case or two when it crossed over with our world. Most recently, I had helped Captain Laure Berthaud handle a case involving magic stones, dwarves, an enchanted prince and dragons! Certainly, my life wasn't boring.

Lately, though, I had been feeling unsettled and unhappy. Like Sherlock Holmes in London, I knew that this happened when I didn't feel my brain was being exercised. And, sadly, I couldn't create exciting cases out of thin air. Right now, those types of cases were thin on the ground.

As I sat pondering what to do, noises began to come through my walls! This should have been impossible, as I lived alone. But, clearly, there was something going on.

I started walking around my beautiful home, checking each room carefully for any intruders. But there was nothing. Not an open window, no shutters banging in the breeze, no wayward critters who had made their way inside through the door. *Rien.*

This was puzzling, but I was a detective! Surely I could figure this one out.

I walked into my formal dining room, a space I rarely used these days. As I looked around, something caught my attention in the corner of my vision. I turned towards the mirror that reflected the large table in the center of the room. Standing behind me was a man in a white suit!

I turned to confront him, but there was no one there!

I looked back in the mirror and there he was again. This time, he waved at me and smiled! I approached the mirror more closely and his smile grew larger. Then, he spoke:

"Finally!" he said. "I've been trying to get your attention for days, but you're very closed-minded for a detective."

I was sure I was hallucinating by now. I'm used to outrageous things, but except for the Magic Mirror kept by Snow White's evil stepmother, men living in mirrors was not one of them.

"Are you really there?" I demanded. "And, who the hell are you if you are?"

"Of course I'm really here," answered the apparition. "I'm a ghost, if you want to know. My name is Marty Hopkirk and I was a detective too, a long time ago—before I died of course. Haven't you noticed I'm speaking to you in English, by the way?"

"What language you're speaking is a lot less interesting to me than the fact that you're speaking at all," I stammered. "Why are you here? How did you get here? What do you want from me?"

"You sure do ask a lot of questions," Marty said in a somewhat snarky tone. "Why don't you invite me into your house so we can have a comfortable chat. I didn't want to intrude more than I've already done without your permission."

"Yeah. OK. Come in and sit down," I told him.

There was a sound like the popping of a champagne cork, and the apparition disappeared from my mirror and appeared in the room next to me. The visitor was a man of medium height with brown hair and eyes, and he was still wearing his very out of date white suit. He held out a slightly transparent hand.

"Go ahead, try to shake it," he said.

I did as he asked, but my hand passed straight though his. There was a mildly unpleasant sensation, halfway between touching a cold steak and being shocked by rubbing your feet on a nylon carpet on a winter's day. Marty laughed.

"Sorry. I couldn't resist. When you've been dead as long as I have, you have to get your jollies where you can."

I glared at my strange visitor. I wasn't sure I particularly cared for his sense of humor.

"Let's go into the salon," I told him.

Then I turned and walked out of the room. Perhaps it was petty of me, but I closed the door before he could walk out with me. He quickly walked through the closed door and stuck his tongue out at me.

"Who's being the silly one now," he said. "I'm a ghost. What did you think was going to happen there?"

I shrugged and led the way into the salon, where I sat down on my favorite armchair. Marty looked around, gave a small jump, floated in the air for a second, then landed on my couch where he stretched out with his feet up in front of him.

"Comfy," he said.

"Now, tell me why you're here and what you want," I said.

I was becoming more irritated at this brash visitor the longer we were together.

"That's a story," he answered. "I guess you could say I'm a refugee of sorts." He closed his eyes and continued. "As I said, I was a private eye in London in the swinging sixties. Ah, those were the days, mini skirts and mini Coopers, Twiggy, the Beatles, the Stones, the world was my oyster.

"One day, I was following a lead and I guess I got too close to the truth, because someone was pissed off and ran me over in the street. That was not a good look for me: road kill. When I woke up from the shock of the crash, I realized that I was still around, even if no one else could see me. That was hard at first, I can tell you. Being totally invisible is no picnic.

"Soon, though, I found my old partner Jeff Randall could see me and hear me! That changed everything. I went back into business with him as a, er, silent partner. I even started to learn a few ghostly tricks as time went on, so even though I wasn't technically there, I was still able to help him and solve cases. It was grand.

"But time moved on. He got older, I didn't. Eventually, he decided to retire to the south of France. So I came, too. We had some good times. At least, I did. I got the feeling Jeff thought I was annoying some-times..."

I had to roll my eyes at that. This guy was pretty clueless for a ghost who had to be close to a hundred years-old by now!

"Anyhoo," continued Marty, totally oblivious to my eye rolling, "one day, Jeff up and died, too. I mean, I should have expected it, but I sort of thought that when he went, he'd be a ghost too, and we could keep on keeping on, y'a know? Instead, he just walked into the light and left me behind.

"I kicked around for a bit, but Jeff's family came and took most of his stuff. I thought I'd head back to Ol' Blighty with them, but I found I couldn't. I seemed tied to France. You may think it's crazy, but I think this Brexit nonsense has something to do with it. A lot of Jeff's posses-sions couldn't get taken back without the proper paperwork, and I think

I'm tied to those items somehow. In fact, I think I'm tied to one particular item…"

He got up from my couch and went over to my bookcase. I had recently gone to a local *depot vente* that specialized in kitschy items from the 60s. Like my visitor, I, too, had loved that era. There was one item I'd had back in the day, which had gotten broken during one of my adventures, and when I saw one in pristine condition at the *depot vente*, I'd had to buy it. Marty was standing in front of it now. It was a perfect, functioning Lava Lamp!

"I used to hide in there when I wanted a little me time," he said. "I think I've become imprinted on it now. So, as long as you have that, you have me! But, you know, things couldn't have worked out better if I'd tried. Imagine me winding up living with another P.I.! How perfect is that? Now I can help you solve your cases. You'll see, I won't be any trouble at all. This will be great!"

I stared at him unable to speak. I wanted to protest, but I couldn't really think of a good argument. After all, I'd worked with other detectives, maybe having a ghostly associate could come in handy?

Just then, my phone rang. There'd been a murder on the Ile Saint-Louis and my old friend, Red Riding Hood, needed my help.

Maybe this could be a chance to try things out with my new partner—the ghost!

Our Canadian contributor, Rod McFadyen, offers here his own take on the hoary theme of the "Yellow Peril," one that nevertheless features a clever twist, casting an entirely new light on it...

Rod McFadyen: *Empire Rising*

Shanghai, 1961

It was after midnight, but the air at the docks was hot and heavy. There was a sense of menace that was almost palpable, making the residents of the area uneasy. They skittered home rather than gathering at their regular gambling dens or watering holes, locking their doors and turning off the lights.

A nondescript warehouse showed an unusual amount of activity for the hour. Goods were normally loaded from there onto the ships during daylight, before sailing down the Yangtze River to other ports further inland, or unloaded from ships returning. The building was typically dark by now but tonight, dim lights flickered inside as shadowy figures moved past windows.

A chauffeured black sedan slid down the alley at the back of the warehouse, stopping before a door and parking behind three other vehicles. A massive, bald, black-clad man emerged from the back seat. He gave cursory glances up and down the alley. Guards posted at each end would ensure there would be no disturbances.

Ming entered the warehouse, taking the stairs to the upper offices, the wooden stairs creaking under his weight. He counted over a dozen men positioned around the periphery of the main floor, at each of the windows and doors, armed with guns, knives and any number of exotic but lethal weapons. And those were just the men he could see.

He arrived at the upper floor and paused at the door. There were more bodyguards in the shadows. In the middle of the room was a single large table with three men already seated.

"You're late," one of the men commented.

"A thousand apologies," Ming said as he sat, no warmth in his apology at all.

"Thank you all for accepting my invitation," he began. "We are all known to each other, so I'll get right down to business. I have a proposal I wish to discuss with you all."

He paused, letting the suspense build.

"China is in turmoil, more so than at any time in its history. Chairman Mao's experiment—his Great Leap Forward—is a disaster. His policies have caused wide-spread famine and millions are starving, while the promised technological advances have not materialized. Meanwhile, the Soviet Union and the United States are thriving and have even taken their first tentative steps towards outer space. China is being left behind to choke in the dust."

Ming looked to the man on his left. He was dressed in rich gold silks and wearing a black skullcap. He had a distinctive moustache and his magnificent green eyes seemed to burn with fire.

"Do you agree, Doctor Fu Manchu?"

"I would have to say that your statement is... accurate," he said, his voice resonant and cold.

Ming then looked at the man sitting across from him. He was dressed in a dark blue tunic with thick silver edging. He was bald and his features were harsh, highlighted by skin that seemed jaundiced compared to the others.

"What do you think, Plan Chu? Although nowadays you seem to prefer to go by the name the casual racists of the West have given you—the Yellow Claw."

The man ignored the jibe and responded, "I can see no flaw in your analysis."

Ming tilted his head to the right. The last figure at the table was dressed in a green robe, with a cowl that covered most of his face, showing only a pair of golden eyes.

"Fo-Hi? Or do you prefer the name of the persona you have built?"

"I have grown accustomed to being called the Scorpion," said the man. "It strikes fear in the ignorant. And I would have to agree with your assessment."

Satisfied with their responses, Ming continued.

"However, disaster always represents an opportunity. Seated at this table are some of the most accomplished and feared men in the world. We each control globe-spanning criminal networks. Our resources are staggering. The advances we've made in the sciences—chemistry, botany, physics, biology and even more arcane fields—are unmatched. The very fact that each of us has devised methods to increase our lifespans unnaturally is a testament to what we are capable of.

"But, for all our power, for all of the plotting over the decades—the assassinations, the blackmail, the manipulation, the destruction—it has come to virtually nothing with regards to our ultimate goals. We have been respective thorns in the sides of the Western government—at best. Our paths have even crossed from time to time, but we squandered any opportunities by squabbling between us, blind to our own missions. If we are to topple Western civilization, our power needs to increase by a considerable degree."

"What are you proposing?" Plan Chu asked.

Ming thought over his next words carefully. "We must become China."

No one spoke for long seconds as his words sunk in.

"Mao and his cronies in the Party are fumbling in the dark. Repression, fear, ineffective bureaucracy and wasteful ideological pursuits are keeping China from making any progress on the world stage. It has no need of external enemies; it is its own worst enemy. But think of the potential sitting at this table," Ming continued, opening his arms. "If a council such as this could rule China, it would become the world's greatest power! A true empire!"

The men looked at each other, assessing the potential of such an alliance.

"I find it ironic that a Mongol such as yourself is the one to suggest a takeover of the Chinese government," Fo-Hi commented slyly.

Ming replied with a grin that could easily serve as a scowl. "My ancestor created the largest empire in history, encompassing both Mongolia and China. I think it would be fitting if I, his descendant, were to surpass him."

"And that plan might succeed, if it were to ever leave this room."

A woman's voice reverberated throughout the room. The last echo of her voice was drowned out by the sounds of guns cocking and knives being drawn as the bodyguards scrambled to look for the intruder.

"Do not bother to look for me; I am not here."

"Madame Atomos!" Fu Manchu said venomously.

Confusion showed in Plan Chu's eyes.

"She is Japanese," Fu Manchu answered the unasked question. "A scientist, possibly as brilliant as anyone seated here, and just as ruthless. She rages against the United States for the atomic bombing of Japan."

"I'm flattered you remember my voice so well since our last encounter," her voice resounded.

"How did you find out about us?" Ming demanded.

"I have resources of my own," Madame Atomos replied vaguely. "It was child's play to plant a secret microphone and radio transmitter here earlier. As I said, your plan might succeed if it went forward. But I cannot allow it. China may be in turmoil, but Japan is only now beginning to emerge from the rubble of the Second World War. I do not want an ascendant China to interfere."

"So, you have come to stop us?" Fu Manchu said. "Have you also planted a bomb along with your radio? Or canisters of poison gas? Or some other exotic means to remove us?"

The men at the table tensed. Her soft chuckle filled the room.

"No. You are all free to go... as long as you go your separate ways."

They exchanged glances around the table, not comprehending this unexpected twist.

"I recorded your discussion," she continued. "If I were to release the tapes to China's leaders, with your plot to overthrow them, you would quickly find yourself outlaws in your own country. You would be cut off from the main source of your resources and bereft of the very purpose of your life's work."

Ming, his ambitious plan crumbling before his eyes, could barely contain his fury.

"Why?" he spat. "Why this subterfuge? Why toy with us this way?"

"As you so eloquently put it, Ming, you have been thorns in the sides of the West for decades. I want you to continue. At a time of *my* choosing, I will deliver the killing blow, but until then, your efforts provide a nice distraction for their agencies. Enjoy the rest of your evening, gentlemen."

Silence filled the room. The conversation was apparently over. The men at the table hesitated at first. Then, all stood up without a further word and left, their bodyguards cautiously filing behind them.

Ming was the last to go, his fists clenched until the knuckles whitened.

Madame Atomos sat on a bench on the wharf, waiting for the ship to begin boarding passengers for the trip back to Japan. She wore a dark coat, sunglasses and a scarf that kept her long dark hair from whipping in the wind. She was middle-aged, but still good-looking enough to attract the stares of many of the men also waiting. Somehow though, they knew not to approach her. Beside her was a satchel containing the precious tapes.

Out of the corner of her eye, she saw a woman sit down on the same bench. Madame Atomos cautiously reached inside her coat for a weapon.

"A weapon will not be necessary, Madame."

She turned to face the woman. She was Asian, beautiful, with jet-black hair, wearing a floral dress that accentuated her stunning figure.

"Who are you?" Madame Atomos asked, her hand paused in her coat.

The woman smiled, showing perfect teeth. "My name is Sumuru. Perhaps you've heard of me?"

"I have. You run an organization similar to those of some men I encountered recently."

"I understand that encounter went very well," Sumuru said, grinning widely.

Madame Atomos tilted her head. "You were the anonymous source of the information about the meeting? Why did you not take care of the situation yourself?"

"I have informants scattered throughout their organizations," Sumuru explained. "I was privy to Ming's proposal and wanted it stopped, but I was unable to do so without endangering those informants. I was aware of your reputation and correctly surmised the motivation that would drive you to act. I hope you forgive me for drafting you to act as my proxy."

"I'm surprised," Madame Atomos said with a nod, respectfully acknowledging the woman's cunning. "From what I know about you, your goals might align with theirs."

Sumuru stared out at the harbor. "I have a different perspective on how a new world order should be, and the place of women in that order, which those men are too misogynistic to entertain. My organization only recruits women. In fact, I could use someone of your scientific expertise and single-mindedness."

She gave Madame Atomos another dazzling smile.

"Someday perhaps," Madame Atomos replied, "but not at the present time."

She said nothing more.

Sumuru sighed and stood.

"I wish you a safe journey, Madame. I suspect our paths will cross again."

She walked away, leaving Madame Atomos alone with her satchel and her thoughts.

After devoting his time to a brilliant series of tales starring Felifax that began in Volume 10 and concluded in last year's installment, Christofer Nigro—like Brian Gallagher and Martin Gately—is moving on with a new story featuring new and old characters, new ideas, and the same thrills that have become his trademark...

Christofer Nigro: *Three the Hardened Way*

A small museum in the vicinity of the Place Vendôme,
Paris, 1920

Officers Bastien Boulinard and Jacques Marquet strode into the museum serving as a temporary display for Queen Victoria's priceless diamond necklace. Their dinner break had ended and, by this point in the early evening, most of the citizens viewing the exhibit for a single franc had cleared out. The two policemen saw that Martial Verdier, the third officers assigned guard duty that day, stood in a corner. He was picking up the slack for his colleagues as they grabbed a meal from the small bakery across the street.

"Perhaps we should not leave Martial here on his own," Marquet told his friend and colleague. "That jewel is worth more than the combined annual wages of the entire Paris police force."

"You worry too much, *mon ami,*" Boulinard rejoined. "We're merely going to saunter a short distance to get some sandwiches. Why, the only people still viewing the exhibit are that young woman with her small child over there. Completely harmless!"

Marquet looked in the direction of the exhibit to see exactly the individuals whom his partner had just mentioned. The young lady was rather tall with a slim build, pretty face, and dressed in a classic Paul Poiret dress with a tight hobble skirt; her golden locks culed under a blue Charlston hat, the back of which was adorned with a grayish feather. The young toddler in her care, whose tiny hand she held, could not be older than two. Boulinard remarked on how adorable the little waif looked in a sailor suit, his small round head partially concealed by a Navy blue dixie cup hat.

Yes, those two visitors were obviously quite harmless. In fact, to underscore this fact, Boulinard approached the attractive mother, wondering if she was perhaps a widow; he would have been even willing to overlook matters if she turned out to be a divorcee or a married woman willing to engage in extracurricular relations.

"Good evening, Madame," he said. "I hope you and your little one are enjoying your visit to the exhibit."

"Oh, most certainly, officer," she replied in a delightful high-pitched voice that was tinged with a slight American accent. "Little Teddy here so loves the pretty sparkling jewels. Their glow is radiant, like a thousand little suns reflecting the light to warm the hearts of the admiring public."

"You most certainly have a way with words, Madame," Boulinard said, smitten already. "And if I may be so bold, the radiance of that royal necklace does not even begin to rival your own."

The lady blushed and gave out a girlish giggle that delighted the policeman. "What a thing to say! You truly warm my heart, officer. If only little Teddy here grows up to be a fine gentleman such as yourself."

"Well, I am pleased to provide the proper role model for gentlemanly behavior," the officer replied, gently flicking his finger across the young child's cherubic face.

Much to Boulinard's surprise, though, little Teddy did not smile. He merely glared at the officer with piercing dark eyes, resembling the buttons on a trench coat, but with some type of indescribable fire to them. This disquieted the officer suddenly felt the inexplicable need to part company with the boy's attractive mother.

"Well, Madame, I am pleased that you enjoyed laying eyes upon the late Queen's jewelry. Do know, however, that the exhibit closes in just a few minutes."

"*Merci*, my gallant sir," the young woman said. "We shall indeed be leaving soon. And thank you for your chivalrous company."

"It was my pleasure," Boulinard replied as he walked to rejoin Marquet.

The latter was standing near another exhibit, a suit of antiquated Viking armor displayed on a huge mannequin which stood a full seven feet in height. This figure had a wild mane of blonde hair that truly evoked the image of a savage but brave Norseman of old.

The calm of the moment was abruptly broken when a beleaguered voice, seemingly belonging to an elderly man, erupted from a broom closet next to the Viking warrior exhibit.

"Help me! Help me please! I cannot breathe in here!" That plea was followed by tortured gasps for air.

"*Bon Dieu!*" said Marquet, who was closest to the broom closet. "Someone is locked in there? I was not aware it even had a lock!"

The policeman ran over to the small compartment and yanked the door open. It was not locked at all, and moreover, it was bereft of any trapped human being. Only a few brooms and a bucket were present.

Marquet became perplexed. "What in…?"

But before he could react further, the frighteningly life-size Viking mannequin raised his mighty fists and brought them down on the policeman. One blow of such powerful force was enough to bring him down, but the faux Viking continued to pummel the felled man with the fury of a berserker.

"Stop!" Boulinard shouted as he went for the gun.

His intended action was thwarted when the toddler produced a sharp knife from his pocket and shoved it into the officer's right leg. It sliced dthrough a nerve, sending the hapeless policeman down to the floor. The little boy then leapt on his back and began stabbing him continuously and mercilessly. The policeman could do naught but scream in agony as his body's precious supply of blood leaked out onto the floor from numerous wounds.

"Do ya think I'm so cute now, cop?" the toddler queried in a squeaky, high-pitched voice during the vicious thrusting of the blade. "This'll teach you to try makin' a play for a little fellow's mom right in front of him!"

"*Arrêtez ou je tire!*" Verdier shouted as he, too, went for his pistol.

But no sooner had the officer brandished it then he was distracted by a desperate child-like voice crying out from behind him.

"Officer, over here! Help! They got me!"

The startled policeman turned around for a second to see that no one was there. That was all the time it took for the young woman to smash him his head with a thick cudgel. Verdier went down and the lady hit him a second time, ensureing that the officer would remain unconscious on the floor.

With the three policemen no longer a concern, the toddler threw off his dixie cup hat and stomped on it with his tiny foot.

"Damn, was it a pain to have to play act as a kid again!" the little man decreed. "Just 'cause I'm cursed to look like one for the rest of my life…"

"That isn't so bad, Mr. Tweedy," the Viking-garbed figure said as he finally ceased the beating that broke more than half the bones in Jacques's fragile body. "You could be freakishly big like me, and that's just as bad."

"Except being freakishly strong along *with* your size isn't such a bad trade-off, is it, Hercules?" the dwarf named Tweedledee queried as used the perforated policeman hat to wipe the blood off his knife.

"Well, not if you say so," the former circus strongman decided. "I mean, you're the brains of our group, Mr. Tweedy. You always know best."

"I hope my performance was up to task, Tweedledee," said the young lady as she doffed the Charlston hat and the blonde wig beneath it to reveal the features of a girlish-looking man. "Though it was just a bit stifling to move about in this hobble skirt and these dreaded high heels. How do the ladies ever get around in such apparel?"

"Stop your complainin', Echo!" Tweedledee insisted as he walked towards the case where the Queen Elizabeth necklace was displayed. "Your knack for throwing and imitating voices did just fine. You made a convincing dame, and it's too bad this Romeo cop didn't get his time with you. It would've been a riot to see the look on his face when he saw what you didn't have up top… and what you *do* have down below. Ha!"

"I am afraid that I lack the presence of mind to answer that, Mr. Tweedy," Echo proclaimed in his natural soft-toned voice as he divested himself of the cumbersome skirt and high heel shoes he had to wear for his latest imposture. "For, as you recall, a certain little Imp has stolen it."

Echo then reached into the cotton Moire Poplin bag that completed his feminine disguise. Out of it he pulled the aforementioned Imp, which was a revolting wooden doll with goat-like legs and a head resembling an old man. The little dummy was then placed on its owner's shoulder, where it so often took up space.

"You better believe I have your mind," came a gruff voice from the direction of the Imp's moving wooden mouth. "And if you want it back, you had best keep me at your side."

"God, that stupid dummy of yours, Echo!" Tweedledee griped as he struggled in vain to reach for the jewels on the four-foot display podium. "If I was tall enough, I'd grab that damned thing from your shoulder and throw it into a fireplace! That way I wouldn't have to hear you making voices for it anymore! It ruins my dinner every blasted night!"

"Oh no, please do not dispense with my Imp, Tweedy!" Echo appealed to the malign dwarf. "If you did so, my mind would be forever lost!"

"No, it wouldn't, 'cause I'd still be here and I'm the only mind you'll ever need!" Tweedledee proclaimed. "And don't you forget that!"

"I... will not," Echo replied, suddenly growing calm.

"I would listen to that one," the Imp concurred. "He and I share a common height, and therefore a large mind that belies our size."

"Shaddup with that thing, Echo!" the frustrated dwarf shouted. "And will ya stop just standing there takin' up space and help me get this necklace?"

"Well, of course, Tweedy," Echo replied as he grabbed the jewels and handed them to his diminutive master.

"Ah, look at these rocks sparkle!" Tweedledee said as he held the necklace before his small face. "They're gonna land us a fortune when we hock them on the black market! I knew coming to Paris was a good idea!"

"Considering how we had to flee America after we killed the Human Skeleton at the circus and left him hanging in the window of that clothing store," Echo noted. "It was perhaps the only idea your great mind could have conjured forth, sir."

"Yeah, well... The point is, our trip here worked out just fine!" the dwarf said. "In the meantime, we all gotta get out of these stupid clothes and get back to the hideout. Sooner or later, someone is gonna come in here and notice these three cops broken and bleeding all over the floor."

"That should not be difficult," Echo said, "as I hid some proper post-caper garments for us right there behind the war exhibit. After all, thinking ahead is what those in our dishonorable but lucrative profession do."

Two hours later, the ex-circus trio of Tweedledee, Hercules, and Echo sat in the spacious apartment hideout they had found near the Porte de Clignancourt. The group's ill-gotten gains had been sufficient to purchase such relatively comfortable living accommodations for the men who had been whimsically but aptly coined "The Unholy Three" by the underworld. The new hit jazz tune *Bye Bye Blackbird* played on a phonograph at the back of the dining room where Tweedledee sat on a small love seat. He continued to admire the glittering jewels of Queen Elizabeth as Hercules stood in the front of the room while Echo relaxed on the main sofa.

"If you gents think this place is good," the malicious dwarf said, "you just wait 'till we get proper payment for this here necklace. We'll be able to afford a whole floor at the Taj Mahal! Maybe the whole entire building!"

"That place is in Germany, right, Mr. Tweedy?" asked the brutish Hercules.

"No, you muscle-bound clod!" Tweedledee said. "It's in India! You know, the land of Hindus and tigers!"

"I wrestled with a tiger once, back at the circus," the giant recalled. "It scratched me."

"Living in such a distant land is a far cry from the world we are familiar with," Echo noted. "Do we truly want to live in such a locale?"

"Who cares where we live, just so long as we're living the life, Echo!" was the small man's answer.

That was when the three loathsome men were startled when a melodious male voice bearing a distinct French accent but speaking in English suddenly emanated from a darkened corner of the residence.

"Or, perhaps you gentlemen would prefer to remain in Paris and work for me," it said. "For under my direction, you will acquire more riches than you ever could working within your own devices."

"Echo!" the dwarf hollered. "Is that you clowning around with your voice-throwing schtick?"

"That was not my doing," the soft-spoken ventriloquist said as he stood up, clearly unnerved.

"Then now you know precisely how it feels when you do this to others, Mr. Echo?" suggested the voice.

Hercules walked in front of Tweedledee with his enormous fists upraised to guard the safety of the small man whom he admired above all others. The dwarf pulled his small but razor-sharp knife from a pocket and pointed the business end in a defensive gesture.

"Don't worry, Mr. Tweedy!" the mighty strongman proclaimed. "I'm gonna protect you, like always!"

"The only one who is gonna be needing protection is the wise guy talking from the shadows!" the irate Tweedledee said. "Now, show yourself! Or, I'll have Hercules here tear the place apart 'till he finds ya! And when he does…"

"Be at ease, *mon ami*," the source of the interloping voice said as the tall, dark-clad figure of a man wearing a masquerade mask, a cloak, and a wide black fedora hat emerged from behind the curtains of the large front windowpane. "And delight in the fact that the antics of you three have come to the attention of the Phantom of the Opera."

Echo breathed an audible sigh of relief. "For a moment there, when he first emerged, I thought it might be that dreadful Judex. In which case…"

"In which case, I would have crushed him, just like I did that cop back at the museum!" the strongman of the trio affirmed.

"So, you might hope, Hercules," Echo replied.

"You say you're the notorious Opera Ghost," Tweedledee stated as he hopped off the love seat, his knife still pointed at the ready. "I heard of you. But ain't you supposed to be haunting that place?"

"Yes, the Paris Opera is my home," Erik said. "But I am far more than a mere ghost, Mr.Tweedledee. I am the most feared assassin in all of Europe. And I have an offer of employment for you three."

"You could've just knocked on our door, big shot!" Tweedledee said.

"That is not the way of one who moves in the shadows and wishes to evade common detection," Erik replied. "I would have thought you would understand this."

"Yeah, yeah, whatever," Tweedledee groused. "But what do we need a job offer from you for when we have the Queen's necklace? We already got it made!"

"But the police will be searching every nook and cranny of Paris to find the culprits," Erik explained, "not to mention the ones who so viciously attacked three of theirs, killing at least one. Are you truly confident that you know this city well enough to avoid capture without my assistance?"

"The Phantom may have a point, sir," Echo advised.

"I'll be the judge of that!" Tweedledee stated. "If you ask me, I think he just wants the jewels! And how did you know what we did just a few hours ago, Mr. Phantom?"

"Rest assured it is not the necklace that I am after," Erik answered. "I am an assassin and a musician, not a thief. As for your question, not much occurs in Paris that I do not find out, and swiftly. That is another reason why you three would prosper under my direction."

"Only one person directs this group," the miniature menace exclaimed, "and that guy is me! Hercules, crush that bag of wind!"

The strongman raised his powerful fists and, with a shout of fury, he rushed at the Phantom to do precisely as commanded. But before he could bring them down on his target, however, the cloaked intruder delivered a punch to the giant's diaphragm with astounding speed. Hercules let out a painful exhalation and was driven back a few inches. The giant could scarcely recall ever being hit so hard, even by the highly athletic performers back at the circus. But he remained on his feet.

As a result, the Phantom followed up with a punishing uppercut to the big man's chin that sent him reeling. Yet, the massive man still remained standing.

"Impressive," the masked assassin said aloud as he realized that he might have a true fight on his hands.

"What are ya waitin' for, Hercules?" Tweedledee shouted. "Dinnertime? Crush that fool!"

The big man ran forward and brought his two piledriver fists down, only to have his target lithely somersault out of the way. The giant's fists instead smashed down against an end table, reducing the wooden structure to splinters.

"Missed him!" Hercules complained. "Where did he go? Where did he go?"

"Up here," came Erik's voice from atop an eight-foot oaken cabinet as the loop of his dreaded Punjab lasso was flung across Hercules's wide neck.

The Phantom braced himself and pulled on the thick rope with all his considerable might. The giant began gagging as his windpipe and trachea were contorted. He nevertheless stood fast and grabbed the rope, pulling it with his own formidable strength. But the Phantom was an expert at this weapon, and he refused to have even such a powerful opponent use it to yank him from his perch. He quickly realized, however, that the act of strangulation against such a foe might take some time, and Hercules was not alone.

"Echo!" Tweedledee shouted. "Get to the side of that cabinet and help me knock it over!"

The ventriloquist did as commanded, running to one side of the tall cupboard while his tiny master dashed to the other. Both men pushed and toppled it over, causing Erik to fall and his lasso's grip on Hercules's throat to slacken. The Phantom landed expertly on both his hands and feet.

Tweedledee scampered towards the dark-cloaked killer with his knife raised. Before he could stick it in his target, Erik kicked him in the sternum, sending the tiny man sprawling across the carpet like a tossed doll.

The Phantom turned when he suddenly heard an incessant knocking at the front door of the apartment.

"Open up! It's the police!"

Erik reacted by quickly getting to his feet and delivering a back-handed punch to Echo's face that sent the long-faced man back against the wall. The ventriloquist slid down to the floor holding his bleeding nose, and the ruckus at the front door immediately ceased.

"A noble effort, Mr. Echo," Erik said, "but I am wise to your abilities."

Luckily for the Phantom, his reflexes were swift, for he barely managed to turn around in time to deal with Hercules's next attack. Erik silently cursed himself for not anticipating the massive man's prompt recovery from near-strangulation.

The seven-foot strongman again delivered his signature move, the punishing downwards blow with both fists simultaneously. Though Hercules had never before failed to thoroughly flatten a person when striking them in that manner, this time would be different... at least, partially.

The Phantom swiftly held out his hands and braced himself with his legs in the space of a split second. Thus, he caught the giant's fists in his palms before they could land on his head or back. Erik was amazed that the force of the blow was strong enough to send him down to his knees. Hercules was comparably astounded that his double-fisted assault had failed to utterly pulverize his target.

"Again, you... impress me, giant," Erik said while struggling against the tremendous force arrayed against him. "I knew... I had correctly chosen your group for the job I now offer."

"You are... rather strong yourself, Mr. Phantom," Hercules graciously conceded aloud.

In the moments it had taken for Tweedledee to get back to his miniature feet, the savvy criminal had been thinking. "All right, enough of this! Hercules, get off him and let the guy give us his offer."

"Are you sure, Mr. Tweedy?" the giant asked as he and the Phantom continued to struggle.

"Yeah, yeah, I'm sure," the dwarf responded. "Let's hear him out. It won't kill anyone to at least do that."

Hercules nodded and backed away. Erik stood back up, straightened out his hat, and proceeded to speak.

"*Merci,* Mr. Tweedlee," the Phantom said. "Your wise decision has spared the spilling of needless blood. Namely, your own."

"Just get on it with, masked guy," the tiny man impatiently insisted.

"That is what I am here for," the cloaked assassin replied. "What I propose is a most profitable job assisting me in procuring a chemical formula from the lab of a mad scientist known as Professor Tornada."

"I think I heard of him," Tweedledee said. "I'm guessing you're referring to the bald one with the twitch who is supposed to be the real bad apple of the bunch."

"Yes, that is the one," Erik confirmed.

"Why do you want that chemical so badly?" the mini-criminal enquired. "What does it do?"

"Word from the underground says that it has restorative powers that are nigh-miraculous," the Phantom replied. "I would risk everything for the possibility of repairing what I was born as."

"Really, now?" Tweedledee pondered quizzically. "You seem as fit as any of those circus acrobats I used to work with. Maybe lots more, 'cause none of them could ever stand up to Hercules. I'd give anything to have your size and strength. What could you possibly want that stuff for?"

"Perhaps it would be best if I were to just show you," Erik stated. "Such a revelation would surpass the descriptive power of any words."

The Phantom took off his hat and, with a quick flip of his wrist, pulled the mask from his face. What the three criminals beheld was a ghastly skeletal visage that was nothing less than a living nightmare.

Tweedledee's button-like eyes widened. "Well... I'll be... damned. Still more handsome than the Human Skeleton, though."

Hercules simply stared with an expression of awe.

One half of Echo's lips sunk down.

"That would indeed be a face that could lose a mother's love," came a gruff voice from the Imp dummy, which sat atop a display table on the other side of the room.

Erik gritted his yellow teeth, barely keeping his composure. "My... mother is said to have perished at the sight of me immediately after my misbegotten birth."

"See?" came the response from the direction of the Imp.

"Echo!" Tweedledee shouted. "Stop talking through that thing before I have Hercules break it to pieces!"

The grotesque goat-legged dummy went silent. "It would seem the Imp has heeded your request, sir."

"Now," the dwarf turned back to the Phantom. "I understand why you want that stuff. You say it will make you look... like a normal man?"

"That is what I am banking on," Erik said.

"Has it been tested?" the small criminal asked.

"It shall be—on me," was the Phantom's reply.

"Ah, OK," Tweedledee said. "Do you think there's a chance that that chemical could help me too? You know, like, make me the size of a grown-up man?"

"Perhaps," the cloaked man responded.

"All right," Tweedledee noted. "Then, if that stuff works for you, will you give me some swigs of it along with the money you're gonna pay us?"

"Of course," Erik said.

"OK, then you can count us in," Tweedledee decided with a rare smile. "So, what's the plan gonna be?"

Not many individuals were aware of the exact location of Professor Tornada's lab. Fewer still knew where he kept vials of his experimental restorative chemical. But word had been out to a select few in the Parisian underground, and that was all that had been required for the info to pass into the hands of France's premier assassin. Also into the Phantom's possession came the knowledge that Tornada was presently out of France on some nameless mission to acquire more components for other experiments.

Hence, there was no better time than the present for Erik to guide his newly-hired trio of malcontents into the lab to purloin the precious concoction. The Phantom would risk all and more to find and test it, but he preferred not to risk having to kill this member of the Tornada family just yet. The man's various experiments had, and may yet again, prove useful to him and the underground in general.

The trio had made short work of the small number of armed guards in the front of the building where Tornada's lab was hidden. The combination of Hercules's muscle, Tweedledee's knife, and Echo's distracting voice made that happen in under ten minutes. Erik was more than pleased to dispatch the head of the security force by looping the Punjab lasso over the man's neck and giving him an impromptu hanging.

The Phantom landed nimbly on his feet as he jumped down from the ceiling loft to continue leading his hirelings to the appointed floor of the building.

"I see you got a kill in too, Phantom," Tweedledee said as he wiped his blood-soaked knife on the sleeve of the guards that Hercules pounded into a heap of broken bones and ruptured internal organs. "Nice one. I just can't believe this Tornada character has his lab in such a swanky building."

"It was set up here by a more respected member of his family," Erik explained. "The Tornada of our concern has sometimes masqueraded as one of them when it has served his interests, and his better-natured kin have reasons to, er, look the other way when this has happened. It is in this particular lab that the formula was hidden by him."

"Yeah, OK," the miniature leader of the trio said. "I heard you got other dangerous people that you employ, and they got good reps. Why did you want us for this gig?"

"Because," the Phantom answered as they trekked up a flight of stairs, "the more in my employ, the better. And while I could have used my Angels or stealth alone to procure the chemical, I needed some way to test your group."

"Wise guy," the dwarf muttered. "You're lucky that you're payin' so well."

The four finally made their way to the door that Erik pointed to indicate as the ingress to Tornada's lab.

"This would be it," the Phantom said. "Now, please do be patient while I quietly pick the lock and sneak in."

"Why waste time with that?" Tweedledee asked. "Not when we got the muscle to do it faster. Hercules, kick the door in!"

"No, do not…"

But the assassin's warning came too late as one forward thrust of Hercules's tree-like leg was enough to smash the locked door clear off its hinges.

"You fool!" the Phantom shouted. "I could have snuck in and out with the chemical. This manner of entrance will alert more security!"

"Now you tell us!" Tweedledee whined.

No sooner had the door been forced down than three guards emerged from a room connected to the lab. This lot, however, were not the typical security officers like the ones dispatched by the foursome on the lower floor. These three men were each completely bald, a bit over six feet tall with the physique of professional athletes, and dressed in one-piece bluish garments resembling the strongman leotards that Hercules himself had often worn during the days at the circus. More unsettling, however, was the fact that their faces, like their bodies, looked totally identical.

"Jeez, were these guys all taken from the same cookie cutter?" Tweedledee remarked.

"In a manner of speaking," Erik proclaimed. "They are synthetic men, the work of Tornada's science. Prepare yourselves, as they will present formidable opposition!"

"Hercules, get 'em!" Tweedledee commanded as he brandished his blade. "Echo, back us up the way you do best!"

The first of the silent synthetic guards clashed with Hercules, who rushed forward to take the brunt of the attack. The two large men grasped each other's hands and attempted to push the other back. To the abject surprise of both, neither would yield a single inch to the other. Hercules pushed as hard as he could while his impassive opponent did the same, but it was the proverbial irresistible force against an immovable object.

Upon this realization the former circus strongman realized he had to change tactics. Though Hercules lacked the brains of his pint-sized boss, he was still not without an inherent cunning, especially where the art of violence was concerned. Hence, he unexpectedly elected to do something he had seen the acrobats he worked with perform numerous times. While firmly gripping the guard's hands, Hercules fell onto his back and kicked his powerful legs onto his adversary's chest, using the momentum to send the synthetic man flying backwards over him.

The guard slammed hard against the wall over a dozen feet away and was momentarily stunned. Hercules took advantage of this to flip back onto his feet and run towards a heavy wooden chair to the side of him. He effortlessly broke off one of the legs and proceeded to use it as a makeshift bludgeon to smash in the bald head of the guard just as he was beginning to recover. After several such thrusts, the synthetic man's skull and brains were in pieces on the floor.

Concurrently to that, another of the guards snatched Tweedledee off the floor in a single hand. His squeeze was clearly intended to crush the tiny malcontent like a tomato. This would have succeeded in a few seconds if not for the voice of the head guard from downstairs that suddenly emanated from the security doorway behind them.

"No! That man is a creation of Tornada! Do not harm him!"

The obviously perplexed synthetic man turned towards the voice to see nothing and no one. This gave Tweedledee the chance to cut the android's wrist with a quick flick of his blade. As one of his opponent's primary veins was ripped open, the dwarf leapt to the guard's neck and slit his throat with an equally fast swipe.

After Tweedledee landed upon being dropped several feet to the floor, he watched the man stumble across the room with blood spraying out of the two gaping wounds. A sordid smirk crossed his plump little face as he realized even this genetically designed powerhouse would bleed out in less than a minute.

"Take *that*, you mindless rube!" Tweedledee said as fresh blood dripped from his blade. "And good show there, Echo! I knew I could count on you!"

The Phantom of the Opera was so determined to reach the shelf where the precious chemical was hidden that he was more than willing to engage the third guard himself. As the synthetic sentry took a devastatingly strong swing at him, Erik deftly ducked under the move, rolled behind the guard, and had his Punjab lasso around the guard's throat from behind.

The Phantom pulled with all his strength, despite knowing that even his great strength would not equal that of this creature manufactured by Tornada's arcane science. However, he did anticipate that the severe crushing of the sentry's airways would disorient the guard just long enough to make his next move. Accordingly, Erik reached for a flask that he had identified as containing methyl alcohol.

The cloaked man emptied the glass container on the guard's eyes, which caused him to fall to his knees as the powerful alcohol burned the delicate orbs. Erik then ran towards a nearby wall where there was hanging an ax that could be used to smash the pane holding a fire extinguisher. With a cry of fury, the Phantom ran towards the pain-wracked synthetic guard and, with one mighty swing of the hatchet, severed the creature's head.

"Jeez lou-eeze," Tweedledee uttered. "That guy don't play around."

"Quite efficient a killer you are, my friend the Phantom," Echo said.

"The chemical," Erik said while tossing the bloodied ax away. "It is located behind that panel over there."

The Phantom's cloak billowed in the air as he rushed towards the cabinet like a humanoid gust of wind. There he expertly jimmied the lock and recognized the blueish hue of the all-important liquid within.

"Ah! Here it is!" Erik exclaimed with indescribable zeal as he picked up the vial and glared at its fluidic contents.

"When do you plan to test that stuff?" Tweedledee queried.

"Now!" Erik replied just before pulling off his mask and gulping down the contents of the vial.

The trio watched in rapt attention as the Phantom's supple athletic body began trembling as if in the midst of an earthquake. The unholy three anxiously anticipated the next few moments to result in their employer's horrific features remolding themselves like organic clay into something normal according to human standards.

Instead, all that resulted was the Phantom falling to his knees and violently vomiting all over the floor for almost a minute.

"Damn it all," Tweedledee whispered to himself, realizing the failure of the chemical.

After the Phantom coughed up the last remnants of the failed formula from his stomach and regained a semblance of composure, Tweedledee spoke to him.

"Well, um, that's a tough break, Erik," the dwarf said. "Since that chemical does nothin' more than make you puke, I guess I won't be trying it either. Maybe you can still sell it as one of those liquids that makes a person clear out their stomach if they get poisoned or something."

"Get out of here," was all the somber and dejected Phantom said while remaining on his knees.

"Ah, sure, no problem," Tweedledee said. "This caper is done anyways. We'll leave you alone now to, um, sulk or whatever. And I hate to bring this up, but, well... you did offer to pay us for helping you get in here, and that didn't hinge on the chemical actually working."

"You shall find your payment on the kitchen table of your accommodations first thing in the morning," Erik said quietly. "Now... go!"

"OK, thanks a bunch and, well... we're off now."

"How sad for poor Erik," Echo lamented as the three left the back entrance of the building.

"Yeah, and just as sad for me," Tweedledee mentioned as they headed down a surreptitious back alley. "But anyways, the Phantom was on target when he said we gotta get out of Paris now that we got the necklace. As soon as he leaves our money in the morning, we're gonna take it and get out of France completely."

"Good idea, sir," Echo agreed formally. "But where can three gentlemen of our nature and vocation retreat to for our subsequent capers?"

"Well, I've heard that England is a great place this time of year," the dwarf answered.

"Then we're off to there tomorrow," Hercules said. "You always know what's best, Mr. Tweedy."

Last year, I wrote that, with John Peel, one never knows what to expect! This is truer than ever with his latest contribution, an allegorical fable, a wicked little tale written in the style of the great French philosopher Voltaire, reusing the characters from his classic Candide, *but with a twist…*

John Peel: *Undying Love*

The 1760s

Of all the loving couples in the world (and I am reliably informed that there are at least several dozen such), perhaps there is none quite as devoted as Candide and his wife Cunegonde. The reasons for the strength of their love are quite simple: Candide is firmly of the opinion that his wife is the most beautiful, most charming and most understanding in the world. As this view is fully shared by Cunegonde—who also considers herself the most beautiful, charming and understanding woman in all of the world—they have a very firm basis upon which to erect their edifice of love. It has been able to withstand all sorrows and misfortunes that the couple has had to face.

And sorrows and misfortunes have, sadly, been encountered a great deal in their still-young lives. Cunegonde was born the only daughter of the Baron of Thunder-ten-Troncke, a position of great privilege and wealth. Candide—also born in the same Westphalian town—came from less exalted parentage, if, indeed, he possessed parents. Rumor supposed that he was the son of the sister of the Baron and some passing noble-man, but, then, rumor supposes a great number of things, some of which are sadly untrue. Be that as it may, Candide was taken in, raised and educated by the Baron, but was always firmly reminded that this was not because he deserved it through the good fortune of being born into the family, but because of the well-known generosity of the Baron. As this generosity was well-known only to the Baron, this explanation was not widely accepted, and the theory of the passing nobleman dallying with the Baron's long-departed sister was the preferred explanation.

Candide and Cunegonde had been raised together almost entirely alone. There was, of course, her brother, the future Baron Thunder-den-Troncke, and the serving maid, Paquette, but they hardly counted to either Candide of Cunegonde. There was also the mysterious Old Woman, who was personal maid to Cunegonde and fiercely devoted to her mistress, but, again, the young couple paid her little heed. The only adult that they did pay attention to was their tutor, the esteemed Doctor Pangloss. Candide, in particular, considered their tutor to be a man of wisdom and great learning, and probably the most intelligent man in the world. Once again, his judgment was shared by its object, as Doctor Pangloss was of precisely the same opinion about himself. He took his duties very seriously, and taught the young people many things, notably his firm belief that all was for the best in the best of all possible worlds.

Candide's opinion on the matter conformed entirely to that of Doctor Pangloss; Cunegonde's views were somewhat shaken after their home castle was raided by a Bulgar army and she was raped and disemboweled. An impartial observer might well understand her reservations after such an experience, and even Candide could hardly fault her for her loss of complete faith.

Now Candide possessed several splendid attributes, it must be confessed. He was undeniably handsome, and his body was strong and in fine shape. He was loyal without question to his friends, and had remarkable tenacity. He was reasonably brave—by which I mean that he was brave as long as it was reasonable to be so, but thought nothing of running rapidly in the other direction when faced by overwhelming strength. And he was invariably truthful. It must be told, though, that this latter trait might not be as helpful as it might sound. It is an interesting question as to whether he was named Candide because of his forthright and candid nature, or whether he was so honest because he felt that he should live up to his given name. In either event, whether the name preceded the nature, or the nature preceded the name, Candide was the most truthful man in the world. And this led to what might well be his only real fault—if fault it was—that he invariably accepted that all other people were as exactingly honest as he was. Once someone informed him of anything, Candide would accept this invariably as being the truth of the matter. Perhaps you or I might hesitate to do the same, but Candide—never!

After many adventures, both in Europe and the New World, and many separations, the lovers were finally united and, together with their friends, settled on a farm back in Europe, on the shores of the Propontis in northern Turkey. By this time Cunegonde had become hideously ugly, but Candide had married her despite this. His sole ambition had become to watch their garden grow.

To his amazement, however, his quiet life was not quite as uneventful as he had expected. After several weeks of marriage, it seemed to him that Cunegonde's ugliness—which had been as intense as had been her previous beauty—began to dissipate. She seemed daily to regain her youthful charms and undeniable attractiveness. He had spoken of the matter to Doctor Pangloss (who had been one of the friends who had joined the happy couple on the extended farmstead), and the philosopher's opinion was simply that this was further evidence that all is for the best in this best of all possible worlds. By this point in his life, however, Candide had developed strong doubts as to the veracity of this philosophy, so he sought further opinions on the matter.

Paquette (who had also joined them in domestic bliss) ascribed the increasing beauty of Cunegonde to the fact that Candide was merely becoming accustomed to her terrible appearance. Candide also found this belief slightly difficult to accept because, despite his admitted naivity, he had never before been known to gloss over faults. And, to be entirely honest (as I feel I should follow Candide's own example), he did rather have a suspicion that Paquette was possibly not the best person to seek out for her opinions on the attractiveness or otherwise of another woman. Despite the lowliness of her birth, Paquette had always held rather an exalted opinion of her own beauty and tended to downplay that of a potential rival.

And the others all had their own comments on the matter. Brother Giroflee had remarked that Candide's discovery that his wife's beauty was increasing went against natural order, as most men complained that their wives grew uglier after they were wedded. Martin and Cacambo, Candide's servants, were of the opinion that they should have no opinions at all concerning the beauty or otherwise of their master's wife. And the old woman contented herself merely with the observation that Candide was—as he had always been—a fool. Candide knew better than to dispute her on this subject.

The result of all of these opinions had left Candide no better off. But he consoled himself with the thought that, whatever the cause, he had come to see that his wife was becoming as beautiful as ever. And, as usual, he had not asked the opinion of the only person who could have told him truthfully what the cause of Cunegonde's increasing beauty was, and that was Cunegonde herself.

We, by good fortune, are not as limited as was Candide, and, as a result, we can (in a manner of speaking) consult with the lady in question. We can quietly creep within the conjugal bedroom of the couple and observe what Candide never has—nor, if Cunegonde can prevent it, that he never will. Once Candide had slipped into his weary sleep—the result of his long, tiring work on the communal farm followed by the enjoyment of his marital relations with his loving wife, Cunegonde quietly roused herself and left the marriage bed. She dressed herself and slipped silently away from the house to venture into the darkness of the night.

I should immediately assure the reader, who might be under some misapprehension as to why a beautiful wife might venture out into the night. This was not, as the gentle reader might mistakenly have assumed, a journey to an assignation with some lover. The reader might consider such suspicions fully justified, given that Cunegonde had spent some considerable time as a courtesan (and compensated most generously for her time and attentions). But no—she was as fully devoted to her husband as he was to her, and the idea of slipping into the bed of some hypothetical lover would no longer even cross her mind.

Her intentions were quite otherwise. Cunegonde was well aware of the nature of her husband, for which she was truly thankful. This was especially so in the matter of his unquestioning acceptance of everything she told him. It did so enable her to avoid certain... difficulties. Following Candide's discovery that she had been raped (multiple times) by the invading Bulgar forces and then disemboweled, he had simply accepted her explanation that it was possible to survive such events. Of course, it was not, and she had not.

Nor had he ever questioned her concerning her friendship with the Transylvanian Prince Rakoczi. She had ostensibly been his slave, and Candide had purchased her freedom. But she had been coached by the Prince in certain matters that she now practiced in isolation. She prowled the night not in search of lovers, but prey. After all, she was the daughter of a Baron, and born to rank and privilege, and that had clearly been the way God had intended matters. And the ones she chose to feed upon were peasants—and heretics to add to that. They were clearly meant by God to be sustenance for her. And their blood was making her more youthful, and restoring her beauty, so that was another sign that everything was working out the way it must.

After all, was not this all for the best, in this best of all possible worlds?

The green-masked Fantômas, who was featured in a trilogy of French films of the 1960s (starring Jean Marais and Louis de Funès), owed more to James Bond than the original dark-clad psychopath created by Allain & Souvestre. That version of the character was recently relaunched by Frank Schildiner and returns here in yet another homage to those 1960s spy films...

Frank Schildiner: *The Specter of Fantômas...*

Undisclosed Location (probably Paris?), 1964

The SPECTRE Council relaxed as the green light flashed across the viewing screen. A light ripple of relieved laughter spread across the chamber as their leader, the massive, terrifying man they knew only as "Number One," slowly stroked his white Persian cat with right hand.

His real name was Ernst Stavro Blofeld and his latest plan, known as Operation Blitzkrieg, appeared to have succeeded. Reaching across his desk, he flicked a switch, opening communications between the strike team and the SPECTRE war room.

"Number Three, report," he said, silencing the room.

The obese face of a bald man whose dentition consisted entirely of gold teeth swam into view. Only Blofeld knew that Roman Orgonetz was a far more dangerous man than anyone else present, save himself. While every member of the inner circle of the Special Executive for Counter-intelligence, Terrorism, Revenge and Extortion controlled a network, Orgonetz's organization was far deeper and more insidious. They—the SMOG—would be a true power in the world one day.

"Number Three to Number One," Orgonetz said, "We intercepted the atomic bombs meant for the American airship. Our people convinced Brigadier General Ripper that the Soviets planned to begin a world war. He ordered full arming of the 843rd Bomb Wing. His actions were later countermanded by General Turgidson and the wing was ordered to stand down. It shall take days before they possess a full inventory of the weapons."

"Excellent work, Number Three," Blofeld said, "Open the canisters immediately so that we may confirm the serial numbers."

"At once, Number One," Orgonetz said. "Our men are performing that act as we speak."

The camera's perspective shifted and the images of three black-clad men appeared. They opened the casing a few seconds later, pulling aside the outer housing of the bomb.

From the steel tube of the bomb emerged music and popping sounds. Confetti exploded above the heads of Number Three and his men as the tune grew louder with each passing second.

"What is this?" Blofeld asked, placing his cat on the desk as he stood and pressed closer to the screen.

"I believe," the eccentric arms dealers Félix Sousse, the representative of SPHINX, said, "that the song is *Entry of the Gladiators* by Julius Fučík."

"Not helpful, Number Fifteen," Blofeld said. "I'm referring to the bomb. Why is there music playing from our bomb?"

One of the black-clad men stuck his head close to the interior, reached inside and handed an object to Orgonetz. The man with the golden teeth studied it for a moment before bringing it closer to the camera. A second later, a white card covered the screen with one word written across it:

Fantômas.

"*Merde!*" uttered Marc-Ange Draco, Number Seven, the leader of the Unione Corse.

"...find that secrecy was paramount in this, Operation Water Ballet," Number Twenty-Two said over the viewer as his two assistants the lovely Linka Karensky and Wen Yurang, completed the loading of the bombs aboard the boat.

"Excellent, Number Twenty-Two," Blofeld said, "Did you encounter any difficulties?"

Count Contini shook his head, started the boat's motor, and said, "None whatsoever, Number One. My assistants were the only ones who knew my plans. This prevented any chances of a leak. Now, I must rendezvous with our freighter for the final segment. Number Twenty-Two, out."

The screen went black, and the SPECTRE Council quietly applauded the success of their most important operation. The theft of a pair of Soviet nuclear missiles had been a masterstroke, one that would lead to several powers soon paying their organization millions in blackmail.

Business resumed for ten minutes before Number Nine, a terrifying woman named Irma Blunt, interrupted the discussion of narcotics trafficking in the United States.

"Forgive me, Number One," she said, "I know you wish to hear the conclusion of my report on our operations involving the Prizzi and Caprice crime families, but we have an emergency. Number Twenty-Two is calling is on Channel D."

"Open Channel D," Blofeld said, flicking a switch that turned his chair towards the television screen.

Count Contini appeared on the viewer, his face a mask of bruises. By his sides, supporting him were his two assistants. The Italian nobleman's single open eye focused upon the screen and fear was visible in the single orb.

"Number One," he said, his normally smooth voice sounding mushy and slurred, "Catastrophe! Just before the operation commenced, *he* attacked me, beat me, and imprisoned me in the trunk of my car. He looked just like me, Number One! He looked and even sounded like me!"

"Who did this?" Blofeld asked, hissing out each word. "And where are our bombs?"

Count Contini's head drooped, and he said in a whisper:

"It was Fantômas."

Mere seconds later, the SPECTRE Council degenerated into a scene of bedlam. Men and women shouted, attempting to air their views on the situation. Accusations flew back and forth and shaking fists threatened greater violence. The mayhem continued unchecked for several minutes before the wall panels slid downward, revealing armed men in black uniforms. Each raised their machine pistols, aiming for the gang leaders that held rank in the underground organization.

The Council members fell silent and Number One, who sat above the group behind clouded glass, cleared his throat. Only his powerful hands appeared visible as he stroked his quietly purring cat.

"Now that we have regained our composure," he said in his mildest tone, "I would have you speak. Number Ten, you were loudest. Please air your views."

Number Ten, a squat former SMERSH killer named Strelik, hammered the tabletop with his enormous fist. Everyone present knew he had been the last Chief Executioner of the infamous spy organization. He was a man capable of any act of terror should he be so ordered.

"Yes!" he said, pounding the table again. "This is treachery! There is no Fantômas! This person was a fictional construct of the French newspapers. And even if he did exist, he died on the *Gigantic* in 1912! And if somehow he survived, he would be, like, 90 today!"

"Then what caused our failure twice?" Blofeld asked.

"This is obvious," Strelik said, crossing his arms and smiling. "Some people at this table seek control of the Council. They have no loyalty to anyone or anything but their own desires. We must interrogate everyone. I shall begin immediately!"

"Shall you?" Number One asked. "Where shall you start, Number Ten."

"With Number Nine, of course! Women lack any loyalty unless beaten soundly," Number Ten said. "I shall tame her for you, sir."

Strelik smiled in Irma Blunt's direction as Emilio Largo, Number Two, rose, raised an air pistol, and shot the former Soviet assassin through the neck. The man gurgled twice before falling over, slowly dying as his lungs filled with blood. Two black-garbed men appeared from the corners of the room and dragged the corpse from sight, a thin trail of blood marking their passage.

"Number Seven," Blofeld told Draco, "approach the head of the Matarese Cartel, offering them Number Ten's seat on the Council. The Shepherd's Boy will serve better than the mad Russian. Until then, we must confront this ridiculous impostor, Fantômas. He hinders our operations and even those fools, THRUSH, might start questioning our might."

"May I suggest we delegate the task to a Russian asset, someone like Krassno Granitski? Or possibly the American martial artist, Bill?" Number Fourteen, a former Gestapo agent named Otto Flick, suggested.

"No," Blofeld said.

"Scaramanga would be a better choice," Number Twelve, a lame man named Gabriel, interjected. "A million per kill is inexpensive in this situation."

"No," Blofeld said.

"You cannot mean to use that overblown Jackal?" Irma Blunt asked as everyone present exchanged obviously concerned expressions at their leader's responses.

"No, none of those," he said, "The problem with each of your suggestions, my friends, is that you think too small. I am not hindered by such failings. In the contingency of another insult by this Fantômas, I plan to engage the services of the new Red Hand. Their members are all trained killers, they're eager to restore their once-proud reputation—and they're inexpensive. They shall find, capture, and torture this thief until he begs for death. Then they shall execute him as we watch."

"The Red Hand? I thought they were our rivals," Largo said.

"Friendly competition. The four men that control their inner circle know that battling us would be their downfall. Therefore, we diplomatically arrange boundaries and lend each other assistance," Number One said. "Now, Number Nine, let us return to the distribution of narcotics in the United States. Do the Corleones still oppose us…"

A week later, after Number Two had garroted another member of the Council, the view screen flashed, and a large letter F appeared across it. Eerie organ music blared for several seconds before falling silent. Mocking laughter followed as the screen flickered and a green masked face appeared. The owner of the mask wore an elegant black suit and tie and his dark eyes appeared filled with merriment.

"Well, well," he said in a deep, melodious voice, "we finally meet, my friends. The pleasure is all yours, for I am Fantômas, and you have proved a most amusing group for me. Your attempts in expanding your power base have not met with my approval. Your lack of respect towards me was your failure."

Blofeld and several others, opened their mouths, but found themselves hushed by a simply raised hand from the green masked man.

"Let us not fence and behave foolishly, you know this to be true. However, I did wish to return something to you," he said while removing a white box with a metal antenna.

Fantômas extended the antenna, pressed a button, and looked towards his camera again. From above their heads, a panel opened, and four human heads fell onto the Council table. The leaders of SPECTRE shrank back from the grizzly items, with only Blofeld moving closer. He examined each face and fell back into his chair, his flesh face pale.

"Yes, Mr. Blofeld, they are the masters of the new Red Hand. I give them to you as an example and a lesson. If you battle Fantômas, you shall receive a worse fate," he said, laughing.

Blofeld closed his eyes, breathed deeply for a moment, and then looked into the viewscreen. He stared at the implacable masked face for a full minute before dropping his eyes.

"What do you want?' he asked in a strangled whisper.

Fantômas applauded lightly as his mocking merriment continued unabated.

"I am glad you learn quickly, Mr. Blofeld. Next, I would be forced to kill several members of your Council as a lesson in proper conduct," he said. "As to my desires, you shall each find a list of assets I require in your jacket's top pockets. Then you may continue with your latest attempt at seizing a nuclear weapon."

Blofeld winced as he pulled the page from his inside pocket, unsurprised that everyone present did so as well. He scanned the list, which was damaging to a small degree to SPECTRE's assets, but not crippling. Fantômas appeared to know everything about their supposedly secret order.

"Done," Blofeld said. "Does this conclude our business?"

"For now," the Lord of Evil said. "But remember: groups such as yours are mere remoras in Fantômas's ocean. Begin believing you are sharks, and you shall be eaten by me. Now, see to the transfer of the assets I requested and you shall have my blessing. Adieu, for now!"

Blofeld stared at his hands for a moment before straightening and pressing a button on his desk.

"Clear those heads from this room. Then we shall hear the details of Number Two's plan…"

Nathalie Vidalinc is both a new writer and a new addition to our crew of contributors. In her first story, she decided to bring together Felifax, Paul Féval fils' *tiger-man, previously used in these pages by Chris Nigro, and Josephine Balasamo, a.k.a, Countess Casgliostro, one of Rick Lai's favorite characters. Some of the more obscure circus characters who appear here were taken from a couple of plays recently translated by Frank Morlock and published in our recent collection,* The Madwoman of Melun...

Nathalie Vidalinc: *The Music Box*

Paris, June 1931

Rama Tamerlane, brought up under the protection of the goddess Kali, the product of the scientific experiments of Edward Sexton, has become famous in India as Felifax, the tiger-man; and in England, as the owner of the extraordinary Rama's Circus & Menagerie. Rama married Grace Palmer, a scientist who found a formula that made him lose his beast-like scent. This story begins in Paris during their honeymoon in June, 1931.

I

The hotel concierge handed Rama an envelope. He opened it in the elevator. It contained a letter written on deluxe bond paper. He and Grace were invited to the Opera by the Earl of Chester for a performance of *La Traviata*.

Back in their suite, Rama threw the letter on the bed with indifference, but this gesture did not escape his wife's attention. The former Miss Palmer was just beginning to enjoy their stay in Paris.

"Oh, *La Traviata*!" she said. "This could turn out to be a wonderful evening."

"Do you know who this Earl of Chester is?" asked her husband.

"No," replied Grace. "It's probably a loyal devotee of your circus who is curious to meet you."

"Something of a mystery, then? I suppose we should go."

Rama sighed. He had learned to appreciate western clothes, pants and long sleeves, but still didn't like to dress up for such occasions.

The pomp of the Paris Opera house appealed to Rama, and he began to no longer regret having had to put on a formal dinner jacket. Grace's visible enjoyment also pleased him. Everything was perfect, right down to the Earl of Chester's box.

"Your Royal Highness!" Grace said, performing a curtsey as she recognized their host.

"Mistress Tamerlane! I am delighted to make your acquaintance!"

The Earl of Chester was, in fact, the Prince of Wales. With him were two younger cousins, a secretary, Countess Josephine de Fénix, who was planning a trip to India and was there for advice, and her escort, General Zaroff. Rama found Zaroff unsympathetic, but the Countess, on the other hand, intrigued him. He thought her to be twenty-five, but Grace, with her feminine instinct, gave her ten more years. They were both wrong.

When the lights began to dim, everyone took their seats. During the intermission, Josephine and Grace talked about fashion while the Prince asked Rama about his circus. Zaroff and the others had gone out in the foyer.

"Mr. Tamerlane, the Maharani of Benares has entrusted me with a gift for your sister Djina, for she knows how much she loves pretty things," said the Prince. "She seemed to be very keen on choosing this gift herself, and, if I understand correctly, the Maharajah, too, is very fond of it. You had some kind of dispute with him, if I remember correctly?" he concluded with an amused smile.

"Nothing that can be set aside, obviously," Rama replied in the same manner.

The Prince made a sign to his secretary, who pulled out of his coat a small package, about two inches wide, wrapped inside a folded cloth.

Rama prepared to unfold it, but Grace stopped him.

"I don't think you should," she said.

"Oh, Grace, please, don't deprive us of the pleasure of looking at a Maharani's gift?" said Josephine.

Rama unwrapped the cloth. It concealed a box of made of gold and enamels with a jungle motif—two tigers made of tiny jewels fighting. There was a small key in the lock. He opened it and a familiar music rang out.

Their unanimous cry of wonder drew the eyes of the neighboring patrons. The two women could not resist handling the magnificent item. Rama noticed the lust in Josephine's eyes.

"Are you a collector, Countess?" he asked.

Josephine closed the box with great care and relocked it.

"There's no point hiding it, is there? I like beautiful objects. If your sister ever gets tired of this music box, let me know and I'll gladly buy it from her."

Rama nodded in ascent.

Later, back at their hotel, the concierge handed Rama two more letters.

"We sure receive a lot of mail," said Grace, grabbing them.

She pocketed the first, having recognized her father's handwriting, but she opened the other.

"It's from the Maharajah of Benares!" she exclaimed. "But how could he know we were here?"

Rama looked at the envelope.

"Though one of his agents, I suppose," he replied. "It's been mailed from London. What does it say?"

" '*You will need this*,' that's all," answered Grace. "And it also contains this."

Inside the envelope was a small key that looked identical to that of the music box.

"It's a duplicate key. Maybe he was concerned we might lose the one that came with the box, or he forgot to give it to the Prince... Strange, isn't it?" she remarked.

Rama took the key and compared it to that of the music box.

"It's not exactly the same," he noted.

"Why don't you try it?" suggested Grace.

"But, darling, locks are made to work with only one key!"

"Try it anyway!" the young woman said, persuasively.

Rama turned the key in the lock of the music box, with the air of someone convinced he is wasting his time, but, to his surprise, he heard a a small click and a tiny hidden compartment opened at the bottom of the box.

Inside was a thin piece of paper. On it were instructions on how to find a package hidden inside the tiger cage at the Cirque Dirko, a small outfit that was currently performing at the famous *Cirque d'Hiver*.

"We shall have to investigate," said Rama. "I've seen their posters on the Colonnes Morris outside, and I'd been meaning to go. It's always good to keep an eye on the competition. What does your father say?" he added, referring to the second letter.

Grace opened it and read it.

"Nothing of great importance. He and Baber are aboard the *Grateful* and spending some time in Deauville. They hope we're enjoying our time Paris, that's all."

"How could we not? We're going to the circus!" said Rama.

II

The next day, Rama Tamerlane and Grace Palmer sat in the shadows in the upper seats of the arena of the *Cirque d'Hiver*. The Cirque Dirko's acts had all been dazzling. Rama had been especially fond of the tiger act and recognized the familiar scent of his feline brother. But a feeling of being watched disturbed him. It originated from somewhere in the audience, but it was impossible to determine who, or where, among the five thousand seats. However, he showed no emotion so that Grace could enjoy the show.

When the clowns concluded with their last pirouette, the couple decided to pay a visit to the menagerie.

As they walked backstage, Dirko, the circus' owner, came to meet them, still wearing his stage costume. He was a robust, jovial, and affable man. He recognized Rama at once.

"Monsieur Tamerlane! What an honor! Have you come to see my tiger?" he asked. "She isn't as beautiful as yours, but I'm still very proud of her."

"Yes, she is very beautiful," said Rama.

Delighted, Dirko took them to the menagerie.

"Here is Zizi, our tamer!" he said, putting his hand on the shoulder of a beautiful young woman.

She bowed low to Rama with her hands clasped.

"It is an honor to meet the noble Son of Kali," she said.

The tiger—India—was resting in her cage. Rama approached her, but the feline let out an unpleasant hiss. He moved closer, and the beast reared up, acting aggressively. Rama was surprised by her reaction. He tried moving his hand closer, but the tiger lunged at him through the bars, roaring, as Zizi cracked her whip.

"It seems as if India is not in a good mood today," she said.

Her look of concern betrayed her surprise. Rama turned to his wife with a confused expression. She took him by the arm.

"We'll come back another day," she said cheerfully without any doubt in her voice.

After exchanging the usual courtesies, Grace led her husband towards the exit.

"Amazing," said Dirko to Zizi. "What do you think?"

"Kali wears two faces," replied the young woman. "She is both death and life, joy and sorrow. Only Brahmins can understand the thoughts of the goddess…"

Back at the hotel, Rama thoughtfully sank into an armchair.

"You understand that what happened was because the serum I've made for you has weakened your scent when you're in that form?" said Grace.

"Yes," replied Rama in a tired voice. "Perhaps we should resume our journey and leave all this behind us…"

Dumbfounded, the young woman took a seat next to her husband.

"Why?" she asked.

"My brethren don't recognize me anymore, Grace. Do you really think it's only because my scent has gone?"

"Absolutely! I'm sure that tiger would have recognized you if you'd approached her as Felifax."

Rama smiled, but didn't seem reassured.

"What about finding that package?" said Grace.

"You're right. I should return to the Circus."

Rama always ended up agreeing with Grace. Truthfully, the blonde woman had him wrapped around her little finger.

III

Dressed all in black, his hair hidden under a turban, a mask hiding his face, Rama walked all around the *Cirque d'Hiver* until he found an unobtrusive spot suitable for climbing.

With his strong hands, he climbed up the wall, proceeded along the gutters, and went down into the menagerie.

Suddenly, a man and a doberman sprang out of nowhere.

"Will you come with me, M. Tamerlane?" politely asked the watchman, who was dressed as a clown.

Rama hesitated. But if he refused and fought back, Felifax might kill the man and his dog. So he followed them. They walked to a large enclosed courtyard, where a group of men and women were dancing to the sound of guitars.

"Are you mad, Rama Tamerlane?" asked Dirko. "Do you really think you can handle my tiger better without my tamer?"

"Yes, I do."

"Zizi will not let anyone into India's cage if the beast objects."

"I understand, but I can do it."

"I think Zizi believes you, but I don't."

"How do you propose we resolve this then?" asked Rama. "I must get inside that cage. I'll do whatever you want."

"Zizi told me about the exploits of the Son of Kali, so I expected to see you again. If you are what you say you are, you will have no trouble fighting Zoltan, our Hercules."

"If that is your pleasure..."

A colossus who was two heads taller than Rama rose from the audience. Rama recoiled slightly, but remained impassive. However, a chuckle went through the group who had caught the gesture.

Rama was younger, lighter and more flexible than Zoltan, so he was able to keep him on his toes for a while. But this wasn't Zoltan's first fight, and the Hercules, now angry, managed to pin Rama against a wall. He ran towards it as if he wanted to walk through it, and crushed Rama against the stone.

Gasping for breath, Rama slid to the ground. Zoltan lifted him up by the neck and smashed his head against the wall. But the young man, clutching the arm choking him, bent his legs and pushed against the wall with all his might.

Zoltan stumbled back, but did not let go of Rama. The Indian could no longer bear his adversary's embrace; his eyes began to change... turning yellow like those of a tiger... then his face...

Zoltan looked at his opponent with fear. He loosened his grip... In an instant, they slid to the ground, still facing each other, ready to pounce. They lunged simultaneously and grasped each other in a violent clash. Zoltan now realized that he was no longer holding an ordinary man; Rama had grown in size and power and his fingers on the giant's back felt like claws.

Zoltan let go of his adversary and, with a hip thrust, found himself at a distance. The Hercules could see that his opponent was no longer the slender young man he'd fought, but a full-fledged tiger-man.

He hesitated, intimidated by Felifax's low growling. Still, he was about to throw himself at him in an act of bravado when Zizi called out.

"I will take you to the tiger, O revered Son of Kali," she said.

The fight stopped. The Circus folks admired this new and magnificent being. Felifax was still angry and showed signs of rage, but he heard Zizi's heart, sensed her loyalty, and calmed down.

When the tiger-man approached India's cage, the tiger stood up to smell him, then lay down on the floor.

Felifax entered, looking for a hidden compartment. It was rather small, with two tiny holes that looked like locks. Fortunately, he had brought with him the two keys to the music box. As he fumbled, trying to insert the right key into the right lock, Felifax almost lost his temper.

Suddenly, there was a lot of barking and shouting outside. Zizi went out to see what was happening.

IV

A new dawn was rising over Paris.

The Circus personnel had just spotted another intruder on the roof and were cutting off his escape.

A few minutes later, Jarry the clown, Oudja the acrobat, and Mercurio the knife-thrower emerged from behind a box, dragging the intruder before Dirko.

"Who are you?" asked the Circus Owner. "What are you doing here? Who are you working for?"

The newcomer looked at them with contempt.

"Mercurio, keep asking our guest these questions until he answers them," ordered Dirko.

The knife-thrower put on a sinister face and passed his blade under the prisoner's nose.

Zizi returned to join Felifax. The Indian had his head close to the tiger's ear. Together, they made a purring noise.

"Are you talking to India, Lord Rama?" she asked.

"Tigers are not very talkative," he replied. "They go straight to the point. I told him you were a friend."

"Thank you, my lord," said Zizi, her face beaming as she bowed.

"What was that ruckus outside?" asked Rama, as he stepped out of the cage.

"Our crew has captured an intruder. They think he was spying on you. Jarry and his dog—whom you already met—had been watching outside. He raised the alarm when the man tried to gain access to the roof. He had nothing on him but a pair of binoculars. Mercurio is questioning him."

The intruder was obviously frightened, but remained silent, even after Mercurio began nipping at his chin with his blade.

"I have nothing to say," he kept saying.

"Are you certain?" said Zoltan, dropping his huge hand on the man's shoulder and squeezing.

The intruder began to sweat.

"What would you say to questioning him in the tiger's cage?" suggested the Hercules to Mercurio.

"OK! OK! Stop! I'll talk!" said the intruder hastily. "My name is Galoubert. I came to see your show. I was just trying to sneak in without paying."

Zoltan was getting restless. Mercurio took out his knives and began to throw them all around Galoubert, missing him only by inches.

"I'm nobody, I tell you!" said the intruder.

Suddenly, the door opened with a bang. Galoubert was startled. Felifax entered. Upon seeing him, the intruder would have melted on the spot if he could.

"I was only paid to watch this guy," he whined, pointing at Rama with his chin.

"Who paid you?" asked the tiger-man.

"Gaston Verdier, the leader of the gang of five."

"Why?"

"I don't know. It's got something to do with a gold music box."

Zoltan and Mercurio turned to Felifax, who was slowly reverting to his human form.

"I've heard of this gang," said Dirko. "They're amongst the worst in Paris. Totally without scruples!"

"Why is this Verdier after the music box?" asked Rama.

"I don't know! I swear!" cried Galoubert.

"Grace!" said Rama, suddenly frightened. "They may be after my wife. She's the one with the box!"

"You should go to her at once!" said Dirko. "Zoltan! Go with him! And Mercurio, you can release this vermin."

After Galoubert was gone, Dirko called Jarry.

"Follow that rascal and don't lose him!" he told the clown. "I want to know where he goes."

V

The taxi stopped in front of the hotel. Rama and Zoltan got out and ran upstairs.

"Grace!" shouted Rama, as he opened the door.

Everything in the suite had been turned upside down. Rama became even more concerned.

"Grace! Grace!" he kept shouting as he searched the suite.

But she wasn't there and he began to calm down. He put the package he'd found in the tiger's cage down on the desk. He'd look at it later.

"The music box is gone," he observed. "It was there on the dresser."

"Do you often leave valuable items in plain sight?" asked Zoltan.

"We were there. Also, who would dare to steal such a repertoried item?"

Zoltan wasn't convinced.

"The concierge! Perhaps he saw Grace?" said Rama.

They ran back downstairs. It turned out that the concierge had seen Grace. She had ordered a taxi to go and visit the haute couture designer Jeanne Lanvin.

"I must tell you," added the concierge, "that a shady character asked me the same question. Obviously, I said nothing. He didn't like it, so I had the porter escort him out."

In the car that was taking them to Lanvin's, Zoltan made a suggestion:

"If Mrs. Tamerlane isn't at Lanvin's, I can get some help. The rest of our staff at the circus can go and look for her. They have many friends in town, and we have a special way of communicating..."

"But Paris is so big..."

Grace Tamerlane had already left Lanvin's by the time they got there, so Rama agreed to Zoltan's proposal. The circus staff gathered, Rama handed out pictures of Grace, and the lot of them spread out into the French capital.

As they were searching the area around the Boulevard Saint-Honoré, Zoltan stopped abruptly. He whistled various sounds and Rama quickly spotted the pattern.

"This way," said the Hercules.

Several circus folk joined them as they arrived at the source of the noise. One of them pointed ahead.

About five hundred yards away, another circus employee was following Grace. But suddenly, he was attacked. A man with a blade leapt at him. He pushed the boy roughly to the ground, approached the young woman, stole her bag, and ran away.

Zoltan ran after him. Rama could feel rage swell within him; it only subsided when he reached his wife.

Grace, still shocked by the theft, was surprised to see her husband appear. She hugged him and pulled herself together. While Zoltan continued his chase, Rama hailed a taxi.

"Was the music box in your bag?" he asked.

"Yes, I was stupid, I didn't want to leave it in the room," she replied. "Oh, Rama, I was so scared…"

"We'll take care of it. These thieves are dangerous. Get back to the hotel, and call Baber!"

"Baber? But why?"

"Please, do as I say," he replied curtly.

The taxi arrived and Grace left. Guided by the circus folk, who hadn't lost the trail, Rama soon found Zoltan standing in front of a maze of small streets in the Quartier Latin.

"I lost him," he explained.

Rama used his sense of smell and soon recognized his wife's perfume.

"Follow me!" he said.

Soon, they spotted their prey in the distance at a crossroad and doubled their pace. But when they reached the Boulevard Saint-Germain, their pursuit ended at a taxi station.

The two dejected men could only return home.

Rama was in a foul mood. He had to find out who was responsible for this attack. Was their adversary only interested in the music box because of its intrinsic value, or because of what it might have been hiding?

Grace was careful not to disturb his thoughts. When the phone rang, she picked it up.

"Rama! A man named Zoltan wants you to meet him at the circus. He said they have a lead!"

VI

Jarry the clown had returned. In the meantime, Dirko had gathered reinforcements. Rama joined them in two unmarked trucks and everyone followed Jarry's directions.

They parked in a small alley, next to a large door.

"Galoubert carried a light with him," explained Jarry, "so it was easy to follow him. He brought me here. He went through that big door over there, and I ran back to report to you."

Rama sensed four persons breathing behind the door. He knocked. Galoubert opened, but he was caught by surprise by Zoltan, who hit him and opened the door wide.

Mercurio grabbed the stunned Galoubert by the collar and sent him flying into the arms of Oudja outside, who tied him up. Meanwhile, the others swarmed into the house. Zoltan sent three more men flying with right and left uppercuts.

A shot rang out; Mercurio had thrown a knife at yet another apache who had been preparing to fire at them; the shot went haywire and the man crumpled to the floor.

Meanwhile, Zizi escorted the few women who were there into a boudoir and locked them up inside.

In less than ten minutes, the circus folks had secured the place. They found Gaston Verdier, the gang leader, just as he was about to flee through a secret passage that led directly to the sewers.

They tied him up and brought him before Rama.

"Monsieur Tamerlane!" said Verdier, with false bravado. "To what do I owe the honor?"

"One of your men stole my wife's purse!" said Rama.

"This is what it's all about?" replied Verdier, somewhat surprised.

"There was a music box inside. I want to know who ordered you to steal it. Who wanted it so badly?"

"Come on, my men steal a lot of stuff. Your wife wasn't targeted. I don't know anything about a music box."

"You're lying! If you know who I am, let me warn you: you wouldn't like my other self..."

As Rama spoke, his breathing became louder. When Felifax began to emerge, Verdier became very place.

"Please, don't hurt me! But I can't tell you anything. They have my daughter. She's everything to me. If I talk, they'll kill her!"

"It's just another trick," grumbled Dirko.

"No," said Felifax. "I can smell he's sincere. Let's go. There's nothing more for us to do here!"

VII

Acting on her husband's advice, Grace had called Baber, Rama's uncle, in Deauville.

He and Sir Eric had immediately set sail for Paris and reached the capital that evening. Rama was pleasantly surprised to see his father-in-law.

"I had time to review the facts of your case," said Palmer. "A name jumped at me—Countess Josephine de Fénix. If the woman you met is whom I suspect, I've already dealt with her in the past. Her real name is Josephine Balsamo, or Josephine Pelligrini, but she is better known as Countess Cagliostro. She was involved in a daring robbery I investigated. A lot of money disappeared that day, as well a beautiful bejeweled gold ewer."

"Why didn't you arrest her?" asked Rama.

"She left, shall we say, a scent, but we no hard evidence."

"That's scandalous!" cut in his daughter.

"Nevertheless, we had no choice but to let her go," Palmer said more sternly. "I think she's the one who hired your thieves. She's used apaches before, against Arsène Lupin in 1894."

"But that's almost forty years ago and she is barely thirty!" said Grace incredulously.

"Yes. She has the reputation of being immortal. That only adds to her charm, I suppose."

"She did exhibit a great deal of interest in the music box," said Rama. "She didn't even try to hide it. But I find it hard to believe she is capable of making such a mistake..."

"What mistake?" asked Palmer.

"To assume that I wouldn't go after her."

"You knew she desired the music box, yet you didn't suspect her. But if you don't mind my asking, what did you find inside that tiger cage?" asked Palmer. "What is this secret you've gone through all this trouble for?"

"Ah, yes!" said Rama, with a grave face. "I haven't opened it yet..."

He went to the desk where he had left the package. He opened it.

Inside was a letter from the Maharajah of Benares as well as a stack of documents. The letter said:

O Most Favored Son of Kali!

Our benighted city must once more beg for your assistance. As you know, the fiendish Edward Sexton died in England soon after his return there. But he had a student, a protégé to whom he entrusted all his dark secrets, and who has come to Benares to continue his master's foul experiments.

We desperately need your help, but the man is cunning and even my palace is infested with his spies. So I have chosen to hide this message in the tiger attraction of Dirko's Circus, which is touring India at this time. I have also entrusted a music box to His Royal Highness that will tell you where to find it, and had my trusted London solicitor mail you the second key that will reveal the box's secret instructions.

If you read this, you are now in possession of the file my investigators gathered about Sexton's evil successor. You will see how great the danger is, not only for India but the world.

Please, Son of Kali, hurry back! We need you!

"It's signed and sealed by the Maharajah himself," said Rama, and there is a post-scriptum: *'Bring the box with you.'* Strange, I wonder why."

Rama handed the file to Palmer, who flipped through it. His horrified face gave away its awful contents. He showed it to Baber and Grace.

"This is terrible!" said Baber.

"Rama, what shall we do?" asked Grace.

Rama took his wife by the shoulders.

"First, we must get the box back. So I shall pay a visit to Countess Cagliostro."

"Be careful," said Palmer. "She is reputed to have a great power of bewitchment."

"That won't work on me," replied Rama.

"I hope so!" Grace said tetchily.

VIII

"Your boy toy is coming" said General Zaroff, leaving his post at the window to lean over Josephine's shoulder.

"I would ask you to leave. We must be discreet."

"What! A tiger-man is coming here and you don't want me to be in the room? You can't be serious, Countess!"

"But I am. Stay out of my business, Zaroff. Or you'll be the one to be hunted."

"Countess!"

"Leave!"

Rama Tamerlane's card was brought to the Countess. She told her manservant to show him in.

"You're hard to find, Countess," he said. "This is the third address I've had to check."

"That's part of my mystery," she replied playfully. "To what do I owe the pleasure of this visit, my friend?"

"You very well know why. I'm not in the mood for games. But I would like for us to remain on friendly terms."

"It's about that music box, isn't it? Is it that important to you?"

"Yes, it is. Besides, you can't use it. You don't have the other key."

"What other key?" replied Josephine. "What are you talking about?"

Rama smiled. This had been his way of finding out if the Countess was more deeply involved in his business; but apparently, greed had been her only motive in stealing the box.

Suddenly, his face contracted. "You are not alone," he said, sensing a threat.

He saw a tiny trace of concern on the Countess' normally impassive but beautiful face.

"Oh, dear," she said emphatically as she stood up and turned around, examining the room surreptitiously. "A servant, no doubt. You don't think I maintain all this by myself, do you?"

Through the many mirrors in the room, Rama saw her expression become hard and threatening, but when she turned around again, she was charming once more.

She came and sat next to him on the sofa.

"Give me back the box, Madame," said Rama sternly.

Suddenly, he changed into Felifax. Always on the lookout, he had just spotted a gun barrel appear behind a narrowly opened doorway.

The Countess rose abruptly and stood before him.

"This is intolerable!" she said with fake outrage, while blocking his view of the doorway. "Leave at once!"

"Give me the box at once, or else… And you may tell General Zaroff to come in."

Rama could feel the Countess' anger growing, almost against her will.

"I didn't know that the General was here," she said with extraordinary bad faith, her gaze impassive, but with an imperceptible smile on her lips, challenging him to question her word.

Faced with such dishonesty, Felifax's fury manifested itself. His feline eyes pierced those of the Countess. His frightening face and threatening growl made her back away.

"Surely the great Rama Tamerlane wouldn't attack an unarmed woman!" she said.

Sensing a trap, the tiger-man pushed her away and, in two strides leapt to the ajar door, flung it open violently and burst into the adjacent room.

Zaroff had been certain he could handle Felifax with his weapon, but when the tiger-man came after him, his survival instinct told him to run. However, he was too late! Felifax grabbed him by the tails of his jacket and lifted him off the ground.

The General was trembling with fear, but his eyes were bulging with rage and spoke of his promise to someday kill this foe.

The tiger-man threw Zaroff against an armoire. The shock caused him to scream in pain. Then Felifax dragged him back into the room where the Countess was waiting serenely, sitting in her comfortable chair. She glared at him.

"So what? I was mistaken," she said defiantly.

"Your bodyguard couldn't protect you. So let's stop this game and give me the box," ordered Felifax.

Zaroff was lying on the ground like a rag doll. The Countess approached Felifax fearlessly, placed her hand on his chest and looked into his eyes.

"This man is nothing to me," she said, breathing the wild scent of her visitor. "But I would very much like for us to remain on friendly terms."

"The box," said Felifax.

She gave it back to him.

IX

The tiger-man left, fearing that another exchange would only make him angrier.

No sooner had he gone out than Zaroff sprang to his feet and ran for his gun. He opened a window and aimed at Felifax, who had just come out of the building.

He had to act quickly and shoot him right through the heart to kill him and yet do as little damage as possible. Through his scope, he saw his prey walk without fear.

He put his finger on the trigger... pressed...

Suddenly, his barrel was deflected. The bullet hit and destroyed the moldings in the ceiling, exposing the joists.

"What's the matter with you?" he spat at Josephine who had caused his shot to go awry.

"I forbid you to hurt that man! I want him—alive!" she replied, watching the feline figure walk away.

Felifax walked towards the Bois de Vincennes. He needed to commune with nature before returning to the world of men. Finally, he hailed a taxi.

When the door to their suite opened, Grace threw herself into Rama's arms. Sir Eric Palmer and Baber felt a great sense of relief.

After the young man had reported his encounter with the Countess and Zaroff, and put the music box back on the dresser, he declared:

"Sexton turned my whole life upside down. I don't want to pursue this matter. I do not wish to give up everything to go hunting for my fellow man. I just want to go on with my honeymoon with Grace."

"This may not be your decision, son," said Palmer, sententiously. "You are already a pawn in a game of which we know almost nothing. Walking away from the table at this juncture might be the most dangerous move of all."

Rama sighed.

"We're going to have to go back to India, Rama, aren't we?" Grace said, looking him in the eye.

"Yes," he replied.

We can always count on David Vineyard to provide us with yet another caper featuring that most wonderful of rogues, Arsène Lupin. However, this clever spy tale is more reminiscent of the thrillers of John Buchan and Talbot Mundy, and is a little different from what we have normally come to expect; nevertheless, it unfolds like a well-oiled machine. Earlier, I mentioned the twin return of Fascinax in this volume; here, the famous black bird makes its second appearance...

David L. Vineyard: *The Gilded Bird*

The Orient-Express, 1927

Captain Hugh North skidded across the surface of the train station made slick by the rain as the Simplon-Orient Express lurched into motion, preparing to leave Istanbul.

Standing in the open doorway of one of the wagons, Pierre Michel, the bored conductor watched him, offering neither support nor derision. Most likely, this was a thirty year-old man who no longer cared about anything other than his train leaving and arriving on time. The conductor watched this passenger's potential fate with a conspicuous lack of interest, though if he made it on board, he would treat him as a king.

Still, he held the door open, and North's long legs carried him across the platform, dodging the people saying good-bye to their loved ones and the luggage carriers moving out of the way.

With a last burst of speed, North flung himself onto the steps, and hauled himself up into the doorway as the conductor made room for him.

"North," he gasped, still breathing hard. "Captain North, the American Consul in Istanbul called ahead to book my passage."

Michel looked at his book, pursing his small lips.

"Yes, Captain Hugh North. I'm afraid that all the compartments were sold out until Zagreb. You can sleep in one of the day cars until then, though."

North nodded. His chest was heaving, but not as badly as before. A near run thing, as Wellington had said of Waterloo, but with any luck, he was the Englishman and not Napoleon in this iteration.

"If you'll indulge me," North said before Michel could go about his business, "but is my friend Mr. Peters aboard?"

This time, the conductor didn't have to consult his book.

"*Oui, Monsieur*," he answered. "Mr. Peters is joining us for this journey. Should I let him know...?"

"No, no," North said, a bit too hastily, "I'll surprise him later."

Michel nodded. Having seen everything, the minor eccentricities of guests aboard the fabled train did not surprise him anymore.

This was the fabled Orient Express and the discretion of its staff was without peer. On board this train traveled the elite of the world, kings and princes, potentates and millionaires. Actors, playboys, thieves, criminals, magnates, confidence men, and, like Hugh North, spies. All found their way from Paris, and across Eastern Europe to the station outside Istanbul through revolution, war, intrigue, and, occasionally, even murder.

Hopefully, that last eventuality could be avoided on this journey.

The romance of the train aside, it had also been the nurturing home of scandal, intrigue, affairs, secret business deals, and more. The late master spy Sidney Reilly and munitions king Basil Zaharoff regularly traveled and did business on this train.

So did Mr. Peters, and on this journey, he was as important as any of the more famous passengers, for tonight Mr. Peters carried death in his wake—papers that would trigger a war across the Balkans that might well draw all of Europe in its wake while it still reeled from the Great War.

North made his way to the lavatory where he stripped off his Burberry, soaked from the heavy rain, and sat about correcting his relative state of disarray. An attendant scared him up a razor, some soap, and a comb, and, from somewhere, a fresh shirt that actually fit. While he dried and polished North's boots and quickly pressed his suit, the American applied the shaving soap and razor musing whether Reilly had ever found himself on this same train in this same lavatory in his underwear while he plotted to avoid a war

The whole affair had started somewhere on the Turkish-Afghan border, at least as far as North knew. Sandy Arbuthnot, Lord Clanroyden, had been slumming in his old wartime hunting grounds, playing at T. E. Lawrence, when he had first come across *it*. In Ankara, he had passed *it* to Tony Hamilton, and Hamilton had passed *it* to Military Intelligence, and, back in London, Sir Pellinore Gwayne-Cust and Sir Walter Harcourt had both confirmed *it*.

North had been in Tiblisi when he'd gotten the call. He'd dropped everything—six months of careful work shot to hell!—and proceeded at once toward Istanbul.

In Istanbul, all the Consul had really known was that there was a man called Peters, a fat man who acted as a kind of go between for another man, someone North knew only from rumor, the mysterious Dimitrios—a fellow with a finger in every pie, behind half a dozen murders and assassinations, revolutions, extremists groups, and countless intrigues, all done in the shadows while Dimitrios kept his hands and nose clean.

Dimitrios made his money from intrigue. Here, he might betray a cause; there, fund the assassination of a key figure, but always for profit. There was money to be made in war for a man like Dimitrios, a man with neither politics nor morals, a man with nothing but a keen eye for the weaknesses of others. Who Dimitrios really was behind this mask, no one really knew, but betrayal and death were no stranger to him.

It was Trevor, the English peer Hamilton had suggested North contact, who had put him onto Peters and Dimitrios on the Viscount's yacht on the Bosphorus over a fabulous meal. Trevor represented no government; he was a sort of Diplomatic Freelance Agent who moved on the outskirts of the intelligence game, but his resources were well respected by those in the know.

"From what your Mr. Hamilton got from Sandy, and what my own sources have told me," Trevor had said, "*it* is a rumor that Dimitrios was able to catch a certain foreign minister of an unfriendly power with his hands bloody plotting a land grab on his neighbor's border, and get it on paper. That's what Peters is carrying, the evidence which, when shown to the government of the aggrieved nation, will no doubt plunge the Balkans into a nice juicy war with Dimitrios funding both sides.

"As for Peters, I can't tell you much about him," Trevor had continued. "He doesn't look like much of an adventurer; in fact, he is a personable raconteur, a man well worth sharing a meal and a drink with, even while he was picking your pocket and slitting your throat. He's by no means exclusive to Dimitrios, but Dimitrios funds his other interests—a bit of a romantic, our Mr. Peters is—a treasure hunter.

"Ordinarily I would handle this myself," Trevor had concluded, "but there is a crisis in Morocco that cannot be ignored, and I sail tonight as soon as we part company. I trust you to complete this business successfully, Captain North. War is a tiresome business, and Europe can ill afford another one. Men such as you and I may not be able to stop a future war, but we can, and must, stop this one."

In the end, or the beginning depending on how you looked at it, Peters had almost given North the slip, booking a flight out of Istanbul, but surprisingly showing up at the ferry crossing to catch the Orient-Express.

North's stomach was still lurching from his mad ride across Istanbul in Trevor's Rolls, then in a powerful motor boat because he'd missed the ferry, and then another wild ride to the Station while the first winter rain of the season had drenched him thoroughly.

Hell, he hadn't yet seen Peters. All he knew was that the man was wearing a bowler, a heavy overcoat with a fur collar, and carried a large heavy black case with him. Almost certainly the papers would be on his person and not in the case, so whatever he carried was of little interest to North.

Clean and dressed again, he made his way to the dining car. He had arranged to be called at the same time as Peters by a well placed bribe to Michel. He would at least get a look at the man.

He arrived in the dining car early enough to pick his seat so he could watch Peters when he entered. Another lone diner was already seated, so North was seated with him. The man was tall and lean, and attractive—a cosmopolitan Turk, impeccably dressed. Before North could speak the man said:

"No need to introduce yourself, Captain North. I am well aware of who you are and why you are on this train."

North tensed. The man raised a hand and a faint smile played at the edges of his lips,

"No, please no need for concern. You see, we are allies of sorts on this trip. You wish to recover a paper carried by a Mr. Peters—at least, that's the name he is using now. And I am here to recover something else he is carrying."

"The black case?" North said.

"Correct. So you see, our objectives are not at odds, and indeed may be combined. But I haven't introduced myself. I'm Colonel Haj."

North couldn't help but be impressed. In the Turkish underworld, Haj was well known; a policeman, a counter intelligence officer, he had a splendid record, a fabulous history, and a ruthless reputation.

"Say we could help each other, Colonel," asked North. "Why don't you simply arrest Peters and take what you want?"

"A good idea, if I could..."

They were interrupted by the waiter with water and the menus. After they had ordered and the waiter had walked away Haj continued:

"I would like nothing better than to arrest Mr. Peters and confiscate what I want and sweat those papers of yours out of him—I no more want war in this region than you do, Captain North—but, alas, his employer, Dimitrios, still has influence in my government with certain ministers who might even be able to end my career. I'm afraid we will have to corner our big rat and outwit him somehow."

A large man entered at the far end of the car. North's eyes barely shifted from Haj, but the man noted it. Knocking a spoon to the floor, Haj bent down to pick it up, managing to glance behind him as he did.

"Ah, our Mr. Peters has arrived. I note the infamous black case is with him. That complicates things. You know, for a policeman, I am contemplating a touch of crime."

North studied Peters as closely as he could without being obvious. The man was jovial with the waiter who obviously knew him; his rich voice and laughter reached well beyond his table, though never rudely. His eyes sparkled with intelligence, and his behavior and style bespoke of money and power, but North's trained eye noted that the clothes he wore weren't quite new, his cuffs were a little frayed, his tie slightly stained, his dark blue pin-striped suit a few seasons out of fashion, and his shoes just a shade worn to the point polish could no longer properly hide their flaws. It suddenly made sense that a man of Peter's obvious appetites would be forced to turn to someone like Dimitrios for funds.

No doubt neither man trusted the other, but this business made for strange bedfellows. Curious alliances were forged, not unlike the one North had just found himself forging with Haj.

North also noted how Peters—he knew it was not his name, but it was simpler to think of him as such—guarded the black case he lumbered to carry and refused all help with it. North had no interest in the man's so called treasure, but if the papers were in there...

"The bird," Haj said.

"Eh?"

"The case. It's a bird, or a figure of one. A golden bird, quite valuable. Our friend Peters stole it. He may even have murdered for it. He's sought it long enough—he and half-a-dozen other cut-throats and back

246

stabbers. I've never seen it myself. I'm not sure many in the modern world have. Peters only received it yesterday. I'm wagering he hasn't opened it to look at it yet. In fact, I'm counting on his saving that moment for later. Our Mr. Peters is an epicurean, not given to satiating his appetites quickly. He'll want to savor the moment."

North hadn't much time for the romance of golden birds, priceless or not. Not with war on the table—one that could very well draw the United States in again. But from his observation of Peters, he agreed with Haj. This was a man who would savor the delicious moment when he finally set eyes on his prize. There might come a time when greed and desperation changed his behavior, but for now, North read him as a man who would prolong his pleasure to better appreciate it, and in his profession, North was a good judge of character—especially that of desperate men.

"If you have a plan, Colonel," North said as the food arrived, "I would be delighted to hear it."

"One is formulating. Your arrival changed my previous plan somewhat, but I suspect for the better. Two heads, as you say in the West... Meanwhile, our food is here. While we indulge, why don't you fill me in on your own plans and what you know of our friend?"

North was still wary, but as Haj could be a valuable ally and a dangerous enemy, he chose the path of least resistance. Without really revealing anything, he laid out his plan of attack, such as it was. He explained his suspicions that Peters carried the papers on his body, either in a recessed pocket or a body belt under his clothes simply because that would make losing them to a thief or a pickpocket less likely. North did not add that he had eliminated hiring either thief or pickpocket based on that deduction.

Haj listened carefully as he ate. Once in a while, he nodded or cocked his head in agreement; twice an eyebrow rose slightly as if he were reassessing his opinion of North based on this conversation.

"Considering how little time you have had to judge our Mr. Peters, I am impressed," he finally declared. "I suspect you are right about his carrying the papers close to his body. I have to admit that even my files on the man are somewhat incomplete. I have a dozen names for him. For a while, he was using the alias of Casper Gutman and worked with a shady fellow named Joel Cairo. I have to admit I am often taken aback by the colorful names these fellows dream up for themselves. Can you imagine trying to avoid the attention of the police with a name like Gutman or Cairo? It sounds like cheap melodrama."

North agreed. In his own business, *noms de guerre* tended to be less colorful and more practical, though there were the likes of Von Grundt, the German they called Clubfoot, or Grim, the American agent in Palestine the locals called Jimgrim, who had colorful sobriquets. Even Paul Dukes had once been called the Scarlet Pimpernel of the Russian Revolution.

Peters/Gutman's main course was arriving to great praise from the fat man for the appearance and smell of the meal, just as North and Haj finished their own. Haj produced a cigar case. They were a Turkish tobacco and a bit harsher than the Cubans North usually preferred, but he took one and held it while Haj lit it for him. Blue gray smoke curled around their heads.

"I think," Haj said, "we should rise when Mr. Peters' dessert arrives and make our way back toward his private compartment. I abused my position to procure a master key from one of the conductors and we should be waiting for our friend when he returns."

North nodded. He had not planned on being this direct, or moving quite this fast, but as his presence had changed Haj's plans, Haj's had changed his. If he could get his hands on those papers and destroy them faster thanks to the Colonel, he wasn't adverse to a little rough stuff. Much as he preferred to use his brain, he welcomed action when it came.

His profession was, by nature, a cautious one, and the war had only made him more so, but he was not unwilling to act, and if Peters objected that was too bad.

Hugh North, train robber, he thought, the Jesse James of the Balkans!

Colonel Haj signed for the check when they had finished, and the two men rose and walked back past Peters. North noticed that, upon closer examination, his deductions regarding the man's clothes were accurate. As immaculate as he might look at a distance, up close there were obvious signs of recent want. That explained why the man might postpone his own dream for the exigencies of money in the pocket, even if it meant dealing with a man like Dimitrios.

They went directly back to Peters' compartment, letting a middle aged woman pass and leave the car before Haj swiftly produced his master key and unlocked the door.

The two men slid inside. North reached up and unscrewed the emergency light which went on when the door was opened. Haj grunted approval as he indicated North should position himself in the doorway of the small wash room to be sure Peters didn't try to run once he stepped in the room.

Haj pulled the curtains down on the windows, even though it was dark outside, and switched off the lights. Then he sat himself facing the entrance.

After that, it was still, the only noise being the clacking of the train across the tracks, a sound that normally would have lulled North into a calming effect. Instead, he felt a faint sweat at his neck, and tension in his spine. He tried to relax, but still felt the tension growing. He hoped Peters was going to be reasonable. He didn't want this to get messy, and he suspected Haj's reputation for being ruthless was accurate. There was a certain energy the man gave off that did not feel like any policeman North had ever known.

He was in unknown territory here, uncertain of either enemy or ally. That wasn't unusual in his profession, but it was always a difficult position. Those damp hairs at the nape of his neck tickled under his collar. He clenched and loosened his fists, shifted from one foot to another. Every noise in the corridor outside registered.

The handle of the door jiggled.

Cool in action as always, all of North's jitters disappeared the instant the door handle moved. His mind went cold and calculating and everything around him seemed to slow down. Years of experience in exactly this sort of business took over his mind and body.

He did not glance at Haj, but he sensed the same tension in the other man. He couldn't see in the darkness, but he imagined Haj was smiling—a grim and dangerous smile.

Peters opened the door. He'd half-stepped in when he sensed something wrong. *The light*. Surely he had left the light on?

His hand rose to turn on the light, but then he hesitated.

North's steel grip closed on Peters' hand.

To his credit, Peters did not cry out. Before he could resist, North had manhandled him into the room; then, when he was far enough in, the agent used his back to slam the door, shoving Peters forward so the fat man stumbled, lost his balance, and had to catch himself before falling.

North heard something heavy crashing to the floor. The black case. In the dark, he sensed Peters scrambling for it.

Haj switched on the light and Peters froze. The barrel of a short blunt automatic pistol was now pointing at his considerable mid section.

"Please, Mr. Peters, be seated," said the Colonel. "My companion and I have business to discuss with you."

Peters' eyes shifted quickly, then his body seemed to relax. A smile played on his lips.

"You have me at a disadvantage gentlemen," he said. "You seem to know me, but I'm afraid I don't have the pleasure."

His eyes shifted from the gun in Haj's hand to North and back.

"I don't suppose you would mind if I made myself a bit more comfortable? For a man of my stature, kneeling on the floor is a bit uncomfortable..."

He gestured toward the seat with a seal-like, perfectly manicured hand.

Haj pointed at the seat opposite him with his gun. Carefully, but with the ease of a much smaller man, Peters rose and sat. He brushed the knees of his suit and fastidiously straightened himself, barely looking at the weapon pointed at him.

"I'm sorry it came to these melodramatics," Peters said, still inspecting his clothes.

North noted that, while he carefully patted himself down, he avoided his inside right pocket. Coincidence, misdirection, or...?

"Personally, I'm a man who prefers talk to action," Peters continued. "I would rather negotiate than engage. I always feel a man who has his wits about him and a good tongue in his head is at an advantage. Now what is it I can do for you? I'm afraid, if it is money you want, you will find my resources embarrassingly sparse at the moment, but perhaps we could come to some agreement?"

Just as he avoided touching his inside pocket, Peters studiously managed not to look at the black case lying on the compartment floor.

"Negotiation is out of the question I fear," Haj said coolly. "You are not a man to be left in a position to negotiate, Mr. Peters—or should I call you Mr. Gutman?"

Peters sagged a little at that.

"So you are not highwaymen," he said. "At least, not ordinary highwaymen. I don't suppose you gentlemen would care to identify yourselves? It would make things much more equitable."

"We aren't concerned with equity either," Haj said. "Do you have the time?" he asked North without taking his eyes off of Peters.

North looked at his wristwatch. "8:22," he replied.

"Ah, an American!" said Peters. "I like dealing with Americans, they are so direct. You know where you stand with an American; there is no European subtly. Americans are..."

"North," Haj said. "If you would be so kind as to pick up Mr. Peters' case."

North nodded, moving forward. He was careful to keep his eyes on Peters as he bent to pick up the case.

The blow that caught him knocked him to the floor. He wasn't knocked unconscious, but thrown to the floor, and, in that instant, as he fought to regain his balance and his senses, the lights went out; then, they were plunged in complete darkness.

They were going through a tunnel and North himself had dealt with the emergency light that should have come on.

Something brushed by him, the heavy black case shifted and was lifted up and he heard Peters grunt and the sound of clothes shifting.

It was a matter of seconds. A figure moved past North's feet, he heard the compartment door open, saw a faint red light from the corridor and the figure of Haj in the doorway, then the door was shut, and North slumped on the floor.

He closed his eyes, and when he opened them, the lights were back on in the compartment.

North sat up quickly. His head swum and he had to stop. When he opened his eyes again, he heard Peters.

"There is no point, my boy," the fat man said. "Your friend is gone, with the bird and the papers." He sounded resigned as if he had half expected this turn of events.

North pulled himself up into a seat. He felt the tender back of his neck. "As soon as I get my feet under me..."

"You'll do nothing, dear boy. Our friend did not strike me as the careless type. He spotted you and me, maneuvered us both into this compartment, timed it perfectly, even down to the oncoming tunnel, and I admit with some chagrin, stuck with perfect efficiency. He will not be lingering waiting for you. I suppose you could explore every compartment on this train, but even then, I doubt you will find him."

North rubbed the back of his neck. "Someone on the train will recognize him. After all, the famous Colonel Haj..."

Peters' soft chuckle broke into a genuine laugh. "Haj? The audacity of the fellow! Haj indeed! You think that a man in my position would be unfamiliar with the real Colonel Haj? No, whoever our friend was, he was neither a policeman nor the real Haj. Why, I saw Haj earlier this evening at the Grand Hotel before I left Istanbul—larger than life, as usual."

When he could, North left Peters. The fat man seemed resigned to his fate as if he had always expected to lose the black case and what it carried. He didn't even report North to the authorities for his part in the night's events. His own position was none too clear, legally, and as he had himself concluded before North left: "I fear I will have to make myself scarce for a time. Dimitrios will not be happy, and he has long arms."

As Peters had suggested, North found no trace of the false Colonel Haj. Had he stayed on the train, or exited unnoticed, somehow? Despite North's close observation, he couldn't be sure. Maybe he rode all the way to Paris atop the train cackling demonically? Whatever the answer, he disappeared without a trace.

North found himself dreading Paris. He could imagine the look on the face of his superiors when he briefed them on his failure. He resignedly prepared for the ordeal. Actions, especially stupid ones, had consequences.

They were pulling into the Gare de l'Est station on Paris when Michel knocked at his door. The conductor handed North a large envelope with his name scrawled on it. He explained that it had been left with the barman with instructions to give it to Captain North when they reached Paris.

Once Michel was gone, North ripped into the envelope. As he hoped, the papers were there. With a sigh of relief, he quickly looked them over, then carefully placed them in his inner Burberry pocket.

He almost didn't notice the slip of paper that had fallen from the envelope when he'd opened it. It read:

Dear Captain North.

I regret the inconvenience I was forced to put you to. My hands were somewhat tied as I will explain. I hope the fact that you now have the papers which compelled you to make this journey will in part forgive my actions. I assure you this was the only way to achieve both our goals. For while you are not a policeman, I could not rely on your fully appreciating my position.

For myself, this was always about the black case and what it contained, or rather what it did not contain.

For some years, I have been involved in the restoration of certain treasures from French history, items lost through time. Among them was a certain golden bird which has been in my possession for some years.

My hope was to keep the reemergence of the bird a secret, but, , earlier this year, I learned that a second bird, a black lead copy of the original, existed. This black bird was still out there and drawing the attention of numerous adventurers like our friend Peters believing it was the real thing.

As you can imagine, it suited my needs to keep the legend alive that the real bird was in circulation, so when I learned that Peters was about to acquire the object, it was in my interest to see that he did not learn its real nature.

That he would contract with Dimitrios to deliver your papers was a complication I could not have foreseen, so when you showed up on the train so obviously on the trail of something, I bribed the conductor and discovered you were a certain Captain Hugh North whose name was not unknown to certain contacts of mine. It was simple enough to put things together regarding Peters' mission for Dimitrios, certain troubles in the Balkans of late, and your sudden arrival.

Thus I became the infamous Colonel Haj, a figure so notorious that no one would dare to question me. I learned long ago that the best place to hide was, as your Mr. Poe suggested, in plain sight, and that no one looks too closely at the police when they suspect a crime is being perpetrated. Peters, on the other hand, almost certainly knew Haj, and was likely to identify me, and I could not be certain of outwitting you both.

Luckily, I travel frequently on that particular train and have memorized certain details that might come in handy. I managed to maneuver us into the compartment in time for the tunnel, and then to strike.

The rest you can surmise. The papers are in your possession and the black bird—well, that benighted object will again play its role in keeping Peters and his ilk busy. It is headed for the Far East again now, and I will see to it Peters, or Gutman, will soon be on its trail.

Who knows, perhaps he will catch up with it again in a more convenient place and time for me than now. He is a dreamer, our Mr. Peters, and the bird, well, it is the stuff of dreams.

I remain faithfully yours,

Arsène Lupin

North patted the papers in his coat pocket reassuringly. His mission was a success after all. War in Europe had been averted, at least for now. Peters was well out of the way, and the man Dimitrios was left alone in the shadows with his intrigues.

All in all, things had worked out surprisingly well, save for a minor headache. He could not speak for the bird, lead or gold, but certainly Arsène Lupin was the stuff that dreams were made of.

Credits

Thirty Pieces of Gold

Starring:	**Created by:**
Joseph Joséphin (Rouletabille)	Gaston Leroux
Olivier Molinier	André Gide
Philippe Roget	Tim Newton Anderson
Inspector Larsan	Gaston Leroux
Inspector Juve	Pierre Souvestre
	& Marcel Allain
Jurgen	James Branch Cabell
Doctor Bull	G.K. Chesterton
Arsène Lupin (Neil Saprenu)	Maurice Leblanc
Sir Dunston Gryme	Gustave Linbach
Fantômas (Gurn, Juan North)	Pierre Souvestre
	& Marcel Allain
Doctor Johannes	J.K. Huysmans
Joséphine Balsamo	Maurice Leblanc
Co-Starring:	
Grenoville	Patrick Suskind
Jerôme Fandor	Pierre Souvestre
	& Marcel Allain
Charles Duroy	Guy de Maupassant
"M" (Mycroft Holmes)	Ian Fleming/
	Arthur Conan Doyle
Doctor Lipsius	Arthur Machen
The Black Coats	Paul Féval
The Brotherhood of the Seven Kings	L.T. Meade
The Red Hand	Gustave Le Rouge
The Si-Fan	Sax Rohmer
Ginochio Gyves	Ellsworth Douglas/
	Edwin Pallander
Madame Chantelouve	J.K. Huysmans
Quentin Moretus Cassave	Jean Ray
Mocata	Dennis Wheatley
Durtal	J.K. Huysmans
Zephyrin Xyrdal	Jules Verne
Thomas Edison	adapted by Auguste

Future Eve	Villiers de L'Isle-Adam Auguste Villiers de L'Isle-Adam
A.J. Raffles	E W Hornung
And:	
Poictesme	James Branch Cabell
The Diogenes Club	Arthur Conan Doyle
Wold Newton	Philip José Farmner
The Gold Coin	Arthur Machen

Tim Newton ANDERSON is a former daily newspaper journalist and PR executive who recently started writing fiction, including a self challenge to write a story a week during lockdown. His story *The Pataphysical Detectives* was published in *Emanations 9: When a Planet Was a Planet* and another story, *Letters to my Daughter*, will soon appear in *Parsec* magazine. He is a member of the London Institute of Pataphysics and an enthusiastic collector of science fiction and fantasy. This is his first contribution to *Tales of the Shadowmen*.

The Long Game

Starring:	**Created by:**
Madame Palmyre	Renée Dunan
Renée	Renée Dunan
Ape O'Connell	Greg Gick
Stavlokratz	Lord Dunsany
Gil-Martin	James Hogg
Major Brabazon-Plank	P.G. Wodehouse
Antinea	Pierre Benoît
King Hiram	Pierre Benoît
Co-Starring:	
Jean Morhange	Pierre Benoît
André de Saint-Avit	Pierre Benoît
Also Starring:	
Edouard, Baron d'Empain	*Historical*
Jean	*Historical*
Rozelle	*Historical*
Harry Houdini	*Historical*
Bess Houdini	*Historical*
And:	
Atlantis	Pierre Benoît
Kôr	H. Rider Haggard
Negari	Robert E. Howard
Opar	Edgar Rice Burroughs

The Crystal Sphere   Lord Dunsany

Matthew BAUGH is the author of oodles and oodles of short stories and several novels, who aspires to keep writing until there are no more stories left to tell. He is represented by Rebecca Angus of the Golden Wheat agency and lives and writes in Torrance, CA. In his spare time he is an ordained pastor and serves the Manhattan Beach Community Church. He is also the author of *The Vampire Count of Monte-Cristo*, and a regular contributor to *Tales of the Shadowmen*.

The Devil Times Phibes

Starring:	**Created by:**
Dr. Anton Phibes	Robert Fuest, James Whiton & William Goldstein
Dr. George Leicester (Fascinax)	*Anonymous*
PC Joseph Cuff	based on Wilkie Collins
Henry Longstreet	based on Robert Fuest, James Whiton & William Goldstein
Lisa	Paul Béra
David Dunwoody	based on Robert Fuest, James Whiton & William Goldstein
Brian Vesalius	based on Robert Fuest, James Whiton & William Goldstein
The Children	Dylan Jones, Sandra Lee Blowitz & John Durren
Co-Starring:	
Vulnavia	based on Robert Fuest, James Whiton & William Goldstein
Numa Pergyll	*Anonymous*
Nadir Kitchna	*Anonymous*
Leonox	Paul Béra
Moses Hargreaves	based on Robert Fuest, James Whiton & William Goldstein
Samuel Whitcombe	based on Robert Fuest, James Whiton & William Goldstein

Atom Mudman BEZECNY is the editor-in-chief of the independent pulp press Odd Tales Productions, a position she has occupied for four years. Her previous publications include the novels *Tail of the Lizard King*, *Deus Mega Therion*, *Kinyonga Tales*, *The New Adventures of the Flash Avenger*, *Flint Golden and the Thunderstrike Crisis*, and *The Return of the Amazing Bulk*, a canonical sequel to Lewis Schoenbrun's superhero film *The Amazing Bulk*. She is also the author of many short stories, including a series starring her original heroine Bloody Mary. Much of her work can be found online for free. She is a regular contributor to *Tales of the Shadowmen*.

The Gift That Kept On Taking

Starring:	Created by:
Ebenezer Scrooge	Charles Dickens
Fascinax	*Anonymous*
Pinkie Brown	Graham Greene
Co-Starring:	
Mr. White	W.W. Jacobs
Also Starring:	
Père Fouettard, Krampus, etc.	*Folklore*
And:	
The Monkey's Paw	W.W. Jacobs

Matthew DENNION lives in South Jersey with his beautiful wife and daughters. He currently works as a teacher of students with autism at a Special Services School. Matthew writes giant monster stories for *G-Fan* magazine and he has recently published three giant monster novels, *Chimera: Scourge of the Gods*, *Operation R.O.C.: A Kaiju Thriller* and *Atomic Rex*. He is a regular contributor to *Tales of the Shadowmen*.

The Telepath of Galicia

Starring:	Created by:
Maréchal	Jean Renoir & Charles Spaak
Jacquemain	Georges Simenon
Simon Hart	Jules Verne
Dr. Cornelius Kramm	Gustave Le Rouge
Yuri Klimkov	based on Maxim Gorky
Professor Mikhail Ossipoff	Georges Le Faure
	& Henri de Graffigny
Countess Irina Petrovski	Arnaud d'Usseau

	& Julian Zimet
Sergeant Mayr	Brian Gallagher
Lieutenant Vuljanić	Brian Gallagher
Prince Wilhelm	based on
	Sir Arthur Conan Doyle
Boris Liatoukine	Marie Nizet
Co-Starring:	
Brion	Michel Corday
	& André Couvreur
Lord Burydan	Gustave Le Rouge
Professor Saxton	Arnaud d'Usseau
	& Julian Zimet
Doctor Wells	Arnaud d'Usseau
	& Julian Zimet
Fritz Kramm	Gustave Le Rouge
The Ténèbre Brothers	Paul Féval
Captain Kronos	Brian Clemens
Also Starring:	
General C.-J. Dupont	*Historical*
A.V. Brune de St Hippolite	*Historical*
General Svetozar Borojević	*Historical*
Władysław L. Jaworski	*Historical*
Józef Piłsudski	*Historical*
Field Marshal Franz Conrad von Hötzendorf	*Historical*
Tsarina Alexandra	*Historical*
Rasputin	*Historical*
And:	
The Lynx Serum	Michel Corday
	& André Couvreur
Vozduhoplavatel	Georges Le Faure
	& Henri de Graffigny
Meyral Effect	J.-H. Rosny *Aîné*
Ling Valley	Allan Balter & Robert Mintz
Kandersfeld	Vincent Tilsley

Brian GALLAGHER has a BA in Politics and Society and lives in London. He works in the media and for many years has written on the politics, economics and many other aspects of Croatia and has been quoted in Croatian and international media. In relation to that he has written extensively on Croatian-related cases at the International Criminal Tribunal for the Former Yugoslavia. He has always been interested in SF, classic horror, comics and is proud to be a lifelong

Doctor Who fan. His latest BCP collection is *The Return of Captain Vampire.* He is a regular contributor to *Tales of the Shadowmen.*

Young Robur in Africa

Starring:	Created by:
Robur	Jules Verne
Thaddeus Frycollin	based on Jules Verne
Tom Turner	Jules Verne
Serafina	Martin Gately
Co-Starring:	
Professor Oxalis	Martin Gately
Walter Trump	John Robinson
Phil Evans	Jules Verne
Also Starring:	
Dr Garett Anderson	*Historical*
Captain Albert Ball	*Historical*
William Joseph Simmons	*Historical*
Lothar von Richthofen	*Historical*

Martin GATELY is the author of the official prequel to Philip José Farmer's *The Green Odyssey (Samdroo and the Grassman* in *The Worlds of Philip José Farmer 4—Voyages to Strange Days).* His writing career commenced in 1988 when he wrote for D C Thomson's legendary *Starblazer* comic. He is also a contributor to the UK's journal of strange phenomena *Fortean Times.* For Black Coat Press, he has provided stories for two collections, *Exquisite Pandora* and *The New Exploits of Joseph Rouletabille,* and contributed to the following anthologies: *Night of the Nyctalope, Harry Dickson Vs. The Spider* and *The Vampire Almanac Vol. 1.* His latest work is an adaptation of Edgar Rice Burroughs' *Pirate Blood* into comic strip form, drawn by Anthony Summey and available on the official ERB website. He is a regular contributor to *Tales of the Shadowmen.*

The Case of Where Does The Time Go?

Starring:	Created by:
Etienne Camparol	André Laurie
Oscar Mazamette	Arthur Bernède
Stella Astarte	Alfred Driou
Spiridon (The Doctor)	André Laurie
Professor Helvetius	Arnould Galopin
The Morlocks	H.G. Wells
Co-Starring:	

Privat	Based on Paul Féval
Inspector Justin Ganimard	Maurice Leblanc
Maurice-Ernest Favraux	Arthur Bernède
Madame Jouvence	Alfred Driou
Doctor Omega	Arnould Galopin
The Timeslip Troopers	Theo Varlet & André Blandin
Also Starring:	
Musidora	*Historical*
And:	
Blinovitch Limitation Effect	Terrance Dicks & Barry Letts

Travis HILTZ started making up stories at a young age. Years later, he began writing them down. In high school, he discovered that some writers actually got paid and decided to give it a try. He has since gathered a modest collection of rejection letters and a shelf full of books with his name on them. Travis lives in the wilds of New Hampshire with his very loving and tolerant wife and a staggering amount of comic books and *Doctor Who* novels. He is a regular contributor to *Tales of the Shadowmen*.

Unknowable Powers

Starring:	**Created by:**
Joel Cairo	Dashiell Hammett
Casper Gutman	Dashiell Hammett
Gockel	Jean Ray
The Horla	Guy de Maupassant
Co-Starring :	
The Black Coats	Paul Féval
Samuel Podgers	Jean Ray
Mattias Tannhauser	Tim Willocks
Gotfried von Kalmbach	Robert E. Howard
Arsene Lupin	Maurice Leblanc
Sam Spade	Dashiell Hammett
Wilmer	Dashiell Hammett
Rhea	Dashiell Hammett
And:	
The Maltese Falcon	Dashiell Hammett
The *Endymion*	Jean Ray
The Wickstead Grimoire	Jean Ray
Sankt Berengonnegasse,	Jean Ray
a.k.a. St. Beregone's Lane	
Marlyweck Cemetary	Jean Ray

Matthew **ILSEMAN** was born in Texas and currently lives in Colorado. He started writing before he could actually write. His mother would write down stories he dictated to her. He has been writing ever since. He contributed a story to *The Many Faces of Arsène Lupin* and once to *Tales of the Shadowmen*.

The Prisoner of Countess Cagliostro

Starring:	Created by:
Irene Chupin (Irene Tupin/Irina Putine)	Narciso Ibanez-Serrador & Juan Tebar
Rochelle	Rick Lai
Orianne	Rick Lai
Josephine Balsamo	Maurice Leblanc
Fabiana Mata	Rick Lai
Wilfreda Tillman (Black Eyebrow)	Rick Lai
Berenice Fourneau (Blythe Furnace/Nevermore)	Rick Lai
Pai Mei / Pah Mei (White Priest)	Lieh Lo
Rylee Balsamo (2nd White Stalker)	Rick Lai
Co-Starring:	
Madame Fourneau	Narciso Ibanez-Serrador & Juan Tebar
Arsène Lupin	Maurice Leblanc
Marguerite Chauvain	Narciso Ibanez-Serrador & Juan Tebar
Catarina Koluchy	L.T. Meade & Robert Eustace
Théophraste Lupin	Maurice Leblanc
The Revenant	Rick Lai
Doctor Cerral	Maurice Renard
Teresa Grévin	Narciso Ibanez-Serrador & Juan Tebar
Violette Mathilde Grévin	Narciso Ibanez-Serrador & Juan Tebar
Blood Flesh	Rick Lai
Legacy	Rick Lai
Jacques Lefebvre	Pierre Grendorn, Arnold Phillips & Werner H. Furst
Kegan Van Roon	Sax Rohmer
Fritz Kramm, aka The Dealer	Gustave Le Rouge

The White Stalker	Rick Lai
Mary Rahilly/Reilly	Valerie Nartin
Doctor Antonio Nikola	Guy Boothby
Isabella Riley/Reilly	Rick Lai
Joseph Alexander Balsamo	Miguel Morayta
Larry Parker	Arthur Conan Doyle
Professor James Moriarty	Arthur Conan Doyle
Dr. Henry Jekyll	Robert Louis Stevenson
Alexandre Cascabel (young circus acrobat)	Jules Verne
Harmonica	Sergio Donati, Sergio Leone, Dario Argento & Bernardo Bertolucci
Kenton Lupin (Allard)	Walter B. Gibson
And:	
Chupin Detective Agency	Emile Gaboriau
The Black Coats	Paul Féval
Wu Fang Clan	James Clavell
White Lotus Tong	Lieh Lo
Temple of the Five Hundred Steps.	Rick Lai
Koga Ninjas	*Historical*
Iga Ninjas	*Historical*
Secrets of the Thirty-Sixth Chamber	Rick Lai
Unbreakable Glass of Yian	Rick Lai
Island of Lynched Women	Robert W. Chambers & Rick Lai
The Purple Sacrament	based on
The House of Crafts	Walter B,.Gibson XXX

Rick LAI is an authority on pulp fiction and the Wold Newton Universe concepts of Philip José Farmer. His speculative articles have been collected in *Rick Lai's Secret Histories: Daring Adventurers*, *Rick Lai's Secret Histories: Criminal Masterminds*, *Chronology of Shadows: A Timeline of The Shadow's Exploits* and *The Revised Complete Chronology of Bronze*. Rick's fiction has been collected in *Shadows of the Opera*, *Shadows of the Opera: Retribution in Blood* and *Sisters of the Shadows: The Cagliostro Curse* (the last two titles are available from Black Coat Press). He has also translated Arthur Bernède's *Judex* and *The Return of Judex* into English for Black Coat Press. Rick resides in Bethpage, New York, with his wife and children. He is a regular contributor to *Tales of the Shadowmen*.

The Taste of Death

Starring:	Created by:
Dr. Robert Chase	David Shore
Dr. Allison Cameron	David Shore
Dr. Eric Foreman	David Shore
Victoria Madsen	Joel Thompson
Percival "Percy" Rose	Craig Silverstein
	based on Luc Besson
Lisa	Paul Bera
Seymour Birkhoff	Craig Silverstein
	based on Joel Surnow
	based on Luc Besson
Michael	Craig Silverstein
	based on Joel Surnow
	based on Luc Besson
Nikita	Craig Silverstein
	based on Joel Surnow
	based on Luc Besson
The Thing	John Carpenter
	& Bill Lancaster
	based on John W. Campbell

Co-Starring:	
Dr. Gregory House	David Shore
Francis Dalvant/Lacana	Paul Bera
Leonox	Paul Bera
Christopher Moltisanti	David Chase
SHADO	Gerry & Sylvia Anderson
	& Reg Hill
UNIT	Derrick Sherwin
	& Peter Bryant
BPRD	Mike Mignola
The Lone Gunmen	Glen Morgan & James Wong
The San Francisco Pods	W.D. Richter
	based on Jack Finney
R.J. MacReady	John Carpenter
	& Bill Lancaster
	based on John W. Campbell
Dr. Felix Hoenikker	Kurt Vonnegut
Clayton "Bloody" Chiclitz	Thomas Pynchon
Reptilian Humanoids	Earl Mac Rauch
Jaime Sommers	Kenneth Johnson

	based on Martin Caidin
Goldine Serafin	John Kohn
	based on Peter Lear
And:	
Princeton-Plainsboro Teaching Hospital	David Shore
Division	Craig Silverstein
	based on Joel Surnow
	based on Luc Besson
Outpost 31	John Carpenter
	& Bill Lancaster
	based on John W. Campbell
Ice-9	Kurt Vonnegut
Yoyodyne Corporation	Earl Mac Rauch
	based on Thomas Pynchon
Q-bombs	Leonard Wibberley

Angel and Hopkirk (Deceased)

Starring:	**Created by:**
The Phantom Angel (aka Rose L'Ange, Briar Rose, Sleeping Beauty)	Randy Lofficier based on Charles Perrault
Marty Hopkirk	Dennis Spooner
Co-Starring:	
Captain Laure Berthaud	Alexandra Clert & Guy Patrick Sainderichin
Sherlock Holmes	Arthur Conan Doyle
Jeff Randall	Dennis Spooner

Jean-Marc & Randy LOFFICIER have collaborated on five screenplays, a dozen books and numerous translations, including *Arsène Lupin*, *Doc Ardan*, *Doctor Omega*, *The Phantom of the Opera* and *Rouletabille*. Their latest novels include *Edgar Allan Poe on Mars*, *The Katrina Protocol* and *Return of the Nyctalope*. Randy has written a number of animation teleplays, including episodes of *Duck Tales* and *The Real Ghostbusters*, and Jean-Marc comics featuring such popular heroes as *Superman* and *Doctor Strange*, as well as (in collaboration with Randy) original characters such as *Robur* and *Tiger & The Eye*. Jean-Marc is currently publisher and edior-in-chief of Hexagon Comics; Randy is a member of the Writers Guild of America, West and Mystery Writers of America.

Empire Rising

Starring:	Created by:
Ming	Henri Vernes
Dr. Fu Manchu	Sax Rohmer
Plan Chu (The Yellow Claw)	Sax Rohmer
Fo-Hi (The Scorpion)	Sax Rohmer
Madame Atomos	André Caroff
Sumruru	Sax Rohmer

Rod McFADYEN has been dabbling in creative writing for a number of years now, although generally doing more dabbling than writing. While an avid reader of books of history, science fiction and fantasy, he is also a fan of the pulp genre and was delighted to come across the French pulp heroes. He's also a sucker for a good cross-over. He has been following the *Tales of the Shadowmen* since the first volume and was finally motivated enough to submit a story.

Three the Hardened Way

Starring:	Created by:
Boulinard	Pierre Souvestre & Marcel Allain
Marquet	Pierre Souvestre & Marcel Allain
Verdier	Pierre Souvestre & Marcel Allain
The Unholy Three (Tweedledee, Hercules & Echo/Imp)	Tod Robbins
Erik	Gaston Leroux
The Synthetic Men	André Couvreur
Co-Starring:	
The Human Skeleton	Tod Robbins
Judex	Arthur Bernède & Louis Feuillade
Professor Tornada	André Couvreur
The Angels of Music	Kim Newman

Christofer NIGRO is a writer of both fiction and non-fiction with a strong interest in pulps, comic books and fantastic cinema, and a regular contributor to *Tales of the Shadowmen*. He may be known to some by his websites *The Godzilla Saga* and *The Warrenverse*, as he is an authority on the subject of *dai kaiju eiga* (the sub-genre of cinema specializing in giant monsters), and the characters featured in the comic magazines published by Warren. He has recently revived and expanded Chuck Loridans' classic site MONSTAAH, and has since been published in the anthologies *Aliens Among Us* and *Carnage: After the Fall*. He is a regular contributor to *Tales of the Shadowmen*.

Undying Love

Starring:
Candide, Cunegonde and all other characters

Created by:
Voltaire

John PEEL was born in Nottingham, England, and moved to the U.S. in 1981 to marry his pen-pal. He and his wife ("Mrs. Peel") and their rescue dog Dickens (named for as favorite author!) live on Long Island, New York. He has written more than a hundred novels, including tie-ins based on shows like *Doctor Who, Star Trek* and *The Avengers* (the one with the *other* Mrs. Peel!). His most popular works are the *Diadem* series (12 volumes so far) and the *Dragonhome* series (a mere 3). Two volumes of his collected short stories are now available from Black Coat Press: *Return to the Center of the Earth* and *Twenty Thousand Years Under the Sea*. He is a regular contributor to *Tales of the Shadowmen*.

The Specter of Fantômas

Starring:	Created by:
SPECTRE	Kevin McClory & Ian Fleming
Ernst Stavro Blofeld	Ian Fleming
Roman Orgonetz (SMOG)	Henri Vermes
Félix Sousse (SPHINX)	Vladimir Volkoff
Marc-Ange Draco	Ian Fleming
Count Massimo Contini	William McGivern
Linka Karensky	William McGivern
Wen Yurang	William McGivern
Irma Blunt	Ian Fleming
Strelik	Ian Fleming
Emilio Largo	Ian Fleming
Otto Flick	Jeremy Lloyd & David Croft
Gabriel	Peter O'Donnell
The Red Hand	Based on Gustave Le Rouge
Fantômas	Jean Halain & Pierre Foucaud based on Pierre Souvestre & Marcel Allain

Co-Starring:	
General Jack D. Ripper	Stanley Kubrick, Terry Southern & Peter George
General Buck Turgidson	Stanley Kubrick, Terry Southern & Peter George
Prizzi Crime Family	Richard Condon
Caprice Crime Family	Chester Gould

Matarese Cartel	Robert Ludlum
The Shepherd's Boy	Robert Ludlum
THRUSH	Sam Rolfe & Norman Felton
Krassno Granitski	Ian Fleming
Bill	Quentin Tarentino
Francisco Scaramanga	Ian Fleming
The Jackal	Frederick Forsyth
Corleone Crime Family	Mario Puzo

Frank SCHILDINER has been a pulp fan since a friend gave him a gift of Philip Jose Farmer's *Tarzan Alive*. Since that time he has written the *Frankenstein* trilogy, the *Napoleon's Vampire Hunters* series (3 vols.), *Irma Vep and the Great Brain of Mars*, and has just embarked on a new fantasy series, all for Black Coat Press. Frank has been published in many other anthologies. Frank works as a martial arts instructor at Amorosi's Mixed Martial Arts. He resides in New Jersey with his wife Gail who is his top supporter. He is a regular contributor to *Tales of the Shadowmen*.

The Music Box

Starring:	**Created by:**
Rama Tamerlane (Felifax)	Paul Féval, *fils*
Grace Palmer	Paul Féval, *fils*
Josephine Balsamo, Countess	Maurice Leblanc
Cagliostro	
General Zaroff	Richard Connell
Dirko	Jules Mary
Zizi	Jules Mary
Zoltan	Nathalie Vidalinc
Jarry	Jules Mary
Oudja	Jules Mary
Mercurio	Nathalie Vidalinc
Galoubert	Xavier de Montépin
	& Jules Dornay
Gaston Verdier	Xavier de Montépin
	& Jules Dornay
Baber	Paul Féval, *fils*
Sir Eric Palmer	Paul Féval, *fils*
Co-Starring:	
Djina	Paul Féval, *fils*
Arsène Lupin	Maurice Leblanc
Edmund Sexton	Paul Féval, *fils*
Also Starring:	

| The Prince of Wales | *Historical* |
| Jeanne Lanvin | *Historical* |

Nathalie VIDALINC is a graphic designer who lives in the Périgord region of France. She is an eclectic reader who loves detective novels, history books, science fiction & fantasy and pretty much everything except poetry. Her favorite English-language author is P. G, Wodehouse. She has written half-a-dozen short stories published in genre magazines and anthologies. This is her first contribution to *Tales of the Shadowmen.*

The Gilded Bird

Starring:	**Created by:**
Captain Hugh North	F. Van Wyk Mason
Pierre Michel	Agatha Christie
Viscount Trevor	G. W. Newman
Colonel Haj	Eric Ambler
Mr. Peters	Eric Ambler
Casper Gutman	Dashiell Hammett
Arsène Lupin	Maurice Leblanc
Co-Starring:	
Sandy Arbuthnot, Lord Clanroyden	John Buchan
Anthony Hamilton	Max Brand
Sir Pellinore Gwayne-Cust	Dennis Wheatley
Sir Walter Harcourt	John Buchan
Dimitrios	Eric Ambler
Joel Cairo	Dashiell Hammett
Adolph Von Grundt (Clubfot)	Valentine Williams
James Schuyler Grim (JimGrim)	Talbot Mundy
Also Starring:	
Sidney Reilly	*Historical*
Basil Zaharoff	*Historical*
T. E. Lawrence	*Historical*
Sir Paul Dukes	*Historical*
And:	
The Black Bird	Dashiell Hammett

David L. VINEYARD is a fifth generation Texan (named for his gunfighter/Texas Ranger great grand-father) currently living in Oklahoma City, OK, where the tornadoes come sweeping down the plains. He has useless degrees in history, politics, and economics, and is the author of several tales about Buenos Aires private eye Johnny Sleep, two novels, several short stories, some journalism, and various non-fiction. He is currently working on several ideas while battling with a three month old kitten for household dominance and the keyboard of his PC. He is a regular contributor to *Tales of the Shadowmen*.

CPSIA information can be obtained
at www.ICGtesting.com
Printed in the USA
BVHW031330301121
622773BV00013B/55